365 Bedtime *Stories*

CHRISTINE ALLISON

Drawings by Victoria Roberts

A John Boswell Associates Book
Broadway Books New York

Broadway Books titles may be purchased for business or promotional use or for special sales. For information, please write to: Special Markets Department, Bantam Doubleday Dell Publishing Group, Inc., 1540 Broadway, New York, NY 10036.

Library of Congress Cataloging-in-Publication Data
365 bedtime stories : fairy tales, myths, folktales, funny stories, comforting stories, heroic stories and more / [edited by] Christine Allison : illustrations by Victoria Williams.—1st ed.
p. cm.
"A John Boswell Associates/King Hill Productions book."
Summary: A collection of stories that vary in length from half a page to one and a half pages with themes matched to various times of the year and intended to be read one every night.
ISBN 0-7679-0096-0
1. Children's stories. 2. Tales. [1. Short stories. 2. Folklore.] I. Allison, Christine. II. Williams, Victoria, Ill.
PZ5.A15 1998
[E]—dc21 98-9894
CIP
AC

Designed by Barbara Cohen Aronica
Drawings by Victoria Roberts

98 99 00 01 02 10 9 8 7 6 5 4

For Loddie

Every princess and knight and good fairy,
all of the hardships and happy endings,
are for you—
with all my love.

Contents

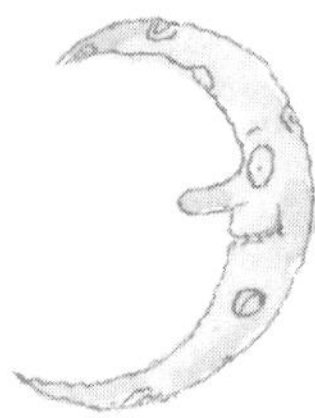

365 Bedtime Stories is the gift of many storytellers. Chief among them was Felicity Buchanan, who not only rewrote an enormous number of the stories but did so with intelligence and enthusiasm. She scoured the library for stories, and her daughter, Caroline, consented on many occasions to hear the stories read aloud. Felicity made a substantial contribution to this book, and for her partnership, I am grateful.

Finding the stories was as much a part of putting this book together as telling them, and for months Tom Peterson poured through dusty archives looking for the wonderful oddball tale. The results of his excellent research are scattered throughout *365 Bedtime Stories*. Tom has the ability to gain a near-instant expertise on any subject, and his research into children's literature and the byzantine world of public domain was inspired. Thanks also to the librarians at the Bradfield Elementary Library and the Dallas Public Library who were tremendously helpful. And I would be remiss if I did not mention Maisie Allison, who found a great deal of material for *365 Bedtime Stories.* She and Gillea Allison, who lovingly gave me moral support, also originated two terrific stories for this book. Loddie Allison helped greatly by listening to the stories night after night after night. . . . Her imagination fired many of the original pieces you will find here. Chrissie Allison, someday you will understand and love these stories, too.

Amy Handy, great copyediting.

Lupe Morales, gracias. You create happiness for my family. This book would not have been completed without you, and I thank you from the bottom of my heart. Heartfelt thanks also to Ginny and David Bauer, John and Marie Peterson, Karen Goodwin, Jenny Lea Allison, Anita Middleton, Carolyn Parlato, Mickie Teetor, St. Jude, and all of the carpool moms in my life. To the amazing John Boswell and Patty Brown, once again, thanks. Barbara Aronica, your talent and good cheer made the design beautiful and the deadline possible. And finally I would like to express deep gratitude and appreciation to Bill Shinker and Janet Goldstein. This book was a blessing.

How to Use This Book

This book was designed to be flexible. Many families will use it as a way to journey through the year, a story a day, holding tight to the format. More often, families will use it as a collection for dipping into, reading from its pages on a more capricious basis. The very breadth of this book guarantees discovery—with stories from all over the world and throughout history, a reading of *365 Bedtime Stories* will escort children to literary places they might not have visited otherwise. While some of the stories in this book will be familiar, many others are well off the beaten track. I hope you will have as much pleasure reading these brief tales to your children as presumably they will have hearing them for the first time.

Will your child love every story in this book? Without a doubt, no. In fact there may be a number of misses. A story or two will have to be read over and over, and others will be rejected as too abstract or too serious or too silly.

Age and cognitive abilities will have a lot to do with this. For the most part, the stories in this book are for children ages two to ten. Obviously a toddler will not understand "The Three Wishes," but he or she will understand that when you pick up a book, it's time to sit on your lap and hear your voice and look into your eyes or at the printed page. Kindergarten teachers say they can tell which children have been read to from those who haven't. Children from reading families will sit attentively during story time; the very presence of a book suggests that something pleasurable is going to happen. Those who have not been read to will wander off because they literally don't know what's in it for them.

By the time the child is six or seven, he or she can enjoy—without fully comprehending—the majority of the stories in this book, especially if you take the time to give a little overview, identifying hard words or new concepts. For instance, I read "The First Day of Fish School" to my five-year-old Loddie the day before her first day at school. She didn't really know what a "school of fish" was, so we talked about fish swimming in formation and I even showed her an underwater photograph from a nature magazine. This little science lesson was followed by the story itself, which I read in a silly way, and she cracked up. The story is about a neurotic fish named Joe who obsesses about everything, and because she could see it in her mind's eye, she enjoyed it.

When do you stop reading to children? Never, I hope. Read to your children as long as they will let you. From time to time, I still read to my ten-year-old daughter Maisie. If we have a book we are both interested in we will sneak fifteen minutes in the early morning, before the mad rush starts, to pull the covers up and read aloud together. I don't read to Gillea, my thirteen-year-old, anymore. She reads to *me.* Whenever she finds an essay or article she wants to share, her first impulse is to read it to me. She doesn't just hand me the book or magazine. She comes into my room and *reads* it. Aloud. To me. Being a mom doesn't get any better.

Whether you are reading aloud or telling a story, don't limit yourself to bedtime. The best storytelling experience I ever had was in an emergency room in a Connecticut clinic. Maisie had ripped open her chin, requiring several stitches. Ever the Roman soldier, Maisie was calm while I was a nervous wreck. I decided to tell her a story to get our minds somewhere else, and though I couldn't tell you what the tale was, I know we were both spellbound. Stories can soothe the soul, whether it is a doctor's visit, or pretest jitters, or a ride to someplace new.

But stories are not just good therapy. They are fun! For years we have told stories around the dinner table, especially when friends and family come over. We use the "roundabout" form wherein each person—from the grandmother to the littlest tyke—adds a bit of the tale as we go around the table. On long road trips or around the campfire, the "roundabout" is one of the most imaginative games of childhood.

Selecting an Appropriate Story

Choosing stories for your child is a matter of common sense. Younger children will enjoy the simpler, more repetitive stories, or those that are very short. "The Gingerbread Man" is one such classic; you can read it to the youngest child every night and soon enough he or she will be able to anticipate the repetition.

From age three on up, a child can follow a very simple plot. Again, I suggest picking a story and reading it even a dozen times to your child so that he or she knows it backwards and forwards. It will become a game for the child to anticipate verse and it will also become a security object of sorts; he or she will know it like a familiar cuddly doll or blanket.

A child from age five on up—and of course, these guidelines will vary by the child—can sustain the interest to hear "Cinderella" or "Jack and the Beanstalk." You will need to explain bits and pieces along the way, and you may need to read stories more than once for your child to absorb them. But with an expressive voice and your own warm presence, your child will be a ready audience.

To me, the most exciting child to read to is one who is a reader. By seven, the age of reason, most children are literate and able to understand right from wrong. This is a wonderful junction in their development. Their comprehension of virtues and vices is growing; they are interested in behaviors represented in the stories, and they identify and empathize. "How could he be so brave?" "Why was she mean to her daughter?" "Who will take care of the little boy?" As our children become more complex and aware, the characters start coming alive, and their actions pose questions and raise issues.

Fables

The simplest fable, such as "The Fox and the Grapes" (page 61), can be read and discussed with a five-year-old, but that child would most likely not have a clue about what is happening in "Pedigree" (page 316). On the other hand, my daughter Maisie, at ten, loved the characters in "Pedigree" and drew a hilarious picture of them all pontificating. The characters in fables are not meant to convey animal nature, but human nature, and their personalities are fascinating.

If the fables seem a bit tough at first, try reading them together and then guessing the moral. The thought process and conversation will take you to interesting moral and ethical places.

Fairy Tales

A fairy tale presumes a family with problems. The story usually starts with one family (for instance, a father, a cruel stepmother, and some siblings) and ends up with the creation of a new family, a couple who marries and who—fingers crossed—will live happily ever after. Fairy tales are imbued with universal power and meaning because they contain truths about relationships, fears, death, and desires. When you read to your child you can explore enormous issues on a soul level, without defenses or judgments.

It doesn't take a lot of imagination to guess why a child might resonate to Jack and the Beanstalk; after all, the child lives in a world filled with unpredictable giants every day. Most children at some point fear abandonment, which is precisely what Hansel and Gretel must overcome in that deep, dark forest. Is the ogre who eats children for breakfast so different from the wrinkled old aunt who says adoringly, "Oh, I could just eat you up?" The figures and forces in a child's life are all new and strange and wonderful and awful. Using the world of make-believe, fairy tales show us who we are.

For the past several years there has been some controversy about fairy tales. Certain scholars, concerned about the portrayal of women, feel that fairy tales demean women, painting them as passive and pretty and not much more. It's absolutely true: strong, positive women don't often appear in fairy tales, which is why it was important to include stories like "Molly Whuppie" and the "Indian Cinderella" in this volume. But it's important to recognize that men get an equally brutal portrayal in fairy tales. By contemporary standards, Hansel and Gretel's father was an accomplice in abandoning children. The men in fairy tales are often passive to the point of being criminal or extraordinarily stupid, married to exasperated shrews. While many of the adults in these stories are failed and flawed, the children are often the repositories of wisdom or perseverance or cleverness. Is this a clue to their enduring charm?

Violence is also an issue in fairy tales. I personally am less dogmatic about the presence of grisly detail in stories than I am about sexist portrayals, and you may find that I have "left in" some violent behavior that offends you or your child. To my mind, sliced-up dragons and children-eating witches are in fact expressive of certain fears and fantasies. However, the cautious reader might want to peruse the traditional fairy tales and folktales before reading them aloud; the traditional stories are the ones that turn up the most gruesome behavior.

The Art of Listening

Some children are born listeners. They can hear a set of complicated directions and repeat them verbatim. They can tell you everything the priest or the rabbi said at services. They are auditory learners. But many more children do not learn this way, and for them listening—focusing on the spoken word—is an acquired skill.

Sadly, for a generation of children raised on television, video games, and movies, the experience of listening to a story—without the aid of lavish illustrations or moving images—is altogether too rare. Simply put, children who are not "read to" miss out. The child who needs elaborate images and lots of sensory input to be entertained has a problem. For this child, the read-aloud experience is crucial.

Listening is not passive. Children who can listen to a story will also know how to listen to a lecture. They will know how to focus and concentrate and their academic experience will be far more successful than children who lack these skills.

The Art of Reading Aloud

Jim Trelease's *Read-Aloud Handbook* changed the national conversation about oral reading. While educators labored over new theories and paradigms, Jim Trelease communicated the simple, powerful truth that reading aloud to children, more than any single factor, made children better readers. Better readers are better students. Better students are more successful in life. One study Trelease shares in his book shows that the United States ranks eighth in the world (interestingly, Finland is first) in reading tests given to eighth-grade students. In this study the two factors that produced higher achievement were the frequency with which teachers read aloud to children, and the time students read for pleasure in the classroom. "Reading aloud serves as a commercial for the pleasures of reading," Trelease says. Human beings are pleasure-centered, and unless reading skills are acquired on that basis, reading likely will not become a lifelong habit.

Anyway, what could be more pleasurable at the end of the day than snuggling up with a book against a mountain of pillows?

Read-Aloud Tools

The most important tool of the storyteller is the voice. When you read these stories to your child, take a moment to collect yourself. Breathe in, breathe out, and then begin. Keep these things in mind:

- You don't have to change your voice dramatically for each character; in fact, overacting can ruin a good story.

- Read slowly, especially descriptive passages, so that your child can absorb it all.
- For action passages you can pick up the pace. Sometimes a rush-rush voice adds excitement.
- The well-placed pause can be very effective. "There, on the other side of the room, was Kate" doesn't carry half the power of "There . . . on the other side of the room . . . was Kate."

When you come across a word that your child does not know, what do you do? Do you stop to explain—and risk breaking the spell? Or do you go on and risk leaving the child in the dark?

Here's the ideal: Most stories in this volume are deliberately short, so you might have time to skim the piece before reading it and set the story up. In this case, if you detect the odd word you can discuss its meaning before you begin, along with some atmospherics on the time and place. Second best: If you don't have time to give a little overview and the story has some unfamiliar words, read the sentence and digress briefly to explain the word. Then reread the sentence and carry on.

The Art of Storytelling

Real storytelling is more than simply reading aloud, and it is a different experience for both the teller and the audience. If, in reading a story in this book, you are inspired to embellish it and make it your own, you will find the experience immensely rewarding. A beginning storyteller should pick an easy one to start, maybe a familiar classic. The "variations" on classic tales included in this book are specially geared to this application; many are presented as jumping-off points for telling the story yourself, not just reading it.

- Read the story through and identify each major event. A storyteller will get key events fixed in his or her memory—maybe even writing them down—to keep order and flow intact.
- If you can imagine the story (kind of like getting a movie running in your head), you will be far ahead of the game. You don't have to memorize stories word for word; all you have to do is get the "movie" in your mind and communicate what you see.
- Unless it is a classic phrase ("I'll huff and I'll puff and I'll blow your house down") you don't have to retain specific language. Be precise and simple with description. Dialogue is very easy to make up as you go along, as long as you know your characters well.
- Tell the same story over and over. Children love to hear a good story as often as you are willing to tell it. The more you tell it, the more you will know it and the better it will be. If you develop a repertoire of standards, you will be amazed how often your child prefers the "story from your mouth" (as my daughter Loddie puts it) over a picture book.

Enlarging the Experience

Finally, if your child has a favorite story, let it take on a life of its own. If your child loves "The Three Bears," make bear cookies or oatmeal together; look up bears in science books and see how they really look; visit bears at the zoo. Do math games in multiples of three; make a shoebox house replica of the three bears' house. If your child really loves a story, have her practice telling it to you or an appreciative grandparent. Children who can internalize a story and present it to an "audience" gain important practice in sequencing.

The applause doesn't hurt either!

JANUARY

January 1
NEW YEAR'S DAY

The Little Match Girl

It was late on a bitterly cold New Year's Eve, and the snow was falling. A poor little girl was wandering in the dark cold streets. She was bareheaded and shoeless, and her bare feet were red and blue with the cold. She carried a quantity of matches in her old apron, and held a packet of them in her hand. Nobody had bought any from her all day long. The poor little girl was hungry and perishing with cold. She was the picture of misery.

The snowflakes fell on her long yellow hair, which curled prettily around her face, but she paid no attention. Lights were shining from every window, and there was a most delicious odor of roast goose in the streets, for it was a holiday.

She crouched for a time beneath the overhang of a roof and drew her feet up under her, but she was colder than ever. She did not dare to go home, for she had not earned a single penny. Her father would beat her, and besides it was almost as cold at home as it was here.

Her little hands were stiff with cold. Oh, one little match would do some good! If she only dared, she would pull one out of the packet and strike it on the wall to warm her fingers. She pulled out just one. *R-rsh-sh!* How it sputtered and blazed! It burnt just like a little candle, and the girl fancied she was sitting in front of a big stove with polished brass feet and handles. There was a splendid fire blazing in it and warming her so beautifully, but—what happened? Just as she was stretching out her feet to warm them, the flame went out, the stove vanished—and she was left sitting with a burnt-out match.

She struck a new one. It blazed up and where the light fell upon the wall, it became transparent like gauze, and she could see right though it into the room. The table was spread with a snowy white cloth and pretty china. A roast goose stuffed with apples and prunes was on the table and—the match went out, and there was nothing but a black wall.

She lit another match. This time she was sitting under a Christmas tree. Thousands of lighted candles gleamed on its branches. The girl stretched out both her hands—then out went the match. All the Christmas candles rose higher and higher, till she saw that they were only the twinkling stars. One of them fell and made a bright streak of light across the sky.

"Someone is dying," thought the little girl, for her old grandmother, the only person who had ever been kind to her, used to say, "When a star falls, a soul is going up to God."

Now she struck another match against the wall, and this time it was her grandmother who appeared in the circle of flame. She saw her quite clearly and distinctly, looking so gentle and happy. "Grandmother!" cried the little girl. "Oh, do take me with you. I know you will vanish when the match goes out. You will vanish like the warm stove, the delicious goose, and the beautiful Christmas tree!"

She hastily struck a whole bundle of matches, because she did long to keep her grandmother with her. The matches made it so bright, and her grandmother had never before looked so big or so beautiful. She lifted the little girl up in her arms, and they soared in a halo of light and joy, far, far above the earth, where there was no more cold, no hunger, and no pain—for they were with God.

In the cold morning light, the poor little girl sat there, with rosy cheeks and a smile on her face—dead. Frozen to death on the last night of the old year. The burnt-out matches were still in her hand.

"She must have tried to warm herself," they said. Nobody knew what beautiful visions she had seen, nor in what a halo she had entered with her grandmother upon the glories of the New Year.

—HANS CHRISTIAN ANDERSEN

January 2

The Twelve Months, Part 1

A BOHEMIAN TALE FOR THE NEW YEAR

Once there was a woman who had in her care two girls. Katinka, the elder, was the woman's own daughter, and she was as harsh in face as she was in heart, but Dobrunka, the younger, who was a foster child, was both beautiful and good. Dobrunka, with her winsome ways, made Katinka appear even more hateful. So the mother and daughter were always in a rage with Dobrunka.

Dobrunka was made to sweep, cook, wash, sew, spin, weave, and take care of the cow, while Katinka lived like a princess. All these tasks she did with great good will, but this only made Katinka and her mother angrier. The better Dobrunka was, the more plainly did their own wickedness show by contrast. As they had no wish to change, they made up their minds to do away with Dobrunka.

On a cold day winter day, when frost castles glistened on the windows and the earth was white with snow, Katinka took a fancy for violets. She called in Dobrunka and said, "Go to the forest, lazybones, and bring me a bunch of violets, so I may pin them to my dress and enjoy their fragrance."

"Oh, sister," gently answered Dobrunka, "I cannot find you any violets under the snow."

But Katinka snapped out angrily, "Hold your tongue and do as I tell you. Go to the forest and bring me back a bunch of violets, or you'll find this door forever slammed shut in your face."

Upon this Katinka and her mother took Dobrunka by the arm and thrust her, without warm winter clothing, out into the cold, and drew the bolt on the door.

The poor girl went to the forest weeping sadly. The giant pines and oaks bowed their branches low, borne down with their icy burdens. There was not a footpath to be found in an white and glittering wilderness, and Dobrunka soon lost her way. To add to her woe, she was freezing and hungry. Still, she trusted that help would come to one who had done no harm.

All at once she saw a light in the distance, a light that glowed in the sky and quivered now and again as if from the flickering flame of some mighty fire. With her eyes fixed hopefully on that light, which seemed to be at the top of a steep hill, Dobrunka began climbing. At the summit, there was a fire, and around it sat twelve motionless figures on twelve great stones. Each figure was wrapped in a long, flowing mantle, his head covered with a hood that fell over his eyes. Three of these mantles were white as the snow, three were green as the grass of the meadows, three were golden as sheaves of ripe wheat, and three were purple as ripened grapes. These twelve figures, who sat there gazing at the fire in perfect silence, were the Twelve Months of the Year.

Dobrunka knew January by his long, white beard. He was the only one who had a cane in his hand. The girl hesitated to speak, but finally addressed them with great respect: "My good sirs, I pray you let me warm myself by your fire. I am freezing with cold."

January nodded his head and beckoned her near the blaze. "Why have you come here, my child?" he asked. "What are you looking for?"

"I am looking for violets," replied Dobrunka.

"Do you expect to find violets in the time of snow?" January's voice was gruff.

"No," answered Dobrunka sadly. "I know this is not the season for violets, but my foster sister and mother thrust me out of doors and ordered me to get them. They won't let me come home unless I obey. Oh, my good sirs, can you tell me where to find them?"

Old January rose, and, turning to a mere youth in a green mantle, give him the cane and said, "Brother March, this is your business."

March rose and stirred the fire with the cane. Suddenly the flames rose, the snow melted, the buds began to swell on the trees, and faint color showed through the grass as violets bloomed. It was Spring!

"Hurry, my child, and gather your violets," said March. Surely such a miracle would satisfy the evil Katinka and her mother, wouldn't it?

January 3

The Twelve Months, Part 2

When Dobrunka returned home with a bouquet of violets, Katinka and her mother, thinking never to see Dobrunka again, were astonished. "Where did you find these?" cried Katinka.

"Up on the mountain," answered Dobrunka, as Katinka snatched the violets from her hand without so much as a thank you.

A few days later, the wicked Katinka began craving strawberries. She summoned her sister, and once again sent her off to the snowy woods on an impossible quest. This time Dobrunka sang as she walked to keep up her courage, and kept her eyes on the hill for the sight of the fire. At length she reached it, where the Twelve Months sat motionless in their places.

"Why have you come again?" asked January. "What are you looking for now?"

"Strawberries, my good sirs. I know it is the wrong time of year," she added sadly.

Old January rose, and turning to a full-grown man in a golden mantle, gave him the cane and said, "Brother June, this is your business."

June rose, stirred the fire, and the earth turned green. The trees were covered with leaves and the birds sang. It was Summer! Dobrunka quickly filled her apron with strawberries and thanked the Twelve Months.

But no thanks did she receive from her sister and mother when she returned home. They devoured the strawberries at once, and sent Dobrunka out the following day for apples.

"You are here again, my child?" asked January. When he heard of her need for apples, he turned to a man with an iron-gray beard in a purple mantle. It was Brother September, who stirred the fire and brought autumn to the earth. A single apple tree stood nearby, bearing rosy fruit.

"Hurry, my child, and shake the tree," said September.

Dobrunka shook it but twice, and hurried home with the two apples. The astonishment of Katinka and her mother knew no bounds. "Apples in January!" cried Katinka. "And where did you get these?"

"Up yonder on the mountain," said Dobrunka. "There is a tree loaded down with them."

"Why did you bring only two? You ate the rest on the way!"

"No, sister. I was only permitted to shake the tree twice."

Katinka did not believe her and drove her from the room. The apples were the most delicious she had ever tasted, and Katinka said to her mother, "I must have more of these. Give me my warm fur cloak. I shall go to the mountain, find the tree, and shake it as long as I like." Her mother tried to dissuade her from going into the wintry forest, but the spoiled girl was determined to have more apples.

Katinka also spotted the light from the Twelve Months' fire and followed it, but when she got there, not knowing who they were, she pushed her way rudely through their midst to warm herself at the fire. January gruffly asked what her business was with them.

"What business is it of yours, old man?" replied Katinka. And without another word, she turned and disappeared into the forest. January frowned until his brow was black as a storm cloud. He raised his cane above his head, and in a twinkling, the fire went out, black darkness covered the earth, the wind rose, and snow began to fall.

Katinka could not see the way before her. The snow beat on her face, and she became hopelessly lost. She called her mother, she cursed her sister, she called out wildly. Still the wind blew.

The mother watched for her daughter at the window for hours. At midnight she put on her cloak and went out to search for Katinka. There were no footsteps to follow, for the falling snow had covered all tracks. And still the wind blew.

Dobrunka sat at her spinning wheel all night, but no one returned. "What can have happened?" she wondered. And in time, winter passed, and summer arrived, but Katinka and her mother never came back to the little house at the edge of the forest. So the house, the cow, and the meadow fell to Dobrunka. By and by, a prince stopped at the house, fell in love, and married her. And through the seasons, no matter how much the North Wind blew and the snow fell, there was always summer in Dobrunka's heart. Joy filled her home, and the laughter of her children made music everywhere.

January 4

The Baby-sitter

Laura Stevens was nine years old, too old, she knew, to need a baby-sitter. But every single time her mother and her father went out, they insisted that Mrs. Thomas stay with her. Laura didn't like Mrs. Thomas. She wouldn't let her stay up late to watch television, she wouldn't let her eat more than three cookies, and she even made Laura play games with her! "I'm not a baby,"

Laura pleaded with her parents. "I'm nine years old. I don't need a baby-sitter. And if you make me have one, I'm going to go to my room and stay there forever."

"Laura," scolded her mother, "you're acting just like a baby. That's why you need a baby-sitter."

Laura sighed. She knew her mother would never understand how hard it was to be nine years old. The reason she had to have a baby-sitter, her mother seemed to be saying, was that she complained about having a baby-sitter. But if she didn't complain, she wondered, would she still have to have a sitter? It was very hard to understand parents.

But no matter what Laura did, every time her parents went out they insisted Mrs. Thomas stay with her. And every time Mrs. Thomas stayed with her, she was very nice to Laura, but made her obey stupid rules. But someday, Laura knew, someday she would be big enough to stay by herself, or at least have a baby-sitter who wasn't so bossy.

One night, as Laura's parents got ready to go out, they told her they had a big surprise for her. Mrs. Thomas had gone to visit her sister in another city. And instead of another ordinary baby-sitter, her parents had hired a brand-new Robo-Sitter! Laura had heard of Robo-Sitters but she had never seen one. They looked just like real baby-sitters, but they were robots, and they could be programmed by parents to set the rules and enforce them. Laura was so excited.

When the Robo-Sitter was delivered Laura was amazed to discover that she looked just a like a real person and even sounded like a real person. Her father used a big remote control to program Robo-Sitter. Pressing all the buttons, he programmed the Robo-Sitter to make dinner for Laura, give her three cookies, help her with her homework, and put her to bed at ten o'clock, a half hour later than Mrs. Thomas ever allowed. And then he programmed the Robo-Sitter to clean the whole house. When he pressed "Enter" the Robo-Sitter's eyes opened brightly and a big smile appeared on her face. When Laura's parents left the house, the Robo-Sitter assured them, "Oh, don't worry about a thing. We'll have a wonderful time."

Laura stood at the window and watched until her parents' car disappeared around the block. And then Laura picked up the remote programmer. It looked just like the control for her computer or her video games. Very quickly, Laura reprogrammed the Robo-Sitter! And then she pressed "Enter."

The Robo-Sitter whizzed around the whole house, cleaning it from top to bottom in less than a minute. Then she raced into the kitchen and returned carrying three whole boxes of cookies, which she handed to Laura. Then she did all of Laura's homework in nine seconds. Then she put Laura's favorite movie in the VCR and got out of the way. Laura sat down in front of the TV set with her box of cookies and pressed the "Off" button. And just like that, the Robo-sitter went to sleep.

Laura ate her cookies and watched her movie. But after a little while, her stomach started hurting and she wanted someone to talk to. She turned on the Robo-Sitter, who immediately cleaned the whole house all over again, brought Laura three more boxes of cookies, and did Laura's homework for a second time. Laura tried to re-program the Robo-Sitter, but was only able to make her do the same things faster and faster and faster. Laura had no choice and finally turned off the Robo-Sitter.

The house was very quiet. For the first time in her whole entire life, Laura was all alone. And it made her feel really strange. She wanted someone to talk to, she wanted someone to play with. She picked up another cookie but her tummy hurt too much so she didn't even want to eat it. She sat very still in her father's favorite chair, watching her movie. But then she heard a loud creak from her bedroom. Maybe it was just the house relaxing, but in her mind it was a person. Oh, she wished Mrs. Thomas was there!

Two hours passed, but they seemed like two weeks. Finally, she heard her father's car driving into the garage. Just as her parents walked in, she turned on the Robo-Sitter, who immediately cleaned the whole house again. "Did you have a nice time?" Laura's mother asked.

Laura smiled. "It was very nice," she said softly, and then added, "but I think I like it better when Mrs. Thomas is here."

—JORDAN BURNETT AND DAVID FISHER

January 5

The Lion and the Old Hare

A HINDU FABLE

In the Mandar mountain there once lived a lion named Fierce Heart, who was continually killing and devouring the other wild animals. Matters at last became so bad that all the beasts of the field and woods held a public meeting, and drew up a respectful proposal to the Lion in these words:

"Your majesty, we were wondering, a few of us here, if it was completely necessary to make a meal of us all. We do not of course want you to go hungry, but we would also like to have a very small say in our fate. Would it be possible, therefore, if we might every day furnish one animal for your majesty's dinner?"

The Lion replied: "If such an arrangement suits you better, all right. I'll give it a try."

So from that time on, one beast was daily allotted to the Lion, and daily devoured by him. At last came the day when it was the turn of the old hare to supply the royal dinner. This old hare, as he went on his way to give himself up, reflected as follows:

"At the worst I can but die, so I may as well take my own time going to my death."

Now it happened that Fierce Heart was unusually hungry and seeing the hare approach quite slowly, he roared out angrily, "How dare you keep me waiting like this?"

"Sire," answered the old hare, "the blame is not mine. I was delayed on the road by another lion who made me swear that I would come back and give myself up to him, as soon as I explained the circumstances to your majesty."

"Come," said Fierce Heart in a great rage, "show me instantly where this villain of a lion lives."

Accordingly, the hare led the way until he came to a very deep well, where he stopped and said: "Let the Lord, the King, come forward and meet his rival."

The lion approached and, looking down into the well, beheld his own image reflected in the water. Whereupon with an angry roar, he flung himself into the well, and perished!

January 6

Baucis and Philemon

AN ANCIENT GREEK TALE

In the ancient land of Phrygia, on a certain hill, there is a linden tree and an oak tree, enclosed by a wall. Not far from the spot is swampy marsh, where a prosperous village once stood.

Now in the days when this village prospered, the god Jupiter and his son Mercury decided to visit this country in human form. They dressed themselves as weary travelers, and went from door to door, asking for lodging and a bite to eat. But all the village's inhabitants turned them away and the gods were becoming quite angry at the rude and selfish people.

The last house they went to was the humble thatched cottage of an old couple, Baucis and her husband, Philemon. They were quick to welcome the gods to their home, and gave them seats of honor at the hearth. A stew was put on the fire, and Philemon brought his guests water with which to wash. They had but a weak wine to offer the travelers, but they set this on the table too.

When the meal was ready, all sat down, and the old folks were astonished to see that as soon as the wine was poured, the pitcher refilled itself. At that moment, both knew they had heavenly guests at their table and were ashamed of their meager hospitality.

But the gods reassured them. "You, alone in this village, were willing to take in weary travelers. This selfish town shall pay for its sins, and only you shall escape the punishment. Leave your house and come with us to the top of the hill."

The old couple hurried to obey, and took their staff to climb up the steep hill. As they turned to look back at their house, they saw their entire village sunk in a great lake. Only their house still stood, and as they watched, it was transformed into a temple.

Jupiter spoke: "Excellent old man, and woman worthy of such a husband, speak and tell us your wishes. What favor have you to ask of us?"

The couple spoke together for a moment and then Philemon said, "We ask to be guardians of your temple. Since here we have passed our lives in love and peace, we wish to take leave of our lives here—and together. I pray that I may not live to see her grave, nor be laid in my own by her."

Their prayer was granted, and they were keepers of the temple for as long as they lived. When they were very, very old, they died peacefully together. They were standing on the hill talking, when Baucis saw Philemon begin to put forth leaves, and Philemon saw Baucis doing the same. For as long as they could still speak, they exchanged parting words. "Farewell, dear spouse," they said together, and at the same moment, the bark closed over their mouths. The trees still stand there, side by side.

January 7

The Shepherd Boy and the King

A GERMAN TALE

There was once a shepherd boy who was known far and wide for his clever answers to every question. The king heard of his wisdom, but he could not believe it, and ordered the boy to court.

When he arrived, the king said to him, "If you can answer wisely three questions I will give you, then you shall be as my own child, and dwell with me in my castle."

"I am ready, your majesty," replied the shepherd boy.

"First," the king asked, "I want to know how many drops of water are in the ocean."

"My lord king," said the boy, "if you could have all the rivers in the world stopped up, so that not a drop could run into the sea, and I could count them, then I might be able to tell you how many drops the ocean contains."

Saying nothing, the king posed the next question. "How many stars are there in the skies?"

The shepherd boy replied, "First give me a large sheet of paper. If I make many points with a pen, close together, then whoever tries to count these points will quickly find his eyes dazzled. If, however, it were possible to count these points, even then it would not be easy to count the stars."

But no one would attempt to count them, so the king asked his third question: "How many seconds of time are there in eternity?"

The shepherd boy answered: "In Pomerania there is a diamond mountain, one league high, one league broad, and one league deep. If a little bird could go once in every hundred years and peck away a morsel from the mountain until the whole mountain was gone, not even then would one second of eternity have passed!"

Then the king replied, "You have answered all of my questions wisely, and from this time forward, all shall treat you as my son!"

The shepherd boy lived the rest of his life in royal splendor and advised the king on many matters.

—BROTHERS GRIMM

January 8

The Necklace of Truth, Part 1

There was once a little girl by the name of Coralie who loved to tell lies. Some children think very little of not speaking the truth, and a small lie—or a great one in case of necessity—that saves them from a duty or a punishment is perfectly acceptable in their eyes.

Coralie was one of this sort. The truth was a thing of which she had no idea. Her parents were deceived by her stories for a long time, but they saw at last that she was telling them lies, and

from that moment forward they had no confidence in anything that she said.

It is a terrible thing for parents not to be able to believe their own child's words. And they worry horribly about what kind of adult this child will grow up to be.

After vainly trying every means to reform Coralie, her parents decided to take her to the enchanter Merlin, who was famous throughout the world and was known as the greatest friend of truth that ever lived. For this reason, little children who were in the habit of telling lies were brought to him from all over in order that he might cure them.

The enchanter Merlin lived in a glass palace with transparent walls, and never in his whole life had he thought of disguising his actions, of causing others to believe what was not true, or even allowing others to believe a lie by being silent when he might have spoken. He knew liars by their odor a mile off, and when Coralie approached the palace he burned vinegar to combat the smell.

Coralie's mother began to explain the vile disease that afflicted her daughter, but her shame was such that she made a rather confused speech. Merlin interrupted her. "I know what is the matter, my good lady," said he. "I felt your daughter's approach long ago. She is one of the greatest liars in the world and she has made me very uncomfortable."

Coralie hid behind her mother's apron at these words, while her parents grew most anxious. They desperately wanted their child to be cured, but they wished her cured gently in a way that would not hurt her.

"Don't be afraid," said Merlin, seeing their anxiety. "I do not employ violence in curing disease. I am only going to make Coralie a beautiful present, which I think will not displease her."

He opened a drawer, and took from it a magnificent amethyst necklace with a diamond clasp. He put it on Coralie's neck, and sent her parents away, saying, "Go, good people, and worry no more. Your daughter carries with her a sure guardian of the truth." Coralie was delighted to be getting off so easily, but then Merlin looked sternly at her and said, "In a year, I shall come for my necklace. Till that time I forbid you to take it off for even a moment. Woe be unto you if you disobey!"

"Oh, it's so beautiful! I'll wear it always!" Coralie might have been less delighted had she been aware that it was the famous Necklace of Truth she wore. The ancients knew of its magical power to uncover lies of all sorts—a power that Coralie would shortly discover for herself.

January 9

The Necklace of Truth, Part 2

When Coralie returned to school after her long absence, her friends admired the necklace at once. "Oh, where did you get it from?" they asked. In those days, one did not admit to having consulted the enchanter Merlin, or everyone would know exactly why. Coralie was careful not to betray herself.

"I was sick for a long time," she said boldly, "and on my recovery, my parents gave me this beautiful necklace." A loud cry rose from her friends. For the diamonds of the clasp, which had shone so brilliantly, suddenly became coarse glass and turned dim.

"Well, yes, I *have* been sick," insisted Coralie. "Why are you all making such a fuss?" At this second falsehood, the lovely amethysts changed to ugly yellow stones. Coralie again heard her friends cry out and saw all their eyes fixed on her necklace. When she looked down, she was terrified.

"I have been to the enchanter Merlin's," Coralie said humbly. Scarcely had she confessed the truth than the necklace recovered its beauty. But the laughter of the little girls so mortified her that she couldn't help saying something to retrieve her reputation. "You are wrong to laugh!" she exclaimed. "He treated us with great respect, and sent his splendid carriage to carry us to his palace. His palace, by the way, is made of jasper and there are so many marvelous things inside that I couldn't begin to tell you—"

The laughter, suppressed with difficulty since she began this fine story, became so boisterous that Coralie stopped in amazement. Looking down once more on the unlucky necklace, she shuddered. At each detail she had invented, the necklace had grown longer and longer till it almost reached the ground.

"You are stretching the truth," cried the little girls.

"Well, I confess . . . we went on foot, and only stayed a few minutes." The necklace instantly shrunk to its proper size.

"And the necklace? Where did it come from?"

"Merlin gave it to me without saying a word, probably—" Coralie had not time to finish. The necklace had grown shorter and shorter, till it choked her terribly and she gasped for breath.

"You are keeping back part of the truth," cried her classmates.

Coralie hastened to alter her words while she could still speak. "He said . . . that I was . . . one of the greatest . . . liars . . . in the world." Freed from the strangling necklace, she began crying, but finished her story. "That was why he gave the necklace to me. He said it was a guardian of the truth, and I have been a great fool to be proud of it!"

"If I were in your place," said one of her friends, "I would send it back. What stops you from taking it off?" Poor Coralie was silent, but the stones began to clatter up and down.

"There is something you have not told us!" exclaimed the little girls in glee.

"I like to wear it!" said Coralie. The amethysts danced more than ever.

"There is a reason you are hiding from us!"

"Well, if you must know—some great calamity will befall me if I take it off."

It didn't take very long at all for Coralie to become convinced that falsehoods were useless for they would be instantly discovered. And as she became accustomed to telling the truth, she became a happier person. The joy of a clear conscience and the peace of mind that truth brought made her grow to hate lies. Soon the necklace had nothing to do, and long before the year had passed, Merlin came to take it back, for he needed the necklace to cure another child of this affliction.

No one knows what became of the wonderful Necklace of Truth after Merlin's death. Perhaps Merlin's descendants hid it. Or perhaps they didn't—which is something children in the habit of telling lies will never know for sure.—JEAN MACÉ

January 10

The Tale of Evan

A CELTIC TALE

At one time there was a husband and wife who lived in a small parish where work had become very scarce. The husband felt he must leave his wife and search for a job. He traveled far toward the east, and at last came to the house of a farmer and asked for work.

"What work can you do?" asked the farmer.

"All kinds of work," said Evan, and they agreed upon three pounds for the year's wages.

When the end of the year came, Evan's master showed him the three pounds and said, "See, Evan, here's your wage, but if you'll give it back to me I'll give you a piece of advice instead."

"Give me my wage," answered Evan.

"No, I'll not," said the master. "I'll explain my advice. *You should never leave the old road for the sake of a new one.*" After that they agreed on another year at the old wages, and at the end of it Evan took instead another piece of advice. And this time it was: *"Never lodge where an old man is married to a young woman."*

The same thing happened at the end of the third year, when the advice was: *"Honesty is the best policy."* But this time Evan would not stay longer; he wanted to go back to his wife. As he was leaving, his master handed him a cake, saying, "Here is a cake for you to take home to your wife, and when you are most joyous together, then break the cake, and not sooner."

As he traveled toward home, he met three merchants from his own parish, coming home from a fair. "Oho, Evan," they said, "glad we are to see you. Where have you been so long?"

"I have been working, and now I'm going home to my wife."

"Oh, travel with us. You'll be welcome," said the merchants. But when they took the new road, Evan, remembering his master's advice, kept to the old one. None had gone far before Evan heard the cry "Thieves!" He ran to the other road and scared away the robbers, and the merchants were terribly grateful. "We are in debt to you, Evan. Lodge with us tonight, as our guest."

But when they got to the inn, Evan said, "First I must see the innkeeper."

"Why do you want him?" asked his traveling companions. "Here is the hostess, and she is young and pretty!" The young woman said her husband was in the kitchen, and when Evan went in there, he found a weak old man turning the spit.

"Oh, I'll not lodge here," cried Evan, again recalling his master's advice. "I'll go next door." Now it happened that the hostess had plotted with a monk to murder the old man and blame it on her lodgers. And it happened that Evan overheard this scheme, and warned the merchants in time. Now they were doubly grateful to him.

At last their roads separated and Evan continued on his way to his wife and cottage. Glad she was to see him, crying, "Home in the nick of time! Here's a purse of gold I've found, and I'm thinking perhaps it belongs to the great lord yonder. But what shall we do with it?"

Remembering the third counsel, Evan said, "Honesty is the best policy. Let us take it to the lord, then."

And though Evan and his wife took the purse of gold to the castle, a dishonest servant there never turned it over to the lord. When the nobleman discovered this some days later, he was so pleased with Evan that he gave him the thieving servant's job for life.

"Honesty *is* the best policy!" exclaimed Evan, as he celebrated his good fortune with his wife. Then he thought of the cake his old master had given him, and the advice to eat it when he was most joyful. And when Evan broke the cake open, lo and behold, inside it were the wages for his three years of labor.

January 11

The Proud Fox and the Young Prairie Chicken

It was breakfast time and the fox was hungry. "My kingdom for a prairie chicken," he thought to himself.

Just then a prairie chicken ambled across the road.

"A tender morsel," the fox said to himself, chuckling with delight. "And a stupid one, too." He walked up to the prairie chicken casually, so as not to alarm her, and bid her a good morning.

"Greetings, little one," said the fox.

"Good morning yourself!" said the prairie chicken, keeping her distance.

"And how is your family on this fine day?" asked the fox.

"So-so," said the prairie chicken. "And yours?"

"My family is doing very well, thank you," said the fox politely.

"Do I know you? You don't look familiar," said the prairie chicken. And then, not wanting to be rude, "What do you do to occupy your days?"

"In general, I just go here and there and enjoy myself. But I used to spend most days learning everything my daddy knows," said the fox.

"Are you saying you know everything your daddy knows?" asked the prairie chicken. "Why, I can't imagine such a thing."

"Yes, indeed I do," replied the fox. "I doubt that there is a slier fox in these parts, and if there is I agree to swallow him without salt or pepper."

"My goodness!" exclaimed the prairie chicken.

"So tell me about you," said the fox. "What have *you* been doing lately?"

"I do very little, really," said the prairie chicken. "From the moment I burst out of that egg, I have been chasing my mommy and eating all of the bugs and seeds she finds. She hasn't taught me much; all I know is to hide when I see a human with a gun or an animal with sharp teeth showing."

The fox was rather uncomfortable with the chicken's last comment and he made a mental note to keep his mouth closed.

"So your mommy taught you how to hide," said the fox. "Well, hiding *is* an art form. I have dozens of ways to hide. What is your own little way?"

"All I do is slip underneath piles of dead leaves," said the prairie chicken. "It isn't very artful. And the bad part is that some of my feathers stick out, though it doesn't really matter because my feathers are the same color as the leaves."

The fox shook his head. "That is not a very intelligent way of hiding," he said, not hiding the insult.

"That might be," said the prairie chicken. "But it will have to do until I learn how to fly—at which point I will never have to hide again."

The fox was wondering what to say next, when a pack of hounds came thundering down the road. The prairie chicken curled herself up and snuggled under a pile of leaves, escaping the notice of the hounds. But the fox stood dumb and in a minute the hounds discovered him and ate him for breakfast. There was not much left of him, except for his bushy tail, which the owner of the hounds saved and used for a little broom.

January 12

The Wild Boar

A wild boar was whetting his tusks against a tree when a fox came passing by. Curious, the fox asked why the boar did sharpen his tusks so. "Why do you spend your time like this? There is neither a hunter nor a hound in sight, nor any danger that I can see at hand," said the fox.

"True," replied the boar. "But when that danger does arise, I shall have something else to do than to sharpen my weapons."

It is too late to whet the sword when the trumpet sounds to draw it.—AESOP

January 13

The Man, the Boy, and the Donkey

A man and his son were going to market with their donkey. As they were making their way down the dusty road, a man passed them and jeered, "What's wrong with you people? Why are you walking your donkey as if it were a dog? Donkeys are to ride upon!"

So the man put his son on the donkey, and the threesome proceeded on their journey to market. They soon passed a group of men. In a loud whisper, one of the men said, "Look at that family. They are spoiling the boy by letting him ride on that poor donkey."

The man and his son heard the remark, and so the boy dismounted and they resumed their journey.

Just about that time, two women walked to the side of the road and the first one shook a long, wrinkled finger at the man. "You should take better care of your boy, mister. It's too hot for him to be walking on those tender feet. Why isn't he riding atop that stupid donkey?"

The man and the boy looked at each other. They didn't know what to do. To please the two women, the boy got back on the donkey and the man, the boy, and the donkey headed down the road.

The threesome had just arrived at the village when a group of people in the town square walked up. "Aren't you ashamed for burdening that sweet donkey with your lazy son? There ought to be a law against such abuse!" they said.

The boy got off the donkey. They thought and thought about what to do. Then the boy had an idea. They cut down a pole, tied the donkey's feet to it, and raised the pole and the donkey to their shoulders. At the Market Bridge, hundreds of people swarmed to see the ridiculous sight. There was laughter and more laughter until the donkey accidentally got one foot loose, kicked out, and threw the boy off balance. The boy dropped his end of the pole and in the commotion, the donkey fell over the side of the bridge. His forefeet were still tied together, so he could not save himself. The boy and the man watched sadly as their beloved donkey drowned.

Try to please everyone and you please no one.—AESOP

January 14

The Pompous Bear

One day a bear named Boffo was padding through the forest when he spotted a pheasant. With a quick swipe of his paw and some very good luck, he managed to catch the bird.

Now Boffo was the kind of bear who liked to impress. It wasn't enough for him to catch his supper; no, the world had to know all of his conquest. He was the kind of bear most of the animals considered a show-off.

"Ho, ho, ho," thought Boffo to himself. "I can't wait to show the other animals how I nabbed this pheasant." The bird was still alive, and he didn't want to mark it, so he held it between his great teeth very carefully, and padded off in search of someone to impress.

By and by, he came upon Rick the rabbit. The rabbit saw the pheasant in old Boffo's mouth and, knowing full well that the bear wanted to boast, he hopped away, his white tail bobbing down the leafy path.

Boffo wrinkled his nose. "Hmrf," he thought to himself. "Next time Rick ignores me I'll catch him for my supper!" A bear could never catch a rabbit, but Boffo was a show-off, even in his private thoughts.

By and by, Freddie the fox came to the clearing where Boffo sat with his pheasant. Rick noticed immediately that Boffo had a bird in his mouth, and he knew Boffo wanted to be acknowledged in the worst way. But the fox was tired of the bear's showing off, and was determined not to give him that satisfaction.

"Say, Boffo, do you think it will rain today?" he asked.

Boffo shook his head "no," hoping that Freddie would notice the pheasant in his mouth.

"Hello, Boffo, I *said,* do you think it will rain today?" the fox pressed.

Boffo did not want to open his mouth for the bird was still quite alive. He shook his head vigorously, as if to say no.

"Let's see," Freddie said teasingly. "When you shake your head side to side, does that mean no?"

Boffo shook his head up and down.

"Oh, I stand corrected. You're telling me that when you shake your head *up and down,* it means no," Freddie said.

Boffo shook his head side to side.

"Well, which is it? Yes or no? Side to side or up and down?" Freddie said impatiently. "Do you think it will rain or *not*?"

"No," said Boffo, in frustration. And with that, the pheasant flew right out of his mouth. Boffo was horrified. And Freddie laughed gaily, all the way back to his hole.

January 15

The Magic Ring, Part 1

A NATIVE AMERICAN TALE

Deep in the forest lived a warrior named White Hawk. The forest was dense and green, and most days White Hawk was content to roam its aisles, but on this day he hiked for miles to see if the forest had an edge.

Indeed it did. After traveling all day, White Hawk came to a clearing where the forest ended and a vast plain of golden grass began. A worn path encircled the forest, forming a magic ring. Curiously, no paths from the plain or the forest led to the ring.

White Hawk was contemplating the ring when he saw a shadow approach, and looked to the sky. Floating down from the heavens was a basket in which rode twelve maidens. The basket landed softly and the girls jumped out, one by one. They were all beautiful but the youngest one was the most beautiful of all, and White Hawk was overcome with desire. Without thinking, he ran out to greet her, but the maidens were filled with fear at the sight of him, and they jumped into their basket and floated away.

"This will not do," White Hawk lamented. All night he laid in bed in his lodge, remembering the youngest maiden, and longing to see her again. He decided to return to the forest's edge the next day to see if he could make her acquaintance. This time, he turned himself into a raccoon, so as not to frighten the maidens.

The maidens floated down in their basket and jumped out and began dancing around the ring of the forest, just as they had done the day before. White Hawk, disguised as a raccoon, jumped out to see them but he so startled them that they raced back to their basket and floated away once more. White Hawk spent another night in his lodge, trying to figure out what to do.

The next day, White Hawk went to the forest's edge. He spotted a tree stump filled with mice. Before the maidens arrived he moved the tree stump to the path around the forest and transformed himself into a little mouse.

When the maidens arrived, it was the youngest who noticed the stump first. "Why, that stump wasn't here before," she observed. Her sisters were having so much fun teasing the mice that they didn't pay attention. They took sticks and killed the mice, laughing at the sport. Just as the youngest maiden was about to kill White Hawk, he willed himself to be human again, and rose up and took her into his arms. The maidens were terrified, and fled to the basket and floated away, leaving the youngest behind.

January 16

The Magic Ring, Part 2

White Hawk knew it would be difficult to woo this maiden who came from a faraway place. He did not force her to be his wife but tried to show her the joys of the earth. He hunted for her and built her a new lodge and did everything he could to help her forget her sisters.

Over time, the young maiden grew to love White Hawk and she bore him a beautiful son. But the maiden, you see, was one of the stars. She still longed for her sisters. She loved White Hawk but Earth was not her home.

One day, while White Hawk was out hunting, the maiden took her son and the two went to the forest's edge. She brought a basket, and went to the magic ring and commanded the basket to take her to the heavens. She sang a song of farewell, and the sweet notes carried in the wind to White Hawk's ear. White Hawk, who had lived in fear that this day might come, knew he had lost his wife and child. He called to them, pleading for their return, but his cries were met with silence. He looked at the sky and watched the basket become smaller and smaller until it was the size of a pea, and then it disappeared.

White Hawk was alone.

For years, the maiden and her son lived in the heavens in happiness. But as her son grew older, he began to resemble White Hawk more, and the maiden began to miss her Earth husband. When she confided this to her father, the Star Chief, he was generous and compassionate. "Invite the man here to live with us," he said kindly. "Have him bring one of every bird and animal he can find."

The maiden and her son returned to earth and found White Hawk, who was overjoyed to see them again. The maiden gave him her father's instructions and White Hawk looked for the rarest and finest examples of each bird and animal he could find. From each creature, he plucked a feather or took a tail or a claw or a wing so as not to kill the beasts unnecessarily. Then the maiden and her son and White Hawk climbed into the basket at the magic ring, and rose to the heavens.

The starry world was overcome with happiness to see the family together, and to celebrate the Star Chief held a great pageant. Each one of the guests received a charm from one of White Hawk's animals or birds: a tail, a claw, a feather, or a wing. Magically, each star took on the form of whatever animal or bird they had chosen. White Hawk's wife chose a white hawk's feather, so he followed suit, and then their son did the same. And to this day, you can see the three white hawks soaring in the sky, never to be separated again.

January 17

The Locust, the Beetle, the Goldfinch, and the Hunter

A CHINESE FABLE

Once upon a time, a certain young prince was walking in the garden behind the royal palace when all at once he heard the song of a locust from the bough of a tall tree. On drawing nearer to the tree, he saw the locust singing the long notes of its little song, quite happy in having found a pleasant place to rest in the morning breeze. The locust did not know that it was in danger from a beetle that had crawled from bough to bough, and was just then raising its body and stretching out its front claws in order to seize upon and eat the locust. But while the beetle's attention was fixed upon the locust, it had no idea that it was in danger itself from a goldfinch, who was fluttering back and forth in the shade of the green leaves, preparing to make a dinner of *it.* And while the attention of the goldfinch was fixed upon the beetle, he little knew that the hunter was standing near with crossbow in hand, preparing to shoot him. And while the hunter's whole attention was fixed upon the goldfinch, he little knew that close up beside him was a deep ditch, nearly full of water. The hunter slipped and fell into the water. The noise of the splash startled the goldfinch, which swiftly flew away. The beetle scurried back into his hole, leaving the locust to sing his song in peace.

January 18

Brave Dan

The whole family had gone out for the evening, leaving Dan, the new pup, all alone. Dan was overjoyed because he had always wanted to be master of the house. Dan had never been the master of anything before, and he liked the idea of being in charge. He trotted proudly through the halls and poked his nose into every room, looking for burglars and other bad guys.

All was quiet until Dan heard a noise. It seemed to come from his master's room: "Tick . . . tick . . . tick . . ." Oh dear! Someone was in the house! Who could it be? Dan wasn't so sure he liked being all alone. Suddenly he heard a loud gong as the clock on the mantlepiece struck one. Brave Dan scampered off as fast as his legs could carry him.

And that was Dan's big night as master of the house.

—ANGELA M. KEYES

January 19

Mercury and the Woodman

A woodman was cutting down trees near the bank of a river and by chance his axe slipped into the water. Immediately, the axe fell to the bottom. The poor man was greatly distressed, for he replied upon his axe to cut trees and earn a living. Now what would he do?

As it happened, the great god Mercury owned the river, and heard the woodcutter's cries of sorrow. When he realized what had happened, he dived to the bottom of the river and brought up a golden axe. "Is this your axe?" Mercury asked kindly.

The woodman, who was scrupulously honest, denied the axe was his. Mercury then dived a second time, and thus brought up an axe of silver.

"Is this your axe?" the god inquired.

But the woodcutter again denied it.

On the third dive, Mercury brought up an axe identical to the one the woodcutter had been using. "Yes, that's mine," the woodcutter said happily.

Mercury was so impressed with the woodcutter's honesty that he made him a present of the other two axes as well.

The woodcutter went home and told all of his companions what had happened. Upon hearing the story, one of the companions wandered over to Mercury's river and pretended to be cutting wood. He then pretended to lose his axe, though really he just slipped it into the river. The man sat down on the bank and made a great production of his sorrow, crying out, "My axe, my axe!"

Mercury appeared as before and asked the man what had happened.

Again Mercury dived down to retrieve the axe, but came up first holding one with a golden handle. "Is this the axe you lost?" Mercury asked.

"Yes, yes, that's the one," the man said in reply. He was about to grasp the golden axe, when Mercury pulled it back from him and refused. Mercury, wanting to punish the man's impudence and lying, walked away in disgust. The man did not even get his own axe back.

Honesty is the best policy.—AESOP

January 20

The Beggar King, Part 1

A JEWISH TALE

The day had started out like any other, with the high priest reading a passage from the Holy Book. Normally, the king slumped over in his chair and snoozed during the reading. But he was semi-awake today, and when he heard the sacred words, his face swelled up in rage.

"For riches are not forever: and doth the crown endure to every generation?" the priest read quietly.

"What?" cried out the king. "Are you saying that my wealth and crown mean nothing? Give me that book!"

To the surprise and horror of the court, the king ripped out the passage from the Holy Book and then threw the book at the wall, while the high priest and all of his courtiers gasped.

"That's enough nonsense for one morning," the king said. "Anyway, I'm late for my hunting expedition. Ready the horses and we will be off."

The king gave a disapproving glare to the high priest and went out to join his hunting party. Very soon into the hunt, the king caught his first glimpse of a glorious wild deer, and he was filled with excitement. Wanting to hoard the deer for himself, he broke from the pack of hunters and followed the deer over hill and dale and then to a river. At the river's edge, he took his clothes off, and wearing nothing but his sword, waded across the river in pursuit of the deer. Suddenly the creature disappeared. The king looked everywhere, but the deer had simply vanished. Just as the king was about to give up, he came upon a young man, clad in a deerskin, asleep beneath an oak tree. The king, who was wearing nothing, jumped back when the youth opened his eyes.

"You were not chasing a deer, but were chasing me in a deer's disguise," said the youth to the naked king. "In truth, I am an angel. I brought you to this moment so that I might be able to teach you a sacred lesson, for your pride has put you in grave danger."

The angel said no more, and then bounded away. Before the king could protest, the angel put on the king's clothes and mounted the king's horse. When the other hunters came up, the angel appeared to them to be the king, and they all retired to the castle.

The king cursed the angel. He stomped and kicked and shook his fist at the heavens. Before long, a woodcutter passing by heard the king's curses and came to see what it was all about.

"What troubles you, man?" asked the woodcutter. "Besides the fact that you are stark naked," he said with a chuckle.

"I am your king," said the king sternly.

"You are a *fool,*" said the woodcutter, starting to walk off. But the king begged the woodcutter for some clothes and the woodcutter, who was a kindly man, took the king home, fed him a simple meal, and sent him on his way in some ragged clothes.

The king made his way back to the palace. When he came to the great door, he told the guards who he was and demanded to be allowed entrance. But the guards just laughed and told the old man to go home. The king now realized his plight was serious and that his punishment for mocking the words of the Holy Book had cost him everything he held dear.

He wandered that night and thought what he might have done differently. He stood at street corners and looked at the poor around him and begged for a little bread and milk. Then he began a wandering that was to last many years.

January 21

The Beggar King, Part 2

The king wandered and begged throughout his kingdom. As it happened, the very poorest treated him with the most kindness. One day he met up with a group of blind beggars, who traveled together and who had lost their guide. They asked the king if he would be their guide, and the king accepted. He was overjoyed because it allowed him a chance to serve others.

The king was a changed man. He was glad to care for his blind friends. Then one day it was announced that the good king (who, remember, was really the angel) was going to give a feast for all of the beggars in the land. The beggars all rejoiced like children. A feast in their honor! From all over the land, they headed for the palace: the crippled, the poor, the rejected.

At the palace, the guards announced that the king would speak to each and every beggar. "This means I will see the angel again," thought the king to himself. He watched as the beggars, one by one, received the angel's blessing. When it was his turn, the king and the angel stared at each other for a long time.

"Are you a beggar?" asked the angel, wearing the king's crown.

"No, your majesty. But I mocked the Holy Book and I am being punished. I am a guide for a group of blind beggars. That is my work."

The angel nodded in recognition. For years, he had longed for this day. "Leave the room, please," he said, gesturing to his courtiers.

The courtiers left and the huge palace hall was now empty except for the angel and the beggar king.

"Dear king, I know you," he said looking deep into the beggar's eyes. "I know, too, that you are a changed man. With pleasure, I return to you your throne."

But the king was no longer interested in power and wealth. "It is not necessary," said the king. "It is true that I have learned humility and wisdom, but the blind beggars now rely on me. I should remain their servant, if you please," the king said.

"You have learned well," said the angel. "But you have a duty to your people. I will provide for the blind ones. Now you must provide for your kingdom."

The angel then removed his fine robes, and put on the ragged clothes of the beggar king. And with this simple exchange of garments, the king was restored to his rightful throne. When the courtiers returned, they could not see a difference. Thereafter, the king ruled with kindness and compassion and his reign lasted for many many years.

January 22

Issun Boshi, the Inchling

A JAPANESE TALE

On a cold rocky island in Japan, an old man and woman lived together under a cloud of sadness, for never had they been blessed with a child. Every morning, they would pray to the Sun in the Heavens, but the Heavens did not seem to care. Just as the couple was about to lose hope, a baby was born to them. He was an intelligent, beautiful, charming child—but he was no taller than a thumb, and so they named him Issun Boshi, which means "The Inchling."

As the child grew older, he became clever and brave but he was still as short as a thumb. One day he announced that he must leave for the great city. His parents were worried because he had grown no higher than his father's ankle, but they knew he needed to make his way in the world. They gathered some provisions: a chopstick for a walking stick, a rice bowl for a hat, a needle for a sword, and a blade of grass for a sheath. Inchling said goodbye.

Now because Inchling was the size of a thumb, it took him thousands of tiny steps just to cross a road. He was starting to wonder if his mission was a folly, when he reached a huge river.

Across the river, high on a hill, he saw the city. He turned his rice bowl into a boat, his chopstick into an oar, and set sail.

When he finally arrived at the city, he was overwhelmed. He had to duck and weave his way carefully so as not to be crushed by boots or the wheels of carts. Soon he came to the most beautiful palace he had ever seen. He wondered how he might announce himself, when a giant boot came down over his head. "Excuse me," Inchling called. "I'm down here, under your boot." The man under whose boot Inchling stood was the Lord of the City. The Lord was charmed with the thumb-sized man and, in turn, Inchling loved to entertain the Lord, dueling a fly with his needle, and dancing on the tip of the Lord's fan. The Lord's daughter, who was a delicate and cheerful princess, also loved Inchling, and they were companions for many years.

One day Inchling went with the Lord's daughter to visit a famous temple. On their way home, three demons—red, green, and black—attacked the princess. The red demon carried a magic hammer. The green and black demons wielded long black rods. Their intentions were evil: *they had come to steal the princess.*

While the rest of the princess's party stood frozen with fear, Inchling leapt forward and screamed, "Never!" with all of his heart. He jabbed the black demon's eyes with his needle, over and over, until the demon screamed for mercy. He then attacked the green demon, who also could not bear the horrible pricks to his eyes. The red demon was not going to be beaten by an enemy as tiny as a thumb, and he lunged for the little warrior with his ugly mouth opened wide. Inchling jumped into the demon's mouth, and began stabbing his gums, until the pain was so great the demon surrendered and fled, without taking the magic hammer.

Inchling was so weak that he was barely able to stand, but he lifted himself up to present the magic hammer to the princess. "Make a wish on this hammer, your Highness, and it will come true," he said in a whisper. The princess ran to her beloved Inchling, and wept. "No, Inchling. This hammer was won because of your bravery. You make the first wish," she said.

Inchling stared up at the Sun in the Heavens. "My wish is that my height would be a measure of my devotion to you." With that, Inchling was transformed into a man who stood above all men.

The princess and Inchling returned to the Lord's palace. Soon after, they married and sent for Inchling's elderly parents, and they all lived together for many good years.

January 23

The Hawk and the Pigeons

Some pigeons had long lived in fear of a hawk, but being always on the alert and keeping near their dove-cote, they had figured out many ways to escape his attacks. The hawk was undaunted and decided to employ a new tactic.

"Doves, doves, doves," he said to them one morning. "Why do you prefer this life of constant anxiety, always on the run, living in fear of me from dawn to dusk? If you would only make me your king, I could protect you from every attack that could be made upon you and you could live in peace once and for all."

The pigeons, trusting his words, called him to the throne, but no sooner was he established there than he exercised his power by eating a pigeon a day. Said the pigeon who yet awaited his turn, "It serves us right. Anyone who voluntarily accepts the rule of an enemy must not be surprised if it is by his hand that they meet their own end."—PHAEDRUS

January 24

Adam and Eve Revisited

Like many folks, the poor old couple did not have it easy. All day they toiled in their dusty garden, just barely making a living. "See how hard we must work," said the old woman, complaining to her husband. "And all because of those fools Adam and Eve. If they hadn't disobeyed God we would be living in a beautiful garden all day, peeling grapes and counting the stars."

The husband agreed. "If you and I had been there instead of Adam and Even, all of the human race would be in Paradise."

The master overheard the old couple as he passed by and he was greatly amused. "Say, there, I could not help but overhear your provocative conversation. How would you like it if I took you to my palace to live and gave you servants and all you could eat or drink?"

"Oh, that would be delightful indeed!" exclaimed the couple in unison. "As good as Paradise!"

"Well, you may come for a visit, if you think so. Only remember that in Paradise there was one tree that was not to be touched. So, at my table, there will be *one* dish that you should not touch," said the master.

"That won't bother us," said the husband. "Why, Eve had all of the fruits in the garden, so why did she want the one that was forbidden? We are used to humble meals so why should it matter if there is an extra dish on the table?"

"Just so we understand each other," said the master. "Remember, you may have whatever you like but if you open that one dish you will be returned to your former life."

"We understand," said the husband and wife together.

The master told his servants to give the peasant couple an apartment to themselves in the castle and to set them a sumptuous table, and to place an earthenware dish in the middle of the table with a small live bird in it. A servant was to stay in the dining hall, so that he would know instantly if the husband or wife opened the dish.

The couple sat down to dinner and praised everything they saw, so delightful it all seemed.

"Look!" said the wife. "That's the dish we are not supposed to touch."

"Better not to even look at it," said the husband.

They went on to have a meal such as they never dreamed of. But as the novelty wore off, they were desirous of something new. And all that was left was the earthenware dish in the middle of the table.

"We might lift it up just a wee bit," said the wife.

"No, don't even think of it," said the husband.

The wife sat still for five minutes and then said, "If we just lifted up the corner of the lid, it could hardly be called an opening, you know."

"Better to leave it altogether and not think about it," said her husband.

Another five minutes passed and the wife could no longer contain her curiosity about the dish. "I should so like to know what the master put in there. Surely it would do no harm to peek."

"Well, I can't guess and can't see why he would care if we looked at it," said the husband.

But when the wife lifted the cover of the dish, she could see nothing. So she opened it a tiny bit more, and the bird flew up.

The servant ran and told his master, and the master came down and threw them out, telling them never to complain about Adam and Eve again.

January 25

The War of the Wolf and the Fox

A RUSSIAN TALE

In a small town in Russia, a man named Pardonya had an aging cat, and his neighbor Nasdalak had an old dog. Both men were ready to get rid of their elderly pets. "Why should I keep our cat any longer?" Pardonya asked his wife. "She's useless!"

"Don't say that!" replied his wife. "Why, she can still catch mice."

"Rubbish! Mice would have to dance on her stomach, and still she probably wouldn't catch one."

Pardonya's wife didn't take his threat too seriously, but their cat did. She had been listening behind the stove, and when her master left she began meowing pathetically. When the wife opened the cottage door, the cat grabbed the opportunity to flee from the house as fast as her old legs would carry her. She did not stop till she reached the safety of the woods.

At the same time, Nasdalak was complaining to his wife that their dog was deaf and blind and no use to them in protecting their house. It was time to put the dog out of his misery. The dog overheard the conversation, which made him feel very sad. When he got the chance, he also fled for the woods.

Now the dog and cat had not been the best of friends back home, but they were quite happy to find each other in the dark forest. They were sitting under a tree, exchanging their tales of woe, when a fox passed by and asked what was troubling them. After hearing how their masters no longer valued them, the fox said, "Alas, that's the way of the world! But I'll help you get back in your masters' good graces if you will only do me a small favor first." And the fox asked for their help in his war with the wolf. "The wolf is on his way to fight me tomorrow, and he has brought the bear and wild boar with him."

The dog and cat agreed to help in the war, for as they said, "It is better to die on the field of battle than to perish ignobly at home."

The wolf, bear, and wild boar arrived at the meeting place first, and the bear decided he would climb an oak tree and be the lookout. At last he spotted the dog, cat, and fox on the march, but told his comrades it would take at least half a day for them to arrive. So the bear took a nap in the tree, the wolf lay down in its shade, and the wild boar buried himself in some straw so that only his ear was visible.

The dog, cat, and fox arrived while they were resting, and the cat mistook the boar's ear for a mouse and jumped on it. The boar awoke in a fright, and ran off into the woods. The cat was even more startled and jumped up into the tree, which woke the bear, who jumped from his branch and landed on the wolf, killing them both.

With the war over, the dog, cat, and fox sauntered home, and on the way the fox caught twenty mice. As they neared Pardonya's cottage, the fox described his plan. "I will lay all these mice out, and one by one, you must put them in front of your master."

"Look here!" Pardonya's wife cried, as the cat brought in the first of the mice.

"Wonders never cease!" said Pardonya. "I never thought that old cat would catch another mouse."

With the cat's job secure, the dog and fox set off for Nasdalak's house. It happened to be the same day that Nasdalak had caught and slaughtered a pig.

"When it gets dark, you must go into the courtyard and bark with all your might. I will take care of the rest."

That night Nasdalak could hear his old dog barking, but he ignored the racket completely.

When Nasdalak's wife went to check on their pigs, she found all of them missing. "Thieves have been here!" she cried to her husband. "Why couldn't you have gotten up when the dog barked?"

The dog was welcomed back to the house, regaining his former position as watchdog. Nasdalak gained a new respect for him, and the fox . . . well, the fox enjoyed a fine meal of pork.

January 26

Looking for Carter Jr., Part 1

I grew up next door to a big family named the Franklins. My mother didn't like the idea of big families. "The Franklins have twelve children and no sense," she would say. Other people would make comments like, "Those Franklins grow like weeds," or "Don't they know about the population problem?"

But I always liked the Franklins. Especially Phillip Franklin. He was my best friend and a great goalie and we were in the same fourth-grade class. Often we would let Carter Jr., the youngest Franklin, hang out with us. After eleven kids, the Franklins had finally named a boy after Carter Franklin, Sr., the dad. Carter Jr. was kind of different. He had almond eyes and squared-off ears and sometimes you couldn't understand him. Phillip said he had Down syndrome and that he was "just a little slow, that's all."

I will never forget the day I became an honorary member of the Franklin family. It was a snowy afternoon and the sky was as gray as an old dime. Phillip and I were walking home from school when Kate Franklin pulled up in her jeep. She was seventeen but she had such a worried look on her face she looked like she was twenty, or even thirty. "Phillip," she called, "it's an emergency, you have to come home right now." I jumped into the jeep with Kate and Phillip and we sped off. Kate explained that Carter Jr. was missing. He had been missing for two hours and the whole family needed to search for him.

Just as we pulled up to the Franklin house, two police cars rounded the corner with their sirens blaring. They came to a stop in front of the Franklin house, and a swarm of Franklins came out of the house, all in their overcoats and mittens and hats. Mrs. Franklin didn't have on a coat or a hat or gloves; just her shirtdress and a thin sweater. Her face was red and her eyes were swollen. "Carter Jr.," she called into the wintry air, but it was so cold the sound didn't carry far. "Carter . . ." she said, and then broke into a sob. The snow continued to come down, making it hard to see.

The police took the important information. Carter was last seen making a snowman in the front yard. He was wearing a red snowsuit. He had on black rubber boots with red trim. The police radioed in the information, and almost on cue, the Franklins broke out in all different directions, calling for their little brother.

I decided to look around the park playground where I knew Carter liked to play in the concrete tunnels. Just the week before he had been there with Phillip and me, and I remembered there was one tunnel he liked to sit in. That was the thing about Carter; sometimes he just liked to sit. But when I went to the park and called for him, no one answered.

It was starting to snow pretty hard, and it was getting darker. I could hear Franklins all over the neighborhood, their calls muffled by the dense snow.

To tell the truth, while most of me sincerely wanted to find Carter Jr., part of me just liked the excitement of looking for someone in the middle of a snowstorm in the middle of the night. Sometimes, while I was calling for Carter, I'd even forget what I was doing, and I'd think about how the snow tasted or how I'd like to go home and eat some warm stew and cornbread, but then I'd remember that Carter Jr. was somewhere lost. That would make me sad, and I would start calling for him louder and louder.

By eleven o'clock, there was still no Carter and more and more police cars pulled up to the Franklin house, and even television crews and newspaper reporters were there. It wasn't fun or exciting any more. It was just sad. Carter wasn't the kind who could afford to get lost. Getting found would be too hard for him.

January 27

Looking for Carter Jr., Part 2

The next morning, I woke up and dug into a big breakfast while my mother looked out the kitchen window at all of the commotion in front of the Franklins' house. "They still haven't found Carter Jr." she said. "That little boy was so precious. . . ."

"I thought you didn't like big families," I said, not understanding my mother at all. I got up from my waffles and pulled on my jacket and snow mask and boots. "I'm going to go look some more," I said. My mother didn't say anything. I think she was crying.

For some reason, I decided to go

back to the park and inspect the concrete tunnels again. Maybe Carter had made his way there. Maybe he was just sitting, waiting for someone to find him. I shoved a dry waffle into my pocket, just in case I found Carter and he was hungry.

The snow was still coming down but the wind had died, and it was so quiet, I felt like I was in another world. I made my way through the gigantic snow drifts slowly but surely towards the park, which was five or six blocks away. When I got to the park I could barely find the concrete tunnels. The snow was at least three feet deep and I slowly pushed my way through it. I got to the first concrete tunnel and tried to dig into the hollow. That's when I saw the black boot with the red trim. I started calling: "Carter, Carter! Carter, answer!"

Then I heard a tiny voice say, "It's snowing."

I dug into the tunnel like a mad dog. Carter was there, hugging himself to stay warm. His nose was red and his eyes were teary but he wasn't crying; he was just cold. He gave me a hug, and I gave him a hug, and I offered him a piece of waffle. Even though he was really too heavy for me to carry, I carried him all across the park and down the street, five or six blocks, to his house. I felt excited and proud and worried and I don't know how I carried him, but I did, my muscles just worked because they had to. I had to get Carter Jr. home.

The local newspaper made a big deal about me and people said I was a hero and my mother and father told me about a thousand times how proud they were of me but I didn't do anything except double check where I had looked before. If I had found Carter the first time I looked in the concrete tunnels he wouldn't have had to spend the night there, so actually, I really messed up. But I didn't say anything because I didn't want to ruin it for the Franklins and plus, I was embarrassed.

The good thing was that the people who didn't like the Franklins and all of their kids seemed to like them better because they almost *didn't* have twelve kids, they almost *lost* one of them, and that made people realize how important each person is no matter how big the family is or what they are like. The Franklins made me an honorary family member, and I still have a photograph of me with all twelve kids, in front of their house, holding Carter Jr.'s boot like a trophy.—CHRISTINE ALLISON

January 28

The Trees Everlasting

A CHEROKEE MYTH

The Creator was pleased when he made all of the plants and trees, but before he finished he wanted to give them a test. The mountains and earth and sky were of an enduring nature, strong and vigilant, and he wanted to know to what degree the plants and trees might be so endowed.

The test was simple. Each plant and tree was asked to stay awake for seven days and nights.

The first night was no problem. Every plant and tree stayed awake, even the tiniest among them.

The second night was too much for the tiny plants and many of them fell asleep standing. On the third night a few more dropped off into slumber, along with some wispy trees and some who were just lazy. Night after night, a few more fell, until the only trees left on the seventh night were the firs, cedars, spruce, laurel, holly, pine, and some herbs.

The Creator was proud of those who endured, and declared that from that day forward the trees would be a glorious everlasting green, while all of the others would lose their leaves in the autumn of each year, and sleep, as was their will, through winter. In this way, strength and endurance were honored for all time.

January 29

The Donkey Prince

There once lived a king and queen who had riches and everything else one could wish for except . . . a child. At last this wish was granted them when a little prince was born.

Now before his birth the queen had offended a wicked witch, who cast a spell on the baby so that his face looked like a donkey's. The queen and king were naturally frightened and upset, but the king said, "He may look beastly but he is still my son, and he will inherit my crown and kingdom."

So the prince grew up to be healthy and strong, and was not so very frightful after all, although he had very big ears. He was a lively, good-tempered little fellow who had a special love for music. When he was old enough, he asked his music teacher if he could learn to play the lute.

"My lord prince," said the music teacher, "I fear I could never instruct you. Your fingers are too thick and clumsy."

But the boy was not to be discouraged, and in time he learned to play as well as his teacher. He was also growing older and beginning to think more of his appearance. His looks made him increasingly miserable, and when he became a young man, he decided to leave home.

After traveling about the world for some time, he came to the country of a powerful monarch who had an only daughter, a most beautiful maiden.

The prince knocked at the gate of the castle and called, "Will you let me in?" But the gate didn't open, so the prince sat down on the steps and began playing his lute.

On hearing the music, the guard looked out and then ran in to the king, reporting that there was a strange animal at the gates playing lovely music.

"Let him come in," said the king.

But as soon as the prince appeared, everyone began to laugh, and he was told to sit with the servants. "No," said the prince, "I may look odd, but I am nobly born. I mean to sit by the king."

On hearing this, the king laughed and said good-naturedly, "So you shall if you wish it. Come here by me." And after awhile he asked the prince, "Well, how do you like my daughter?"

The prince replied, "Very much indeed. She is the most beautiful maiden I have ever seen."

"Sit by her side then, if you will," said the king.

The prince then talked with the princess so politely and kindly that she quite forgot how beastly he looked, and began to like him very much.

He stayed at the castle for some weeks, growing fonder and fonder of the princess, but at last he said to himself, "What's the use of staying here? I may as well go home."

He went to make his sorrowful good-byes to the king, who had grown to love him. The king asked, "Why do you wish to go? Stay here and I'll give you whatever you want. Do you want jewels or money? Shall I give you half my kingdom to keep you here?"

"No," replied the prince, shaking his head sadly.

"Ah," the king exclaimed, "perhaps you want to marry my daughter?"

A smile transformed the face of the ugly young prince, and he said, "Oh, that is all I desire! If I only thought she could love me."

But of that there was no doubt, for the wonderful music and the gentle ways of the prince had made the princess quite forget his looks. So the marriage was celebrated with great pomp and splendor, and at the wedding, instead of a bridegroom with the face and long ears of a donkey, there stood a handsome young prince. A good fairy had come to the prince the night before the ceremony, and with her wand she cast off the evil spell that had disfigured the prince.

The king could not believe it was the same person but the princess knew, for she had loved him for his goodness, not his looks. They lived together in great happiness for many, many years.

January 30

The Princess and The Pea

Ever since the prince was a young boy, he knew he wanted to marry a princess. While many beautiful ladies lived in the kingdom, few claimed to be princesses, and even fewer really were princesses. Frankly there weren't any princesses in his kingdom at all.

This meant the prince had to travel. He traveled near and far, high and low, but still no princesses. A lot of ladies wore crowns for decoration but that didn't make them princesses. A lot of ladies had fancy long dresses, but that didn't make them princesses. How am I supposed to know if a princess is real? the prince wondered, rather discouraged about it all. Weary from the search, he came home.

The night he arrived home, there was a terrible storm. In the midst of the thunder and lightning someone banged loudly at the city gate. The old king went to open the gate and there stood

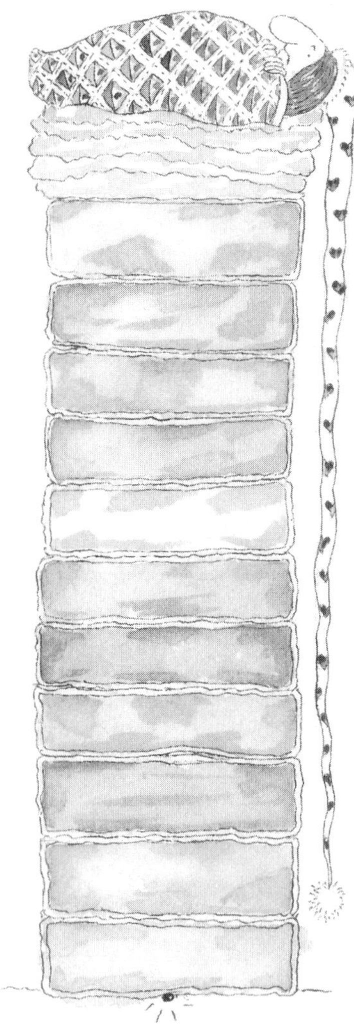

a princess. She was drenched and matted, but insisted in a gentle tone that she was indeed a princess, and asked if the king would be so kind as to let her in.

The queen doubted the girl's story. But being a real queen and therefore having a charitable spirit, she invited the "princess" in to dry off and spend the night. While no one was looking the queen put a tiny pea under the bottom mattress. She then placed thirty additional mattresses on top of the pea, followed by a tower of feather pillows.

"Here, dear," said the old queen. "Sleep tight."

In the morning, the queen asked the "princess" how she slept. "May I be honest?" the princess asked the queen. The queen nodded, suddenly interested in what she had to say.

"It was awful!" the princess said. "I hardly slept at all! There was something hard and rock-like under my mattresses, and now I am bruised all over."

The prince ran in when he heard the news, followed by the old king. "She must be a real princess," exclaimed the prince. "No other person would be so sensitive to the world as to be wounded by a pea buried under thirty mattresses (and a host of feather pillows)."

Happily, the prince took the princess for his wife, and the pea was placed in a royal gallery, where it may still be seen.—HANS CHRISTIAN ANDERSEN

January 31

Aesop and the Donkey

"The next time you write a fable about me," said the donkey to Aesop, "why not have me say something wise and sensible? I am tired of being the clown in all of your tales."

"Something sensible about you?" exclaimed Aesop. "What would the world think? People would call *you* the moralist, and *me* the donkey!"

FEBRUARY

February 1

The Seed from Mars

On the first of February, in the year 2020, Jesse Taylor Stevens and Charlie Ann Brown were walking along the road when they saw a great white streak in the sky. It came towards them, closer and closer, and settled gently on the ground in front of them. Jesse and Charlie Ann carefully moved close to it. On its side they saw written: SPACE CAPSULE FROM MARS! HANDLE WITH CARE!

Jesse picked up the capsule and put it in his backpack. Then the two of them raced to the space laboratory in the middle of the city. Everyone was incredibly excited about this find. On the front page of every newspaper and every television news program it was the biggest story of the year. Because Jesse and Charlie Ann had found it, they were permitted to open the capsule. When the top was unscrewed, Jesse reached in and took out a video. Charlie Ann reached in and removed an audio cassette tape. There were many other interesting items in the capsule, and as Jesse reached into it again he accidentally pulled out a tiny seed. It was green and red, and almost immediately, it started growing.

"It's a monster," someone screamed and everybody except Jesse and Charlie Ann ran out of the room. Within minutes, the entire world had been notified that a seed from Mars had started growing.

Nobody knew what this seed would become. Many people believed it would became a monster, which had been sent here to take over the earth. The president ordered the entire army to surround the building. The Air Force had planes flying overhead prepared to fight the Martian invader. The presidents and prime ministers of every nation on earth met to try to figure out a way to stop this threat to life on earth.

In the little room Jesse and Charlie Ann watched very closely as the seed began to grow. It grew very slowly. It seemed to be growing straight up.

Days passed, then weeks. No one on earth could think about anything but the strange seed from Mars. Almost every person living within hundreds of miles had packed their belongings and left their homes. Eventually, the only people left in the entire city were Jesse and Charlie Ann.

Thirty one days after the space capsule had been opened the seed finally made a sound. "Crrrkkkk."

"Something's happening!" Jesse yelled. "Hide!" And he ran to hide behind a big table. But Charlie Ann stood there, unable to take her eyes off the seed.

"Crrrkkkk," it went again, and suddenly it split in half. Charlie Ann closed her eyes. She was afraid of what was going to happen, afraid that when she opened her eyes, a giant Martian would be standing in front of her.

"Binggggg!" came a sound from the most beautiful purple and maroon rose Charlie Ann had ever seen. A lovely, sweet aroma filled the room. "You can come out now, Jesse," she said. "The Martians have sent us a gift."

—JORDAN BURNETT AND DAVID FISHER

February 2

GROUNDHOG DAY

Casey's Big Day, Part 1

For Casey, today was no ordinary day. It was Groundhog Day, his coming out party, his debut, his fifteen minutes in the sun—or the clouds—as it were. Today for the first time, Casey would venture up from the Great Hole while the whole town of Bloomington watched to see if he would cast a shadow.

For about a hundred years, Casey's family had lived in a small Pennsylvania town where people took Groundhog Day more seriously than most. The tradition went like this: if it was sunny on February 2 and the groundhog saw his shadow, it would be a long, hard winter. But if was dark and gray and his shadow couldn't be seen, then the people supposed that an early spring would come to their little farming town.

To the groundhogs, it was all pretty silly. The furry animals had kept careful records and discovered that the shadow formula held true only 28 percent of the time. Still, the groundhogs liked the attention. After all, what other animal has a holiday named in its honor? Thus the groundhogs cheerfully went along with the tradition and each year let one of their young ones have the honor of climbing up through the Great Hole so the townspeople of Bloomington might make their dubious weather prediction.

As it happened, the honor this February went to Casey. The problem was that Casey, who was seven in groundhog years, was starting to get nervous, as in scared of his own . . . shadow. What if he made a fool of himself? What if it was rainy and his fur got all matted down, and the people thought he was a wet rat? A thousand fears raced through his mind, and before long, poor Casey was a nervous wreck. He was so nervous, he confessed his fears to his big brother, J.B. This was a terrible mistake because J.B. was the worst tease a brother could have.

J.B. was a teenage groundhog, and teenagers like nothing more than to tease their little brothers and sisters. But J.B. was the *worst.* When Casey told J.B. he was nervous, J.B. just smiled.

"To tell the truth," J.B. said, not telling the truth at all, "a *lot* of groundhogs think you're going to mess up. After all, there will be huge television cameras and newspaper reporters and lots of noisy schoolchildren just outside of the Great Hole. Chances are you'll get stage fright. Say, did anyone ever tell you about the time one of us got trapped and put in a cage? That's what happened to poor Uncle Casey, who, as a matter of fact, was . . . your namesake!"

"My namesake?" asked Casey, who did not like the way this was shaping up. "Nobody ever told me I was named after anyone. And what traps? What cages? I thought the townspeople *liked* groundhogs."

"Sure they like groundhogs," J.B. said. "They like groundhogs *in their stew.* That's what happened to Uncle Casey because he was too scared and too slow. He was only seven at the time," J.B. said, and then slapped his paw on his forehead. "Wait a minute . . . this is a remarkable coincidence . . . aren't you . . . seven years old?"

Casey nodded weakly, while J.B. shook his head in mock amazement and continued.

"Gosh, I kind of hate to be the one to tell you about this," J.B. said, loving every minute of it, "but before Casey, that is, *Uncle* Casey, had his big day he got very nervous. Why, he felt exactly the way you do now! At first he tried to get out of the whole thing by pretending to have the sniffles; he faked a few coughs so that everyone would think he was too sick to do the honors. But it was obvious he was just scared. 'It's your big day and that's that,' Grandpa told him. Uncle Casey started to run away, but Grandpa pulled him back and then gave him a kick and Uncle Casey went flying up through the entrance of the Great Hole. He landed right on his face in front of the whole town. The people started laughing at him, and he felt so foolish, he just lay there, like an overturned statue. Before any of us realized what was happening, a farmer grabbed Uncle Casey and shoved him into a cast-iron stew pot! A few minutes later, we could smell groundhog stew cooking on a nearby stove."

J.B. rubbed his eye, as if to dry a tear. "It a shame you never were able to meet old Uncle Casey . . ."

February 3

Casey's Big Day, Part 2

Casey could not believe it. He had to get out of this shadow business and fast. He checked his watch. In half an hour it would be time for his fifteen minutes of fame and then—he nearly fainted at the thought—his untimely demise in a cast-iron stew pot.

Casey's head was spinning until his father interrupted his thoughts. "Good morning, son," Casey's father said, patting him on the back. "All ready for your big day?"

J.B. excused himself from the room. "Uh, er, not really," Casey said. "As a matter of fact, Father, I don't feel very well," he said, clearing his throat loudly and making a rather pathetic coughing sound. "Maybe I should go rest somewhere."

"I hope you're not going to run away like J.B. did when he was your age," Casey's father said, with a little grunt. "He'll always be embarrassed about that whole episode."

"What are you talking about?" asked Casey. "J.B. ran away? You mean . . . he didn't do it? *He didn't show up for his big day?*"

"Why, no, son. I'm surprised he never mentioned it to you. When he was little, J.B. practiced for weeks for Groundhog Day, and at the last minute he pretended he was sick, coughing just like you were a few moments ago. Then he disappeared. We actually had to send up a replacement.

"Between you and me," Casey's father went on, "he was awfully nervous. I know he always acts tough, but sometimes J.B. on the outside isn't exactly who J.B. really is on the inside. He'll always regret not showing up that day," he explained.

Casey had just learned something quite amazing. He was quiet for a moment, and then asked, "Dad, where did you get my name? I mean, do I have a namesake? Was there ever an *Uncle* Casey?"

"Uncle Casey? Why, no, son. Where did you ever get an idea like that?" his father replied.

"Oh, never mind," Casey said. "Actually, I feel much better now. Is it time for me to make my debut?"

Casey's father looked at his watch. "Just a few more minutes, son. Let's get J.B. and your mother and all of the relatives together for a group shot before you go up. I'll get my camera."

"And I'll get J.B.," Casey thought to himself. "Boy, oh boy, will I get J.B.!"

And with that Casey bounded down the path to the Great Hole. Casey was no longer afraid of making a fool of himself. He had learned that one of the main things in life is just to show up. With his head held high, he stood in the pouring rain—before television cameras and newspaper reporters and noisy children—enjoying every moment of his big day.

—CHRISTINE ALLISON

February 4

The Miser

A miser, to make sure of his property, sold all that he had and converted it into a great lump of gold, which he hid in a hole in the ground. He was so proud of the gold that he continually went to visit and inspect it.

This roused the curiosity of one of his workmen. The workman, suspecting that there was a treasure, went to the hiding spot when his master's back was turned. Sure enough, he discovered the great lump of gold and stole it. When the miser returned and found the place empty he wept and tore his hair. But a neighbor who saw him in his extravagant grief said, "Don't worry any longer but take a stone and put it in the same place and pretend it is your lump of gold. In truth, you never meant to use it—the one will do you as much good as the other."

The worth of money is not its possession but its use.—AESOP

February 5

The Half-Chick

A SPANISH FOLKTALE

Once there was a handsome black Spanish hen who had a large brood of chicks. They were all fine, plump birds except the youngest. He was a strange, queer-looking creature, quite unlike his fluffy brothers and sisters, for he had only one leg, one wing, half a head, and half a beak.

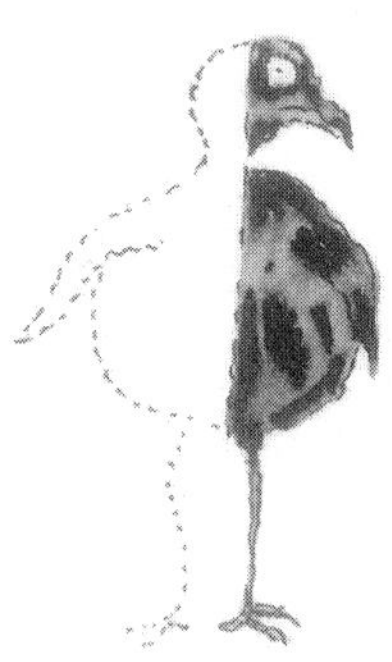

The mother was astonished by him from the moment he chipped his way out of his shell. She said sadly, "My youngest is only a half-chick. He will never grow up to be a tall handsome rooster who will rule over a poultry yard of his own like his brothers. This poor little one will have to stay home with me." And she named him Medio Pollito, which is Spanish for half-chick.

Now even though Medio Pollito looked like a helpless chick, his mother soon found he was anything but that. He refused to stay by his mother's side, and when she called him to return to the coop he pretended he could not hear her, as he had only one ear. As he grew older, he became more and more willful and other chickens thought of him as quite rude and disagreeable.

One day he announced to his mother, "I am tired of this life in a dull farmyard, with nothing but a corn field to look at. I'm off to Madrid to see the king."

"To Madrid, Medio Pollito!" cried his mother. "Why, you will never make it!"

But Medio Pollito would not be discouraged, and quickly said his good-byes to everyone. "When I have a fine courtyard of my own at the king's palace, I shall perhaps ask some of you to come and pay me a short visit." And off he stumped down the road that led to Madrid.

On the way there, he passed a stream, all choked up with reeds and water lilies. "Oh, Medio Pollito," called the stream. "Do come help me by clearing away these weeds."

"Help you, indeed!" answered Medio Pollito. "Do you think I have nothing better to do?" And he stumped away, hoppity-kick, on the road to Madrid.

That night he came to a fire that some gypsies had left burning low in the woods. "Oh, Medio Pollito," cried the fire. "In a few minutes, I will go out. Please put some sticks on me."

"Don't trouble me," answered Medio Pollito. "I am off to Madrid to see the king."

The next morning, Medio Pollito found the wind all tangled in the branches of a large chestnut tree. But when the wind asked for help, Medio Pollito said, "It is your own fault for going there. I can't waste time helping you." He stumped away quickly, for the towers of Madrid were in sight.

He found the king's palace, and planned to wait till His Majesty came out and noticed him. But as he walked past a window, the king's cook saw him, grabbed him, and plopped him in the soup pot.

How wet and clammy the water felt as it slid over Medio Pollito's head! "Water, water!" he cried in despair. "Have pity on me, and do not wet me like this." But the water replied, "You would not help me when I was a little stream and now you must be punished."

Then the fire heated up the water, and Medio Pollito began to dance from side to side of the pot. "Fire, fire! Do not scorch me like this!" he cried. "You would not help me in the woods," said the fire.

Just then, the cook opened the lid to see how the soup was doing. "I didn't notice before, but this chicken is quite useless," exclaimed the cook, and, opening the window, he threw Medio Pollito out.

But the wind caught him, and whirled him through the air so quickly that Medio Pollito could hardly breathe. "Oh, wind," he gasped, "if you hurry me along like this, you will kill me. Do let me rest." The wind did not listen. "When I was caught in the chestnut tree, you would not help me. Now you must be punished." And he swirled Medio Pollito to the tallest church in the city, and there he left him fastened to the top of the steeple.

There stands Medio Pollito to this day. If you go to Madrid and visit the tallest church there, you will see Medio Pollito perched on his one leg on the steeple, with his one wing drooping at his side, gazing sadly out of his one eye over the city.

February 6

Sleeping Beauty

A GERMAN TALE

There once were a king and queen who lived in sadness because they had no children. But after a great many years, as if by a miracle, the queen gave birth to a baby daughter. Seven fairies were asked to be godmothers to the child, and plans were made for a magnificent christening at which each would give the princess a gift of talent or beauty or virtue that would insure her happiness and good fortune.

After the christening ceremony a great banquet was held in honor of all the fairies. At each of their places the king had set gifts of gold and precious jewels. Just as everyone was sitting down at the table, a very old fairy entered the hall. The king had not invited her because he thought she was dead. The king ordered that a place be set for her at his table but he did not have the gold and jewels for her, as he did for the others. The old fairy regarded this as a great slight, and she began to mumble threats and curses under her breath.

One of the young fairies who sat nearby began to worry that the old fairy would cause some harm to befall the infant princess. As the other fairies were making their gifts to the princess, the young fairy hid behind a curtain, hoping to be the last to make a gift, so that she could undo whatever evil the old fairy might wish upon the princess. After the other fairies gave the princess grace and musical ability and beauty beyond compare, the old fairy stepped forward. Quivering with rage and spite, she declared: "The princess will prick her finger on a spindle and die." The guests were struck dumb with horror until the last fairy, who had been hiding behind the curtain, cried out, "No, Your Majesty. The princess will not die of this wound." She explained that she did not have the power to totally undo the older fairy's wish but she *could* alter it so that the princess would only fall into a deep sleep. The princess would sleep a hundred years and be awakened at the end of that time by a prince.

In a desperate attempt to prevent either prophecy from being fulfilled, the king ordered all the spindles removed from the kingdom. Anyone found using a spinning wheel was to be put to death.

One day when the princess was about fifteen, the king and queen were away from the castle for a day. The princess was amusing herself by exploring the castle. At the top of the tower she came upon an old woman servant using a spindle. She had never heard of the king's ban on spinning wheels, and was fascinated and wanted to try her hand at spinning. No sooner had she touched the spindle then she pricked her finger and fell to the floor in a swoon. Nothing the old woman or any of the servants or courtiers could do would revive the young girl.

When they returned, the king and the queen saw that their worst fears had been realized. The princess was carried into the most beautiful room in the castle and laid upon a bed with elegantly embroidered coverings. There she was left to sleep in peace.

The good fairy who had changed the old fairy's wicked curse heard the news of what had happened and hastened to the palace in a fiery chariot drawn by dragons. She touched all the people who worked in the castle with her magic wand, as well as the princess's dog, Puff, causing them to fall asleep with the princess. The king and queen left the castle, which soon was enveloped by a vast forest of trees.

A hundred years later, a prince was hunting in the countryside around the castle. He inquired about the thick hedges and trees that surrounded it, and was told the story of the sleeping princess, deciding that he would be the one to awaken her. He made his way to the castle and found the rooms crowded with sleeping people. At last he came to the princess, who was as beautiful as ever. As he gazed at her, she awoke. "Is it you my prince? You have been so long in coming," she said.

The prince and the princess were enchanted with each other. It seemed as if in her slumber the princess had dreamed of this prince. They talked for hours, then dined on a feast prepared by the servants, who like the rest of the palace staff were fully awake now.

After the feast, the prince and the princess were wed in the palace chapel, and the next morning traveled to the city ruled by the prince's father. They were welcomed warmly.

February 7

Sleeping Beauty, Variation 1

In the French version of "Sleeping Beauty" the prince leaves his bride after the wedding and returns to his parents' castle. He does not tell his parents of the marriage for two years but continues to sneak away to see the princess in the forest. Two children are born, whom the prince hesitates to introduce to his mother even after the public announcement of his marriage following the king's death. It is rumored that the queen mother has ogreish tendencies, which, soon after finally meeting the grandchildren, she demonstrates by ordering the chief steward of the castle to serve first one grandchild and then another for her dinner! The steward manages to protect the children and their mother from the ogre, who eventually ends up in a vat of poisonous brew that she had prepared for her grandchildren and their mother. Then, at last, the king and the family live in peace.

February 8

Sleeping Beauty, Variation 2

The somewhat more widely known version of "Sleeping Beauty" by the Brothers Grimm features thirteen fairies, including the evil one. The princess is called Briar Rose, and when she falls asleep the king and queen sleep along with her.

The prince awakens her with a kiss, and as he does, the evil fairy's spell is broken and everyone in the castle awakens to celebrate together. The prince and Briar Rose are married a few days later and live happily in "peace and joy until they die."

February 9

The Travelers and the Purse

Two travelers were making their way through a crowded village when the first one spotted a purse on the ground.

"This is my lucky day!" he exclaimed. "This purse weighs so much it must be filled with gold."

The traveler inspected the bag and, sure enough, it contained gold.

The second traveler said, "Do not say 'my' lucky day. This is 'our' lucky day. We are traveling together and we must share fortunes and misfortunes alike."

"On the contrary," said the first traveler. "This is my bag, my gold, and my lucky day. You will get none of it."

Just then a crowd of people ran up to the two travelers. "Thief! Thief!" they cried, pointing to the first man holding the purse of gold.

"Wait, wait, I can explain," said the traveler. Then he looked to his companion and said, "Tell them what happened. Explain that I just found it," he said.

"But no," said the second traveler. "You just told me it was your bag, your gold, and your lucky day."

Do not expect others to share your misfortune if you do not also share the good things that come your way.—AESOP

February 10

The One-Eyed Doe

A doe who was grazing near a lake had but one eye. Knowing that she must be vigilant against possible enemies, she decided to keep her eye towards the land, thinking that hunters were more likely to come from that direction.

But some sailors rowed by in a boat and, seeing her, aimed from the water . . . and shot her. "Oh, what a quirk of fate," said the doe as she lay dying. "I was safe on the side of the land from where I expected to be attacked but found an enemy in the lake, from where I presumed I would find my protection!"

Our troubles often come from places where we least expect them.—AESOP

February 11

The Very Sick Lion

A lion had grown very old and now was so weak he could not hunt for his prey. So he laid himself up in his den, breathing in a labored way, allowing the world to believe he was on his death bed. Only it was a trick!

Word soon spread among all of the beasts that the lion's days were numbered, and so the animals came to pay their last respects. Those who came with a friend were safe, but those who came alone were not so lucky, because the lion would kill anyone who came up to his bedside. In this way, the lion grew fatter and fatter every day.

The fox, who was very clever, began to suspect the lion was up to no good. It didn't make sense that a dying lion would get fatter and fatter every day. When he came to visit his fat majesty, the fox stood at quite a distance. Then he asked how the lion was faring.

"Oh, dear fox, is that you?" asked the lion in a weak voice. "Come closer and speak a kind word into this poor lion's ear."

But the fox would have none of it. "I offer you all kindnesses, Your Majesty, but excuse me if I cannot stay, for I can't help but notice all of the footprints here in your den. The footprints lead to your bed, but only in that one direction. I fear your death bed might mean my death instead." And with that, the fox gave a quick bow, turned, and ran with great speed far away.

Make sure you know your way out of every circumstance you enter.—AESOP

February 12

PRESIDENTS' DAY

The Cherry Tree

When George Washington was about six years old, he was given the gift of a hatchet. As you might guess, he was extremely fond of the tool and would chop down everything in sight.

One day, as he wandered about the garden amusing himself by hacking his mother's peasticks, he found a beautiful young English cherry tree of which his father was most proud. He tried the edge of his hatchet on the trunk of the tree and tore the bark so grievously that it died.

Some time after this, his father discovered what had happened to his favorite tree. He came into the house in great anger, and demanded to know who the mischievous person was who had cut away the bark. Nobody could tell him anything about it.

Just then George, with his little hatchet, came into the room.

"George," said his father, "do you know who killed my beautiful little cherry tree in the garden? It was priceless to me."

This was a hard question to answer. For a moment, George did not know what to do. But then, quickly recovering himself, he cried, "I cannot tell a lie, Father! I did it with my little hatchet."

The anger drained from his father's face and he took the boy gently in his arms, saying, "George, that you are not afraid to tell the truth is worth more to me than a thousand trees, even if they blossomed with leaves of silver and gold."—M. L. WEEMS

The Story of the Two Cakes Who Loved Each Other in Silence

A LOVE STORY FOR ST. VALENTINE'S DAY

On the shop counter lay two gingerbread cakes. One was in the shape of a man with a hat, the other was of a maiden without a bonnet. Both of their faces were on the side that was turned up, for they were to be looked at on that side and not the other. On the left the man wore a bitter almond—that was his heart. The maiden was honeycake all over.

As they were only samples, they stayed on the counter for a long time. And, at last, they fell in love with each other. But neither told the other, as should have been done, if anything was to come of it.

"He is the man and must speak first," thought she. But she was happy, for she knew he loved her.

His thoughts were more extravagant. He dreamed that he was a real street boy, and that he had four pennies of his own, and that he bought the sweet maiden and ate her up.

So they lay on the counter for weeks and weeks, and grew dry and hard.

But the thoughts of the maiden became ever more gentle and maidenly. "It is enough for me that I have lived on the same table with him," she said, and crack! she broke in two.

"If only she had known of my love," thought he, "she would have kept together a little longer."

"And that is their story, and here they are, both of them," said the baker, for it was he who was telling the story. "They are remarkable for their curious history, and for their silent love, which never came to anything. There they are for you." So saying, he gave the man gingerbread cake, who was yet whole, to the little girl, Joanna, and the broken maiden cake to the little boy, Knud.

But the children were so impressed with the story that they could only look at them; they could not eat them up just yet.—HANS CHRISTIAN ANDERSEN

February 14

ST. VALENTINE'S DAY

A Valentine for Christopher

Christopher never liked Valentine's Day.

It started when he was in kindergarten. He had just learned his letters and his mother made him sign twenty-two cards "Love, Christopher." It took six whole days to get the job done and his hand got really sore. "Would it be okay if we changed my name to 'Chris'?" he asked his mother. "Don't worry. It'll be better next year," she assured him. Christopher's mother liked to think positive.

But it didn't get better. When he got older, Valentines got him in lots of trouble. Everybody knows Valentine cards don't mean anything. Everybody but Alice Pugh. In third grade, Christopher, without thinking, gave Alice a card that said "Peas Be My Podner." Immediately she told the whole class that Christopher had a crush on her. Alice smelled like peanut butter and never combed her hair and her last name was Pugh. No one on the *entire planet* could have a crush on her. It was the most embarrassing day of his life.

But all of that was history. Christopher had much bigger problems than Alice Pugh. It was February 13, and Christopher was getting on an airplane with his mother and father. They were flying to Atlanta because Christopher's dad got a new job and now they were going to live there. His new school was going to be twice as big as his old school. Christopher considered it a terrible sign that his first day would fall on . . . Valentine's Day.

The plane ride, which should have been a special occasion, was just okay. Christopher got to drink as much soda as he wanted and the flight attendants gave him three extra bags of peanuts, but even that didn't lift his spirits much. He spent a lot of time looking at the clouds and feeling sorry for himself. A new town, a new house, a new school. Why did everything have to be new?

On the way to their new house, Christopher and his parents drove by the school, which was as big as a factory. "Think positive," his mother said, giving him a hug. "When your father and I were househunting, we met your teacher and saw your classmates. They are so excited to have a new student."

So Christopher tried to "think positive." He woke up the next morning and tried to imagine everyone talking excitedly about meeting "the new student." He tried on about five different pairs of shorts and T-shirts until he got the right one. He practiced smiling and saying "hi" in the mirror. He even flossed. He felt ready, as ready as he could be, until he got to school and started walking down the hall to his classroom. Who was he fooling? Nobody was excited that he was coming. Nobody even knew he was there! When he finally found his classroom, he just stood at the door. The bell rang, and he just stood there. At last a dark-haired woman came out of the classroom. "You must be Christopher," she said. "I'm your homeroom teacher, Mrs. Sanders. Come, let me show you to your desk."

Mrs. Sanders led Christopher into the classroom and walked him to his new desk. On top of the desk was a huge heart-shaped card with "HEY CHRISTOPHER" in big bold letters across the top. "I know you're a bit old for this, but we thought we'd make you a Valentine card to welcome you on your first day," Mrs. Sanders said.

"After gym class we're going to have a little party in your honor."

Christopher looked around the room. Actually, the students seemed pretty normal. He got a nod, a smile, a wink, a silly salute, and lots of other friendly looks. The teacher introduced him and then began to discuss the day's activities. While she spoke, Christopher looked down at the card on his desk. It was signed by everyone in the class. Some wrote jokes; others drew funny cartoons. One person did his initials in really cool graphics. There were even some phone numbers on it.

It was a great card.

Maybe, Christopher thought, Valentine's Day is something you don't understand until you're older. He'd have to think about that. All he knew for certain was that, right now, things were looking up. Even if it was Valentine's Day.—CHRISTINE ALLISON

February 15

Apollo and Daphne

AN ANCIENT GREEK MYTH

Daphne was the god Apollo's first love, and he happened to fall in love with her all because of a cruel trick played on him by Cupid, the god of love. At that time, Cupid was still a young lad, and when Apollo saw him one day playing with his bow and arrows, he mocked him. "What are you doing with weapons of war, saucy boy? Leave them for hands worthy of them! Do you not know of my conquests?"

Cupid took offense at Apollo's words, and as the god walked away, Cupid said, "Your arrows may strike all other things, Apollo, but mine shall strike you." Then he took two arrows from his quiver. One had a gold tip, and it would make its victim fall passionately in love. The other was tipped with lead, and whoever was struck by this arrow would spurn all affection.

Daphne was the daughter of the river god Peneus, and her delight was woodland sports and the hunt. Cupid struck her with the lead arrow, and he shot Apollo through the heart with the golden arrow. Apollo now fell desperately in love with Daphne, but she would have nothing to do with him.

Each time Apollo caught sight of her beautiful face, he was seized with longing and wanted nothing more than to make her his wife. Daphne fled every time he came near her, and grew most distraught when he tried to speak of his love.

Apollo was despondent. "It is for love I pursue you. I am the son of Jupiter, and I know all things, present and future. I am the god of song and the lyre. My arrows fly true to the mark, but alas, an arrow more fatal than mine has pierced my heart! I am the god of medicine, and know the virtues of all healing plants. But I suffer a malady no balm can cure."

One day Apollo caught up with her in the forest, and began to plead his case once more. In her fear, Daphne cried out, "Help me, Peneus! Open the earth to enclose me, or change my form, which has been nothing but a curse to me."

As she spoke, a stiffness seized her limbs, and her skin began to be covered by bark. Her hair became leaves, and her arms branches. Her feet stuck fast in the ground to become roots. All that was left of her human form was its beauty. Apollo stood amazed, then he touched and kissed the bark. "Since you cannot now be my wife," he said sadly, "you shall be my tree. I will wear you for my crown, and the Romans shall weave you into wreaths to represent their conquests. And, as eternal youth is mine, you also shall always be green."

And the nymph Daphne, now changed into a laurel tree, bowed her head in grateful acknowledgment.

February 16

The Three Little Pigs

There once was a mother pig who was very poor and had to send her three little pigs out to seek their fortunes.

The first little pig met a man who gave him some straw to build himself a house. He lived happily in the house until a wolf came along and knocked at his door.

"Little pig, little pig, let me come in!" demanded the wolf.

"Not by the hair of my chinny-chin-chin," replied the pig.

"Then I'll huff and I'll puff and I'll blow your house in," said the wolf. So he huffed and he puffed and he blew the house in, and chased away the first little pig.

The second little pig met a man who gave him a bundle of sticks to build himself a house. He lived in the house until the wolf came along and knocked at his door.

"Little pig, little pig, let me come in!" demanded the wolf. The pig refused, just as his brother had done. The wolf proceeded to huff and puff and to blow his house in, and then chased away the second little pig, too.

The third little pig met a man who gave him a load of bricks to build himself a house. This little pig built a fine house and lived in it, just as his brothers had lived in theirs. Eventually, the wolf came along and knocked on his door, demanding to be let in. Of course, the little pig refused. The wolf said he would huff and he would puff and he would blow the house in, but as much as he huffed and puffed, nothing happened.

The wolf rested for a few moments and then asked the little pig if he would just let the tip of his nose in.

The pig, who was no fool, refused.

The wolf asked if he would just let the wolf's paw in, or the tip of his tail.

Again, the pig refused.

"Then I will climb on your roof and come down your chimney," the wolf threatened.

The pig immediately made a fire so hot that the wolf could not possibly come down the chimney. Finally the wolf retreated.

The third little pig, being perfect in almost every way, invited his mother to join him, and they both lived happily in the little brick house for many years.

February 17

The Three Little Pigs, Variation

The preceding was a soft version of "The Three Little Pigs." The story has a bit more edge when the first two pigs are gobbled up. When the wolf confronts the third pig, the pig sets the pot to boil in the fireplace. The wolf mounts the roof, falls down the chimney, and boils to death. In this variation, the laziness of the first two little pigs, who built their homes of mere straw and twigs, is emphasized and contrasted with the rewards of the third little pig's industry. The message: those who work hard survive.

February 18

The Bundle of Sticks

The countryside was worn from the ravages of famine and war. Though the times were difficult, the five sons made it worse by fighting and bickering with each other.

One day, the father could take it no more.

"Are you boys crazy?" asked the father. "Outside people are dying of battle wounds and hunger. Why do you add to the misery?"

Then the father had an idea. "Bring me a bundle of sticks," he asked the oldest son.

The oldest son gathered the sticks, and his father asked him to break them.

The boy tried and failed.

And so he asked the second son, who also failed.

The third son failed, and then the fourth.

Finally, the youngest son, who was wise and good, untied the bundle of sticks and pulled out a single stem.

"Father," he said, "I know now why you asked us to break up this bundle. When we fight amongst ourselves and are divided, we are like a single stem and break easily." The boy snapped a stem in two. "When we stand together, like this entire bundle, we are strong. Standing together, it will be impossible for our enemies to cause us harm."

The father marveled at the young boy's wisdom, and encouraged the other brothers to understand.—AESOP

February 19

Intelligence and Luck

A CZECH TALE

Once upon a time, Luck met Intelligence on a garden bench. "Move over and make room for me!" commanded Luck. Intelligence was inexperienced in the ways of the world, and didn't know who ought to make room for whom. "Why should I move?" asked Intelligence. "You're no better than I am."

"Shall we have a wager on that?" replied Luck. "Let us see who is the better man by who performs best. See that peasant's son plowing the field over there? Enter into him, and if he gets on better through you than through me, I'll always make way for you whenever we meet." Intelligence agreed at once, and immediately entered the boy's head.

As the boy, whose name was Vanek, felt his new intelligence, he began to think: "Why must I follow the plow all the days of my life? I can go somewhere else and make my fortune more easily." He quit his work and went to his father, telling him he was tired of the peasant's life and wanted to learn to be a gardener. Shortly thereafter, Vanek apprenticed himself to the king's gardener, and soon knew more than the older man did.

Vanek made the king's gardens so beautiful that the king began to stroll in them each day with the queen and his only daughter. The princess was a very pretty young lady, but at the age of twelve she had suddenly stopped speaking, which greatly saddened the king. He had issued a proclamation that promised her hand in marriage to the young man who caused her to speak again. Many princes and lords had already tried and failed. "Why shouldn't I try my luck?" thought Vanek the gardener.

He presented himself at the palace and was led to the royal chambers. Now, the princess had a clever little dog she was very fond of, and Vanek began at once to speak to the little dog, ignoring the princess entirely. "I have heard, doggie, that you are very clever, and I come to you for advice. We are three companions traveling together, a sculptor, a tailor, and myself. We had to pass the night in a dangerous forest, so we took turns keeping watch. While it was his turn, the sculptor carved a damsel out of a log, just to pass the time away. When it was the tailor's watch, he took out needle and thread and made the damsel clothing. I got up to take my turn and asked what the meaning of this was. The tailor explained and said, 'If you become bored, why don't you teach her to speak?' And by dawn, I had actually taught her speech. But then each of us wanted to possess the damsel. 'I made her,' said the sculptor. 'I clothed her,' said the tailor. And I, of course, pressed my claim too. Tell me, therefore, doggie, to which of us does the damsel belong?"

The dog said nothing in response, but the princess suddenly spoke up: "To whom can she belong but to yourself? What's the good of the sculptor's damsel without life? What's the good of the tailor's clothing without speech? You gave her the best gift, life and speech, and so she belongs to you."

"You have spoken rightly, princess," said Vanek. "I have given you speech again and a new life, and therefore you belong to me."

Now the king offered Vanek a generous reward but had no intention of marrying his daughter to a peasant. Vanek began to insist that the king keep his word, and so offended his majesty that he was seized and bound and sentenced to be executed.

When he was taken to the place where his head would be chopped off, Luck was waiting for him. "See where you have gotten this man!" Luck said to Intelligence. "Let me take over."

As soon as Luck entered Vanek's body, the executioner's sword broke, and before another sword could be obtained, the royal carriage drove up. The princess had convinced her father that he must keep his word, and the king had further agreed to make Vanek a prince.

As the royal carriage departed from the wedding, Intelligence happened to see Luck on the road ahead, and quickly bent his head down and slunk off to the side. And from that time forth, it is said that Intelligence has always given a wide berth to Luck whenever they meet.

February 20

Mother Lark's Lesson

Once there was a family of young larks who lived in a corn field. In early spring, the field was nothing but a muddy slab, lined with the promise of a thousand seeds. The seeds sprouted, and from the sprouts, young plants grew, stretching themselves to the blue sky.

It had been a fine season for growing, and the larks spent it nestled in the tall plants, feeling happy and safe. But now it was harvest time. Reapers would come to cut the tall plants down to the ground. The larks would have to find a new home.

Mother Lark gathered her brood. "Children, when corn is reaped, we will have to head south. Whatever happens, we must be ready. Your work is to listen to the farmer and tell me exactly what you hear. From his words, I will know when the field will be reaped."

"But what are we listening for?" asked one.

"Just listen," said Mother Lark. "Listen and tell me what you hear."

And so they did. The larks posted themselves at every corner of the corn field so they would not miss a word. Sure enough, the farmer appeared the next morning with his wife, and the twosome walked the rows of corn. "It looks as though the corn is nearly ripe," he said. "Let's tell our friends that we need help so we can get this corn reaped." The farmer's wife agreed, and they left for town to ask for help.

That evening, the larks told their mother exactly what they had heard.

"If the farmer is counting on his friends for help, then we can relax," said the Mother Lark. "They will surely ignore him. Listen again tomorrow. We've no need to pack our things yet."

And so they did. Again, the larks posted themselves at each corner of the field. The farmer's friends did not show up, and at mid-day, the farmer and his wife strolled up and down the rows of nearly ripe corn.

"Nothing's been done!" the farmer exclaimed. "So much for our friends. Let's call in our neighbors," he said to his wife. "The corn is turning riper and riper, and we must begin to harvest."

Once again, the larks reported what they heard to their mother. They told her that the farmer had called for the neighbors to pitch in for the harvest.

"Well, we have all of the time in the world, then," Mother Lark said. "If the farmer thinks the neighbors are going to come to his aide, he's in for a surprise."

The next day, as their mother had foreseen, no work was done, and the larks' home was undisturbed. When the farmer and his wife came to survey their corn field, the birds circled their heads to listen carefully.

"Dear wife, what kind of neighbors do we have? They didn't lift a finger for us! It's time to bring in the cousins. This corn is going to harvest itself if we don't hurry up," the farmer said.

The larks were concerned. They told their mother what they'd heard. "He's called for the cousins," they told her, worriedly. "Surely his family will not let him down."

The Mother Lark shook her head. "I know this farmer's family. I am sorry to say that the corn will rot in the husk if he thinks his family will help him," she said.

The sun grew hotter and hotter, and the corn was now perfectly ripe. If the farmer lost more time, his crop would die. The larks listened expectantly the next day to find out what the farmer would do when he saw that the cousins had not so much as looked at the corn field.

"What is wrong with the world?" asked the farmer, as he saw that his cousins had disregarded his pleas for help. He turned to his wife and said: "That's it! We can no longer wait for our friends, or our neighbors, or our family. Hire some reapers and we will begin the work ourselves!"

When the larks heard this, they raced back to their Mother, who for the first time listened intently.

"Well, then, the day has come," said the Mother Lark. "It's time for us to be off. When a farmer decides to take care of his own business, you can be sure the work will be done."

And so the corn was reaped, and the larks moved on.

February 21

Simeli Mountain

A GERMAN TALE

There were once two brothers, one rich and the other poor. As often happens, the rich one shared none of his good fortune, and the poor brother was often hard-pressed to feed his wife and children.

As the poor brother pushed his wheelbarrow through the forest one day, he noticed a great, treeless mountain that he was quite sure had not been there before. While he stood there staring in amazement, twelve wild-looking men approached the mountain. Believing they were robbers, he climbed a tree and waited to see what they would do.

As the twelve men came to the foot of the mountain, they cried, "Semsi mountain, Semsi mountain, open!" And the mountain opened down the middle, and they went in, the entrance shutting behind them. After a short time, however, the men came out carrying large sacks, and turned and faced the mountain, calling, "Semsi mountain, shut thyself!" The entrance quickly closed and the twelve men went away.

The poor brother was most curious to see what was hidden inside, so he walked to the mountain, and called, "Semsi mountain, open!" Within he found a great cavern filled with silver and gold and great piles of pearls and other sparkling jewels. "Should I take any?" wondered the man. "My family is very hungry." At last he decided to fill his pockets with gold but leave the gems where they were. He ordered the mountain to open, and he left to retrieve his wheelbarrow.

This stroke of luck made life for his family much easier. And it gave the man much joy to share his good fortune with the poor in his village. In time, the money ran out and the man borrowed a bushel measure from his brother and returned to the mountain. Again, he left the most valuable treasures in place, and took only what he needed for his family.

When it was necessary to go to the mountain for a third time, he went to his rich brother's house to borrow the bushel measure again. Now the rich brother had become quite curious about his brother's change of fortune and thought perhaps the bushel had something to do with it. So he put sticky tar at the bottom of the bushel and when his brother returned it, he found a gold piece stuck to the bottom.

He asked his brother where the money came from and the poor man told him everything. At once the rich brother went to the mountain himself to gather up all the treasures.

No bushel would do for him! He went to the mountain in his carriage, expecting to bring back a great load of wealth. "Semsi mountain, Semsi mountain, open!" the rich brother cried. The mountain opened up for him, and the rich brother was overwhelmed by the piles of treasure inside. When he had as much as his arms could carry, he thought to take a first load outside, and then come back for more.

But in his greed and excitement, he forgot the right words. "Simeli mountain, Simeli mountain, open!" Of course the mountain stayed shut. The brother became alarmed, but the more he thought about it, the more confused he got, and all of his commands to the mountain were useless.

That night the mountain opened and out came the twelve wild men. "Aha, we have caught the thief!" they cried. "We know you have been here before!

But you will not leave here alive this time!"

Then the rich man cried, "It was not me before! It was my brother! Take back your treasure! What good is it to me now?" But in vain the rich man begged for his life and learned too late the price of greed. The wild men chopped his head off, and the mountain never opened again.—BROTHERS GRIMM

February 22

The Wolf and the Crane

One day a wolf was greedily wolfing down his lunch and a bone got stuck in his throat. The wolf was filled with pain, and went running up and down the aisles of the forest, screaming and gesturing wildly for assistance.

"Help me, help me," he cried, nearly choking. "I have a bone stuck in my throat! Help and I will give you a grand reward! A reward, I say! *Help!*"

Most of the animals paid the wolf no mind, privately taking pleasure in his pitiful circumstances. But a crane was moved by his pleas, in particular the promise of a reward. "I believe *I* can help you," she offered.

The crane's long beak made the perfect tool for removing the bone from the wolf's throat, and she extracted the bone with little effort. Having drawn out the bone, she gingerly asked for compensation. "Are you prepared now to give me a reward?" she said.

The wolf looked at her, shocked. "Surely, you are joking," he said with a sneer. "To ask for any reward other than that you have put your head into a wolf's jaws and brought it out safe again marks you a fool. Be off, I say, or I will reward myself . . . by having you for dessert!"

Being charitable in hopes of a good return can backfire.—AESOP

February 23

The Fox and the Grapes

It was a hot summer day, and a fox had been strolling through the orchard for hours. He was hungry and thirsty. The fruit of the trees had withered from drought and pests, and the pond was dried up. For a moment, the fox thought he might die from the heat. Then, almost miraculously, he came upon some lovely grape vines that had been trained on a high branch of a nearby tree.

"Grapes, how delightful," thought the fox. "Just the thing to quench my thirst."

He jumped up to grab a cluster of grapes but to no avail. He tried again. Nothing. He drew back several paces and then took a running jump—and missed.

Then he went to look for a stick long enough to knock off some of the grapes. He looked everywhere, but he couldn't find the right stick.

After trying a few more running jumps, the fox walked away. "Oh, forget it," he said to himself. "The grapes are probably sour anyway."

It is common to fault what we cannot have.—AESOP

February 24

The Steadfast Tin Soldier

Once upon a time there were twenty-five tin soldiers who were brothers, for they had been cast from the same piece of tin. They shouldered their muskets and looked straight before them, and their uniforms were splendid in red and blue. Each soldier was exactly like every other, except one, for he had but one leg. He had been cast last of all, and there had not been enough tin to finish him, but he stood as firm on one leg as the others on their two.

The first words the twenty-five brothers heard was "Tin Soldiers!" for they had been given to a little boy for his birthday, and he clapped his hands with glee as he opened the soldiers' box. He set them out on a table that held many other playthings, including a delightful cardboard castle. In the doorway of the castle stood a lovely little cardboard lady, with a dress of gauze and blue ribbon attached with a tinsel rose. The little lady stretched out both her arms, for she was a dancer, and she lifted one leg so high that the Tin Soldier could not see it at all. He thought that, like himself, she had but one.

"That would be just the wife for me!" he thought. "But she is very grand and lives in a castle, while I have only a box to offer her. Still, I must try to make her acquaintance."

He watched her carefully all day. She never lost her balance nor wavered from her spot. That evening all the playthings were put away and the people of the house went to sleep. Now the toys began to play at "visiting" and at "war" and at "having dances." The only two who did not stir were the Tin Soldier and the Dancing Lady. She stood straight up on the points of her toes, and he never took his eyes off her for a moment. A Jack-in-the-box spoke sharply to the Tin Soldier, telling him to keep his eyes to himself, but the Tin Soldier pretended not to hear. "Just you wait till tomorrow, then," said the bad-tempered Jack-in-the-box.

The next morning the little boy placed the Tin Soldier in the window, and whether it was a draft or the ill wishes of the Jack-in-the-box that did it, all at once the Tin Soldier tumbled out of the window and fell three stories to the ground.

The little boy and a servant came to look for him, and though they almost trod upon him, they could not see him. If the soldier had shouted, "Here I am!" they would have spotted him, with his bayonet stuck in the paving stones, but he did not think that was dignified to do in full uniform.

Soon it began to rain heavily and the gutters of the street were filled. Two boys passed by and saw the Tin Soldier. "He must have a boat ride!" they cried. The boys made a boat out of newspaper, put the Tin Soldier in the middle, and sent him sailing away down the gutter. The paper boat rocked up and down and spun left and right so that the Tin Soldier trembled, but he kept his composure and didn't move as the paper boat was swept into a long, dark storm drain.

The current ran faster and faster there, and the Tin Soldier could hear a terrible roaring noise up ahead. His boat started to fill with water, and he thought of the Dancing Lady he would never see again, when suddenly he was swallowed by a fish. The fish rushed about for a time, but then all was quiet, and the Tin Soldier saw a flash like lightning. Someone called out loudly, "Look, a tin soldier!"

The fish had been caught, taken to market, and brought to a kitchen, where the cook was cutting it open. And wonder of wonders, the Tin Soldier found himself in the house he had left just that morning.

He was returned to the playroom, where the dancer still stood resolutely on one leg. He looked at her, and she at him, but they never said a word. At this moment, the little boy, for no particular reason, flung the Tin Soldier into the fireplace. The soldier felt as if he were melting away, but he kept his eyes on the little maiden, and managed to keep himself erect, shouldering his musket bravely. Suddenly a door was opened, and the draft caught the Dancing Lady so that she fluttered straight into the fire.

When a maidservant cleaned the fireplace the next morning she found nothing but a small tin heart and a spangle.—HANS CHRISTIAN ANDERSEN

February 25

Stone Soup

Long ago, in a foreign land, three soldiers were returning home from a war. They were tired and hungry, and all they could think about was how good it would be to have a steaming bowl of soup. Eventually, they came upon a handsome little village.

"Ah," sighed one of the soldiers, "how wonderful it would be if the villagers would offer us a bowl of soup and a bed to sleep in." But the war had taken its toll, and food was scarce. The poor villagers viewed the soldiers with deep suspicion and as they approached, doors were locked and the villagers frowned.

Suddenly the first soldier had an idea. "Do not hate us," he said in a clear voice. "We do not want your food or gold but only a large black pot so we might prepare our famous stone soup."

Stone soup? the people wondered.

"Stone soup," the soldier went on cheerily. He winked at his two companions and said loudly, "Is it time to build the fire, gentlemen?" The soldiers nodded and though they, too, were puzzled, they helped to build a fire. Not long after, a young man emerged from his cottage, bearing a large black soup pot filled with water. The soldiers thanked him many times, and began to search the roadside for stones. When the finest stones were located they went into the pot, and the soup began to boil.

Now the villagers, peering through their curtained windows, found this a most peculiar event and, overcome with curiosity, one by one they unlocked their doors and made their way to the soup pot. Once he had the crowd's attention, the soldier leaned over the pot, took a deep sniff, and in a stage whisper said, "Hmmm . . . something is *missing.*" He turned to the villagers. "I understand that you have

no food to spare, but if we had some salt and pepper, this soup would be vastly improved." "I'll fetch it," said a little girl, scampering off to fetch the seasonings. After the soup received the salt and pepper, the soldiers took another great sniff. They were in agreement. The soup did taste better, but it needed a touch of fresh spring onions. The farmer's wife was glad to oblige, and returned straight away with a bundle of onions.

And so it went. The soldiers would sniff the soup, and politely observe how much better it would taste if only it had a handful of carrots, a few stalks of celery, a potato or two, some barley to thicken it, some milk to enrich it. Each time they would shake their heads and lament that there was no use wishing for what you could not have, and a villager would slip off quietly and return with whatever ingredient was called for.

The soup began to smell good, quite good, and one of the soldiers observed that if there were but a few chunks of meat in it, it would smell just like the stone soup they had made for the king the week before. "The king?" the villagers murmured among themselves. *The soldiers had dined with the king?* The people were so excited now that they brought out all kinds of food from hiding, and suddenly there was enough food and drink for a feast. When the soup was ready, the entire village shared the meal, and then danced until the moon came out. The soldiers were hailed as heroes and invited to sleep in the most comfortable beds the village had to offer.

The next morning, the soldiers went on their way, their arms brimming with little gifts and provisions for their journey home. The villagers cheered and waved farewell from their curtained windows. Who ever would have imagined that stone soup could taste so good?

February 26

Prunella, Part 1

There was once a little girl who lived near an orchard with plum trees. Each day, on her way to school, she would pick a plum and put it in her pocket for lunch. Everyone called her Prunella.

Now the orchard belonged to a witch, and eventually the witch spotted Prunella gathering plums. She seized the girl by the arm and cried, "You

little thief! I have caught you and now you shall pay!" She dragged the girl to her house, and there she kept Prunella as her servant for years.

Prunella grew into a beautiful young woman, but her loveliness and her gentle nature did not change the witch's determination to punish her. In fact, the witch grew more vengeful. One day, she called Prunella and said, "Take this basket to the well, and bring it back to me filled with water. If you fail, I will kill you."

Prunella took the basket and let it down into the well again and again. But of course the water streamed out each time. In despair, Prunella gave up and began crying bitterly. Suddenly she heard a voice by her side, asking, "Prunella, why are you sad?"

Turning around, she saw a handsome young man looking kindly at her. "Who are you? And how do you know my name?" cried Prunella.

"I am Bensiabel, the son of the witch. I know she is determined you shall die, but I promise I shall prevent her from carrying out her wicked plans. Will you give me a kiss if I fill your basket?"

"No," said Prunella. "I cannot give a kiss to the son of a witch!"

"Very well," said the youth sadly. "But I will fill your basket anyway." And when he dipped the basket in the well, the water stayed in it.

Prunella brought the basket back to the witch, who turned scarlet with rage. "Bensiabel must have helped you," she screamed. Prunella looked down and said nothing.

The next day the witch gave her a sack of wheat, telling Prunella she expected her to have made bread by day's end. If not, she would kill her. Now it was impossible for Prunella to grind all this wheat, make dough, and bake bread in the short time she had. She started bravely enough, but soon realized how impossible her task was. Through her tears, she heard a familiar voice. "Prunella, Prunella, do not weep. If you will give me a kiss, I will make the bread for you."

"I swear I will not kiss the son of a witch, even to save my life," replied Prunella.

Bensiabel took the wheat and made bread anyway, and when the witch returned, all was ready. Now the witch's fury knew no bounds. "Bensiabel must have been here!" she cried. "But I will win in the end." Prunella looked down and said nothing.

The following day the witch called Prunella and said, "Go to my sister's house, which is across the mountains. She will give you a casket to bring back to me." The sister was even more wicked, and the witch was sure Prunella would never leave her house alive. But Prunella did not know this, and she set off cheerfully enough, little suspecting the fate that awaited her.

February 27

Prunella, Part 2

On her way across the mountains, Prunella met Bensiabel, who asked where she was going. When she described her task, Bensiabel looked horror-stricken. "You poor girl!" he cried. "You are being sent straight to your death! Give me a kiss and I will save you."

But Prunella's answer was the same. "I will not kiss the son of a witch."

"Nevertheless, I will save your life, for I love you better than myself," said Bensiabel. Then he continued, "Take this loaf of bread, this piece of rope, and this broom with you. When you get to the witch's house, a fierce bloodhound will be at the door. Throw him the loaf of bread. When you pass the dog, you will see a woman in the courtyard trying to lower a bucket in the well with her braid. Give her the rope. And in the kitchen you will find another woman trying to clean the hearth with her tongue. To her, you must give the broom. The casket will be on top of the kitchen cupboard. Grab it quickly and leave the house at once."

Prunella listened carefully to his instructions and did exactly as he said. But at the last moment with the casket under her arm, she was discovered by the witch. "Kill that thief!" the witch cried to the woman in the kitchen.

"I will not!" said the woman. "For she gave me a broom to clean with. You made me clean the hearth with my tongue!"

Then the furious witch called to the woman at the well, "Grab the thief and throw her down the well and drown her. Do as I tell you!"

"I will not drown her," said the woman, "for she gave me rope to draw water. You made me use my hair."

The witch shouted at the dog to devour Prunella, but the dog also refused to obey her order. "You starved me, but she gave me a loaf of bread."

And so Prunella escaped and brought the casket back to her mistress, who almost choked with anger. "Did you meet Bensiabel on the way?" she screamed. But Prunella said nothing. "We shall see who wins in the end," exclaimed the witch. "There are three roosters in the hen house. One is yellow, one black, and one white. If one of them crows during the night, you must tell me which one it is. If you make a mistake, I will eat you up."

Bensiabel came that evening and stayed in the room next to Prunella's. Sometime after midnight, one of the roosters crowed. "Which one was it?" screamed the witch from her chambers.

Trembling, Prunella knocked on the wall and whispered, "Bensiabel, tell me, please!"

"Will you give me a kiss if I tell you?" he whispered back. Prunella again refused, and Bensiabel sighed. But he told her, "It was the yellow rooster."

Now the witch had come to Prunella's door, waiting for her answer. When Prunella told her it was the yellow rooster, the witch stamped her foot and gnashed her teeth in anger.

Near dawn a rooster crowed again. This time Bensiabel hesitated when Prunella begged for help. He hoped she could forget he was a witch's son, and promise to kiss him. But then Prunella cried, "Please, Bensiabel, save me! The witch is coming to my room!"

Bensiabel leapt from his bed and flung open the door to his room. He did this with such force that the door threw his mother backwards. She fell headlong down the flight of stairs and was killed.

Forgetting her vow, Prunella threw herself into Bensiabel's arms in gratitude. And at last she was touched by his goodness and his kindness toward her. She agreed soon after to become his wife, and they lived happily ever after.

—ADAPTED FROM ANDREW LANG

February 28

The Spindle, the Needle, and the Shuttle

A GERMAN TALE

A young girl, who had been orphaned as a baby, lived in a little cottage at the edge of a village with an old woman, who took care of her and brought her up to be industrious and pious.

The girl earned enough by spinning to support herself and the old woman. Then, in the year the girl turned fifteen, the old woman fell very ill. Calling the girl to her bedside, she said, "Dear daughter, I feel that my end is near. I leave you this cottage. With the needle, the spindle, and the shuttle, you can earn your bread." Then she blessed the maiden, and added, "Keep God always in your heart, and you will never go wrong." A few days later, the old woman died.

After this the young girl lived in the cottage quite alone, working diligently at her spinning and weaving. The blessing of the old woman seemed to rest upon all she did, for she made enough money for her own wants, with a bit left over for the poor.

It happened about this time that the son of the king was traveling about the country in search of a bride. The prince could not take a poor woman as a wife, but he also did not care much for riches. So he had decided to try and find a bride who was both the richest and poorest.

When he came to the girl's village, he inquired first for the richest maiden in the place, and then asked, "Who is the poorest?" A villager directed him to the cottage of the young maiden.

Riding through the village, the prince passed the stately house of the richest family. At the door sat a finely dressed young woman, who made a curtsey to the prince as he rode by. The prince looked at her but said not a word, and rode on, without stopping, to the cottage of the poor maiden.

She was not seated at her doorway, but was diligently working away inside. The prince peered in the window of the cottage for a time, watching her at her spinning wheel. Presently she glanced up, and seeing a gentleman looking at her through the window, she began to blush and turned back to her work. And so the prince got back on his horse and rode away.

The girl kept at her spinning, but her thoughts were on the handsome prince, though she knew not who he was. She began to sing a curious song the old woman had taught her: "Spindle, spindle, run away; fetch my lover here today." To her astonishment, the spindle leaped from her hands and rushed out of the house. She followed it to the door and watched as it danced merrily across the fields, trailing behind it a bright golden thread.

Having no longer a spindle, the girl took up her shuttle and began weaving. The spindle, meanwhile, continued on its way, and just as the thread ran out, it caught up with the prince. "What do I see?" he cried. "This thread will lead me to good fortune, no doubt." So he turned his horse around and followed the trail of the golden thread.

Back at the cottage, the girl was at her loom, recalling more of the song: "Shuttle, shuttle, thou art free; bring my lover home to me." At those words, the shuttle ran to the door sill and began to weave the most beautiful carpet ever seen.

The maiden now had nothing left to work with but the needle. And as she sewed, she sang another tune: "Needle, needle, while you shine, make the house look neat and fine." All at once, the needle sprang from her fingers and flew about the room. Suddenly the table was covered with fine green cloth, the chairs with velvet, and curtains of heavy silk appeared at the window.

Just then the prince arrived, having followed the golden thread to the cottage. In the doorway, he stepped upon the beautiful carpet and entered the elegant room. There the maiden sat, and even in her homely dress, she looked as lovely as a wild rose.

"You are exactly what I seek!" the prince cried. "At once the poorest and richest maiden in the land. Will you come with me and be my bride?"

She did not speak, but held out her hand to him. He kissed her hand, led her out, and rode away with her to his father's castle.

Their marriage was celebrated with great splendor and rejoicing. And the spindle, the needle, and the shuttle were kept in a place of honor in the treasure chamber ever after.

—BROTHERS GRIMM

MARCH

March 1

The Wind and the Sun

One morning the wind and the sun entered into a dispute as to which was the strongest of the two. After much discussion, they agreed to a test: whichever could persuade a traveler to take off his cloak first would be considered the more powerful.

The wind began blowing with all of his might, harder, stronger still, so that trees were bent nearly to the ground. But the more he blew, the tighter the traveler clutched his cloak.

Then the sun broke out, his welcome beams clearing the air, and the traveler, feeling warm and relaxed, took off his cloak straightaway. The sun was therefore decided to be the stronger, and since then it has been deemed that persuasion is better than force and that the sun with its mild and congenial approach made far greater gains into a man's heart than the force of the harsh and merciless wind.—AESOP

March 2

The Selfish Giant

A TALE FOR EASTER

Every afternoon, as they were coming from school, the children used to play in the Giant's garden. The Giant had been away for seven years, visiting his friend the Cornish Ogre.

It was a lovely garden, with soft green grass, flowers, and twelve beautiful peach trees. The birds sat on the trees and sang so sweetly that the children used to stop their games to listen.

But one day the Giant came back and found the children playing in his garden. "What are you doing here?" he cried in a very gruff voice. The children ran away.

"This is *my* garden," said the Giant. "I will allow nobody to play in it but myself." And he built a high wall around it. He was a very selfish giant.

Then spring came to the country. But in the garden of the Selfish Giant it was still winter. The birds did not care to sing in it as there were no children, and the trees and flowers forgot to bloom. The only people who were

pleased were the Snow and the Frost. "Spring has forgotten this garden," they cried, "so we will live here all year round."

The Snow covered the grass with her great white cloak, and the Frost painted the trees silver. They invited the North Wind to stay with them. He roared all day about the garden, and blew the chimney pots down. "This is a delightful spot," he said. "We must ask the Hail on a visit." The Hail, whose breath was like ice, came and rattled on the roof till he broke most of the slates.

"I cannot understand why Spring is so late," said the Giant, as he looked out at his cold, white garden. "I hope the weather will change." But Spring never came.

One morning the Selfish Giant was lying in bed when he heard lovely music, and thought the King's musicians were passing by. It was only a linnet outside his window, but it had been so long since he had heard birdsong that he had forgotten the sound.

When he looked out his window, he saw a most wonderful sight. Through a hole in the wall, the children had crept in, and they were sitting in the branches of the trees. So glad were the trees to have the children back again that they had covered themselves in blossoms.

But in the far corner of the garden, one poor tree was still covered with snow. A little boy was standing beneath it. He was so small he could not reach the branches, and he was crying bitterly.

The Giant's heart melted. "How selfish I have been! Now I know why Spring passed me by. I will put that poor little boy in the tree, and then I will knock down the wall and my garden will be the children's playground for ever and ever."

When he went into the garden and the children saw him, they were frightened and ran away, all but the little boy, for his eyes were so full of tears that he did not see the Giant coming. The Giant took him gently in his hand and put him up into the tree, which broke out at once into blossom. The little boy flung his arms around the Giant's neck and kissed him. And when they saw that the Giant was not wicked any longer, the other children came running back. "It is your garden now, children," said the Giant, and he took an ax and knocked down the wall.

All day long they played, and in the evening the children came to bid the Giant good-bye. "But where is the boy I put into the tree?" The Giant loved him best because he had kissed him.

The children said they had never seen him before, and the Giant felt very sad.

The years passed. The children came to the garden every afternoon and played with the Giant. But the little boy whom the Giant loved was never seen again. The Giant was very kind to all the children, yet he longed for his first little friend and often spoke of him.

In time the Giant grew very old and feeble. He could only sit in his armchair and watch the children at their games.

One winter morning he glanced out his window as he was dressing. He did not hate Winter now, for he knew it was merely the Spring asleep. Suddenly he rubbed his eyes in wonder and looked and looked at the farthest corner of the garden. A tree was quite covered with lovely white blossoms and underneath it stood the little boy he had loved.

The Giant hastened to the garden in great joy, but as he came near the child, his face grew red with anger, and he asked, "Who hath dared to wound thee?" For on the palms of the boy's hands and on his little feet were the prints of two nails.

"Tell me," cried the Giant, "so that I may take my sword and slay him."

"Nay," answered the child. "These are the wounds of Love."

"Who art thou?" asked the Giant, and in awe he knelt down before the little boy.

The boy smiled and said to him, "You let me play once in your garden. Today you shall come with me to *my* garden, which is Paradise."

And when the children came that afternoon, they found the Giant lying dead under the tree, all covered with white blossoms.

—ADAPTED FROM OSCAR WILDE

March 3

The Month of March

AN ITALIAN FAIRY TALE

Once upon a time there lived in Italy two brothers. The elder, named Cianne, was as rich as a lord, and the younger brother, called Lise, was so poor he had barely enough to live on. Cianne, though rich in fortune, was poor in spirit, for he would not give his brother a lira, even to save his life. Poor Lise set out to wander the world and scrape out a living.

One wet, cold night Lise came to an inn, where he found twelve youths seated around a fire. Taking pity on Lise, who was shivering from the cold, they beckoned him to come sit by the blaze. While he was warming his hands, one of the young men, who had a sad and cross look, was watching him closely. "Well," he suddenly growled out at Lise, "what do you think of this weather?"

"I think that each month of the year must perform its duty," replied Lise. "But in winter, when it rains and snows, we want the sun of summer, and in August we grumble with the heat and long for rain. Now if our wishes could come true, all nature would be upside down. Therefore, let us leave heaven to its course and each month to its job."

"You are a wise young man," said the youth. "But you cannot deny that this month of March is ill natured, with all this frost and rain, wind and storm."

"Why, you are not fair to the poor month," answered Lise. "You tell only of its ills and do not speak of the benefits of March. It heralds the spring, and starts all life growing again."

The youth was greatly pleased when he heard what Lise said, and his face lost the sad look and became bright with happiness. For this youth was March himself, and the others were his eleven brothers. He was so grateful to Lise for trying to see the good rather than the evil of the month that he sought to reward him. Giving Lise a beautiful little box, March said, "Take this and if you want anything, only ask for it, and open the box and you will see it."

"Thank you, thank you!" said Lise, and went to sleep with the box under his head.

The next morning, Lise took his leave and set out on his way. It was windy and snowy, and poor Lise began to wish he were traveling in a carriage. Remembering the box, Lise opened it and instantly a carriage appeared. When he wished for a meal on his homeward journey, a feast fit for a king was spread before him. Velvet garments were his for the asking.

Lise called on his brother, Cianne, who could not believe his eyes. "Where did you get these sudden riches?" Cianne asked. Lise told him of the youth at the inn, but not of their conversation.

Cianne hastened to the inn the very next day and found the twelve youths still there. Now when the sad youth asked him the same question about March, Cianne replied, "Confound the miserable month! It stirs up ill humors and brings sickness to our bodies. It would be a blessing if it were dropped from the year!"

March, who heard himself thus slandered, controlled his anger, though his face clouded with fury. When Cianne was about to depart, March presented him with a fine whip, saying, "Whenever you wish for anything, say, 'Whip, give me a hundred,' and you will receive your reward."

"I am sure this is a magic whip," Cianne said to himself, as he hurried home. "And it will bring me gold!" Once in his chambers, he cried, "Whip, give me a hundred!" Whereupon the whip gave him more than he bargained for on his legs, his back, and his face. Hearing his yells, Lise came running to help Cianne and could stop the whip only by opening his magic box.

"How did this happen?" asked Lise, and Cianne told him the whole story. "You well deserve the punishment," said Lise. "For you have always been greedy for gold. You should watch what you say for you never know whom you may hurt with your cruel words." But he put his arm around his brother and added, "But do not worry. There is enough in my box for both of us to share. We will forget the past and begin again."

When Cianne heard his brother's generous offer, he cried out, "Oh, my brother, forgive me for my past unkindness. I truly deserve the gift March gave me."

So the two brothers lived together for the rest of their days and shared their good fortune, and from that time Cianne spoke well of everyone, for his heart was filled with love.

March 4

The Short Tale of the Rabbits Who Went Out to See the World

Two white rabbits lived in a hutch in our backyard. One sunny morning, One said to the Other, "Let's go out to see the world."

So they did. They went up the alley to the front garden. Here the grass was growing fresh and green.

"Ah," said the Other to the One, "the world was made for us. The world is one big cabbage leaf! Taste it!"

Just as they put their noses down to nibble a bit of it, a dog poked his nose through the fence and said, "Bowwow."

"Uh oh," said One to the Other, "I think the world belongs to *him*. And he may have it!"

The two white rabbits scurried back to their safe hutch and there they stayed, eating cabbage leaves and leaving the world alone.

—ANGELA M. KEYES

March 5

The Marvelous Donkey

AN ITALIAN TALE

A poor widow made so little from her weaving that she and her son were close to starving. At last the widow decided she must ask for help from her brother-in-law, a steward at a distant castle. She sent her young son on this mission, and when he reached his uncle, he asked, "Please, can you help us? I am too young to make any money and we are dying of hunger!"

"You should have come sooner!" said his uncle, a kindly man. "I will give you something that will support you always. Take this donkey home with you. You have only to put a cloth beneath him, and he will fill it for you with coins. But don't tell anyone about him and don't let the donkey leave your side!"

The lad had to stop at an inn that night, for his home was some distance away. When he asked for lodging, he insisted that his donkey stay in the room with him. The innkeeper found this a peculiar request, and so he peeked through the keyhole that night and saw the donkey laying money. "I would be a fool if I let this marvelous animal escape me!" thought the innkeeper. So he found another donkey of the same size and color, and switched animals while the boy slept.

The boy resumed his trip but soon began to suspect that all was not right with his marvelous donkey. And sure enough, the donkey laid not a cent. Back the lad went to the inn and accused the innkeeper of stealing his donkey. But the innkeeper threw him out, crying, "How can you say such a thing?

We are all honest people here! Go away, before I have you arrested!"

In tears, the boy returned to his uncle and told him of his misfortune. "You should not have stopped at the inn," said his uncle. "But I have another present I can give to you and your mother. This looks like an ordinary tablecloth, but if you spread it out and say, 'Tablecloth, make ready,' a marvelous meal will be laid out before you."

The youth thanked his uncle profusely, and set out for home, but young and foolish as he was, he stopped at the same inn again. He asked for a room, but told the innkeeper he needed no meals, which made the man suspicious. He spied on the boy that night and discovered the secret of the magic tablecloth. Once more, the dishonest innkeeper made a clever switch, and the boy was none the wiser till he asked the tablecloth to make a meal the next day.

Now the lad was in despair and dreaded going back to his uncle with the terrible news that he had been robbed once more. The uncle would have had every right to refuse to help him any longer. After all, he had warned the boy about the inn. But he was a kind soul, and he decided to give his nephew a gift that would help him retrieve his stolen goods. It was a stick the boy was to hide under his pillow. Should anyone try to rob him, he only had to say, "Beat, beat!" and the stick would thrash the person until the boy commanded it to stop.

The boy returned to the inn, and the innkeeper had his eyes on the stick at once, feeling sure it possessed some magical properties. The boy pretended to sleep that night, and when he heard the innkeeper creep into his room, he whispered, "Beat, beat!" Blows rained down on the innkeeper without mercy, and the boy refused to halt the stick until his donkey and his tablecloth were returned.

Finally successful at his mission, the boy returned home. And with the help of the donkey and the tablecloth, he and his mother never went hungry again.

March 6

The Marvelous Donkey, Variation

Another slightly different approach to this story is presented in *The Donkey, The Table, and the Stick,* an English folktale. This story centers on the travails of a young man named Jack, who had a cruel father. Jack loved a young woman in the village, and so to marry her and escape his father's beatings, he went off to seek his fortune.

He escaped at night. On the road he met an old woman gathering wood. She liked Jack and offered him a job as her servant. Jack agreed, and worked for her for a year and a day.

At the end of that time, he asked for his pay, and the woman gave him a donkey named Neddy. Neddy was a very special donkey, she explained; if Jack pulled on the donkey's ears, the donkey would bray and silver and gold coins would tumble out of her mouth.

Jack and Neddy went to an inn and the two spent the night. Jack ordered the best of everything, but the innkeeper wanted to be paid in advance. When the innkeeper saw how Jack got his money, he wanted Neddy for himself, so in the middle of the night he switched another donkey for Neddy.

Jack rode out the next day without a clue that he was on a different donkey.

Jack went home, thinking that his amazing donkey might endear him to his father. But when he tried to demonstrate, the donkey did nothing. "Get out!" screamed his father, and he chased Jack with a pitchfork. Jack ran to the next village and stopped at a carpenter's shop. The carpenter agreed to hire him for a year and a day. At the year's end, the carpenter gave Jack a special table. When Jack said, "Table, be covered," at once it would be covered with food and drink. Naturally, Jack was thrilled. But stupidly, he stopped at the same inn to spend the night. The innkeeper spied on Jack and saw him using his magic table. In the middle of the night, the innkeeper switched Jack's table for another.

Thinking that his father might be impressed with his magic table, Jack went home. But when he tried to demonstrate the table's unique powers, nothing happened. Jack's father hit him on the head with an iron skillet, and Jack ran away again.

On the road Jack found no work but he did help a stranger walk across a toppled tree spanning a river. The stranger pulled a limb off the fallen tree and fashioned a walking stick out of it. The stranger advised Jack that if anyone angers him, all he must do is command, "Up stick, bang him."

Jack stopped at the inn again and commanded his stick to whack the innkeeper until he returned the donkey and the table. Once he regained his donkey and his table, Jack returned home to show his father, but his father had died.

With the house now to himself, Jack became wealthy. The village girls were suddenly very interested in Jack. Jack was loyal to his first love, but announced that he would marry the wealthiest girl in town. He instructed all of the eligible girls to assemble at his house the next day and to bring all of their wealth in their aprons. Jack's sweetheart was very poor and had only a few pennies to carry in her apron. All the girls stared at her disdainfully and even Jack brushed her aside. Then he instructed his stick, "Up stick, bang them." The stick knocked all of the girls to the ground, and Jack grabbed their money as it fell. He poured all the money into his sweetheart's lap. "Clearly you are the richest of all," Jack declared. "I will marry only you."

March 7

Hercules and the Wagoner

It had rained for days so it was no surprise, really, when the farmer's wagon wheel got stuck in the mud. The horses pulled and pulled but they could not budge the load an inch, and soon the wagon began sinking.

"The horses are worthless," grumbled the farmer, climbing down from the wagon. He looked up and cursed the rain, blaming everyone and everything around him.

Then he shook a fist at the gods. "Hercules, help a poor man surrounded by stupid beasts and bad fortune."

To his shock, Hercules appeared.

"If you are a true man, you will put your shoulder to the wheel and budge the wagon forward with your wits and might. If you stop complaining and try to help yourself, I will come to your aid."

The farmer, shaken and fearful, pressed his shoulder to the wheel and the wagon popped out of the mud. Soon the farmer was moving forward, happy and enlightened by what he had learned.

To solve a problem you must take a first step.—AESOP

March 8

Cinderella

There was once a man who married a proud and haughty woman after his first wife died. She had two horrible daughters, while the man's daughter was as fair and gentle as her mother had been.

The stepmother forced her husband's daughter to do all of the housework and to wait upon her and her daughters. Whenever she had a free moment, the hardworking child would sit quietly in the chimney corner among the cinders. Her stepsisters came to call her Cinderwench, or sometimes Cinderella.

One day it was announced that the king's son would give a series of balls for the fashionable people of the realm. Cinderella's two sisters were invited and immediately started planning what they would wear. To tease Cinderella, her sisters cruelly asked if she wouldn't like to go to the ball. But Cinderella wouldn't even dream of such a thing. What would she wear?

On the evening of the ball, Cinderella helped her sisters dress and fix their hair. When they left, she sat down by the fire and cried. She was not a person who pitied herself, but for some reason she had wanted to go to this ball very much. Instantly, her fairy godmother appeared and asked her why she was so unhappy.

"I wish, I wish I could . . ."

"I know," said the fairy godmother. "You want to go to the ball—and you shall!"

Cinderella was instructed to find a pumpkin in the garden. She did so, and when her fairy godmother touched it with her wand, it turned into a golden coach. The godmother sent her to find six live mice, and these were turned into a set of fine horses to draw the coach. The fairy godmother selected from the rat trap the rat with the longest whiskers, to be transformed into a fine fat coachman to drive the golden coach. Six lizards were brought in from the garden by their tails, to become six footman dressed in livery who jumped up behind the coach just as footmen are supposed to do.

It seemed Cinderella was all set to go except for her ragged clothes. With one touch of her fairy godmother's wand these were turned into a gown of gold and silver, embroidered with jewels. For Cinderella's feet there were the prettiest glass slippers ever worn by any princess. Just as Cinderella was mounting her coach, the fairy godmother warned her that she must return at midnight, otherwise her coach would once again become a pumpkin, her horses mice, her coach a rat, her footmen lizards, and her clothes nothing but rags.

Cinderella promised she would not be late and set off for the ball, dizzy with happiness.

For some mysterious reason, the king's son seemed to be waiting for her at the palace. He did not let her out of his sight the entire evening. Everyone at the ball was completely dazzled by the loveliness of the unknown princess. When Cinderella heard the clock strike twelve, she graciously bid everyone goodnight and went off in her golden coach.

Her fairy godmother was pleased that Cinderella had come back just in time. Cinderella could not stop talking and laughing and dancing about; it had been the most wonderful night of her life. There was to be a second ball the following evening. Cinderella asked if she might go once more and the godmother agreed.

The next night, the two sisters went off to the ball and Cinderella followed shortly afterward, dressed in even more exquisite attire. Once again, the prince was captivated by her. Cinderella was enjoying herself so much she completely lost track of time. Suddenly she heard the clock strike twelve. She fled the palace, running so fast down the stairs that she lost one of her glass slippers. The prince followed but he lost sight of her and was left with only her shoe.

Cinderella's coach had disappeared and she had to run home in her ragged clothes. When her sisters came home, they talked endlessly of the ball and the mysterious disappearance of the princess.

A few days later, the king's son announced that he would marry the woman whose delicate foot fit the glass slipper. A courtier took the shoe from house to house, and all of the eligible young ladies tried it on. Finally, the courtier arrived at Cinderella's house and the sisters tried to stuff their bulky feet into the little slipper.

"May I try it on?" Cinderella asked gently. Her sisters laughed scornfully but the courtier lifted the slipper to Cinderella's foot and, of course, it fit perfectly. Instantly, her godmother's spell was upon her again and Cinderella was transformed into the beautiful, elegantly dressed lady she had been at the ball.

Her sisters recognized her immediately and begged her pardon for all of their former unkindness. Cinderella forgave them. The courtier took Cinderella to the palace, where the prince vowed he would love her forever and asked for her hand in marriage. Cinderella invited her sisters to live in the palace, and not long afterwards, changed by Cinderella's simple goodness, they were married to two lords of the court.—ADAPTED BY PERRAULT

March 9

Cinderella, Variation 1

There are many powerful versions of Cinderella and often the variant centers on a different character device. The Zuni Indians feature the fairy godmother as a wild turkey; in the Scottish version the fairy role is Cinderella's dead mother who appears as a sheep. Other versions change the nature of the trial itself. A Native American version of the story—most often called "Indian Cinderella"—features a warrior named Strong Wind who can make himself invisible at will and always fights on the side of good. The most common retelling of this is by Cyrus McCormick.

Strong Wind shared his hero status with his sister (although neither she nor the Cinderella figure are given a name) and the two roamed the world doing mighty deeds. When Strong Wind decided it was time to marry, his sister developed a trial to determine the most suitable woman. They would summon all the eligible maidens in the country. The one who was able to "see" Strong Wind would marry him. Because the warrior really could make himself invisible, "seeing" him required either unique powers, or the honesty to admit that one cannot see him, honesty being the authentic power sought here.

A long line of maidens came to "see" Strong Wind. His sister gave the test, and the maidens all lied and said they could indeed see the warrior. But when asked to describe him they were at a loss. *"Do you see him?"* "Yes." *"Of what is his shoulder strap made?"* The maidens usually guessed rawhide. *"With what does he draw his sled?"* The maidens usually gave wrong answers like hide of a moose, a pole, or a great cord.

Then along came a family of three sisters: two cruel older sisters and one beautiful younger sister whom they treated very badly. They were the daughters of a great chief, and their mother had died. The younger wore only rags, and her sisters had cut off her long black hair and burned her face with coals so she would be scarred. Like most fathers in fairy tales, their father had no idea of their cruelty. The older sisters told him that their younger sister did all of the hair cutting and face burning to herself, and he believed them.

Like all of the other eligible maidens in the country, the two older sisters sought to marry Strong Wind, so they went to take the "test." Naturally, they failed. When the younger sister said she too wanted to take the test, they laughed at her and called her a fool. But Strong Wind's sister was kind-hearted towards the little sister. When asked, "Do you see him?" the young girl told the truth and answered no. Strong Wind's sister was very pleased—for the first time someone had spoken the truth. She asked again, and Strong Wind, who also realized that this maiden was truthful, revealed himself to her. When asked what drew his sled, she correctly answered a rainbow; she also saw that his bowstring was made of the Milky Way. Because she was honest and passed the test, the young girl was invited to take her position at Strong Wind's side. And so they were wed.

March 10

Cinderella, Variation 2

In the Japanese version of Cinderella, there are only two sisters. Instead of going to a ball, they wanted to go to the Kabuki theater. They do not have to take a slipper test or an honesty test, but rather the would-be bride must compose a classical song on the spot. The song must respond to an image the lord has created by putting a plate on a tray., pouring salt on the plate, and placing a single pine needle upright in the salt.

After contemplating (too briefly) the image, the mean stepsister, "Broken Dish" (Kakezara), blurted out:

Put a plate on a tray
Put some salt on a plate
Stick a pine needle in the salt
It will soon fall over.

Since she failed to follow any of the rigid rules of the meter, she knew she had failed, and she was so enraged with herself and clumsy in her anger that she hit the lord on the head as she ran out of the room.

Then "Crimson Dish" (Benizara), the Cinderella figure, managed the meter and poetics ably:

A tray and a plate, oh!
A mountain rises from the plate,
On it, snow had fallen.
Rooted deep in the snow,
A lonely pine tree grows.

March 11

Funny Bunny

Once there was a bunny who liked to tell jokes. While all of the other bunnies were out foraging for lettuce and carrots, Funny Bunny would go to the pond and look at his reflection in the still water, and practice stand-up comedy. Many of the jokes were about his mother and she did not like them at all. Sometimes he would tell stories about his sisters and brothers and exaggerate what really happened, and they would be very embarrassed. His parents had told him to stop, to get serious, to quit all of this funny business, and for a day or two he would but then he would let out a little quip like "hare today, gone tomorrow" and it would start all over again.

One day, Funny Bunny decided to go to the Farmer's Market to get some new material. There would be lots of human beings there, and crates of vegetables and fruits, and he thought the excitement of it all would inspire him to think of some new jokes. All of the other bunnies had gotten up early to nibble some lettuce and carrots in a nearby garden. But when they got to the garden, they were in for a terrible surprise. The farmer was waiting there to trap all of the bunnies and put them in cages and take them to the market to sell for rabbit stew!

Of course, Funny Bunny knew nothing about this. He was lost in his own thoughts, hopping around the market, trying to stay out of the way of all the tennis shoes and sandals. It was tricky to maneuver unnoticed in a crowd of human beings, but Funny Bunny didn't care. He loved humans. He loved the way they laughed, but most of all, he loved the sound they made when they clapped their hands. He had often dreamed about going to upstate New York and opening at a club in the Catskill Mountains, pacing back and forth on a stage with a hand-held microphone in front of a room full of human beings who were laughing so hard they had to hold their sides. Funny Bunny dreamed big. He was that kind of bunny.

Funny Bunny was trying to think of some puns when he saw it: across the way in the stall next to the rhubarb there was a cage filled with all of his bunny friends and family. All of his sisters and brothers were there, his dad and his mom, his bunny school mates and their parents. The sign above said: LIVE BUNNIES! WHY NOT HAVE STEW TONIGHT?

Funny Bunny could not believe it. This was no laughing matter; this was serious. But what could he do? How could he save the bunnies? "I'm just one bun, a fab rab to be sure, but this is no time for comedy," he thought to himself.

All at once he had an idea. Maybe it *was* time for comedy. As it happened, Funny Bunny had in his vest pocket some plastic glasses with a nose and moustache. He put them on, crossed the way, and stood in front of the cage filled with bunnies. When no one was looking, he unfastened the latch, then motioned for the bunnies to leave one by one, without drawing attention to themselves.

Then he got up on a crate in front of the cage, and cleared his throat. "Excuse me, excuse me, can I have your attention?" he asked.

A few people turned to look at the little bunny, who was standing on two legs and holding a carrot like it was a microphone. He tapped the top of the carrot. "Testing—one, two, three—testing," he said. He blew into the carrot-microphone. More passers-by stopped to see where the little bunny voice was coming from.

"Ladies and gentlemen, I am sorry about the sound system today; but I promise we will get to the *root* of the problem," he said, elbowing the air and then pointing to the carrot. "Okay, but seriously, humans . . ." As Funny Bunny gathered a crowd of astonished human beings, his bunny friends and family silently crept out of the cage. Everyone was so transfixed with Funny Bunny and his jokes that no one noticed the bunnies escape.

In the crowd of humans was a hotel manager from Middletown, New York, a middling sort of town just outside the Catskill Mountains. He was always on the lookout for new talent, and he thought that Funny Bunny might be a good warm-up act. After all the bunnies had fled for safety and Funny Bunny was sure his family was gone, the rabbit told a hilarious joke about his mother. The crowd applauded and Funny Bunny believed it was the greatest moment of his life. But then it even got better because the hotel manager lingered and asked Funny Bunny if he would like to be a warm-up act at his hotel in the Catskills. He told the rabbit he loved all of his jokes, but that the nose and glasses and moustache would have to go.

—CHRISTINE ALLISON

March 12

The Elf Who Stayed Out Too Late

In a beautiful rose there lived a little elf. With a fairy microscope, you could see his wings reaching from his shoulders to his feet. Without it, you couldn't see him at all.

One day when he went out into the sunshine to play, he had such fun that he forgot all about getting home in time. He flew from flower to flower. He danced on the wings of a passing butterfly. Best of all, he measured how many steps it would take to cross all of the roads made of veins on the geranium leaf.

It was this that delayed him so long. Before he knew it, the sun was down, dewdrops sprinkled the leaf, and the night began to darken. The poor little elf was very frightened indeed. He began to shiver with cold. He grew so numb that he could hardly spread his wings to fly back to the rosebush.

But he made it.

Just as the beautiful rose was closing her petals for the evening, he dived into her warm heart, and fell right to sleep.—ANGELA M. KEYES

March 13

The Fairy Frog

A JEWISH TALE FOR PASSOVER

When Hanina read the messenger's note, he felt a chill. "Please come at once, my son," the note read. "There's very little time." It was signed by his father in handwriting that was barely readable.

Hanina said goodbye to his wife and traveled that afternoon to the bedside of his mother and father. They were dying. They were both weak and pale but there was joy in the room. "We are about to go to the next world," said his very old father, "but we are leaving in peace. We have had a beautiful life and we are honored to leave this world, just as we lived in it, together." His father instructed him to mourn for the customary seven days, which would end on the eve of the festival of Passover. "On that day go to the marketplace and purchase the first thing that is offered to you, no matter what it is or how much it costs," his father said. "In time, this purchase will bring you many blessings."

Hanina promised his father he would obey the strange instructions.

The couple died on the same day and after a week of mourning, on the day before the Passover festival, Hanina went to the marketplace. Within minutes, a craggy bearded man approached him, carrying a silver box. "Buy this, my son. It will bring you many blessings," he said. Events were happening just as his father had foretold. Even though the silver casket cost a thousand gold pieces—almost every bit of money Hanina had—he purchased it and took it home. On the first night of Passover, he placed it on the table and opened it. Inside was a smaller casket. When he opened it, out jumped a little frog.

Hanina's wife could not believe he had spent their entire fortune on the frog. Worse, the frog ate like a pig. It devoured everything in sight, and when Passover had ended in eight days, it had grown to an enormous size. Soon Hanina had to build a little shed for the frog to live in.

As you can guess, Hanina was very uncomfortable with this situation. The frog ate so much that he and his wife had no food left for themselves. They had to sell furniture and other possessions just to keep the frog supplied with food. When at last there was nothing left to sell, Hanina's wife, for the first time, let her emotions show. A tear rolled down her cheek.

To her amazement, the frog, which was now bigger than Hanina, spoke. "Dear wife of Hanina, you have treated me like a prince. Ask me for anything and I will carry out your wishes," he said. "Food?" said the woman, weakly. "Could we please have something to eat?"

At once there was a knock at the door and a huge basket of food was delivered. Hanina stood dumbfounded. "A frog that speaks and can perform wonders must have much wisdom to share. Will you teach me what you know?" he asked the frog. The frog agreed, but he was a strange teacher. He wrote out the Law and seventy languages on little strips of paper and ordered Hanina to eat the paper. As Hanina devoured the knowledge he became wise in all matters. Soon he was known throughout the city as a very learned man.

"I have one more gift to repay your kindness," said the frog. "Come to the forest with me and you shall see many wonders."

When Hanina, his wife, and the giant frog arrived in the center of the forest, the frog made an announcement. "All ye who live in the caves and streams and trees, come forward. Bring forth your precious stones and herbs and roots."

Hanina and his wife could not believe what happened next. From all directions came birds and animals and insects bearing gifts. Each one of the many thousands placed a gift at the feet of Hanina and his wife. "All of this is yours," said the frog, motioning to the hill of jewels and herbs and roots. "The precious stones will keep you in luxury and the herbs and roots will allow you to heal humans of every disease and injury."

Hanina and his wife looked in awe at the sight, and then turned to the frog. "But who are you?" Hanina's wife asked.

"I am the fairy son of Adam. I have the power to become any creature I like," he said, and then smiled. With that, he bowed, and before their eyes became smaller and smaller and smaller. Then, a tiny frog once again, he jumped off into the woods.

Hanina and his wife became great healers. People from all over the world came to be cured of their illnesses and fears, and the couple received them with wisdom and compassion.

March 14

The Bronze Pig

In Florence, Italy, there is a little street called Porta Rossa, and there stands a fountain cast in the shape of a pig. Clear, fresh water pours from its snout, which shines as brightly as bronze can, for it is polished daily by schoolboys and beggars who lean on it while getting a drink. The rest of the pig's body is green with age.

It was a winter evening with a full moon, and the tops of the hills that surround the city were covered with snow. In the gardens of the duke, a ragged little boy sat under a large pine tree. He was hungry and thirsty, and though he had held out his little hand all day, no one had dropped anything into it. A watchman who was closing up the garden gates drove the little boy out, and for a time he stood on a bridge over the River Arno, staring into the water and dreaming.

He then walked to the fountain and, putting his arms around the bronze pig's neck, he drank water from its shining spout. Nearby he found some lettuce leaves and a few chestnuts and they were his dinner. It was late and the streets were deserted, so the boy climbed on the pig's back and fell asleep.

At midnight the metal animal beneath him moved and said very distinctly, "Little boy, hold on tight, for I am going to run!"

Thus began the strangest ride anyone has ever taken. The pig first ran to the Piazza del Granduca. The bronze horse, on which the duke was mounted, neighed loudly when it saw them. When the pig reached the arcade of the Palazzo degli Uffizi, where the nobles of Florence gathered for masked balls, it stopped. "Hold on tight," the pig told the boy, "for now we are going up the stairs." Half joyful and half fearful, the boy clutched the neck of the pig tighter, and did not answer.

They entered the long gallery, which the boy knew well. The corridor contained many lovely statues and the walls were hung with paintings, all of which seemed brighter and more alive than they had appeared in daylight. But the most magnificent moment, one the boy would never forget, was when the door to one of the smaller rooms opened. Here was the beautiful marble sculpture of a woman. She moved her lovely limbs, and the dolphins at her feet arched their backs and leaped about. The world knows this sculpture as the Medici Venus.

The bronze pig walked slowly through every room, giving the little boy a chance to see everything with new eyes. "Thank you!" whispered the boy, as the pig went bumpity, bumpity down the stairs.

"The thanks are to you!" said the pig. "I have helped you and you have helped me, for only when an innocent child sits on my back do I become alive and have the strength to run as I have tonight. It is only into church that I'm not allowed to go, but we can peep through the doors."

And away they ran through the streets of Florence to the Church of Santa Croce. The portals of the church opened by themselves. All the candles on the great altar were lit and the marble clothes on the statues seemed to move. Their heads appeared to turn and look out at the deserted square, where the only thing illuminated by the candlelight was a bronze pig, with a boy mounted on his back.

The boy suddenly heard the wind whistling in his ears, and a loud bang as the doors of the church closed. Then he lost consciousness.

The next thing he knew was that he felt cold. He was awake and it was morning. He was sitting—almost falling off—the bronze pig, which stood as immobile as ever in the Via Porta Rossa.—HANS CHRISTIAN ANDERSEN

March 15

The Green Children

AN ENGLISH TALE

Almost nine hundred years ago, a strange and wondrous event occurred in the village of St. Mary's of the Wolf Pits, though this is not a story about wolves.

It is a story about a boy and a girl who were found by village people near a wolf pit. The children had arms and legs, indeed they were really quite normal looking except for their deep green eyes and the color of their skin, which was wholly different from human skin, for the children, you see, were *green.*

When the children emerged from the wolf pits, they seemed confused. They stared at the townspeople as if they were creatures from another world. No one could understand their speech. They were frightened and not even a soft and tender mother could calm them.

The villagers had never encountered anything strange, let alone green children, and so they took the boy and girl to the home of Sir Richard de Calne. Every village has a respected individual, a wise woman or man, and for St. Mary of the Wolf Pits, Sir Richard was the one. When he saw the children he was enchanted but he was also mystified. He knew that the children had not eaten for a time, so he had bread and honey set out for them. They cried but they would not touch the food even though it was clear that they were tormented by hunger. Chickens and sausages were presented, but the children turned from that, too. Then, by chance, a farm woman brought in a basket of broccoli. The children seized the green food and fed on the long stalks with great delight. For a long time they would taste no other food.

The children stayed at the home of Sir Richard, who took good care of them. At first they would only eat green food, and the boy became very weak and prone to illness. For months he refused to eat foods that were not green and though he ate spinach and green beans and lettuce and brussels sprouts, he eventually died. The girl knew that she would need to eat many different foods and so she did, and she became stronger. Soon she lost her green pallor, and eventually her skin became more like those of the people around her.

She learned the language of the villagers, which was a combination of French and English, and then one night with many villagers around her, she told how she had arrived in their midst.

"I lived in a quiet, dim place," she began. "There was very little light, only the soft light like that which shines after sunset."

"Was it far away?" the villagers asked.

"I cannot say," she replied. "It was not here, in the upper world, I know that. We were somewhere below. It was gray all of the time, though we could always see a place of light, this place of light, in the faraway distance."

"Was your mother green like you were?" asked the villagers.

"I do not remember my mother or much about where I lived or who I knew. I only know that all of the people and even the animals were green. My brother and I were tending our green flocks when we heard bells ringing. They were the bells from your church tower, I suppose. The sounds were so sweet, we followed them, as if in a trance. We came to an opening and we were overwhelmed by the glaring light and the sudden warmth of the air and so we lay in a confused state for a long time. Then we heard the noise of the villagers who had come upon us. It was all of you and we were terrified and wished to fly, but we were so weak we could only allow ourselves to be caught."

Sir Richard was among those listening.

"If you wish to return to your world, I will gather the most able men and we will find the opening from which you came, dear child," he said to the little girl, though he really did not want her to go.

"But you know I cannot," she said. "Each day I forget more and more about my past life, and it is almost that it does not exist."

The green child never returned to her home. Some of the villagers dug into the wolf pits to see if there was a tunnel or a passage or road of some kind, but nothing was ever found. The green eyes of the children still haunt the villagers, and the mystery of their origins was never solved.

March 16

The Trees and the Ax

A woodman came into the forest to ask the trees to give him the small amount of wood he needed to make a handle for his ax. It seemed so modest a request that the trees agreed to it at once, and it was settled among them that the plain, homely ash would furnish what the woodman wanted.

No sooner had the woodman fitted the staff to his purpose that he began chopping away, toppling first the noblest of trees in the forest. One by one, he took down tree after tree, without explanation or apology.

The oak, now seeing the whole matter too late, whispered to the cedar, "We have made a fatal mistake. What seemed like a small concession will cost us all our lives. In sacrificing our humble neighbor, we brought about the ruin of all."—PHAEDRUS

March 17

ST. PATRICK'S DAY

The Last Snake in Ireland

AN IRISH TALE

Everybody has heard the tale of how the blessed Saint Patrick drove the snakes out of Ireland, but not everyone knows the trouble the saint had with the very last one. This cunning snake could not be talked out of the country, nor induced to drown himself, and Saint Patrick was fit to be tied.

Then the saint had an inspiration, as saints are wont to do. He had a strong iron chest made with formidable bolts and took a stroll to the snake's hidey-hole. The snake, who understandably had some animosity towards the saint, began to hiss and show his teeth at his approach.

"Oh, snake," said Saint Patrick, "don't fash yourself so. 'Tis a nice house I've had made for you, for which you'll be grateful in the winter. You can come out and look at it whenever you please."

The snake, hearing these reassuring words, thought it was possible that even though Saint Patrick had driven out all the other snakes, he meant no harm to himself. So he emerged from his hole to inspect the house, but was immediately suspicious of the bolts, which were nine in number.

" 'Tis a nice warm house, you see," said Saint Patrick, "and 'tis a good friend I am to you."

"I thank you kindly, Saint Patrick, but too small it is I think for the likes of me," replied the snake, and he began to slither away.

"Too small!" said the Saint. "Stop, if you please, I'm sure 'twill fit you, and I'll bet you a gallon of ale that if you'll only try to get in, there'll be plenty of room."

The snake was as thirsty as could be, and the thought of doing Saint Patrick out of all that ale was a delightful one, so swelling himself up as big as he could, into the chest he squirmed, and all but a little bit of his tail fit. "There, now," said he. "I've won the ale, for you can see the house is too small."

Then Saint Patrick came to slam down the heavy lid of the chest. When the snake saw it coming down, in went his tail like a shot, for fear of having it chopped off. And Saint Patrick began at once to secure the nine iron bolts.

"Oh, Saint Patrick, won't you let me out?" cried the snake. "For I've lost the bet fairly, and I needs must pay you your due. A gallon of ale, wasn't it?"

"Let you out, my darling?" said Saint Patrick. "To be sure I will, but I haven't time right now, so you must wait till tomorrow."

He took the iron chest with the snake in it and pitched it into the biggest lake in Ireland, where it lies to this day. And it is the snake struggling down at the bottom that makes the waves upon it. Many is the man who has heard the snake crying out from under the water, "Is it tomorrow yet?" which, to be sure, it never can be.

March 18

The Wolf and the Lamb

A wolf was lapping up water at the head of a running brook when he spied a stray lamb paddling, at some distance, down the stream. "That lamb certainly would be a tasty lunch," he thought to himself. More than anything he wanted to seize her, and so he thought to himself how he might justify his violence.

"Villain!" he said, running up to her. "How dare you muddy the water I am drinking!"

"What are you talking about?" the lamb responded. "I do not see how I am disturbing the water, since it runs from you to me, not from me to you."

"Be that as it may, it was but a year ago that you called me many bad names," retorted the wolf.

"Oh, sir, you mistake me for someone else," said the lamb. "A year ago I was not even born."

"Well, it was not you, then, it was your father, and that is all the same," said the wolf. "In any case, it is no use trying to argue me out of my supper." Without another word, he fell upon the poor lamb and tore her to pieces.

Wicked creatures can always find excuses for their deeds.—AESOP

March 19

The Wolf and the Seven Little Kids

A GERMAN TALE

There once was a nanny goat who had seven kids and, like all mothers, she loved them very much. One day she was going into the woods to fetch food, but she called them around her first and said, "Children, while I am gone, beware of the wolf. If he gets into the house, he will eat you up. He often disguises himself, but you will know him by his rough voice and his black feet."

The kids said, "Oh, we will be very careful, dear mother."

The nanny goat set off, but before long, someone knocked at the door and called, "Open the door, dear children! Your mother has come back and brought something for each of you."

The kids knew quite well by the voice that it was the wolf. "We won't open the door," they cried. "You are not our mother. She has a soft, gentle voice, but yours is rough, and we are sure that you are the wolf."

The wolf gnashed his teeth and went back to his lair. There he ate a lump of chalk, which made his voice softer. He returned to the nanny goat's house and knocked at the door. "Open the door, children! It's your mother!"

But the wolf had put one of his paws on the windowsill, where the kids could see it. They cried, "Our mother has not got a black foot as you have. You are the wolf!"

Then the wolf ran to a baker and forced him to put flour on his feet. The baker suspected that the wolf was up to no good, but he was too frightened not to obey.

Now the wolf went for the third time to the door, knocked and said, "Open the door, children. I have something for you!"

The kids cried, "Show us your feet first so we are sure you are our mother."

He put his paws on the windowsill, and when they saw that they were white, they believed him and opened the door.

Alas! It was the wolf who walked in. The kids were terrified and tried to hide themselves in the nooks and crannies of the house. But the wolf found all but the youngest kid—who had hidden in the clock case—and swallowed them, one after the other. When he had satisfied his appetite, he took himself off and lay down in a meadow nearby, where he soon fell asleep.

Not long after, the nanny goat came back from the woods. Oh! what a terrible sight met her eyes! Tables and chairs were overturned, and the covers and pillows torn from the bed. She called her children by name, one by one, but no one answered. At last when she came to the youngest, a tiny voice cried: "I am here, Mother, hidden in the clock case."

She brought him out, and he told her that the wolf had come and devoured all the others. You can imagine how she wept over her children.

When she had no more tears left, she took her only kid outside with her, and they happened upon the meadow where the wolf lay under a tree, making the branches shake with his snores. More than that, they could plainly see movements in his distended belly.

"Oh, heavens!" thought the goat. "Is it possible my poor children are still alive?"

She sent the kid to the house to fetch scissors, needle, and thread. Then she cut a hole in the wolf's side, and hardly had she begun, when a kid popped out its head, and as soon as the hole was big enough, all six jumped out. None of them were in the least bit injured for, in his greed, the wolf had swallowed them whole. The overjoyed mother hugged them, then said, "Go and fetch some big stones, children, and we will fill up the wolf's body while he sleeps."

The seven kids brought stones as fast as they could and stuffed the wolf with them until he could hold no more. The mother quickly sewed him up without his having noticed a thing.

When the wolf finally roused himself, he was terribly thirsty and decided to go to a spring to drink. But as soon as he moved, the stones began to rattle and roll inside him. Then he cried, "What's the rumbling and tumbling that sets my stomach grumbling?"

When he reached the spring and bent over to drink, the heavy stones dragged him down and he was drowned.

When the seven kids, who were hiding in the woods nearby, saw what had happened, they began to sing, "The wolf is dead! The wolf is dead!" And they and their mother danced joyfully around the spring all day long.

—BROTHERS GRIMM

March 20

The Wolf and the Seven Little Kids, Variation

A Yiddish tale collected from Jews who migrated to Canada from Poland and Russia by Edith Fowke uses the same plotline: mama leaves the children alone and warns them not to let anyone gain entry to the home. This tale, "A Granny Who Had Many Children," features the granny of several children who warns them that a bear—in Yiddish, "Berele" (Bear-uh-luh)—might come and eat them up. The children secure the cottage, but to no avail. The Berele attempts to be clever at first; he knocks on the door, and says, "Children, children open the door and I'll give you some blackberries." The children reply no, they have their own. The bear offers blueberries. The children have their own. The bear then resorts to brute strength and threatens to break the door in. The children answer, "We are not afraid. We'd rather listen to Granny."

Listen though they might, the angry bear breaks into the house and eats all the children except for the youngest, named Heshela, who hides in a little bottle. (She is apparently quite small.) When Granny comes home, she calls for the children. No one answers. Heshela finally emerges from the little bottle and tells Granny the whole story.

Intent on getting her children back, Granny tries to coax the bear. First she calls, "Berele, Berele, come to me." He refuses. She offers him some delicious milk pudding. The milk pudding does not gain his interest. Granny finally promises to tickle the bear's ear. For this, he will come. He bounds out of the forest and lays his head in Granny's lap and she proceeds to tickle his ears, first the right one, then the left one. While he enjoys this, Granny whips out a sharp knife and snips open his stomach, and all of her children pop out. She takes them home, scrubs them well, puts clean clothes on them, and sends them to school.

March 21

The Lion and the Donkey

One day the lion was strolling down the forest aisle. All of the animals bowed or lowered their eyes in respect except the donkey, who brayed a nasty remark as the lion passed him by.

Though the lion felt the heat of rage for just a moment, he said nothing.

He would not honor the stupid donkey with even a word of recognition.

If a fool troubles you, ignore him.—AESOP

March 22

The Ugly Duckling

One beautiful summer day, a mother duck sat among the reeds of a little pond, hatching her brood of ducklings. The last one was taking a long time to hatch. Finally, the egg opened and out tumbled the baby. He looked nothing like his brothers and sisters. He was big for a duckling, gray instead of yellow, and just plain ugly. His mother thought perhaps he was a turkey chick but found, to her amazement, that he swam as well as any of her other little ones.

When the mother duck took the ducklings to the farmyard, the other animals made fun of the ugly duckling and commented on his strange looks. Even after the other ducklings adjusted to life in the farmyard, the ugly duckling was insulted and teased by everyone. This hurt his feelings terribly so he decided to run away.

That night he stayed in a marsh where some wild ducks lived. The next morning, when the wild ducks saw him, they thought he was so ugly that they liked him and so invited him to stay. Just at that moment, two hunters' shots rang out, and a big hunting dog came splashing into the swamp. The dog gave the duckling a curious sniff, then splashed on by. He was so ugly, even the dog wouldn't touch him.

The duckling wandered on until he came to a miserable little cottage with a light on inside. An old woman lived there with her cat and her hen. The duckling hoped to stay a while but the cat and the hen thought he was so ugly they shooed him away. When the old woman found out he couldn't lay eggs, she didn't want him around either.

Soon autumn came. The leaves began to flutter from the trees and it grew colder. The poor duckling was very unhappy.

One evening he saw some birds flying south. He thought they were the most beautiful, graceful creatures he had ever seen. The duckling found a lake to swim in, but as winter came, the circle of water grew smaller and smaller, turning to ice. To his horror, the duckling got caught in the ice, but a farmer saw him and released him, and took him home for his family. The children wanted to play with the duckling but they were too rough. They spooked him and he flew into the flour barrel, creating a cloud of flour, and nearly got stuck in the butter tub. The children laughed, but the farmer's wife was furious and chased the duckling out of the house.

Alone again, the duckling made his way through the woods, wandering through the cold, hard winter.

When spring came, the duckling flapped his wings and flew up into the

sky. Riding the wind, he saw three swans, as beautiful as any creatures he had ever seen. He felt a tremendous call to join them even though he thought they might peck him to death because he was so ugly. Still, he flew down into the water and headed for the swans. As he did, he caught sight of his reflection in the water. He could not believe his eyes. His neck was curved and graceful. His wings were thick with white feathers. He was a swan. The other swans welcomed him as one of their own. "Look, a new brother! And the most beautiful of all," they said.

He did not tell them that he had never dreamed of such happiness when he was just the ugly duckling.

—HANS CHRISTIAN ANDERSEN

March 23

That's a Lie

Once upon a time there was a king who had a daughter who was a dreadful liar. The king announced that he was awarding her hand in marriage to the man who could tell such outrageous stories that the princess would say, "That's a lie!"

Well, many young men came and failed miserably, for the princess was so accustomed to spinning tall tales that their lies didn't faze her. Three brothers were among the last to try. The two oldest went first, but fared no better than the others. The third brother, named Boots, found the young lady holding court in the farmyard.

"Good morning," he said. "And thank you for nothing."

"Good morning," said she. "And the same to you. I'll bet you haven't such a fine farmyard as ours. Do you know that when two shepherds stand at either end of it and blow their horns, one can't hear the other?"

"Ours is far bigger," answered Boots. "For by the time a newborn calf gets from one end of our yard to the other, she is ready to be milked."

"I dare say," said the princess. "Well, but you haven't such a big ox as ours. When two men sit on either horn, they can't touch each other with a twenty-foot pole!"

"Stuff!" said Boots. "Is that all? Why we have an ox who's so big that when two men sit on either horn and each blows his great mountain trumpet, they can't hear one another."

"Is that so?" replied the princess. "But you haven't as much milk as we do, I'll bet. We milk our cows into great pails, and empty them into great tubs, and make cheeses the size of wagon wheels."

"Oh, you do, do you?" said Boots. "Our cheeses are as big as a great house. We once had a mare to tread the cheese during the making, but she tumbled down into the cheese brewing vat and we lost her. After we had eaten this cheese for seven years, we came upon the mare, alive and kicking. Now that we had her back, I was going to ride her to the mill, but her backbone snapped, so I took a young spruce tree and put it into her for a backbone. But the sapling kept growing, and it grew into such a tall tree that I climbed up to Heaven on it. When I got there, I saw the Blessed Mother sitting there weaving ropes, and just then, the spruce broke, so She let me down by one of her ropes. Somehow, I was lowered into a fox hole, and who should sit there but my mother and *your* father making shoes for some reason, and I so surprised them that my mother gave your father such a whack on the head that his whiskers curled."

"That's a lie!" shouted the princess. "My father wasn't there and he never did anything like that."

So Boots was rewarded with the princess for his wife, and half the kingdom besides.

March 24

The Farmer and the Stork

After the long winter, the farmers finally were planting their fields. This made the birds exceedingly glad, for now there would be millions of seeds to steal! While some of the birds were cautious, the cranes were daring; they stole seeds from right under the farmers' noses. The cranes considered stealing a fine art and a sport, and on this morning, they asked a simple-minded stork to come along for the fun.

The stork went along, not knowing what the cranes were up to. But the party ended abruptly when the birds all got tangled in the meshes of the farmer's net, who had set the trap for just that purpose.

When the farmer discovered the birds in his trap, the stork pleaded for mercy.

"Please, farmer, sir, I am a stork. I come from a good family that is honest and true. I went along with the cranes, but I had no idea they were going to steal from you," the bird said.

"You may come from a good family, but I caught you with the birds who were stealing. Therefore you will receive the same punishment!" replied the farmer.

You are judged by the company that you keep.—AESOP

March 25

Venus and the Cat

Once a cat fell in love with a young man. It was not the kind of love pets have for their masters, but boy-girl love, and so the cat asked Venus, the goddess of love, to transform her into a girl. The goddess was moved by the cat's passion and so she transformed her into a fair maiden. When the young man met the fair maiden he was overtaken by her beauty and charms, and took her home to marry.

As they were sitting in his castle, Venus, who was a curious and sometimes meddling goddess, wondered whether in changing the cat's form she had also changed her nature. To test the cat she set down a mouse before her. The girl, forgetting her new condition, started from her seat and pounced upon the mouse as if she would have eaten it on the spot. The goddess, disappointed that the cat was such a poor actress, changed the fair maiden back into a cat again and the young man fled in horror.

What is bred in the bone will never be out of the flesh.—AESOP

March 26

The Fisherman and the Little Fish

It was spring and the snow on the mountain was melting, and the river was rushing.

"The ice has melted and now at last I can fish," thought the fisherman, who had not had a good meal in days. He went up to the river's edge and threw his line in. He cast again. The river was freezing!

The cold water made the fisherman even weaker, and now all he could think of was a bite of sweet white fish meat. Still, he did not catch a fish.

Finally, after several hours in the deep, icy waters, the fisherman felt a tug on his line. He hooked the fish, and pulled in a tiny silver trout.

It was tiny indeed. No bigger than his finger!

The fish spoke, "Please, good sir, do not kill me. I am so tiny that it is not worth soiling your basket with so minor a fish. If you spare me, I will grow and when I am bigger I will make you a much better meal."

The fisherman thought about the fish's proposal, but only briefly. Then he threw the fish into his basket. "A hungry man would be a fool to give up even a bite of fish. You might be tiny, but I would rather swallow you than nothing at all."

A gain—however small—is better than an empty promise.—AESOP

March 27

Molly Whuppie, Part 1

AN ENGLISH TALE

Once upon a time there was a man and a woman who were terrible parents. They had dozens of children and just couldn't manage, so they decided to get rid of them. They didn't kill them or anything, they just left them in the forest, with no food or supplies, only the clothes on their backs. That was how Molly Whuppie and her two older sisters ended up in the middle of nowhere.

After Molly and her two sisters were dumped unceremoniously in the woods, they walked and walked, looking for a helping hand. Finally they saw a light, and it turned out to be a house. They knocked, and a woman answered the door.

Molly, who was the bravest of the three, did the talking.

"Uh, hello, ma'am. We are lost and we wondered if we might have a bite to eat and perhaps some shelter for the night," she said.

"I would love to have you as my guest," said the woman, "but you see my husband is a giant and he likes to eat humans, and if you stay here he will surely kill you."

Just our luck, thought Molly to herself. But she didn't say anything.

The woman felt sorry for the girls. She had a soft spot in her heart for them because she had three daughters of her own, albeit half-giant, half human. Then she had an idea: "I know. Why don't you come in and have some milk and bread and sit before the fire. When my husband gets home, you can run off before he even knows you are here," she said.

The three girls thought it was an excellent idea, and so they sat down to their bread and milk.

But before they even got settled, a dreadful voice said, "Fee, fie, fo fum, I smell the blood of some earthly one."

Good timing, thought Molly, swallowing her last chunk of bread.

She started to grab her sisters when the giant appeared. "What have we here, wife?" he said.

"Just three lassies who were cold and hungry. Don't worry about them, dear. They were just about to *leave,*" she said, emphasizing the "leave" as if to hint that the girls should get out of the house as quickly as possible. But before the girls could leave, the giant ordered them to stay. He then ate an enormous meal.

The three sisters were commanded to sleep with the three half-giant, half-human sisters, which Molly thought was a strange setup but she didn't say anything. To be on the safe side, though, she decided to keep one eye open all night.

After the giant finished stuffing huge amounts of food into his face, he came around to each bed. He put a rope around the necks of Molly and her sisters, and then put little gold chains around the necks of his own children. Then he went to sleep.

Molly didn't like the rope and gold chain business, so she switched them, putting the gold chains on her sisters and the ropes on the giant's children.

Sure enough, in a few hours, the giant woke up and groped his way in the dark, feeling for the ropes. He pulled out all of the girls with the ropes around their necks and battered them until they were dead. Unbeknownst to him, he had killed his own daughters. But he went back to bed, thinking he had managed well.

Molly thought it would be foolish to stick around to see the giant's reaction when he discovered that he had murdered his own daughters, so she woke up her sisters and helped them slip out of the house.

They got out safe and ran and ran and never stopped until morning.

March 28

Molly Whuppie, Part 2

Molly and her sisters were weary so they decided to rest by a brook. When the sun came up they saw a grand house in the distance. It turned out to be a king's house.

Molly was bold, so she took her sisters there and told the king about their experiences with the giant. The king was impressed. "Well, Molly, you are a clever girl, and you managed well. Let's see if you can go back to the giant's house and get the sword that hangs over his head. If you get the sword, I will give your eldest sister my first son to marry." Molly somewhat regretted telling the king about the giant in the first place, but since he was a king, she said she would try.

Molly slipped back into the giant's house that night, and crawled under his bed. He ate an enormous meal and then went to bed. When she was sure he was completely asleep, Molly slowly crept out from under the bed and reached over his head and grabbed the sword. She was squeezing out the door when the giant awoke and began chasing her. She ran and she ran until she came to the "Bridge of One Hair." Giants cannot cross the "Bridge of One Hair," and she laughed as she crossed to her freedom. "Molly Whuppie, you better never come again!" screamed out the giant, shaking his big fat fist.

Molly took the sword to the king, and her eldest sister married the eldest son.

The king was pleased with the sword. "You're a clever girl and you've managed well, Molly. Let's see if you can go back to the giant's house and get the purse that lies under his pillow. If you get the purse, I will give your second sister my second son to marry." Molly was thinking she was glad to have only two sisters at this point. But the king had asked, so she said she would try.

Molly slipped back into the giant's house that night and crawled under his bed. He ate an enormous meal and then went to sleep. When she was sure he was completely asleep she slipped her hand under the pillow and got the purse. She was climbing out the window when the giant awoke and began chasing her. She ran and she ran until she came to the "Bridge of One Hair." She laughed as she crossed to her freedom. "Molly Whuppie, I'm warning you: you better never come again," called out the giant, who this time was in a red-faced rage.

Molly took the purse to the king, and her second sister married the second son.

The king was pleased with the purse. "You're a clever girl and you've managed well, Molly. Let's see if you can go back to that giant's house and get the giant's ring that he wears on his finger. If you get the ring, I will give you my favorite son to marry." Molly was not so sure she wanted to marry anybody but since the king asked, she said she would try.

Again she slipped into the giant's house and waited under his bed. When he fell asleep, she slipped the ring off his finger and started to tiptoe out of the house. Suddenly the giant awoke and grabbed Molly. "I've got you now, Molly Whuppie. If I had done to you what you had done to me, what would you do to me?" he asked.

Molly thought for a moment and then answered: "Well, I am sure that I would put me in a sack with a cat and a dog and needle and thread and shears and hang me on a wall, and go to the forest and get a huge stick and beat the bag with that stick until I were dead."

So the giant put Molly and a cat and a dog and a needle and thread and shears into a sack and hung it up and went to the woods to get a stick.

As Molly had known, once the giant was out of the house his wife came in to see what was going on. When she finally noticed the bag hanging, Molly sang out, *"Oh, if you could see what I see!"* And then again: *"Oh, if you could see what I see!"*

The wife got curious and begged Molly to hang her up in the sack so she too could see. So Molly took the shears and cut a hole in the sack and put the giant's wife in, and sewed up the whole thing with her needle and thread.

When the giant returned with the stick he beat the sack, and even though his wife was calling, "It's me, dear, stop, it's me," he kept on beating the sack until the wife was quite dead.

Molly slipped out of the house and brought the ring to the king. She married the king's favorite son and never saw the giant again.

March 29

The Hermit and the Mouse

A HINDU FABLE

In the forest of the Sage Gautama there once dwelt a hermit named Mighty-at-Prayer. Once as he sat at his frugal meal, a young mouse, dropped from the beak of a crow, fell beside him. The hermit took the mouse tenderly and fed it with rice grains and treated him like a friend. Some time later the hermit saw a cat chasing his new little friend, intending to devour it. The hermit, using his saintly powers, changed the mouse into a large vigorous cat. The cat, however, soon found himself troubled greatly by dogs, and so once again the saint changed the mouse, this time into a dog.

As they dwelt in the forest, the dog was always in danger of prowling tigers and accordingly the hermit changed him into a tiger, all the time thinking of him and treating him as nothing more or less than a mouse. Even the country folk as they passed by would say, "That a tiger? Not he. He is nothing but a mouse that the saint has transformed." The mouse, hearing this, became angry and said to himself, "So long as my master lives the shameful story of my origin will be remembered and I will bear ridicule and scorn."

With this thought in mind, he was about to take the saint's life when the saint, who had the power of reading creatures' thoughts, turned the ungrateful beast right back into a mouse.

March 30

The Two Bad Bargains, Part 1

A SERBIAN TALE

In days gone by there lived a couple who had only one son, named Vladimir. Now Vladimir was a boy both strong and of good courage, yet he had such a big heart that he was constantly being waylaid by a person or an animal in need. When Vladimir grew to manhood, his father, a merchant, gave him his own ship to command, and told him to sail about the world and grow rich.

Vladimir put to sea with great hopes, his head full of visions of great fortunes, but he was not gone many days from port when he met a vessel swarming with savage pirates. From the vessel he heard much weeping and wailing. He bravely hailed them and asked what was wrong aboard their ship. The pirates had captured many slaves, whom they were taking to the slave market in Istanbul. Vladimir could not help himself: "How much are they worth—your shipload of slaves?"

And the captain of the pirates answered, "As much as all of your cargo!"

Vladimir's dreams of fortunes grew fainter as the weeping of the chained slaves tugged at his heart and he cried out, "I will trade all my merchandise for those poor creatures!"

Of course the captain agreed readily, and Vladimir soon had a ship full of slaves. As each came aboard, he asked where they came from and told them they were now free. An old woman was the last to get on, and at her side was a pale and beautiful maiden. The old woman wept, "Our home is so far away that we can never get back again.

This maid is the only daughter of a mighty king, and I am her nurse. Please, let us just stay with you."

Vladimir set the other former slaves ashore at the first opportunity, but he felt such pity for the maiden that he married her and sailed for home. When he arrived with an empty vessel, a penniless wife, and an old woman to show for his voyage, his father was furious.

"My foolish son!" he cried. "What have you done? I gave you valuable cargo and you have come back with nothing but two empty mouths to feed!" And with these words, he threw Vladimir out of the house and told him never to return.

Vladimir and his wife, Helena, and the nurse lived in great poverty in a rude hut, but the young couple had come to love each other dearly, and so were happy in spite of their circumstances. In time, the father's heart softened, and he took pity on his son and welcomed the couple back to his home. He even entrusted another vessel to Vladimir. "But you have seen the consequences of your last foolish bargain, my son. Do not repeat your folly!"

Vladimir was full of gratitude and, leaving Helena in his father's care, he set out to make his fortune at last. But at the first port he stopped at, he was unlucky enough to see a procession of prisoners at dockside. At their head was a white-haired old man, being driven harshly along by soldiers. "Where are you driving these poor creatures?" cried Vladimir.

"They cannot pay the king's taxes," said the soldiers. "They shall rot in prison till they do!"

Now Vladimir, remembering his father's words, tried to turn away from the pitiful sight, and set about selling his cargo, but the look of those poor prisoners was ever in his heart. For the life of him, he could not turn away. He went straight to the chief magistrate of the city and gave him all his merchandise to settle the prisoners' debts and set them free. Then he sailed home with an empty vessel and not a single copper to show. Falling at his father's feet, he told him what he had done and begged his forgiveness. Eventually Vladimir's father relented and received him back in his home. And in time, he even gave him a ship loaded with finer goods than the two before.

"Behold," said Vladimir's father, "your last chance to win a fortune!"

On the prow of this new ship, Vladimir had painted a portrait of his wife, Helena, and set sail once more with high hopes and great dreams.

March 31

The Two Bad Bargains, Part 2

Vladimir sailed for months and at last dropped anchor in a great city where a mighty king dwelt. Many citizens came down to the docks to see what Vladimir had to offer and the king himself paid a visit to this foreign merchant. But as the king neared the ship he saw the portrait of the beautiful maiden on the prow, and could not believe his eyes. "Stranger," he cried to Vladimir, "how did this maid come to grace your ship?" Vladimir told him all his tale, and when he finished the king had tears in his eyes. He embraced Vladimir and said, "That girl is my only child, stolen from me these many years!"

The king took Vladimir to the palace to tell the queen the good news. Vladimir was proclaimed the heir and there was great rejoicing among the people. Only the king's chief minister was silent, for he had been promised the princess in marriage when she was but a child, and he had no intention of losing her now that she was found. After giving Vladimir many gifts for his family and an even finer ship than he had arrived in, the king bade him sail for home and bring Helena and his parents to court.

Vladimir was eager to obey but he begged the king to send one of his ministers back with him so that his father might not disbelieve the strange tale he would tell. Now who should the king send but his chief minister? And all through the voyage, the minister said to himself, "Once the girl is safe in my power, I'll make an end to this troublesome fellow."

Arriving home in splendor, Vladimir surprised his father for once. "You must have learned at last to make a shrewd bargain!" the father cried. But Vladimir smiled and answered. "No, my good fortune is due to my first bad bargain." So he told his father his story, and Helena was overjoyed at the thought of seeing her mother and father again. In just a few days, they set off for the distant kingdom.

Now the chief minister had found Helena ten times more beautiful than he even remembered, and he was more determined than ever to get rid of her young husband. One dark night, he summoned Vladimir to a lonely spot on the deck. The young man came with no thought of evil, but as he drew near, the minister seized him and threw him overboard. The next morning, Helena and the parents were overcome with grief to find Vladimir apparently lost at sea.

Meanwhile, Vladimir was carried along by the waves and dashed upon a barren rock. For fifteen days and nights he sat there, with no way to get off his lonely refuge. Finally he spotted a small boat coming his way. As the man grew nearer, Vladimir recognized the face of the white-haired old fellow who had marched at the head of the prisoners, and the old man recognized him and made straight for the rock. Once he rescued Vladimir, he took him to a village where all the prisoners still lived. They welcomed him as a hero, and gave him new clothing and food for his journey to Helena's homeland.

For thirty days more Vladimir traveled, till his clothes were as ragged as before and his face hardly recognizable with its long beard. When he reached the palace, the guards refused to let him in. Vladimir was close to tears. The king, his chief minister, and Helena passed by him just then, and Helena noticed the wedding ring on his finger. Her face grew pale and she asked where he had gotten it. "How can you speak to that dirty beggar?" asked the minister, dragging her off. But Helena told her father she had recognized her husband's wedding ring, and begged him to send for the beggar and find out how he had obtained it. As soon as Vladimir arrived and Helena could look him in the eyes, she knew him. She threw herself in Vladimir's arms and there was great rejoicing.

When the king heard of his minister's treachery, the minister was publicly disgraced and banished forever. And after they had all been reunited and living very happily for some time, a little bird whispered into the ear of Vladimir's father, "After all, is it so fruitless—your son's kind of bargaining?"

APRIL

April 1

APRIL FOOL'S DAY

Jean Sotte, Part 1

There once was a fellow who was such a fool that everyone called him Jean Sotte. In the bright daylight he would light a lamp, and then when it turned dark he would put it out. In summer he would wear a greatcoat and in the winter, well, he would parade about nearly naked. To make a long story short, Jean Sotte did everything the opposite.

Now the king at that time was a fun-loving man named King Bangon. King Bangon loved a good laugh and silly tricks amused him more than one might expect in a grown man. But he was the king and kings can do what kings want to do, and so one day, the king invited Jean Sotte to his court.

From the moment Jean Sotte entered the room, there were snickers.

"Tell me, Jean Sotte," said the king, looking around the room to make sure everyone was paying attention. "They say Compair Lapin is your father. Is this true?"

"Why, yes, he is," Jean Sotte replied.

An attendant spoke up. "But I thought Compair Bouki was your father," he said.

"But no," called out a woman. "I heard it is Renard who is your father."

"You are all correct," said Jean Sotte. "They are all my fathers. Each time one of them passes, he says, 'Good morning, my child.' I believe, then, by their own admission they are all my fathers."

Everyone laughed, especially the king. Finally, when he had collected himself, he said, "Jean Sotte, I need your help. Tomorrow morning I want you to bring me a bottle of bull's milk. My daughter is sick and she needs it for medicine."

Now everyone knows that bulls cannot make milk, and so there were many muffled giggles. But Jean Sotte was not put off. "No problem, Your Majesty. I will bring some tomorrow."

"Good, good," said the king. "And one more thing. I want you to come again, in one month's time, on April first. On that day, I will ask you to guess something. If you guess correctly, I will give you my daughter's hand in marriage. But if after three guesses you do not succeed, I will have to cut off your head."

There were murmurs in the audience. Most people thought the king's dare rather cruel. It was not kind to set up a fool like that for his own death. But a king can do what a king wants to do, so no one said a thing.

When Jean Sotte got home, he told his mother about his meeting with the king. She started crying when she heard of the king's proposition. She knew her son was a fool but she loved him nonetheless, and she begged him not to go to the palace the next day.

But the next day, Jean Sotte left the house with an axe on his shoulder. He was going to meet the king and that was that. At the palace he climbed a great oak tree and began to cut down its branches. One of the servants came out and said, "Hush, fool. You are disturbing everyone."

"Send out the king," Jean Sotte demanded, in a voice that startled the young servant.

When the king came out, Jean Sotte explained that he was cutting branches to get bark to make some tea for his father, who had given birth to twins the day before.

"What? Your father gave birth to twins? What kind of a fool do you take me for?" the king asked.

"But Your Highness, yesterday you asked me for a bottle of bull's milk. If you were right, I am right also," he said.

The king gave Jean Sotte a long, hard look. "You are not as foolish as you would like us to believe," the king said. "I will see you in a month and we will see which one is the April Fool."

April 2

Jean Sotte, Part 2

As the first of April neared, Jean Sotte tried to prepare for his meeting with the king. Meanwhile, the evil Compair Bouki was plotting against the poor fool. "I see an opportunity here," said Compair Bouki. "After all, no matter how hard he tries, Jean Sotte will fail and his head will be cut off. With Sotte gone, who will have his horse? It is better that I should profit and get his horse."

So Compair Bouki, in a scheme to get Jean Sotte's horse, took a basket full of poisoned cakes and put them on the bridge where he was to pass. He knew that Jean Sotte loved sweets and would be tempted by the cakes. "Once he is dead, I will take his horse," Compair Bouki figured.

Now Compair Lapin liked Jean Sotte, and in fact he owed the fool a favor, because Jean Sotte had freed him from a trap one day. So at daybreak on April 1, when Jean Sotte set out for the palace, he waited for him on the road and told him, "Jean Sotte, I must warn you: do not eat or drink anything on your way to the palace. And when the king asks you to guess, your answer will be what I am going to tell you. Come here," he said, motioning Jean Sotte to his side, and he whispered into the fool's ear.

As Compair Lapin told Jean Sotte what to say, Jean Sotte laughed. "Yes, yes," he said, "I understand."

"Now don't forget me when you are famous and marry the princess," he said to Jean Sotte as the fool walked out of his view. "And remember," he yelled, "pay attention to all you see on your way. *Look on all sides and listen well.*"

Jean Sotte started off again and finally arrived at the bridge. The first thing he saw was a basket of little cakes. They smelled delicious and were very tempting. But instead of stuffing his mouth, which was his first impulse, he decided to feed a cake to his horse, to see if they were harmful. Minutes later, the horse fell down dead on the porch.

"If I had not listened to Compair Lapin, I would now be dead," Jean Sotte thought to himself. "I will now heed his advice and pay attention to everything I see."

Before leaving the bridge he dragged his horse into the river and as it was carried away by the current three buzzards alighted on the horse and began to eat him. "Compair Lapin told me to listen and look, but my dead horse is all I see. Nevertheless, I will remember this—it could be something I could ask the king."

When Jean Sotte arrived at the king's palace fifty men had already been beheaded for failing to answer the riddle.

Here was the king's question: "What is it that early in the morning walks on four legs, when he grows up walks on two, and when he is old walks on three legs?"

Jean Sotte told him it was a child that walked on four legs; when he grew up he walked on two; and when he was old he had to use a cane, which made a third leg. The crowd gasped.

"You have guessed correctly," said the king. "My daughter is now yours. Now ask me anything in the world. If I do not guess correctly, then I will give you my kingdom and my fortune."

Jean Sotte replied, "Today I saw a dead creature who was carrying three live beings on him. The dead did not touch the land and was not in the sky. What was it?"

The king guessed at a thousand things but finally had to give up. Finally, Jean Sotte told him, "My horse died on the bridge. I threw him into the river and three buzzards alighted on him and were eating him as he floated downstream. They did not touch the land and were not in the sky."

The audience in the court began to clap softly, then louder and louder. Jean Sotte had done it! Everyone saw that Jean Sotte was no fool at all. He married and after a while governed the whole kingdom. He made Compair Lapin his prime minister.

April 3

The Wise Fool

Dayal was the name of the simpleton in a village in India. Everyone always laughed at Dayal, and found ways to play jokes on him. One day a villager held out ten paise in one hand and one banknote, a rupee, in the other, and asked Dayal which hand he wanted. Now it takes a hundred paise to make up one rupee, but Dayal picked the ten paise.

When word of this joke spread, all the villagers laughed and wanted to test it for themselves. Over and over they teased Dayal. "Do you want the ten or the one?" And invariably he took the ten paise coins. They would laugh, and then Dayal would laugh too, for he always joined in laughter, even when it was at his own expense. Perhaps Dayal believed that metal was more valuable than paper, or perhaps he was fooled by the numbers, thinking ten had to be greater than one. No one in the village knew, and no one bothered to ask him.

The day came when Dayal fell very sick and was thought to be dying. The village healer went to visit him, and found him weeping. The healer was moved by his tears, for Dayal had always been a man of laughter. "Why do you weep?" the healer asked.

"I feel great regret for what I have done all these years," said Dayal. "I have cheated and deceived people who have been kind to me! Of course I know that one rupee is worth more than ten paise. Any fool knows that! But that first time, I chose the paise because I didn't want to take advantage of the man's generosity. And after that, I always chose the paise because I knew that if I were to choose the rupee, people would stop offering me the choice at all. Thus by always choosing the ten paise, I earned a great many rupees!"

And so the village fool was really the wisest man in the village.

April 4

What the Good Man Does Is Always Right

A TALE FROM NORWAY

Once upon a time there was a man named Gudbrand who had a small farm with two cows. The man and his wife lived very happily together, for they understood each other well, and she thought him the ablest and cleverest man around.

One day the wife said to Gudbrand, "Do you know, dear, I think we ought to take one of our cows into town and sell it, that's what I think. For what do we want with more than one cow, and we ought to have some more money in hand." The couple had a hundred dollars put aside, but that was all. Gudbrand thought his wife made good sense, so he set off at once to town with the cow.

But when he got to town, there was no one who would buy the cow. "Well, never mind!" Gudbrand thought. "At worst, I'll bring her back home." After he had gone a bit of the way back to his farm, he met a man with a horse to sell, and Gudbrand swapped with him. A little farther on, he encountered a man driving a fat pig before him, and Gudbrand thought a pig might be even better to have than a horse, so he swapped again. As the miles went by, he made other trades: the pig for a sheep, and the sheep for a goose. As the day was almost done, Gudbrand was growing hungry, so he sold the goose for a shilling, and used the money to buy food.

Gudbrand had reached his neighbor's house by now, and the neighbor asked, "How did things go with you in town?"

"So-so," said Gudbrand, and he told his whole story.

"Ah!" answered his friend. "Your good wife will give you a piece of her mind, I wager."

"Well," said Gudbrand, "I think things might have gone much worse for me. But whether I have done wrong or not, I have such a kind wife, she never has a word to say against anything I do."

"Oh, this I don't believe!" exclaimed the neighbor.

"Shall we bet on it?" asked Gudbrand. "I have a hundred dollars. Will you bet the same?"

The two agreed on the wager, and when Gudbrand went home, his neighbor followed, so he could stand outside the door and listen.

"Good evening, dear!" Gudbrand said to his wife, and she asked how his day had gone.

"Not much to brag of," replied Gudbrand. "No one bought the cow, so I swapped it for a horse."

"For a horse!" said his wife. "Well, that was good of you. Now we can drive to church."

"Ah, but I've not got the horse after all. Further down the road, I traded it for a pig."

"You did just as I should have done myself! A thousand thanks! Now we can have bacon. And what do we want with a horse? People would say we had gotten too proud to walk to church."

"But I've not got the pig either. I swapped for a sheep."

"Why, you do everything to please me! Now I shall have both wool and clothing and meat."

"But the sheep I traded for a goose after all."

"How you think of everything! I have no spinning wheel, nor carding comb. But I have often longed for a roast goose. Besides, we shall have down for pillows."

"But, dear, I was forced to sell the goose for a shilling because I feared I would starve of hunger."

"God be praised you did so! Heaven be thanked that I have got you back safe again. You who do everything so well that I want neither goose nor sheep, nor pig nor cattle."

Then Gudbrand opened the door and said, "Well, what do you say now? Have I won the hundred dollars?" And his neighbor was obliged to agree that he had.

April 5

How Nan and the Moon Went for a Walk

One evening as Nan started out for a walk the white moon in the sky went before her.

"Why, the moon is coming, too," said Nan, and she stood still because she was so surprised. The white moon stood still, too. Nan walked on faster. The white moon went faster before her. At the corner, Nan turned to go home. Now the white moon was behind, but it followed her even to the door. Nan looked up before going in, and the white moon looked down at Nan.

That night, before she jumped into bed, Nan looked out the window. There in the starry sky was the moon gazing down at her.

"Were you waiting for me all of this time, moon?" asked Nan. "I can't come out until tomorrow night. We'll have another walk then."

And they did.—ANGELA M. KEYES

April 6

The Most Powerful Person in the Whole World

"Who is the most powerful person in the whole world?" Mrs. McGrath asked her fifth-grade class. Immediately everybody's hands were raised high into the air. This was such an easy question. "Jennifer?" Mrs. McGrath said.

Jennifer said, "The most powerful person in the world is my father. He does anything he wants to do." And then she admitted, "Well, most of the time he does what my mother wants him to do, or what I want him to do, or what my little brother wants him to do. So maybe he's not really the most powerful person in the world."

"I know," Kurt screamed. "I know, Mrs. McGrath."

"All right, Kurt, please tell the class."

Kurt was sure he was right. "It's Arnold Schwartzenegger. He won all the contests for lifting more weight than anybody else and then in the movies he beat all of the bad guys." But then Kurt paused and sighed, "But since they were only movies, I guess he really isn't the most powerful person in the world." Kurt frowned.

But immediately Angela raised her hand. She was positive she knew the answer to this question. When Mrs. McGrath called upon her, Angela explained, "The most powerful person in the whole world is the president of the United States. He makes all the laws that we have to follow, and people all over the world listen to him." And then she admitted, "But he does have to listen to the senators and the representatives, so maybe he isn't really the most powerful person in the whole world."

The classroom was silent. This was a much more difficult question than anyone had thought. Then Mark raised his hand. When Mrs. McGrath called on him, he said, "I think the most powerful people in the world are the tiny little people who live inside batteries and spin the tiny wheels to produce power that makes the batteries work. Because without them we wouldn't be able to run our games and flashlights and radios and telephones and everything. Without them, we would all be powerless." Everybody laughed at that, but then Mark finally admitted, "But those little people aren't real, they just exist in stories, so maybe they aren't the most powerful people in the world."

Everyone sat very still, hoping Mrs. McGrath wouldn't call on them. This was a very hard question. Finally, Mrs. McGrath looked around the room and called, "Josie?"

Josie was the shyest girl in the whole class. She almost never raised her hand and she certainly did not like having to answer hard questions. She thought and thought, but couldn't answer this question. "I . . . I . . . I . . ." she said, but no other words came out.

Mrs. McGrath smiled. "Very good, Josie, that's exactly right. You are the most powerful person in the world because you have the power to change your own life whenever you want to. That was very good."

Josie smiled and felt wonderful inside. And she never told anyone the truth.

—JORDAN BURNETT AND DAVID FISHER

April 7

The Queen Bee

A GERMAN TALE

A king once had two sons who were considered clever, yet they wasted their time on foolish pleasures. These two had a younger brother, whom they mocked because he was quiet and simple, and they used to say that a simpleton such as he would never make his way in the world.

One evening, however, they took him for a walk with them, and on the way they passed an anthill that the elder brothers wanted to overturn. But the simple brother said, "No, no, leave the little creatures in peace."

Next they came to a lake on which ducks were swimming, and the brothers wanted to catch one or two for dinner. But the simpleton stopped them, saying, "No, I cannot bear that you should kill them." So the ducks were left to live, and the three brothers walked on to a woods, where there was a bees' nest in a tree, full of so much honey that it ran down the trunk. The two brothers wanted to light a fire under the tree to smother the bees so that they might take the honey, but again the youngest prevented them.

At last they came to a strange castle, and they went in and found a door with three locks. The center of this door had a window, and inside they could see a very old man sitting at a table. He let the eldest brother in, and showed him a stone table, on which was engraved these words: "In the woods, under the moss, are scattered the pearls of the king's daughter. They are a thousand in number, and whoever can find them all in one day before the sun goes down will release the castle from its enchantment. But if he should not succeed before sunset, he will be turned into stone."

The eldest brother was determined to try. The next day, though he searched till sunset, he found only a hundred pearls, and so was turned into stone. Despite this, the second brother also accepted the challenge. He found only a hundred more, and was also turned to stone.

At last it was the turn of the simple brother, who had little confidence in himself, and went into the woods and sat down on a stone and wept. As he sat there, he saw the ant king, whose life and kingdom he had saved, approach him. In gratitude for his act, the king and his five thousand ants offered to find the pearls, and soon they were piled in a heap before the brother.

On returning to the castle, the young man found a second task awaiting him. It was to fetch the key to the princess's bedroom from the bottom of a lake, into which it had been thrown. He went to the shore of the lake, wondering what to do, when the ducks swimming there recognized him. When they heard his problem, they dove to the bottom of the lake and retrieved the key for him.

The most difficult task of all awaited the youngest brother. He was told to enter the chamber of the king's three daughters and discover which one of them was the youngest and most beloved. All three were sleeping and looked exactly like each other. There was but one way to distinguish them: before they went to sleep, the eldest had eaten barley sugar, the second a little syrup, and the youngest a spoonful of honey. As the brother wondered how to know, the queen bee, whose community he had saved from fire, flew in the room. Quickly she discovered who was the youngest from their breath, and the young man knew which one to awaken. No sooner had he done so than the enchantment on the castle was lifted.

The simple brother married the youngest daughter of the king, and became king himself after her father's death, which shows that it is better to be simple and kindhearted than clever and cruel.—BROTHERS GRIMM

April 8

Lazy Jack

AN ENGLISH TALE

Once upon a time, there was a boy named Jack who lived with his widowed mother in a dreary cottage in the countryside. The mother earned a poor living by spinning, but Jack was lazy and earned nothing. At last his mother lost all patience with the boy and told him that if he did not find some work, she would turn him out of the house.

"Dear me!" thought Jack. "What a pass I have come to."

He went out and hired himself for the day to a farmer. The farmer gave him a penny for his labor, and Jack was well pleased. But he was not used to handling money, and he lost the penny on the way home.

"You stupid boy," said his mother. "You should have put the penny in your pocket."

"You're right," agreed Jack. "That is what I shall do next time."

Jack hired himself to a dairyman the following day. At the end of the afternoon, Jack was given a jugful of creamy, warm milk, and putting it into his pocket, the lad walked home.

"I did as you said, Mother," called Jack, stepping indoors, but when he lifted the jug from his pocket, he found he had spilled all the milk on the journey home.

His mother groaned, "Don't you know you should have carried it on your head?"

"You're right again, Mother," agreed Jack. "I'll do that next time."

A day or so later, Jack worked for another farmer. In payment, the farmer gave him some cream cheese. Jack put the cheese on his head and walked home. But the sun was shining, and the cheese melted and ran through Jack's hair and over his shirt.

"You fool!" shrieked his mother, who liked cream cheese. "You should have carried it in your hands." Jack swore to follow her suggestion the next time.

Jack then worked for a baker whose cat had recently had kittens. "Take a kitten for your payment, Jack," smiled the baker.

Jack tried to carry the kitten carefully in his hands, but it scratched Jack so much he had to let it go. And once again he arrived home with nothing.

"You stupid boy," said his mother, when Jack told her what had happened. "You should have tied it with a piece of string and pulled it behind you."

Jack, a good-natured lad, agreed and promised to take her advice.

His next job was for a butcher, who paid him for his work with a shoulder of mutton. Jack tied the mutton to a string and pulled it along behind him all the way home. By the time he reached there, the meat was not fit to eat.

"You ninny," sighed his mother. "You should have carried it on your shoulder."

"Why didn't I think of that? Thank you, Mother," Jack smiled.

On the following Monday, Jack hired himself to a herdsman, who gave him a donkey in payment. Now the donkey was heavy, but Jack was strong, and with much heaving and grunting he pulled the donkey onto his shoulder and set off for home. On the way he passed the house of a rich merchant, who had a rather strange daughter.

The girl had not laughed even once in her life, and the doctors had said she would never be cheerful until she saw something she thought was funny.

Now the merchant was fond of his daughter and, wishing to see her happy, he had promised her hand in marriage to any young man who could make her laugh.

The merchant's daughter happened to be looking from her window as Jack stumbled past carrying the braying donkey. The girl had never seen anything so ridiculous, and she burst out laughing. The merchant was delighted and, inviting Jack in, asked if he would like to marry the girl and accept a fine dowry.

Jack agreed, and he and the merchant's daughter lived happily together for the rest of their lives. Since Jack was a kindhearted fellow, he saw that his old mother had everything she needed.

And his mother, being a wise soul, never called him lazy or stupid again.

April 9

The Lion, the Fox, and the Donkey

The lion, the fox, and the donkey once joined together in a hunt and agreed to share the spoils afterward. When it was over, the lion very generously asked the donkey to work out the portions due to each of them. The donkey took great pains to divide the portions evenly, then asked his companions to choose the ones they wanted.

But the lion did not like the idea of equal portions. His eyes flaring with rage, the lion delivered a mighty blow of his paw to the donkey and killed him instantly. Then the lion asked the fox to divide the spoils once more. The fox piled all of the booty into one large heap, except for a small morsel, which he set aside for himself.

The lion looked pleased. "I like the way you did that," he said. "That's what I call a fair division of the spoils. How did you come by such talent?"

"Actually, I learned it from the donkey," said the fox, very humbly.

—AESOP

April 10

Honor, Fire, and Water

A FRENCH FABLE

Once upon a time, Honor, Fire, and Water set out to travel in company.

As it was to be an expedition of pleasure and discovery, they foresaw the possibility of getting separated on the road, and made arrangements by which they might be sure of meeting again.

Fire explained that although in general he was visible enough, he sometimes was concealed from view. "But even if you miss my light," he said, "whenever you see smoke, you will be sure to find me." Water also instructed his friends as to certain marks by which his whereabouts could be readily ascertained—look, he said, where the grass is the greenest and the evening mists rise in the air. It remained for Honor to give his companions some clue of the same kind. But he confessed, with a sigh, that the only charge he could give was to keep him constantly in view and never lose sight of him. "Watch me," he said, "and never let me go. For if you lose me, I promise sadly, you will never find me again."

April 11

How the Manx Cat Lost Her Tail

A TALE FROM THE ISLE OF MAN

It was starting to rain, and Noah was calling the animals to his ark. Everyone was accounted for but one cat who was out mousing around. The cat was a good hunter, but she was having trouble locating a mouse. She had no idea they were all with Noah.

Noah looked at his list. He saw that he was short just one cat.

Rain. More rain.

"That's it," thought Noah to himself. "Who's out is out, and who's in is in."

And with that he was just closing the door when the cat came running up, half-drowned, squeezed in, just in time. But Noah had slammed the door as he ran in and cut off her tail, so she got in without it, and that is why Manx cats have no tails to this day.

April 12

Boots and His Brothers

A NORSE TALE

Once upon a time there was a man who had three sons, Peter, Paul, and John. John, the youngest, was known as Boots. This was a very poor family, and the man told his sons over and over that they must go out into the world to earn their bread, that there was nothing for them at home.

A short way from their cottage was the king's palace, and right outside the king's chambers a mighty oak had sprung up, blocking all the light. Many men had tried to chop it down, but as soon as one chip flew off the oak, two grew in its place. This did not please the king, nor was he happy that he had no well, as many of his subjects did. Unfortunately, the palace lay high on a hill, and any man that tried to dig a well hit solid rock in just a few inches of digging.

So great was the king's frustration that he had offered his daughter's hand in marriage and half his kingdom to the man who could both chop down the oak tree and dig him a well.

As you can guess, this offer produced many a man who came to try his luck. But the oak grew bigger and stronger, and the rocky hill grew no softer.

The three brothers, with their father's blessing, also set off to try their hands at the tasks. They hadn't gone far before they heard something hacking and hewing away in the forest.

"I wonder now what it is that's hewing away up yonder?" said Boots.

"You're always so full of your wonderings," replied his brothers. "What is so strange about a woodcutter in the forest?"

"Still, I'd like to see what it is," said Boots, and he went up the hillside toward the noise, and there he found an ax, hewing all by itself at a fir. "Good day," said Boots. "So you stand here all alone and hew, do you?"

"Yes, I've hacked away a long, long time, waiting for you," said the ax.

"Well, here I am at last," said Boots, and he picked up the ax and took it with him. His brothers jeered at him and asked what wonder he had found. "Oh, just an ax," said he, and they kept walking till they came to a steep spur of rock. Up above, they heard something shoveling and digging. Boots, of course, wondered what the noise was.

When he investigated, he found a spade working all alone. Boots took the spade along with him, and when his brothers inquired what strange and rare thing he had found, he said, "Only a spade."

They went a good way till they came to a brook, where they stopped for a drink. "I wonder where all this water comes from," Boots said to his brothers.

"I wonder if you're right in your head," answered Peter and Paul in one breath. "Have you never heard how water rises from a spring in the earth?"

"Yes, but I've still a fancy to see where this brook begins." Boots had to climb a hill to follow the brook, which got smaller and smaller as it rose, till it ended at a great walnut, from which the water trickled. Boots picked up the walnut and stopped its hole with a plug of moss, then rejoined his brothers, who made jokes at his expense for the next few hours.

Finally they came to the king's palace, and Peter and Paul were the first of the brothers to try and fell the oak. Instead, they caused it to grow even more, and as the king was irritated by this, Boots almost didn't get his turn. "Hew away," he said to his ax. The ax made the oak chips fly and it wasn't long before the oak was down. Next, Boots pulled out his spade and had a well dug in a flash. Then he took out the walnut, unplugged it, and the king soon had a well filled to the brim with water.

Boots, as you can guess, got the princess and half the kingdom too, and his brothers were heard to say, "Well, after all, Boots wasn't so much out of his mind as we thought."

April 13

The Wolf and the Baby Goat

Kid, the baby goat, was finally getting his horns.

The horns made him think he was a grown-up goat, and about that he was very wrong. He was reckless, and one evening as the sun was setting in the sky and the flock was making its way home from the pasture, he decided to stay back and get in an extra nibble of the delicate spring grass.

His mother called for him, but he did not answer. A while later, when he lifted his head and looked up. The flock was gone.

Oh, no! He was alone!

The sun was sinking quickly now and the shadows blurred, and it was suddenly dark. Across the pasture, a cold wind carried odd night noises from animals and insects.

Kid was scared. Worse, he had the terrible sensation that he was being watched.

He started bleating for his mother, but no one answered.

Suddenly, a wolf appeared.

That's it. I'm finished, thought Kid. He managed to squeak out a greeting.

"I know you intend to eat me, Mr. Wolf, and it's my own fault, really. I stayed back from my flock and now no one could possibly save me! Would you please play a song on your pipe? I would like to dance to be happy one last time."

The wolf figured a last dance would not hurt anything and anyway he liked the idea of having a little music before dinner. So he started up a merry tune and the kid began to dance.

The wolf did not think before he acted.

Meanwhile, as the flock was moving homeward the evening air carried the wolf's tune across the pasture, and the goats and their shepherd dogs pricked up their ears. They recognized the tune: it was the song the wolf played before he was going to have a feast. The feast, no doubt, was their beloved little kid.

The shepherd dogs and the goats raced to the kid's side, and chased the wolf for miles.

The wolf felt like a fool.

He had played the piper to please the kid when he should have stuck to the butcher trade.

Don't take your eyes off of your purpose.—AESOP

April 14

The Philosopher, the Ants, and Mercury

A philosopher who was standing on the shore witnessed the shipwreck of a vessel. To his horror, he saw the ship crash and sink; all of the crew and passengers drowned. Raising his fist to the heavens, he called out in anger, thinking that perhaps for the sake of one criminal who might be sailing on the ship, the gods had allowed so many innocent persons to perish.

As he was indulging his anger and these reflections, he found himself surrounded by a whole army of ants, near to whose nest he was sitting. One of them climbed up and stung him, and he immediately trampled them all to death with his foot. Suddenly Mercury appeared to him. Striking the philosopher with his wand, Mercury said, "Who are you to sit in judgment of the Gods when you—without a moment's thought—in a similar manner treated these poor ants?"—AESOP

Hodja in the Pulpit

A TURKISH TALE

Hodja was a master preacher, but sometimes he was confusing. One Friday he addressed his congregation with these words: "I beg you to tell me truly, O brothers! O believers! Tell me if what I am going to say to you is already known to you!"

This puzzled even the oldest and the wisest of the people. So the answer came, as in one voice, from his congregation that they did *not* know, and that it was *not possible* for them to know what the Hodja was going to say to them. "Then," said the preacher, "of what use to you or to me is an unknown subject?"

He then descended from the pulpit and left the mosque.

The following Friday his congregation, instead of having decreased, had greatly increased, and their anxiety to hear what he was going to say was felt in the very atmosphere.

The Hodja ascended the pulpit and said, "O brothers! O believers! I beg you to tell me truly if what I am going to say to you is already known to you."

The answer that came to the Hodja was so spontaneous as to suggest it had been planned. They all shouted, "Yes, Hodja, we do know what you are going to say to us."

"That being the case," said Hodja, "there is no need either of you or me wasting our time." And, then, descending the pulpit, he left the mosque.

On the following Friday, Hodja again mounted the pulpit and saw that his mosque was so crowded that not a nook or corner in it was empty. He

addressed his congregation in exactly the same manner. "O brothers! O believers!" said he. "I ask you to tell me truly if what I am going to say is already known to you."

And again the answer of his overflowing congregation had evidently been prepared beforehand, for one half of them rose and said, "Yes, Hodja, we do know what you are going to say to us," and the other half rose and said, "O Hodja, how could we poor ignorant people know what you intend to say to us?"

The Hodja answered, "It is well said: and now if the half who knows what I am going to say would explain to the other half what it is, I would be deeply grateful. Then of course, it will be unnecessary for me to say anything."

Whereupon he descended from the pulpit and left the mosque.

April 16

Hodja in the Pulpit, Variations

In different cultures, the preacher is depicted as an engaging combination of cleverness and naivete. Hodja is a Turkish preacher, a trickster, but beloved nonetheless.

Storytellers can change settings on the preacher-as-trickster motif. In Harold Courlander's "Terrapin," a black preacher in the South saves "a powerful lot of time" when he uses the method in the previous Hodja story, concluding: " 'Pears to me that if you all know what I'm talking about, ain't no use of my sayin' a word.' "

As Atelia Clarkson and Gilbert B. Cross point out in *World Folktales,* settings for the Hodja motif can vary and are not confined to a church or mosque. One story they identified took place in the Ozarks at a secret lodge meeting. There is a guard and fine badges but no "secret wisdom." A wise man collects $25 and asks if the boys know "holy words." No one does, and he concludes that the crowd is not ready for the "secret wisdom." Another $25 is collected on another evening and the answer is now "yes." Another $25 produces the wisdom that the lodge brothers are all "brothers in the bond. . . . Them that knows is obliged to tell them that don't know." Once again, those who feign knowledge are duped.

April 17

The Fish and the Ring

AN ENGLISH TALE

Once upon a time there was a mighty baron who was a great magician and could predict the future. One day, when his little boy was four years old, he looked into the Book of Fate to see what would happen to him. To his dismay, he found that his son would wed a poor maid who had just been born in York. Now the baron knew the father of the baby girl was very poor and had five children already. The baron rode to their cottage and found the father, rather downcast, sitting by the front door. So he went up to him and said, "What is the matter, my man?"

The father replied, "Well, your honor, the fact is I've five children already, and now a sixth's come, a little lass, and where I'm to get the bread to fill their mouths I don't know."

"Don't be downhearted," said the baron. "I can help you. I'll take away the last little one, and you won't have to bother about her."

"Thank you kindly, my lord," answered the man, and brought his baby girl out and gave her to the baron. The baron took her and rode to the banks of the nearby river, and threw her in.

But the little girl didn't sink. Her clothes kept her afloat for a long time, till she washed ashore in front of the fisherman's hut. The fisherman felt sorry for the poor little thing, and took her in, and she lived there until she was fifteen years old, and had grown to a fine, handsome young woman.

One day it happened that the baron and some companions went hunting near the same river, and stopped at the fisherman's hut to get a drink. The girl came out to serve them, and they all noticed her beauty. One of them said, "You can read fates, Baron. Who will this lovely girl marry?"

"That's easy to guess," said the baron. "Some yokel or other. Come here, girl, and tell me of what day you were born."

"I don't know, sir," said the girl. "I was picked up from the river fifteen years ago."

The baron froze. He knew who she was, and later he rode back and told the girl, "Young lady, I will give you a small fortune if you will but take this letter to my brother in Scarborough."

Now the letter, which the girl could not read, said: "Dear Brother: Kill the young woman who is carrying this note immediately. Yours affectionately, Humphrey."

The girl agreed to go, and on her journey, she stopped at an inn, which was beset by robbers while she slept. She had no money, but the robbers read her letter and felt sorry for her. The chief of the robbers wrote a new letter that read: "Dear Brother: Let the young woman carrying this note marry my son immediately. Yours affectionately, Humphrey."

She traveled on to Scarborough and the home of the baron's brother, a noble knight with whom the baron's son was staying. When the brother received the letter, he ordered the wedding to be held that very day.

Soon after, the Baron came to his brother's castle, and was chagrined to find the very thing he had plotted against had come to pass. He took the girl for a walk and planned to throw her over the cliffs by the sea. But she pleaded for her life and said, "If you will spare me, I will never see you or your son again."

The baron took off his gold ring and threw it into the sea, saying, "Never let me see your face until you can show me that ring."

The poor girl wandered through the countryside until she came to a great noble's castle, where she was given work as a kitchen maid.

Now one day who should she see coming up to the castle but the baron and his son, her husband. She hoped they wouldn't notice her in the kitchen, and set to cleaning a huge fish that was to be boiled for dinner. As she was cleaning it, she saw something shiny inside. What had she found? Why, it was the baron's ring that he had thrown into the sea.

When the fish was served in the hall, the guests praised the cook and the lord sent for the girl to accept their compliments. She put the baron's gold ring on her thumb, and went up to the hall.

The guests were surprised to see such a young and beautiful cook, and no one was more surprised than the baron. But when he saw the ring on her thumb, he decided that he could no longer fight Fate, and he announced to all the company that this was his son's true wife. And so they rode home to the baron's castle and lived happily ever after.

April 18

The Fox and the Goat

A fox fell into a well. For hours he pondered how he should get out again. He had nearly given up hope when a goat came to the place and, wanting to drink, asked the fox whether the water was good.

"This is too good to be true," thought the fox to himself. Amazed that the goat was so stupid that he had not figured out that the fox was trapped, he said nothing about his predicament. Instead he answered, "Actually, my friend, the water is *so* good that I can not get enough of it and, fortunately for you, the water is so plentiful there is enough for both of us."

That was enough encouragement for the goat, who, without thinking, jumped right into the well. The goat drank and drank the pure water and after satisfying his thirst asked the fox how he usually climbed out of the well.

"Quite simple," replied the fox. "And since there are two of us, it will even be simpler. Just rear up and place your front feet against the side of the well and bend your horns forward. I will easily mount your back and jump right out," the fox advised.

The goat, again without thinking, did just as he was told and the fox nimbly climbed up his back and with one jump from the goat's horns was safely out of the well.

"Now it is your turn to help me out," said the goat.

But the fox was already well on his way. Leaving the goat stranded deep in the well, he called back, "My friend, if you had half as much brains as you have beard, you would have looked before you leaped."

—AESOP

April 19

The Beggar's Curse

There was once a farmer from France who traveled to the annual Pardon, which was held in the town of Rumengol. The Pardon was a day on which poor beggars were treated like kings. This farmer knew his duty, but was not about to carry it out pleasantly. For he was an ill-tempered man, and as he drew near Rumengol, he grew more and more irritated by the beggars who lined the roadside. "Alms to the poor!" they cried, again and again.

One beggar in particular revolted him. The man was covered with sores and boils, and obviously had not washed for many a year. "Remember your duty to the poor!" the beggar whined as he followed the farmer down the road. At last the angry farmer raised his stick and struck the beggar, knocking him into a ditch. "May you wander to Rumengol for seven years," yelled the beggar in fury. "And on your return to your fireside may fresh trouble await you."

The farmer pressed on, paying no attention to the beggar's curse. But the next day, on his way home from the Pardon, he was surprised to find himself back in Rumengol after having walked several miles towards home. With an expression of disgust at his carelessness in taking the wrong path, he retraced his steps. Yet after scarcely half a league, he was again on the outskirts of Rumengol.

He slept that night under a hedge, determined to be more clearheaded tomorrow. But every path he took led him back to Rumengol. Terrified and exhausted, he continued mechanically to walk, week in, week out, month in, month out. His shoes wore out, and then he walked barefoot. His clothes fell gradually to pieces till he had nothing but a shirt left. And still, in heat and cold, in sunshine and in storm, he walked. Food became scarce, and he became lean and haggard. But still, in starvation, he walked. And for seven long years, he fled from Rumengol, only to find himself, a dozen times a day, back where he had started from.

At the end of his strength, he knew suddenly one night that he would finally be going home the next day. And so he did. No one recognized the scarecrow he had become, as he staggered into the village he had left seven years before. A group of people were gathered around the door to his house. From within, he could hear the sound of a newborn baby.

"What is happening here?" he asked someone.

"Away with you, filthy beggar!" exclaimed one of the onlookers. "And mind your own business." But another person took pity on him, and told him the good wife inside had just given birth.

"But her husband . . ." cried the farmer.

"Is at her bedside," answered someone.

"But I am her husband, you fool!" said the farmer. "Let me in!"

"Fool yourself!" said an onlooker, restraining the farmer. "Her first husband has been dead these seven years, killed by a wolf as he returned from Rumengol. This is her second husband."

In vain did the farmer tell his sad story. The villagers just laughed at him, then drove him out of town. "Is there any man more miserable than I?" wailed the farmer. And sorrowfully, he walked blindly into the forest, and was never seen nor heard of again.

April 20

The Old Woman and the Tramp

A SWEDISH TALE

There was once a tramp traveling through a forest. Houses were few and far between, and the tramp had resigned himself to finding no shelter for the night, when he saw some lights through the trees ahead. He had come across a cottage with a fire burning at the hearth. How nice it would be to warm himself there and get a bite to eat! Just then an old woman came up to him and said, "Good evening! Where do you come from?"

"South of the sun and east of the moon," replied the tramp. "And now I am on my way home."

"You must be a great traveler, then. What is your business here?"

"I seek shelter for the night."

"I thought as much, but you may as well get away from here, for my husband is not at home and my place is not an inn."

"My good woman, you should not be so cross. Humans should help each other!" said the tramp.

"And who helps me?" replied the woman. "I haven't got a morsel in the house. No, you'll have to look for shelter elsewhere." But the tramp wasn't easily discouraged, and besides he suspected the woman wasn't as poorly off as she insisted. Soon he'd persuaded her to let him stay the night.

She grudgingly offered him the floor, and the tramp, being a man of rhyme, said, "Better on the floor without sleep than suffer cold in the forest deep."

He made himself very agreeable and waited for a bit to ask for something to eat. "Where am I to get it from?" replied the woman. "I haven't eaten myself all day."

"Poor old granny," said the tramp. "You must be starving. Lend me a pot, will you?" The old woman was very curious and wondered what the tramp could offer her, so she gave him a pot.

He filled it with water, put it on the fire, took a large nail from his pocket, and dropped it in the pot.

"What's this going to be?" asked the old woman.

"Nail broth," he said. Now this was a marvel to the old woman, who thought it would be a fine meal for poor people to know how to make. The tramp told her to watch him closely as he stirred.

"This generally makes good broth," he said. "But this time it will likely be thin, as I have been using the same nail all week. If I just had a handful of oatmeal to put in, that would help."

"Well, I may have some somewhere," said the old woman, and, sure enough, she did.

The tramp added it and commented, "This broth will be good enough for company, but if I only had a few potatoes and a bit of salted beef, it would be fit for gentlefolks." And what do you think but the old woman found some of both, which the tramp put in, while she kept staring at him. He was really a wonderful man, that tramp! Imagine making a fine meal with just a nail!

All at once the tramp took out the nail and said, "Now it's ready, and we'll have a grand feast. Of course, a dram or two and a sandwich would go quite nicely with it. But what one has to go without, it's no use thinking about." Lo and behold, the woman went straight to a cupboard and produced a brandy bottle, dram glasses, butter and cheese, and smoked beef.

She was in such a merry humor at

having learned an economical way to make soup that she made a great fuss over the tramp and insisted he take her own bed to sleep for the night.

In the morning, she gave him coffee and a dram, and sent him on his way with a bright dollar piece. "And many thanks for what you have taught me. Now I shall live in comfort, since I've learned to make broth with a nail."

"Well, it isn't very difficult if only one has something good to add to it!"

The woman waved the tramp on his way, thinking how rare such a clever person was.

April 21

The Old Woman and the Tramp, Variation

"The Old Woman and the Tramp" can have a variety of endings. In the French version the traveler is a missionary who uses a stone from the fireplace to begin soup preparation. (To establish even more credibility, he even looks for a couple of additional stones to add to the soup once it is made, making it "ah, perfect.") An ax is used as the key ingredient in the Russian version of the tale. Once the soup is made the old woman asks if the traveler will eat the ax. The traveler is quick-witted; he replies that it is not "quite tender enough."

April 22

Mercury and the Sculptor

The god Mercury wanted to know how the people on earth regarded him and so he put on a disguise and went to a famous sculptor's workshop. He browsed around all of the statues and began asking the sculptor for prices. He first asked about Jupiter. "How much for the God of the Gods, Jupiter?" Mercury asked.

The sculptor replied that the statue could be purchased for a drachma.

"And how about Juno? How much for a statue of Juno?" asked Mercury, more curious still.

"Now that would be a bit more," answered the sculptor. "For Juno I would need two drachmas."

Mercury then spotted his own image. He put the question to the sculptor. "How much for this statue of Mercury then?" he asked.

"Well," said the sculptor, "if you will buy Jupiter and Juno, I'll throw in Mercury for free."

Those who care how the world values them are always disappointed.
—AESOP

April 23

The Fox and the Monkey

At the beginning of the new year, all the animals held a meeting to elect their ruler. It was a festive occasion, and on this particular night the monkey was asked to dance.

The monkey was a fool, but he danced so well and entertained so thoroughly that the animals begged for more and more. Before long, they were all so carried away by the excitement of the dancing monkey that they elected him their new ruler.

Only one animal, the fox, did not vote for the monkey. The fox knew the monkey was a fool and thought that the animals were even more foolish for electing a monkey as their ruler. The fox spent day and night fuming over the monkey king. One day while he was out pacing in the woods, he came upon a trap with some red meat in it. He ran to find the king.

The monkey was in the animal palace, dancing as usual, when the fox rushed in.

"Your Highness," the Fox said breathlessly, "I have discovered some rich treasure, treasure fit only for a king. Please come at once to receive your due."

The monkey stopped dancing and followed the fox eagerly to the forest. When the stupid and greedy monkey saw the trap with the red meat in it, he grasped for the meat—and was instantly caught.

"No true king would have been so foolish and greedy about a scrap of meat," said the fox disdainfully. "You cannot even take care of yourself, let alone the animal kingdom."

Upon his return, the fox called for a special election to replace the monkey.

The fool may rise to the top but eventually he will get caught.—AESOP

April 24

Fair Maiden Looks at the Mirror

Lily Chen was the youngest of five sisters, and her grace was so great it was said she could melt snow on the mountaintop just by thinking it should be so. One after the other, her sisters married and had children, but Lily was never interested in marriage, and because her mother and father adored her so, they did not attempt to press her into a life she did not desire. For the time, they were content to have their beloved daughter's laughter and grace fill their home.

Lily understood the world and its creatures: animals, mountains, people, trees, even invisible things like the wind and, in turn, all creatures were drawn to her. When she was just five years old and beginning to take lessons, all sorts of cats and dogs and birds would follow her to school and then home. Her tutor was a silver-haired woman, feared and hated by most children, but Lily, who saw evil in no one, did not despise the cranky old woman in any way. The tutor was disarmed by Lily's generosity of heart, and it softened her own. Lily was not simply a good person, she was goodness itself.

One night Lily had a dream. She dreamed she looked into a mirror that was oval, shaped like a hand. Instead of seeing her glossy black hair, she saw a tiger. She was not afraid of the tiger, because she was not afraid of the world or any of its creatures, but she was curious.

The next night the maiden again dreamed about the mirror, and in her dream appeared the tiger once more. It was as if the tiger emerged from her fingertips, and she felt enormous compassion for it, and stroked it gently, taming it, and then woke up. This time, she was so intrigued with her dream that she wanted to ponder it, and so she laid in bed all morning. As you can imagine, Lily rarely stayed in bed, and so her mother and father thought she was ill, and the birds peered into her window, and the cats and dogs came to her bedside, and when they asked, "Lily Chen, whatever is wrong?" she laughed and said, "Please don't worry. It is just that I have had for two nights a dream that I am attracted to and I want it to come back, because I want to know what happens next." The maiden was filled with such grace she could summon nightfall, and she did so she could sleep again, to find out what would happen in her dream.

The dream returned. And once again the maiden picked up the mirror, stroked the tiger, and in her dream the maiden looked again into the mirror, but this time she could see distantly an iron bridge. The iron bridge led to a place known and unknown to her but wherever this place was, she knew deeply that she wanted to cross the bridge, to go where it would take her.

The next morning, her mother and father, and the birds, cats, and dogs came to stay with Lily, who now had not left her bed for three days. She told them of the mirror and the tiger and the iron bridge. Lily had a faraway look in her eye, and light seemed to be in her hands and all around her, not the kind of light you see with but light you can almost feel. The maiden's mother and father worried, and the birds were still and the cats and dogs were calm. Lily Chen was becoming distant; she could think only of her dream.

On the fourth night, Lily dreamed again of looking into the mirror, and then stroking the tiger, and seeing the mirror again, from which an iron bridge emerged. On this night, a gray cloud covering the moon filled her mind's eye; she saw the moon visible, then invisible, then visible again as the cloud passed, and then she woke up. As she told her parents of her dream, their heads bent low and their eyes filled with sorrow. Lily's mother and father knew it was time for her to pass into her next life, and that their fair daughter who so loved all creatures had been given the grace to prepare. Lily's mother and father summoned all of the sisters and their children, the family all stayed with her as her light grew dim, and then each said good-bye.

On the fifth night Lily dreamed of the mirror, and the tiger she so gently stroked, and the iron bridge, and the gray cloud covering the moon, and then the fair maiden's dream ended.

Not far off, a monk struck a bell, and as its sound grew dim, Lily Chen, who was goodness itself, disappeared.

—CHRISTINE ALLISON

The Lion, the Wolf, and the Fox

A lion king, growing old, lay sick by his cave. All the beasts had come to visit him, except the fox. The wolf, thinking he had a chance to ruin the fox, accused the fox of disrespect. "Can you imagine that the fox thought so little of you that even on your deathbed he did not pay a visit?" urged the wolf to the lion. The lion, though weak, agreed that this was a grave insult and was furious.

At that very moment, the fox came in.

Sensing that the wolf had somehow maligned him, the fox quickly began to defend himself.

"Your honor, I apologize for the terrible delay, but I have been meeting with physicians all over the land in search of a cure for your illness," said the fox.

At this the lion perked up. "Well, did you find one?" he demanded to know.

"Why, yes, dear king," replied the fox. "We first must find a wolf, and remove his skin alive, and then take the skin and wrap it around you for warmth." The fox pretended to look around for a wolf, and upon seeing his enemy, pointed a paw in his direction. "My goodness, we are in luck. There's a wolf now!" he said, faking surprise.

The wolf was at once taken and skinned, whereupon the fox said to him with a smile, "You should have moved your master not to ill, but to good will." The conniving wolf, regretful too late, looked up at the fox and then died.—AESOP

Three Questions

In a far-off country, there was once a parish priest who owned a mill. And in that country there was a king who was bent on challenging the power of the church. He called the priest to his castle and said, "A priest ought to know many things. You must tell me the answer to three questions: How long is the road to heaven? Exactly how much am I worth? And what precisely am I thinking of? I will call you back here for the answers in three days, and if you cannot tell me, I will have your head."

The reverend father returned home very sad and became sadder with each succeeding day. The miller noticed his dejected air and asked him why he was troubled. "If you will but tell me your problem, sir, I am sure I can help you." So the priest told the miller how he had to answer the king's questions, how he had searched through his learned works in vain, and how he was sure the king would be chopping off his head.

"If you will give me your mill," said the miller, "I will put on your robe and appear before the king in your place." The priest, who would have given ten mills in exchange for his life, agreed.

The miller asked his wife to take all the string she had in the house and roll it into a ball. Toward the end of the string, he tied a knot for a mark. Then he set off for the king's castle.

Admitted to the king's presence, the miller-priest said, "Here I have the exact measure of the road to Heaven. If you do not believe it is exact, test it yourself." And he showed him the knot in the ball of string. "You also wished to know how much you were worth.

Well, our Lord was sold for thirty pieces of silver. I would say you are worth twenty-nine pieces. You certainly do not think your value is greater than that of our Lord's, do you?"

This display of wisdom astonished the king. The miller-priest continued, "And you wished also to be told what was on your mind. It is this: you believe that I am the priest, but I am not. And you are reflecting on these things I have just told you."

The miller told him who he was and the king was greatly impressed with his cleverness, so impressed that he sent the priest packing and installed the miller in his place.

Of course, one of the duties of a parish priest is preaching. When the time came to give a sermon, the miller climbed into the pulpit and shouted, "Like the others! Like the others!" And he kept this up for as long as one would expect a sermon to last. After church that Sunday, many parishioners complained to the king. What kind of priest was this? He spent the entire sermon shouting, "Like the others!"

"If he preached like the others," the king replied, "then I am satisfied."

Some days after this, the miller was invited to preach at a neighboring parish. This presented a problem. "Like the others!" might not satisfy them. So he took the pulpit and declared, "He who hears me will be saved and he who hears me not will be damned." Then he began to move his lips as if he was preaching and he pounded the pulpit for emphasis. But of course no one heard anything and the parishioners looked at each other in confusion. An old lady awoke just as the "sermon" was coming to an end and, rubbing her eyes, she said, "How well he preached! What a beautiful sermon!" All were astonished that she alone had heard the clergyman's words and they thought it better not to discuss the subject further.

So the miller-priest prospered, and in fact became very rich with his mill and his parish. The real priest, however, became poor and lost all his standing in the community.

Goldilocks and the Three Bears

Once there were three bears: a papa bear, a mama bear, and a baby bear. Like most bears, they enjoyed a hearty breakfast, only on this particular morning their breakfast, thick porridge (Mama's specialty), was far too hot to eat. "This porridge won't be ready to eat for days," Papa said, complaining, as usual. "Let's take a walk."

Ordinarily such an outing would be of little or no consequence, but on this particular morning a girl named Goldilocks also decided to take a walk. And that's where the trouble began.

Actually Goldilocks had not just taken a "walk," she had wandered far from home, directly contradicting her mother's wishes. Her mother had warned her that children got lost every day of the week and that she better not be one of them, but here she was, lost. She was thinking about how much trouble she was in when she came upon a tiny cottage in the woods. "I'll just go see who lives there," she said to no one in particular.

Goldilocks knocked on the door. "Hallooo . . . is anybody home?" she asked. But no one answered. And so she knocked again. "Is anybody home?" she asked. But, still, no one answered. Finally she knocked one more time. "Yoo-hoo. Anybody home?"

No one answered and so she let herself in.

Goldilocks now found herself in a charming parlor, which is sort of a front room for receiving visitors. In a row were three chairs: a big chair, a medium-sized chair, and a little chair. She plopped into the big chair. "This chair is much too big," she said, though no one was there to hear her. She tried out the medium-sized chair. "This chair is much too hard," she said, wondering who should prefer such an uncomfortable chair. She then tried the little chair. "Gosh, this chair is just right," she said. And she rocked and rocked and rocked until she broke it.

Goldilocks didn't seem too concerned about breaking the chair, mainly because she was starving. While most people might have made some attempt to put the chair back together, Goldilocks just poked around, hoping to find some food. In the dining room was a long table set for three. There were three bowls of porridge: a big bowl, a medium-sized bowl, and a little bowl. She sampled a spoonful from the big bowl. "Yuck!" she said. "This porridge is much too hot." She then took a taste from the medium-sized bowl. "Oh, no," she said. "This porridge is much too cold." At last she tried the contents of the little bowl. "This porridge is just right," she said with delight. And she ate it all up!

Goldilocks was starting to feel a little

sleepy, so she mounted the stairs to see if she could find a place to lie down. She opened the door and found a room with three beds in a row. She was starting to see a pattern. "Uh-huh," she said. "This bed is much too big." She tried the medium-sized bed and, sure enough: "This bed is much too hard," she said. Even before she tried the little bed, she knew it would be the perfect one. She climbed in, pulled the covers up to her chin, and nestled her curls into the lace pillow: "This bed is just right," she said dreamily, and with that she fell asleep.

Just about that time, the three bears returned to their tiny cottage, hungry from their morning walk. The door was wide open and Papa immediately sensed that something was wrong. "Just our luck," he began to complain. "We leave for ten minutes and someone breaks into the house." He tore into the parlor. "Somebody's been sitting in my chair," he bellowed. Mama had to admit he was right. "Somebody's been sitting in *my* chair," she said. Then baby bear made a painful discovery: "Somebody's been sitting in *my* chair *and broke it!*"

The three bears ran into the dining room, only to have their worst fears confirmed. They were hungry, but someone had beaten them to breakfast. "Somebody's been eating my porridge," roared Papa bear. "Somebody's been eating *my* porridge," echoed Mama. "Somebody's been eating *my* porridge *and ate it all up,*" lamented the littlest one.

The three bears raced up the stairs to their bedroom, where nothing was as they'd left it. Once again, the intruder had sampled it all. "Somebody's been sleeping in my bed," growled Papa bear. "Someone's been sleeping in *my* bed," said Mama bear. "Somebody's been sleeping in *my* bed," said baby bear, "and *here she is now!*" Three sets of big brown eyes stared at the sleeping child. Goldilocks stirred, and when she opened her eyes to the sight of three staring bears, she jumped out of bed, ran down the stairs, dashed through the dining room, and bolted out the parlor and into the woods. She was running so fast that before she knew it she was at her mother's doorstep. Knowing this was one adventure she would never hope to repeat, she apologized tearfully to her mother and promised that her wandering days were over.

April 28

Master of All Masters

AN ENGLISH FOLKTALE

In olden days, young men and women went to fairs to hire themselves out as servants. At one particular fair, a girl was hired as a maid by a funny-looking old gentleman. When she got to his home, he told her he wished to teach her the special names he used for things around his house.

He began by asking, "What will you call me?"

She replied, "Master or mister, or whatever you please, sir."

"You must call me 'master of all masters.' And this?" he asked, pointing to his bed.

"I would call it a bed or couch," she answered.

"No, that's my 'barnacle.' And what do you call these?" he demanded, as he gestured to his pants.

"Why, I would call them trousers, or whatever you please, sir."

"In this house they are 'squibs and crackers,' " said the odd gentleman. "And what would you call this? A cat, I suppose?" he asked as he pointed to his pet.

"Why, yes, cat or kitty, sir."

"You must call her 'white-faced simminy.' And this now," said the man, as he waved at the fire in the fireplace. "What name would you give this?"

"I would say fire or flame, or whatever you please, sir."

"From now on, it is 'hot cockalorum.' And what's this?" he asked, pointing to a bucket of water.

"Why, it's water, sir."

"No, 'pondalorum' is its name." Now the man waved his hands to include his whole house. "You would call all of this—what?"

"House or cottage, or whatever you please, sir."

"You must learn that here it's known as 'high topper mountain,' " insisted the man.

In the middle of the night, the new maid rushed to her master's room and shook him awake. She was obviously very frightened as she cried, "Master of all masters, get out of your barnacle and put on your squibs and crackers. For white-faced simminy got a spark of hot cockalorum on her tail, and unless you get some pondalorum quickly, high topper mountain will be all on hot cockalorum."

April 29

The Fisherman Who Caught the Sun

A HAWAIIAN TALE

Many years ago, the Sun used to burst forth from the ocean at dawn and race so swiftly across the sky that he would fling himself over the top of the great fire mountain and sink down again into the ocean before half a day's work was done. Sunset followed so quickly on sunrise that men began to complain, "Alas! The Sun, in his great hurry, is cheating us. We have not daylight enough to finish our hunting and fishing, to build our canoes, and gather our yams, bananas, and coconuts. Night comes on and finds our work but half done."

Then a brave fisherman rose up and said, "I shall go to the Sun and teach him to make his journey as he should.

He shall no longer race across the sky." The fisherman's friends warned him that the Sun was a powerful foe, but the man said, "I do not fear the Sun." And be began plaiting long ropes to make a snare and told his friends, "In this snare I shall catch him."

So when the Sun had run its mad race for the day and left the world to night, the fisherman got into his canoe and sailed out into the Pacific Ocean. Far he sailed and farther through the shadows, down the silvery path that the moon lit up across the dark waste of the waters. Thus he came to the very edge of the Earth, to the spot where the Sun would soon burst forth when he rose from under the ocean. And there the fisherman set his snare and waited.

The darkness began to fade into gray. Bright jewels of light flashed now and again from the ocean. Purple and rose appeared in the sky, and a small rim of the Sun peeped up to touch the white crests of the waves into fire and set all the ocean aflame. Still the fisherman waited, in his rocking canoe at the edge of the world.

In another moment a flood of gold streamed over the Earth and the whole great Sun burst forth to begin his wild race across the sky. But he had bolted straight into the snare and was tangled in its meshes. Then the fisherman rose in his canoe, and pulled the ropes tight in his hands.

The great Sun raged! He flared and flamed, but the fisherman held on fast. "Sun," he cried, undaunted, "from this day forth you shall travel at proper speed. You shall no more race across the sky. You must give a man a day that is long enough to finish his work."

The rage of the Sun grew scorching, withering, blasting. He struggled with all his might to be free. But the fisherman braced his feet, balanced his rocking canoe on the waves, and held to the ropes with a grip that would never, never yield. At last the Sun saw he had met his master, and softened his glare and stood still. "I promise," he said. "I will race no more, but will travel steadily over the sky."

When he had promised this, the fisherman set him free but he did not remove all the ropes. Some he left fastened securely at the edge of the world in order to bind the Sun to his promise.

The fisherman went home and was hailed by his people as their savior, for now they were able to finish their day's work, since the Sun kept his word.

But to this very day, when the Sun rises or sets, you may still see the ropes hanging down. Those brilliant rays that seem to anchor the Sun to the sea are in truth the meshes of that snare by which the fisherman bound him.

April 30

Daughter of the River Rhine

If you travel down the River Rhine, just above the city of Koblenz, you will see an immense rock that suggests in its shape and grandeur a throne. In a certain way, it *was* a throne, though no fair royalty reigned there. For upon the rock once lived a water nymph, whose beauty and evil brought thousands of men to their death.

Her throne, the Lorelei Rock, is where this story takes place.

The Lorelei Rock was positioned so that men, even at a great distance, could see the luminous nymph. Her ivory skin, white-gold hair, and pale pink lips were renowned throughout the world, and from every point fishermen and sailors would come to hear her sweet song and inhale her fragrance, which rode over the tops of the waves to their crude wooden boats.

Many tried to resist her, but none succeeded.

The son of Count Palatine thought he would be different. His name was Ronald and he was a courageous young man who had triumphed in war and found foolish the claims that the water nymph could not be overcome. It seemed absurd to Ronald that so many from his kingdom had died because of "a song and sweet smell." Privately he also liked the idea that he might capture the nymph and take her for his wife. So he asked for his father's blessing to pursue her.

His father, though wary, agreed.

Ronald's plan was simple. He would hire some fishermen to take him to the Lorelei Rock, climb it, and seize the beautiful nymph. After making arrangements, Ronald and two fishermen set out in a sturdy boat. As they approached a curve in the river where stood the Lorelei Rock, Ronald saw the nymph for the first time. She was poised high on the rock, combing her silken hair and singing her faint melody. Ronald's senses began to drift, and soon all he could think of was getting to the nymph.

"Faster," he urged the fishermen. "Row faster, I must see her now."

The fishermen were not fools. They kept their pace steady and slow. But the count's son was bursting with desire. "Faster," he demanded.

Unfortunately, Ronald was possessed. All at once he jumped out of the boat and attempted to swim to the rock, but like thousands of others, was swept away by the currents and his own madness.

The count, upon hearing his son had drowned, was broken-hearted. He was also in a rage. "The water nymph must go if it takes my entire army," pledged the count.

He sent five of his mightiest soldiers to capture the nymph of Lorelei. Cleverly they approached the rock in the dark so they could see nothing and would not be tempted by the nymph's beauty. When they were almost to the top, she spotted them. "Look at me and die," she said, cursing their cleverness.

The soldiers looked away so they would not so much as catch a glimpse of the nymph's face.

"Come down or you will perish like the thousands of men you destroyed," yelled one of the soldiers.

"You fools, you cannot touch me," hissed back the nymph. "I am the daughter of the Rhine. No ill can come to me for the river will kill you first."

With that she tore the pearls off her neck and told the current to take each pearl to her father to let him know she was in danger.

Within minutes the currents turned into a whirlwind, and a stallion made of foam emerged and carried the nymph down the river and out of sight.

The nymph did not return. When the soldiers told the count she had fled, he was pleased, though still sorrowful over the loss of his son.

MAY

May 1

MAY DAY

Little Ida's Flowers

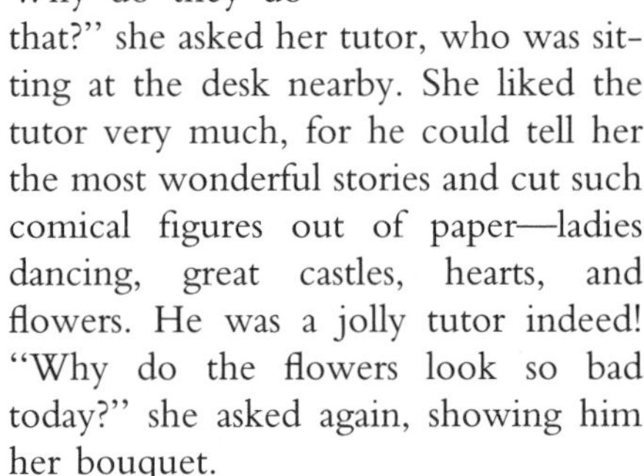

"My poor flowers are quite dead!" said little Ida. "They were so pretty last night, and now all the leaves hang faded and withered. Why do they do that?" she asked her tutor, who was sitting at the desk nearby. She liked the tutor very much, for he could tell her the most wonderful stories and cut such comical figures out of paper—ladies dancing, great castles, hearts, and flowers. He was a jolly tutor indeed! "Why do the flowers look so bad today?" she asked again, showing him her bouquet.

"Do you know what is the matter with those flowers?" said the tutor. "They were at a ball last night and that is why they hang their heads so!"

"But the flowers cannot dance!" said little Ida.

"Yes, indeed, they can," replied the tutor. "When it is dark and we others are asleep, they jump merrily about. They have a ball almost every night."

"May children go to that ball?"

"Oh, yes," said the tutor. "Especially the tiny daisies and lilies of the valley."

"Where do the most beautiful flowers go to dance?" asked little Ida.

"You have been outside the town gates near the great castle, have you not, where the king lives during the summer, and where the beautiful garden is? You may be quite sure that out there some very wonderful balls take place."

"I was in that garden yesterday with my mother," said Ida. "But there were no leaves on the trees and not a single flower left. Where are they? Last summer I saw so many."

"They are inside the castle," the tutor told her. "As soon as the king and all the court ladies and gentlemen return to the city, the flowers immediately run up out of the garden and into the castle, and there they have such merry times! You ought to see! The two most beautiful roses seat themselves on the throne. They are the king and queen. Then all the flowers come in and the ball begins. The blue violets make believe they are naval cadets, and dance with the hyacinths and crocuses, whom they call young ladies. The tulips are elderly ladies, who watch over the younger set."

"But does no one punish the flowers for dancing in the king's castle?" asked Ida.

"No one really knows anything about it," said the tutor. "Of course a steward lives in the castle during the winter, but as soon as the flowers hear his heavy keys jingling, they become very quiet and hide themselves. 'It smells like flowers here!' says the old steward, but he cannot see a single one."

"But then I should not be able to see them either!" cried Ida.

"Oh, yes," said the tutor. "When you go out there again just be sure to remember to look through the window and you will certainly see them. That is what I did today. A long yellow Easter lily was lounging on the sofa. She was one of the court ladies."

"Do the flowers in the botanical gardens also go there? Can they travel a long distance?"

"Of course! They can fly if they want to. Have you not seen the beautiful butterflies, some red, some yellow, some white, that look so much like flowers. That is what they once were, but they leaped from their stalks high

in the air, and beat with their leaves as if they were little wings, and away they flew! And because they behaved themselves nicely, they were given permission to fly about in the daytime, too. They did not have to go home again and sit quiet on their stalks. And thus the leaves at last became real wings."

The tutor had not noticed that Ida's governess, who tended to grumble a great deal about the tutor, had walked in the room while he was talking. "What nonsense to put into a child's head!" the governess said. "Nothing but stupid fancies!"

But Ida, who had been laughing and clapping her hands a moment before, did not find what the tutor had told her fanciful at all.

—HANS CHRISTIAN ANDERSEN

May 2

The Wild Swans, Part 1

Far away, where the swallows fly in winter, lived a king who had eleven sons and one daughter, Elise. The eleven princes went to school, where they wrote upon golden slates and used diamond pencils. They could recite just as well by heart as they could read from books. Their sister sat upon a little footstool made of looking glass, and she had a picture book that had cost half the kingdom to buy. Oh, they were very happy children. But it was not to last.

Their mother being dead, the children's father remarried, and to a very wicked queen who was not at all kind to her stepchildren. She sent Elise into the country to live with a peasant couple, and it did not take her long to make the king believe so many bad things of the boys that he no longer cared for them.

"You shall fly out into the world as great voiceless birds" was the curse of the wicked queen. But her spell was not quite as bad as she would have liked, for the princes were turned into eleven beautiful wild swans. With strange, sad cries, they flew out of the palace into the forest.

Poor Elise spent many years in the peasants' cottage. The days went by, one just like another, except that Elise grew more and more beautiful. When she was fifteen, she was summoned to the castle, and when the wicked queen saw how lovely she was, her anger was great. She would have turned Elise into a swan too, but she did not dare, for the king was expecting to see her.

Instead, the queen put toads in Elise's bath. These toads were cursed, and were to make Elise as homely and stupid as they were. But when Elise got in the bath, the toads were transformed into scarlet poppies, for the girl was too pure and innocent for the enchantment to have any power over her.

The wicked queen then grabbed Elise and put evil-smelling ointments on her face and tangled her beautiful hair. The king did not even recognize her and cast her out of the castle, saying she could not possibly be his daughter.

Poor Elise wept, thinking sadly of her eleven brothers, who were the only ones who could have helped her. Her determination to find them grew as she made her way back to the forest. Night had fallen and she had quite lost her way, so she said her evening prayers and went to sleep.

May 3

The Wild Swans, Part 2

When Elise awoke the next morning, she met an old woman who gave her something to eat from her basket of berries. Elise asked if she had ever happened to see eleven princes ride through the woods. "No," said the old woman. "But yesterday I saw eleven swans with golden crowns upon their heads flying towards the sea."

It was several more days travel to the sea, and Elise was not at all sure that there was a connection between the swans and her missing brothers. But she trudged on, and when she got there, the sight of the rolling waves brought her great peace. "I will be as untiring as the sea," she thought. "And my heart tells me that sometime the sea will bear me to my beloved brothers."

As the sun was setting that night, Elise saw eleven white swans headed towards the shore. Elise hid behind a bush and watched as the sun sank below the horizon and the swans suddenly shed their feathers and became eleven handsome young men. She recognized the princes at once and their reunion was most joyful.

"We have to fly about in the guise of swans as long as the sun is up," said the eldest brother. "When it goes down, we regain our human shapes."

"Is there nothing that can be done to free you from this spell?" cried Elise.

"Oh, it would be much too hard," the brothers said. "For you would have to take the stinging nettle, which can only be gathered in churchyards, and crush it with your feet to make flax. From this flax you must weave eleven coats of mail with long sleeves. If you throw these coats of mail over us, the charm will be broken. But if you speak once after you begin this work, even if it takes years, we shall perish. Our lives will hang on your tongue." After telling her this, they had to leave for the lonely rock in the sea that was their home in exile.

Elise was thankful to hear that there was a way she could free her brothers and resolved to begin at once. She made a home for herself in a cave and gathered many horrid nettles with her delicate hands. They burst like fire and blistered her badly, but she suffered it willingly for her brothers.

Elise had finished but one coat of mail when a hunting horn sounded nearby. A group of huntsmen, led by their king, came upon Elise and her bundle of nettles. He was struck by her loveliness and he was the most handsome of kings. "How came you here, beautiful child?" he asked.

Elise shook her head and dared not speak. Her brothers' lives depended on her silence. "Come with me," the king said. "You cannot stay here." He lifted her upon his horse and she wept, but he took her to his castle just the same.

At the castle he created a chamber for her that was like the cave. The bundle of flax lay there and the finished coat hung on the wall. She kissed his hand in gratitude, but could not confide in him.

His love for Elise grew and he married her, despite the protests of his archbishop, who believed her to be a witch. Elise was also growing very fond of him, yet she could not tell him of her love. More than a year passed by, and Elise was almost finished with her labors. Meanwhile, however, the archbishop had succeeded in convincing the king that his bride was a sorceress and must be executed. Elise could not say a word in her defense.

Ten shirts had been completed and the eleventh was halfway done as Elise was led to her execution. Just then eleven wild swans perched upon the executioner's cart and Elise hastily threw the shirts over the swans, who immediately became eleven princes. The youngest brother, though, still had a swan's wing, as his shirt lacked a sleeve. "Now I may speak!" Elise cried. "I am innocent."

Elise fainted at these words for the strain on her had been terrible, but the eldest brother explained their curse and Elise's suffering to the king, who loved her now all the more. Elise's beloved brothers were given honored positions in the kingdom, and all lived happily together for many, many years.

—HANS CHRISTIAN ANDERSEN

May 4

The Fox and the Stork

One day a fox invited a stork to dinner, which is odd when you think of it. Anyway, the fox was a bit stingy and not at all a good host, and so he offered his guest some thin soup in a shallow dish.

The stork had a long, thin beak. It was impossible for her to get even a drop of the soup. So while the fox lapped up the soup the stork just sat there. "Do you not care for the soup?" inquired the fox slyly. "Is it not seasoned to your liking?"

The stork said little. But she was thinking hard while the fox ate up all of the soup.

"Now I must repay your kindness and have you dine at my home," said the stork with a twinkle in her eye.

The fox agreed to dine at the stork's home the following day. When the fox arrived he found to his dismay that dinner was served in a tall, long-necked vessel. The stork easily inserted her beak into the vessel and lapped up the thick soup. But the fox, with his short snout, could not get a drop. Unable to enjoy the dinner, the fox excused himself, thinking that he could hardly fault the stork for her trick. The bird had outfoxed the fox!

May 5

The Magic Horns

A TALE FROM AFRICA

This story begins with a sad little boy who lives in a village in Africa filled with huts, like mushrooms on a golden plain. Women and girls are busy making pots and weaving and pounding grain. Children are playing in the veldt, while men are readying for the hunt. Look closer: you can see him. He sits alone.

When the boy was born his mother died and since then he has been alone. Watch him: when he sees the children pulling at their mothers' legs or wrapped in their strong brown arms, he feels hungry . . . hungry for a mother. Hoping one will take him, he tries to please the women of the village. He brings a gift of firewood to one. He weaves scraps of string for the next. The women yawn and shrug their shoulders. They ignore him.

The boy cannot find a mother among these people. So he slips out of his hut one night, steals one of the bulls, and disappears from the village.

The boy and the bull travel through the dark blue night. In the morning they rest. They are startled: a herd of cattle led by another bull are heading their way. The boy's bull warns him, "This bull will challenge me."

There is a terrible fight. Fortunately, the boy's bull is triumphant.

The boy and the bull travel on through the golden veldt. At the end of the day, another bull appears, and again the boy's bull is challenged. But the boy's bull is tired from the earlier battle and the long day's journey. This time the boy's bull warns him, "I am very tired and it is likely I will be killed. Do not be sad for I will still be with you." The boy's bull gives him instructions. "If I die, you must cut off my horns. Keep them with you and touch them whenever you need anything. Whatever you ask for, you will receive."

The boy's bull fights as hard as he can, but he cannot win the struggle with the second bull. When he finally collapses, the boy weeps for his friend. Our boy is sad. He has lost the only companion he ever had. But he remembers what the bull said, and carefully re-

moves the horns from his friend's dead form.

As the day turns to night, the boy comes upon a village. He goes to the first hut and asks a stranger if he might spend the night. "You may stay in my hut but we have no food to offer," said the stranger.

The boy says, "Food will not be a problem." He touches one of his horns and instantly a feast is set out between the stranger and the boy.

The stranger eats the food greedily. Seeing that the horns were magical, he stays awake while the boy sleeps, and secretly exchanges an old pair of bull's horns for the boy's magic horns.

In the morning, the boy thanks the stranger and leaves, carrying the wrong horns!

The stranger, meanwhile, gets straight to the task of asking the magical horns for everything he can think of. This man is greedy. He asks for food and riches and jewels and clothing, but the horns do not respond. When he realizes the horns obey only the young boy, the stranger becomes frightened, thinking the boy might have dangerous powers.

The boy is still on his journey and getting tired. He touches his horns to ask for a blanket to sleep on. But nothing happens. He realizes he has the wrong horns. The stranger tricked him! The boy journeys back to the stranger's hut and demands his horns.

"Take them, take them," whimpers the stranger, who flees in fear of the boy. The boy shrugs, and touches his horn to ask for some food to eat. He sleeps in the stranger's hut again that night.

The boy decides to trek back to his own village. "At least I know the people there," he thinks to himself. The boy is sad. By sunset, he is back in his home village.

He asks for some water.

"Get out of here, you filthy orphan," says one villager, waving him away.

The boy sees a woman and asks for some water.

"I have no water to spare for a beggar in rags," she says.

The boy remembers his precious horns, and touches them, and asks to be clean and to have fine clothes.

At once, he is fresh and dressed in finery!

Dressed as someone who seems important, the boy calls again on the villagers. This time they welcome him with figs and drink and salted meats. He appears so wealthy that he is treated like royalty, and eventually he is given the most beautiful girl in the village to marry.

The boy never forgets who he is. He lives to be an old man. Whenever an orphan or a beggar comes to him, he opens his home and cares for them, using his magic horns. He is happy at last.

May 6

King of the Cats

The sexton's wife had been waiting for her husband for hours. She and her big black cat, Old Tom, made a fine pair, half asleep in front of the fireplace, shifting into wakefulness every now and then, seeing no one, then drifting back asleep.

Suddenly the door burst open and the sexton came rushing in. He had a crazed expression on his face and he was asking, "Where's Tommy Tildrum? Where's Tommy Tildrum?" in such a wild way that both his wife and the cat looked at him to know what on earth was the matter.

"Oh, but I've had such an adventure," said the sexton. "I was digging away at old Mr. Foryce's grave when I took a break and I guess I must have dropped asleep, waking up only when I heard a cat's meow."

"Meow!" said Old Tom in answer.

"Yes, just like that. When I looked over the edge of the grave, can you guess what I saw?"

"Oh, tell," said the sexton's wife eagerly.

"Why, nine cats all dressed like Old Tom here. They were carrying a small coffin—a cat's coffin!—and every third step they took they all cried meow."

"Meow!" said Old Tom again.

"Yes," said the sexton. "Just like that! Well, anyway, the cats, you see, were walking towards me, closer and closer, and their eyes were all beaming green light and the closer they got, the more fear I could feel because it wasn't right what was happening, something felt like it wasn't right. They kept making that sound, meow. . . ."

"Meow," said Old Tom again.

"Yes, you've got it, old cat," said the sexton. "Then they all came and stood opposite Mr. Foryce's grave, where I was standing, and they stopped and they all stared at me. But wait, look at Old Tom: he's staring at me just the way they did."

"Go on, go on, tell your story, old man," said the sexton's wife.

"Where was I?" he asked. "Oh, yes, they all stood staring at me and then one of them stepped forward and said, 'Tell Tom Tildrum that Tim Toldrum's dead,' and that's why I burst in here asking you whether you knew a Tom Tildrum. How can I tell Tom Tildrum that Tim Toldrum is dead if I don't even know who he is?"

"Ahhhh!" screamed the wife just then. "Look at Old Tom, look at old Tom."

And well he might look, for the cat was all puffed up and staring strangely at the sexton. The truth had hit Old Tom: "What—old Tim is dead! Then *I* am King of the Cats!"

Old Tom rushed up the chimney and was never seen again.

May 7

King of the Cats, Variations

Many folktales use cats as central characters. The many variations of this tale focus mainly on the replacement of different whimsical names for the cats: in England, "Molly Dixon is dead," in the Ozarks, "Old Kitty Rollins is dead." Other names replace Tom and Tim with Dildrum and Doldrum.

May 8

The Astronomer

An astronomer used to walk out every night to gaze among the stars. It happened one night as he was wandering through the outskirts of the city, his thoughts wrapped up in the skies, that he fell into a well. The astronomer hollered and yelled like a madman until a young man heard his cries and ran to help him.

Listening to his story, the young man said, "Dear astronomer, I applaud your desire to solve life's riddles but while you are trying to pry into the mysteries of the heavens, you might pay more attention to what's right under your feet!"—AESOP

May 9

The Imp Tree, Part 1

AN OLD ENGLISH FOLKTALE

King Orfeo of Winchester had many virtues, but he was most admired for the love and devotion he had for his wife, Queen Heurodis. The king and queen were an inspiration, and for years there was a remarkable peace.

One hot summer afternoon, the beloved queen was walking in the orchard and became very drowsy. She lay down under an imp tree and fell asleep.

While she slept, a dream entered her being. She dreamed that two knights came to her side, demanding that she meet with their lord and king. In her dream, the queen, of course, refused. Soon after, the knights returned, accompanied by their king. He was the King of the Fairies! And, oh, what followed: in his train were a thousand knights and ladies dressed in pure white riding snow-white steeds. The king wore a crown that was studded with every kind of jewel and by his side was a blazing white horse. The horse seemed prepared for some unknown rider, for the saddle was empty.

The queen now dreamed that she was commanded to sit on the magnificent white horse. This filled her heart with fear and excitement, but the fear dissolved as she and the Fairy King began their procession through the fair country. Oh, if you could see the country of the fairies! It is filled with banks of flowers and pleasant waters. On a green terrace overlooking many orchards and rose gardens stands the Fairy King's palace. The Fairy King showed these things to Heurodis, and then gently returned her to the imp tree. But as he started off, he made her promise to return to the tree at the same time the next day—or he would kill her.

Heurodis fled back to her king and when she told Orfeo of her dream, he was furious. He swore that the next day he would post thousands of soldiers around the imp tree to protect his beloved from the Fairy King. When the time came, the king and his knights stood around the queen like a ring of living steel but, in spite of all this, King Orfeo and his knights were foiled. Lovely Heurodis was snatched from them before their very eyes. They did not even see where the queen was taken, and King Orfeo was left reeling with anger and despair—and no queen.

May 10

The Imp Tree, Part 2

It all happened so quickly that King Orfeo still could not believe that his beloved queen had been stolen by the Fairy King. He searched the upper earth from end to end, but found no trace of her footsteps. The once proud man became a man defeated. He removed his crown and left his palace at Winchester with only his harp in hand. Often he wandered the forest, sorrowing for his beloved and playing on his harp. He sang with such beauty and grief that the foxes and bears and squirrels would gather around him to give his heart comfort. They were enchanted with his song and moved to pity by his brokenness.

One day the weary king heard a rustle in the forest and then the sound of trumpets. He followed the sound and came upon the Fairy King, followed by his knights, their swords drawn as if they were off to war. He then saw sixty lovely ladies riding on their pure white steeds, each with a falcon in her bare hand. In the midst of them, to his wondrous eyes, was his beloved queen, Heurodis!

Orfeo was determined to follow them; he was determined not to lose his queen again. They rode for miles and miles until they came to the fairest country he had ever seen. In the midst of it all stood a palace of a hundred towers, with walls of crystal and windows coped and arched with gold. The walls of the palace were embedded with emeralds and rubies and sapphires and diamonds, and in the sun the kingdom was filled with rainbow light. Orfeo was overwhelmed.

Cautiously, the tattered Orfeo entered the palace hall, where he found the Fairy King on his throne. When the Fairy King saw the stranger, he was enraged. The king's fury filled the palace like a terrible storm, and Orfeo did not know what to do, so he began to play his harp. As he played, the Fairy King calmed down. He had known beauty in the land and in his subjects, but he had never heard music like this and he was entranced. As the Fairy King swayed to the sound in delight, another figure entered the palace hall.

It was Heurodis! She had heard the sweet sound of Orfeo's harp and she knew her true king had come to take her home. Just as she came upon her husband, the Fairy King asked Orfeo what he might offer in return for the sound of such sweet music. To this, Orfeo called out:

Heurodis!

The Fairy King obliged and gave the queen back to Orfeo, and Orfeo and Heurodis, having been apart so long, were overjoyed. Hand in hand they walked together through the wilderness back to Winchester, where they lived and reigned together in peace and happiness, never again to rest beneath the fateful imp tree.

May 11

The Face in the Mirror

A JAPANESE FOLKTALE

On their wedding day, a young Japanese farmer decided to give his wife a gift. The gift was a mirror, and it delighted his wife because she'd never seen her reflection before except in the waters of a pond or stream. When she looked in the mirror and saw her lovely face, the young woman laughed with joy. The farmer was joyful, too; he knew he was fortunate to have such a wife.

After a few years, the young wife gave birth to a baby girl. But the birth was difficult and the young woman died. The farmer, grief-stricken, put all of his wife's belongings away, including her beloved mirror.

The mirror lay in a chest for many years.

The daughter grew, and with each year she looked more and more like her mother. One day, when she was almost a woman, her father took her to a quiet garden and told her about her mother and the mirror she so loved. The girl was curious and could not contain herself. She dug into her mother's old belongings and found the mirror. She lifted the mirror in front of her face and looked deeply into it: "Father, father, come," she cried. "It is mother. Her face is in the mirror."

The face in the mirror was the girl's own, but her father said not one word.

He could not speak. Tears were streaming down his face.

May 12

The Hare and the Tortoise

The hare, quite frankly, was a braggart. He bragged about many things, and on this occasion he was bragging to a gathering of forest animals about how fast he could run.

"I am faster than any of you," he said with a sneer. The animals rolled their eyes as if to say, "Here he goes again." And indeed, the hare fully intended to press his case until he got a rise out of one of his fellows. "Ha, ha, ha. Ho, ho, ho. I am the best, yes, I am the best. Why doesn't someone challenge me?" the hare said. "What are you . . . *scared*?"

The animals were not scared but they were sure tired of listening to this hare. Still no one said anything. Finally, the tortoise said simply, "I am not scared. I will challenge you." The animals turned to the tortoise in amazement. He was not exactly famous for his speed.

The hare was very amused. "This is a great joke," he said. "Why, I could run circles around you the whole way," he said, cracking up again.

"Right, right," said the Tortoise. "Shall we begin?"

The hare agreed so the course was fixed and the start was made.

The hare was an exceptional runner and he darted out of sight. He ran a few laps and then, to insult the tortoise, he lay down to take a nap. It was a warm afternoon and the hare fell into a deep sleep.

The tortoise was very much awake. He made tiny, painstaking steps, plodding in the sun without complaint. When the hare suddenly awoke from his nap, the tortoise had just crossed the finish line.

The hare broke into a frenzied sprint, but it was too late.

Slow and steady wins the race.—AESOP

Cornelia's Jewels

A STORY FOR MOTHER'S DAY

It was a bright morning in the old city of Rome many hundreds of years ago. In a vine-covered summer house in a beautiful garden, two boys were standing. They were looking at their mother and her friend, who were walking among the flowers and trees.

"Did you ever see so handsome a lady as our mother's friend?" asked the younger boy, holding his tall brother's hand. "She looks like a queen."

"Yet she is not as beautiful as our mother," said the elder boy. "She has a fine dress and many jewels, it's true, but her face is not noble and kind. It is our mother who is like a queen."

"That's true," said the other. "There is no woman in Rome who is so much like a queen as our own mother."

Soon their mother, Cornelia, came down the walk to speak with them. She was dressed in a plain white robe. Her arms and feet were bare, as was the custom in those days; and no rings or chains glittered about her hands and neck. For her crown, long braids of soft brown hair were coiled about her head; and her tender smile lit up her noble face as she looked into her sons' eyes.

"Boys," she said, "I have something to tell you."

They bowed before her, as Roman boys were taught to do, and said, "What is it, Mother?"

"You are to dine with us today, here in the garden, and then my friend is going to show us that wonderful casket of jewels of which you have heard so much."

The brothers looked shyly at their mother's friend. Was it possible she had still other rings besides those on her fingers? Could she have other gems besides those which sparkled in the chains about her neck?

When the simple outdoor meal was over, a servant brought the casket from the house. The lady opened it. Ah, how those jewels dazzled the eyes of the wondering boys. There were ropes of pearls, white as milk and smooth as satin; heaps of shining rubies, red as glowing coals; sapphires as blue as the sky that summer day; and diamonds that flashed and sparkled like the sunlight.

The brothers looked long at the gems. "Ah," whispered the younger, "if only our mother could have such wonderful things."

At last, however, the casket was closed and carefully carried away.

"Is it true, Cornelia, that you have no jewels?" asked her friend. "Is it true, as I have heard it whispered, that you are poor?"

"No, I am not poor," answered Cornelia. As she spoke, she drew her two sons to her side. "Here are my jewels. They are worth more than all of those beautiful gems."

The boys never forgot their mother's pride and love and care and in the after years, when they had become great men in Rome, they often thought of this afternoon in the garden. And the world still likes to hear the story of Cornelia's jewels.

—ADAPTED BY JAMES BALDWIN

May 14

Five Peas in a Pod

Each one of us sees the world differently. Even peas. Yes! Even peas. Once there were five peas who lived together in a shell that was shaped like a crescent moon. The peas were green. The shell was green. And so the peas believed the whole world was green, for what did they know except what they saw?

The sun shone and made the shell warm. The rain came and made the shell soggy and cool. Inside, the five little peas were getting bigger and bigger.

One day one of the peas said, "This can't be what life is all about. I, for one, am very uncomfortable squeezed up next to all of you plump little peas. Surely there is more room outside of this green shell." But the other peas just looked at him and shrugged.

Pretty soon, the shell started turning yellow. The peas became yellow. The peas were very puzzled. "Why has our world turned yellow? This is very strange. Strange, indeed!"

Then one day the peas were jolted by an enormous tug. Their little shell was torn right off the vine and they were put into a pocket, although they had no idea it was a pocket. They just knew that suddenly they were rolling this way and that way.

"What has happened?" they wondered. "And what will happen next?"

Just as they were wondering about their future, a loud cracking noise startled them, and their shell was strung open and the five little peas rolled out into the bright sunlight. They were nearly blinded! A little boy, who of course appeared to be a giant to the tiny peas, rolled them around in his warm, sweaty hand and stared at them with huge brown eyes. "I can use these peas for my pea shooter," they heard him say. Suddenly one of the peas was plucked up and placed in a narrow tube. A strong wind came and the pea was flying through the air. "I'm flying, I'm flying," he called out. "Catch me if you can!"

Then a second pea was hurled through the air. "To the sun and beyond," he cried with joy as he was sent flying.

Pea after pea went for its grand ride, the great adventure of its life. When the last pea was shot from the pea shooter, it bounced off an old sill on an attic window and fell into a little crack filled with moss and soil. The moss closed around him and there he lay. Stuck.

"Oh, dear. This is terrible," said the little pea. "I liked it better when I was flying."

But the little pea was never going to fly again. The moss and the soil now owned him and were part of him, and soon the pea fell into a deep sleep and dreamed a beautiful dream about becoming a lovely plant, with tender leaves and sweet blossoms.

Now in the attic there lived a woman and her little daughter. The little girl had been sick for a long long time. Each day, the woman worked for hours and hours to earn enough money to buy food and medicine for her precious child. She tried in every way to make her daughter strong again.

One morning it was spring. The sun was shining through the attic window and a sunbeam made a warm place on the floor. The mother pushed the little girl's bed closer to the window so she could look and breathe some fresh spring air.

"Mother, Mother, come quickly," the little girl said. "There's a little green thing at the window. See it swaying in the wind?" "Why," said her mother, "that's a little pea that has taken root in the moss and is putting out green leaves. Let's give it some water. It can be your very own garden."

Every day the little girl watched her pea vine grow and it seemed to nod and smile at the girl as if to say, "This warm sun will make you grow, too." Bit by bit the girl seemed to feel better and grow stronger. As the little vine grew, so did the child. One day, from a tiny bud, the pea plant made a beautiful pink blossom, and on that day the little girl's cheeks turned a rosy pink, too.

At last one day the girl got out of bed and began to walk. It was the first time in a whole year that she had been out of her bed. She leaned out the window and gently placed her cheek against a blossom on her pea vine. "You made me well," she whispered.

The little pea vine could not speak, but it made a whiff of sweet perfume to let the child know that it heard her. "This is even better than flying," the little pea thought to himself. And he looked at the world and tried to see everything he could see. Then he drifted back into his beautiful dream.

—HANS CHRISTIAN ANDERSEN

May 15

The Gingerbread Man

An old woman and an old man lived a quiet life in a quaint village. The two were happy in most ways; the old man spent most of his time in the garden, and the old woman spent most of her time baking delicious cakes and cookies.

On this day the old woman had decided to bake gingerbread and had a bit of ginger dough left over. On a lark, she formed the dough into the shape of a little man. She gave the little man arms and legs, and used raisins to make two eyes and a nose and a little mouth that curved up into a mischievous smile.

The old woman popped the cookie man into the oven. After a while, she heard something rattling at the oven door. She opened it and out popped the little gingerbread man she had made!

Before she knew it, he had scampered out the kitchen door.

"Run, run, as fast as you can, You can't catch me, I'm the gingerbread man," called out the gingerbread man.

The old woman chased him into the garden, where her husband was digging. The old man put down his hoe and joined in the chase, but they could not keep up with the speedy gingerbread man. "Run, run, just as fast as you can, you can't catch me, I'm the gingerbread man!" As the gingerbread man ran down the dirt path he passed a cow. The cow called out, "Stop! I want to eat you!" But the gingerbread man laughed and said, "I've run from an old woman and an old man. You can't catch me, I'm the gingerbread man."

The cow joined the old woman and the old man in pursuit. Soon they all passed a horse. "Halt!" called out the horse. "I want to eat you." But the gingerbread man just gave him a wink and said, "I've run from an old woman, an old man, and a cow. Run, horse, run, as fast as you can. You can't catch me, I'm the gingerbread man!"

Now the gingerbread man was followed by the old woman, the old man, the cow, and the horse. The odd parade now passed a crowd of haymakers. The haymakers were hungry, and they also were curious to hear a cookie that could talk, especially when it said, "I've run from an old woman, an old man, a cow, and a horse. Run, haymakers, run, as fast as you can. You can't catch me, I'm the gingerbread man."

The haymakers joined the odd chorus of men and women and beasts, all chasing after the little cookie. The gingerbread man ran through the fields, and there he passed a fox. The gingerbread man was very full of himself now, and did not know how sly a fox can be. He called out, "Run, run, as fast as you can. You can't catch me, I'm the gingerbread man." The fox wanted to eat the cookie as much as anyone, but he was very clever. He replied, "But why would I want to catch a gingerbread man? *I* only wish you well."

The gingerbread man suddenly had to stop because he came to a wide, fast-moving river. The fox saw that the gingerbread man—followed by an old woman, an old man, a cow, a horse, and some haymakers—was in trouble, so he went to the gingerbread man's side and offered to help. "Here, jump on my back and I will carry you across the river and away from those who would harm you," the sly fox offered.

The gingerbread man had no choice, so he jumped on the fox's back and the fox began to swim. They reached the middle of the river, where the water was deep. "Can you stand on my head, gingerbread man?" the fox said. "Hurry, otherwise you will get wet!"

The gingerbread man moved forward to the fox's head, but the current began to move swiftly and the gingerbread man was close to drowning.

"Quick," called the fox, "move to the top of my nose." The gingerbread man complied, straddling the fox's long snout. But when the two reached the bank at the far side of the river, the fox tossed back his head and the gingerbread man was thrown up and down—right into the open mouth of the fox! "Oh, no, I'm a quarter gone!" he said, slipping down the fox's throat. "Oh, no, I'm half gone!" he said, his voice fading. "Oh, no . . ." the gingerbread man said. Then silence. The fox enjoyed the cookie immensely, and the gingerbread man was never heard from again.

May 16

The Gingerbread Man, Variation

The best-known version of "The Gingerbread Man" (retold here) was first published in *St. Nicholas* magazine, which brazenly propounded the idea that children's literature didn't have to be didactic or inspirational to be worthwhile; it could (and perhaps, should) simply be fun.

"The Gingerbread Man" *is* simply fun and various cultures have replicated the story using native baked goods, such as Johnny-Cakes, Scottish bannocks, Russian buns, or American pancakes.

The gingerbread man wails, "Oh, no, I'm a quarter gone!", the runaway bannock's last words are "Oh, ye're nippin's, ye're nippin's," and the pancake doesn't even get a parting shot—he is devoured in a single gulp.

May 17

The Origin of the Mole

A RUSSIAN FOLKTALE

Once upon a time, a rich man and a poor man had a field in common, and they sowed it with the same seed at the same time. The poor man's crop flourished, but the rich man's seed did not grow. So the rich man tried to claim that part of the field where the grain had sprung up, saying, "Look now! It's my seed that has prospered and not yours!"

The poor man protested, to no avail. The rich man told him, "Come into the field at dawn tomorrow and we will ask God to judge between us."

While the poor man went home, the rich man dug a deep trench in the poor man's part of the field. Then he called his son and made him lie down in the trench. "Look now, my son! When I come here tomorrow morning and ask whose field this is, you must pretend you are God and say that it is the rich man's."

He covered his son with a blanket of straw and left for home. Many people from the village went to the field in the morning, and once they were assembled, the rich man cried, "Speak, O God! Whose field is this? The rich man's or the poor man's?"

"The rich man's! The rich man's!" cried a voice from the middle of the field.

But God himself was among those gathered there and He said, "Do not listen to that voice, for the field is truly the poor man's." Then God told the people how they had been deceived and said to the rich man's son, "Stay where you are and sit beneath the earth all of your days, so long as the sun is in the sky."

And from that moment on, the rich man's son became a mole, and that is why the mole always flees the light of day.

May 18

The Donkey and the Lap Dog

A donkey and a dog belonged to the same master. The donkey was tied up in the stable and had plenty of corn and hay to eat, and was as well off as a donkey could be. But the dog received even better treatment. As he was always sporting about, hugging and kissing his master in a thousand amusing ways, the dog had become a great favorite and was even permitted to sit in his master's lap.

From the donkey's viewpoint, the whole thing was terribly unfair. All day the donkey was drawing wood and all night he worked in the mill. Certainly he was surviving, but his life was hard and it grieved him to see the dog living in such luxury and ease.

One day he had an idea. He broke from his halter and went rushing into the hall, kicking and prancing about in a strange attempt to act just like the little dog. He swished his tail and frolicked about, but he upset the table where his master was having dinner, breaking it in two and crushing all of the plates and bowls. Stupidly, he kept it up and would not stop until he jumped into his master's lap, pawing him with his rough-shod feet.

Seeing their master in terrible danger, the servants interfered. Once they released their master from the donkey's hugs and kisses, they beat the donkey with forks and knives. The donkey, wincing from the attack, knew he had made a foolish calculation. In anguish he cried, "I have betrayed myself and my lot, and now I will surely be cast out. Why did I pretend to be someone I was not?"—AESOP

May 19

The Comb

A RUSSIAN FABLE

A loving mother bought a good, strong comb to keep her little boy's hair in order. The child was so pleased with his new present that he would not let it out of his hands. Whether playing games or learning his alphabet, he was all the time drawing the comb through his soft, thick, golden curls. And what a wonderful comb it was! It did not pull out his hair, but glided through so smoothly and easily that it never even got caught in it!

One day, though, the boy lost the comb. He had been playing and romping until he had gotten his hair in a terrible tangle. No sooner did the boy's nanny start to comb his hair than the boy began to cry and scream. "Where is *my* comb?" he cried. "I want my comb now." He would not let anyone touch his hair without *his* comb.

At last the comb was found. But when they tried to draw it through his hair, it could not be moved either backward or forward, for the boy's hair had not been combed for weeks and was a matted, tangled mess. The comb pulled the hair out by the roots and brought tears of pain to the boy's eyes.

"How wicked you are, bad old comb. I hate you now forever," cried the boy. But the comb replied, "My dear boy, I am the same comb I always was, only your hair has become badly tangled." Whereupon the foolish young child flung his comb out the window and into a river. He could not bear so simple a truth and in doing so lost a friend.

May 20

The Worm of Lambton

In England long ago there were only very rich people and very poor people and no people in between. The rich people were few in number and therefore the object of much gossip. The gossip was often mean-spirited, though certain people deserved it.

The Lambton family, heirs to Lambton castle, was one such deserving family.

The son of Lambton was a waste of a good soul. He drank wine all day, used terrible language, and he held most of the world in contempt, as if he were superior to everyone.

One day he went fishing and as usual did not catch any fish. He did, however, get a tug on his line, and when he saw that it was just a worm, he tossed it over his shoulder. The worm landed in a well, which to this day is called Worm Well. Shortly thereafter the son of Lambton went off to join the Crusades, which everyone hoped would either build some character in him or finish him off for good.

While the son of Lambton was off at war, the worm was growing in the well to a disturbing size. It grew until it was the size of a walking stick, and then slithered out of the well. It fed on whatever it could, growing and growing, until it could wrap itself around a giant hill five times.

The worm was a zoological wonder, but it was also a horrible menace. It began to eat woodland animals and then farm animals. As its appetite increased for more and more creatures, so too did it increase in size.

Pretty soon, the people had to flee the land.

Once the worm polished off all of the animal life in the kingdom, it turned its eye to Lambton castle.

There was no leadership in the castle because the son of Lambton was still at the Crusades, and the lord of Lambton was weary and old, and besides, his servants and knights did not respect him. Without a leader, there was panic, and the servants started throwing chickens out the windows and shooing cows into the fields to appease the giant worm's hunger.

An occasional knight or brave man tried to slay the worm, but each one met his own death. The worm wreaked havoc for seven long years, and the few people who remained were filled with hunger and despair. Everything was a terrible mess.

One day, the son of Lambton returned from the Crusades.

He had grown up to be a man of good character, though he was rather put out that the place had gone to weeds in his absence. He surveyed the empty village, the ravaged fields, the castle in near ruins, and he was annoyed. He had been away for a mere seven years, and the place had completely fallen apart!

When he learned about the worm, and the many knights and brave men who had met their death fighting it, he decided to go to the Wise Woman of Chesterle Street to get some advice.

"Why are you asking me for advice?" she asked, annoyed as he was.

"This really is all your fault." She proceeded to tell him how the worm got its start. "If you want to get rid of this thing, put on your best armor, stand in the middle of the river, place your sword in your hands and all of your trust in God. Kill the worm. After you slay the worm, you must also kill the first living creature you meet on your way back to the castle. If you don't, no one in your family will die a happy death for *nine generations.*"

It didn't sound very complicated, so the son of Lambton made preparations. He secured his best armor, sharpened his finest sword, prayed to God, and arranged for an old dying dog to be rushed to him once he slayed the worm, so that it might be the living creature sacrificed.

Then he set off for the river and did as he was told. After a fierce battle, he killed the worm and sliced the monster into many bits, all of which flowed down the river and away from the kingdom. He blew his bugle to signal that the deed had been done, and returned to the castle to complete his mission and pierce the old dog as a sacrifice.

The aged father heard the sound of the bugle and knew his son had triumphed. In his excitement, though, he forgot about the sacrifice, and ran out to greet him. Frantically, the son waved his father away and called for the dog, but his father thought he was motioning him, and instead came faster and faster to his son.

The lord of Lambton arrived at his son's side just a few paces ahead of the dog.

"Now what do I do?" pondered the son of Lambton, not a little irritated with his father. He plunged his sword into the old dog. "No one will know who reached me first," he figured.

The kingdom returned to its prosperous and peaceful self, but the fate of the Lambton family was set. For the next nine generations, the lords of Lambton all died terrible and painful deaths.

May 21

Old Monarch's Tale

A TALE FROM THE AMERICAN WEST

Old Monarch was said to be the largest buffalo in the world. At the time that Buffalo Bill brought him to a park in Nebraska, he was already very old, though he never would tell his age. And he was one of the smartest beasts that ever roamed the western plains.

Boys and girls would come on school trips to see Old Monarch, and sometimes he would agree to tell them stories. On this particular day, Old Monarch was reminiscing about his first contact with settlers. "I think it was in 1860," he began, as he scratched his head while trying to recall the date. "That's when I first saw cattle west of Omaha. The telegraph line was being built from the Missouri River to the Pacific Coast, and cattle were used, instead of horses, to haul the supplies. Lumbering big fellows they were!

"I was just a little buffalo calf then and didn't know what fear was. I was on my way to see these beasts up close when I saw a man on an Indian pony coming toward me at a gallop. I saw he had something bright in his hands, and he was stopping and raising the object to his shoulders. Then a little puff of white smoke would come out, and a buzzing noise, like a bumblebee, would whiz by me. He got pretty close to me, and then I felt a stinging sensation. It flashed through my mind that I had been shot, for I recalled hearing my grandmother tell of how a Sioux wounded her this way.

"I looked at my side and saw a red stream trickling down. I ran for dear life, and finally threw the hunter off my track. Well, I had a sore spot for a while, but I was young and strong. And while I was recovering, I had more time to study the strange cattle.

"One night while a number of them were grazing up a canyon, I went and introduced myself. At first I couldn't understand a single word they said, but soon I picked up similarities between their language and mine. If they said, 'Oo-oo-oo-oo,' I replied 'Oo-oo-oo-oo,' and the sounds were almost identical. The next night I went back and learned several more words, and by the end of a week I could understand cattle talk pretty fair.

"The humans laying the telegraph line moved their camp several times over the summer and I moved with them, though I always stayed in the hills in the daytime to avoid hunters. But after it got cold in the fall, the telegraph crew started running out of cattle feed, so they turned about twenty big, strapping oxen out on the range to fend for themselves.

"The moment they were on their own, those oxen got scared, and one of them, Old Baldy I think he was called, told me in confidence afterward that he had expected they would starve to death.

"Here was a chance to show them even a wild buffalo has a heart. I told them if they would trust me, I'd take them down to a canyon on the Clearwater where there was good water and plenty of grass year round. Old Baldy spoke for all of them when he said, 'Lead us there!'

"The next spring, while we were out one day nipping the soft new grass, we saw two horsemen riding toward us, and in a moment they were rounding us up. 'Golly, but these cattle are in fine shape!' said one of the men. 'Good enough for beef,' replied the other, and by that I knew it was time for me to get out of there.

"That night I quietly slipped away from the herd and headed north, to where I knew I could find my own folks. So that's how it all started, or so I heard Buffalo Bill say. If it weren't for Old Baldy and his friends, maybe the western plains would still be empty today!"—EUGENE O. MAYFIELD

May 22

The Birds, the Beasts, and the Bat

Once upon a time there was a fierce war waged between the birds and the beasts. For a long while, the issue of the battle was uncertain and no one knew which side would win. The bat, taking advantage of his natural ambiguous nature, kept aloof and remained neutral.

Soon it appeared that the beasts would win the war so the bat joined their forces and appeared active in the fight. But when a successful rally was made by the birds, the bat switched over to the birds so he would count among the ranks of the winning party.

Once peace was made the bat's conduct was so condemned by both parties that neither birds nor beasts would acknowledge him. The bat, therefore, was excluded from the terms of the truce. Ever since, he has lived in holes and corners, never daring to show his face except in the duskiness of twilight.—PHAEDRUS

May 23

Thumbelina, Part 1

Once upon a time there was a woman who wanted a child very much, so she went to a fairy for help. "I would so love a tiny baby!" she said. "Can you tell me how to get one?"

"That can be easily managed," said the fairy. "Here is a grain of barley that is different from the kind that grows in the fields. Plant it in the flowerpot and see what happens!"

The woman thanked her, gave her twelve pennies, and went home to plant the seed. Immediately up sprang a beautiful flower that looked something like a tulip, but the petals were tightly closed.

"That is a lovely flower," said the woman, and she gave it a kiss. When she did so the flower opened, and in the middle, upon the velvet green stamens, sat a delicate little maiden. She was scarcely half as long as a thumb in height, and so she was called Thumbelina.

Thumbelina was given a beautifully polished walnut shell for a bed, and violet leaves for a mattress and a rose petal for a blanket. During the day, she amused herself at the kitchen table, where the woman had placed a plate of water. On the water floated a tulip leaf, and on this the little maiden could sail from one side to the other, using two white horse hairs as oars. It was a very pretty sight. She could sing also, and so softly and sweetly that nothing like it had ever before been heard.

One night, as she lay in her bed, an old toad came hopping in through the window. The toad, all wet and ugly, hopped over to where Thumbelina slept on the table. "What a pretty little wife she would make for my son!" thought the toad, and she picked up the walnut shell and hopped back out the window and into the garden. There flowed a stream where the toad lived with her son.

He was even uglier than his mother. When he saw the pretty little maiden, all he could say was, "Croak, croak, croak!"

"Be quiet," said his mother, "or she will wake up, and then she might run away. We will place her on one of the water lily leaves out in the stream while we prepare a bridal chamber in the mud for the two of you. It will be like an island to her, and she won't be able to escape."

Thumbelina woke early in the morning, and began to cry bitterly when she saw where she was. In a little while the toads swam out to fetch the little walnut bed. The mother toad bowed before her. "This is my son, little lady. He is to be your husband, and you will live happily together in the mud."

The sight of the toad's son made Thumbelina cry even harder. The little fish who swam around the water lilies had heard the toad's words, and when they popped their heads out of the water and saw the wonderfully pretty little maiden, they felt very sorry that she had to go live with the ugly toads. "No, this must never be!" the fish said. And so they chewed through the stalk that held the lily pad in place and Thumbelina floated quickly downstream.

The lily leaf traveled farther and farther till it reached another land. A graceful white butterfly fluttered around Thumbelina and at last alighted on the leaf. Thumbelina was pleased to see him, and happy now that she was out of reach of the toads. She took off her sash and tied one end of it around the butterfly and the other to the leaf, and now she glided much faster, for the butterfly was pulling her.

Just then a big beetle came flying along and grabbed Thumbelina around her slender waist, taking her up to a tree. The lily leaf floated on downstream, for the butterfly was still attached. Thumbelina was terrified for herself, but even more worried for the white butterfly, for if he could not free himself he would perish of hunger.

May 24

Thumbelina, Part 2

Once the beetle had Thumbelina up in the tree, he seated her on a leaf and gave her some honey to eat. After a while, all the beetles who lived in that tree came to visit her. "She has only two legs! How ugly that looks!" said one. "She has no feelers!" said another.

The beetle who had captured Thumbelina was soon convinced by his friends that she was ugly and too like a human, and he would have nothing more to do with her. He flew her down from the tree and set her on a daisy, saying she could go where she liked. Thumbelina wept at the thought that she was so ugly that the beetles shunned her, though in fact she was really the loveliest creature imaginable.

During the summer, Thumbelina lived alone in the forest, with only the song of little birds for company. She wove herself a bed with blades of grass and hung it up under a broad clover leaf for protection from the rain. But as the months went by and it began to turn chilly, the clover leaf shriveled up. Thumbelina was dreadfully cold, for her clothes had torn and were no protection at all.

Next to her forest home was a grain field, which had been cut down to stubble. She struggled to cross the field—and for someone her size it was like making her way through dense jungle—and came at last to the door of a field mouse, who had a little den beneath the stubble. Thumbelina stood before the door and begged for a handful of barley. "You poor little creature," said the field mouse. "Come into my warm room and dine with me." The field mouse was quite taken with Thumbelina, and offered her a home for the winter if she would keep house and tell stories.

One day the field mouse announced that a neighbor would be visiting. "He is very rich and learned, wears a beautiful black velvet coat, and has a splendid house with large rooms. If you could only have him for a husband, you would be well provided for indeed."

Thumbelina was not at all interested in the visitor, as he was a blind old mole, but the field mouse sang his praises constantly. Unfortunately for Thumbelina, the mole fell in love with her sweet voice. He dug an underground passageway from his house to theirs, so they could visit frequently. He warned them, though, not to be alarmed by the dead swallow lying in the long, dark corridor. It didn't bother the mole in the least because he had a very low opinion of birds, but Thumbelina was greatly saddened.

That night she wove a carpet of hay and covered the dead swallow with it, then lay her head on the bird's breast to say farewell. What should she hear but "thump, thump!" The swallow was not dead after all, only benumbed by the cold.

For many nights after, Thumbelina brought the swallow more covers, and food and drink, and nursed him back to health with care and love. Very soon, spring arrived and it was time for the swallow to leave. He offered to carry Thumbelina off with him to the woods, but she knew that would make the field mouse very sad, so she answered, "No, I cannot."

The mole, meanwhile, had become intent on marrying Thumbelina, and she was not allowed to go out in the sunshine anymore, but had to stay below weaving clothes for the wedding. The field mouse brushed aside all her objections, telling her that a poor girl ought to be thankful for so splendid a husband.

On the day before her wedding, Thumbelina had permission to go outside a final time. "Farewell, bright sun!" she cried. "Greet the swallow for me if you see him." Just then, she heard "tweet, tweet" above her head. It was her friend on his way to warmer lands. The swallow listened to her sad story, and had no trouble this time convincing her to leave with him.

Thumbelina seated herself on his back and tied her sash to one of his strong wings. Then the swallow rose in the air and flew for many days to a beautiful country, where the sun always shone, and where lemons and oranges hung from trees. The swallow's home was in a nest atop a pillar of a marble palace by a lake. "But it would not do for you to live here," he said, and told her to choose one of the lovely white flowers that grew in profusion by the palace. He would set her down there.

"That will be delightful," Thumbelina said. But how surprised she was to see a tiny man in the middle of the flower she had picked. He was as transparent as if made of crystal, and not much larger than Thumbelina herself. On his head he wore a gold crown and he had delicate wings at his shoulders.

All flowers have angels—tiny men and women who dwell inside them—and he was the king of all the flower angels. Of course he found Thumbelina to be the prettiest little maiden he had ever seen, and asked her to be his wife and queen. And when she consented, she was given a splendid wedding gift—a pair of gossamer wings. Now Thumbelina could fly from flower to flower, and her days to come were filled with bright sunshine and much happiness.

—HANS CHRISTIAN ANDERSEN

May 25

The Little Chicken

Once there was a very little chicken. He had little chicken legs, little chicken feathers, and even a little chicken beak. Because he was so small, all the other chickens made fun of him. And no one wanted to play with him. When the other chickens chose up sides for chicken games like "Who Can Squawk the Loudest" or "Hen Peck," the Little Chicken was always the last one picked. This made the Little Chicken very sad, and sometimes late at night, when he was all alone in his coop, he would cry chicken tears and his feathers would get all soaked.

The meanest chicken in the entire flock was named Eggbert. Everybody was afraid of him. Whatever Eggbert told the other chickens to do, they would do immediately, and no one would ever open their beak to object. Eggbert loved to make fun of the Little Chicken. When all the chickens went out to play he would always try to make the Little Chicken do silly things. "Why don't you . . . go look in the farmer's window!" Eggbert said.

The Little Chicken knew that the farmer got very angry whenever any of the animals looked in his window. "I don't want to," he replied.

"Ha!" Eggbert laughed. "You're just a little chicken!" and all ten of the other chickens laughed at the Little Chicken. The Little Chicken walked away sadly.

That night his father, Bigtime Rudy Rooster, put a warm wing around his shoulders and told him not to listen to Eggbert. "Don't listen to him," he said. "Be your own chicken."

Every day the same thing would happen. And throughout the entire barnyard the animals laughed and laughed. Each time an animal refused to do a task, the other animals called him a "little chicken." They were not very nice.

One day all the chickens went for a long walk. When they reached the highway, Eggbert looked at the Little Chicken and said, "Why don't you cross the road?"

The Little Chicken saw the big trucks go roaring past, and the cars whizzing past, and even the racing motorcycles and he knew crossing the road would be very dangerous. "I don't want to," he said.

Eggbert laughed. "You're just a little chicken," he said and all the other chickens laughed. Then Eggbert said to the others, "Let's just leave him here. Come on." And he led them onto the road.

Not one of them made it across the road. The trucks and the cars and the motorcycles never even saw them and never slowed down.

That night, safe at home, the Little Chicken nestled under the wing of his dad, and knew that sometimes it could be really hard to be a Little Chicken, but that his dad was right, no matter what others say, you have to be your own chicken.

—JORDAN BURNETT AND DAVID FISHER

May 26

Madschun

A TURKISH TALE

Once upon a time there lived in the hills a woman and her son. The young man was not more than twenty but he had not as much hair on his head as a baby. Old as he looked, however, he refused to get a job, and to his mother's grief, he spent all his time doing nothing.

On a fine summer morning, he was lying as usual half asleep in the little garden in front of their cottage when the sultan's daughter came riding by. The youth lazily raised himself up to look at her, and that one glance changed his life forever. "I will marry her and nobody else," he thought, and he ran to his mother. "You must go at once to the sultan and tell him that I want his daughter for my wife."

"What?" shouted the old woman, thinking he was crazy. "Do you really expect the sultan to give his daughter to a penniless, no-account baldy like you?"

"Do as I bid you," the son cried, and he tormented her day after day till she had no choice but to put on her best clothes and go to the palace. It happened to be the day the sultan met with the public, so she had no trouble gaining admission. But when she finally got to meet the sultan, she didn't know what to say. Finally, she began, "Do not think me mad, O Excellency, but I have a son who would not give me a day of peace until I came here and asked for your daughter's hand in marriage."

The sultan, as it happened, had a liking for anything unusual, and this woman's request was certainly that.

"Tell your son to come to the palace," he said. The woman stared in astonishment at such a reply, but swiftly bowed her way out of the chamber and hurried home.

But when the sultan saw the bald head of his daughter's suitor, he was no longer amused and thought quickly of a way to rid himself of this unwelcome fool. "The man who wishes to marry my daughter," he announced, "must first collect all the birds in the world and bring them into the gardens of the palace." These words filled the young man with despair. How was he to trap all those birds? And even if he did, how was he to carry them back to the palace? Still, he did not intend to give up on the princess without a struggle, and he left the palace and headed out into the desert.

After wandering for a week, he came across a holy man who noticed that he was troubled. The youth described his problem, and the holy man said, "Do not despair. It is not as difficult as it sounds. Two days' journey from here, there stands a cypress tree. Sit under it, in the darkest shadows, and keep very still. Soon you will hear a mighty rushing of wings and all the birds in the world will come nestle in the branches. When all is quiet again, say 'Madschun!' The birds will be forced to remain in their perches, and you will be able to place them all over your body and thus carry them to the sultan."

All went according to plan, and the sultan was mightily surprised to find a strange feathered figure at the palace a few days later. "I have done your bidding, O Sultan. Now give me the princess!"

The sultan answered hurriedly, "Yes, yes, you have pleased me well. Only one thing remains to turn you into a proper husband. That head of yours, you know—it is so very bald! Get it covered with nice, thick, curly hair and I will give you my daughter. You are so clever you'll have no problem."

Well, not only was it a problem, but it was impossible for the young man to grow a head of hair. For weeks he sat in despair at his mother's cottage, until the day he heard that the sultan's daughter was going to marry another man. He secretly made his way into the palace, where he found the bride and bridegroom about to sign the marriage contract. "Madschun!" the youth whispered. And instantly all in the room were turned into statues.

The sultan was overwhelmed with sorrow. His sorcerer advised him that to undo the magic he must honor the bargain he had made with the bald young man. Once promised his bride, the youth called out, "Let the victims of Madschun be free!" To everyone's great relief, most especially the bald young man's, the statues returned to life, and the princess placed her hand joyfully in that of her new bridegroom's. He never did grow hair, but she found him to be a proper husband just the same.

May 27

A Caterpillar's Tale

A caterpillar had crawled up on a twig. It looked the twig over, then fastened itself tightly to it by its hind legs and began twisting itself and moving its head up and down. Every time the caterpillar's head moved, it left behind something that looked like a glistening thread of silk.

An ant crawling nearby stopped and looked in wonder. "What in the world are you doing?"

"I'm making a house," the caterpillar said, as it paused to rest for a moment.

A bee that had lighted close by began to buzz with laughter. "Will you tell me, if you please, what sort of house that is?" he cried.

"The only sort of house I know how to make," the caterpillar answered humbly.

"I never heard of anything so absurd. Why don't you hunt about and find a hollow tree or a good hive and live in that? Then you would be safe."

"Or you might find a hole under a stone," said the ant. "That's a very good place."

The caterpillar shook its head, then it set to work again.

The bee and ant went on their way. "A poor sort of house indeed," each one thought.

Up and down the caterpillar's head moved, weaving and weaving. Now the silk was like a thin, silvery veil. Through the veil you could still faintly see the caterpillar moving.

At last the veil grew so thick that you could only guess that the caterpillar might still be at work inside. The bee came by that way again, and stopped to look at the little house. Then it flew down to the anthill. "Miss Ant, come out here," it buzzed. "I've such a joke to tell you! That caterpillar we were watching has finished its house, and has forgotten to leave any door."

"That's too bad," said the ant. "I'm afraid it will starve."

But the caterpillar did not die. It was not even hungry. It was fast asleep in its little cocoon house, knowing not whether the sun shone or the rain beat down. It was snug and dark inside.

Many days and nights passed, and at last what had once been the caterpillar began to stir and wake. "How strange I feel!" said the thing to itself. "I must have light and air!"

One end of the cocoon was very soft and loose, and through this end what was once the caterpillar pushed its way out. How weak it felt! Fastened to it on each side were two crumpled wet things, which it began to move feebly up and down. As it moved them it felt its strength returning and the crumpled things began to spread and dry. Broader and broader they spread until they were strong, velvety wings, two on each side. They were a lovely soft brown color, with a pinkish border along the edges. In the middle of each of the lower wings was a glistening spot, like the "eye" on a peacock's feather.

This thing was no caterpillar. It was a beautiful winged moth. Presently it spread its wings and floated softly down to earth. It did not fly far, for it had not its full strength yet. As it happened, it alighted on the anthill, where the ant was busy hunting for food. It stopped its work to stare with awe at the wonderful stranger. "You beautiful thing," said the ant, "where did you come from?"

"Don't you remember the caterpillar that made its house on the twig above?"

"Oh, yes, poor thing, it must have died long ago."

"I am that caterpillar," said the moth gently, as the ant looked at it in wonder.

Just then the bee who had laughed at the caterpillar's house buzzed by and heard the news. "Well, well!" it said. "So that was what you were about—growing wings in your queer house!"

The moth stirred itself and said, "Now I must go and find a shelter under a rock or in some hollow tree until the sun goes down. But tonight—ah, tonight! I shall come out to fly wherever I like!" And it waved its great wings and flew softly out of sight.

The ant and bee sat looking after it. "And to think," cried the bee, "that I didn't understand what the caterpillar was doing! I suppose everyone knows his own business best."

May 28

Little Red Riding Hood

A GERMAN TALE

Once there was a sweet little girl who was loved by all who knew her. Her grandmother was particularly fond of her and always made her wonderful presents. One day she made a pretty red cape with a hood. The child loved the cape and wore it often, and so she became known as Little Red Riding Hood.

But today grandmother was ill and the whole family was worried about her. Little Red Riding Hood's mother packed a basket of cakes and butter and asked Little Red Riding Hood to take it to her grandmother. "A visit will do the old woman good," her mother said. The child agreed cheerfully and set out along a path through the woods.

She had not gone far when she met a wolf who greeted her politely. "Tell me, where are you going on this fine day?" he asked, thinking he would like to eat her up.

"I'm headed to see my grandmother, who is very ill," Little Red Riding Hood replied.

"Why don't you pick her some pretty flowers," the wolf suggested, thinking it might delay the child. The child thought it was a good idea and lingered among the flowers while the wolf ran straight to grandmother's house.

The wolf wasted no time gulping grandmother right down. Within minutes he had put on her flannel nightgown and cap, and climbed under her covers.

Soon Little Red Riding Hood arrived at grandmother's house and was surprised to notice the door ajar. She let herself in.

"Good morning, Grandmother," Little Red Riding Hood said, thinking she looked a little strange today.

"Why, Grandmother, what big ears you have," she called out, wondering why she had never noticed them before.

"The better to hear you with, my dear," said the wolf, lying in bed, disguised as grandmother.

"And what big eyes you have," Little Red Riding Hood continued, feeling more uneasy than ever.

"The better to see you with, my dear," said the wolf, who was starting to drool.

"And, Grandmother, what big teeth you have," said Little Red Riding Hood.

"The better to eat you with," said the wolf, and he lept up from the bed and gobbled Little Red Riding Hood all up.

Just at that moment a woodcutter was passing by and heard all of the commotion. When he saw the wolf asleep in Grandmother's bed he knew something terrible had happened. He killed the wolf with one blow of his axe, then cut him open. As soon as he did, out stepped Little Red Riding Hood and Grandmother.

They were very grateful to the woodcutter for saving them. They invited him to share the cakes and butter, and Grandmother started feeling much better.—BROTHERS GRIMM

May 29

The Frogs and the Old Serpent

A HINDU FABLE

In a deserted garden there once lived an old serpent named Slow-Coil. He was so very old that he could no longer catch mice or other animals for food. As he lay one day by the edge of a pond, a certain frog saw him there and asked, "Are you so old, serpent, that you no longer care to eat?"

"Leave me, kind sir," replied the reptile. "The troubles of a poor wretch like me could not possibly interest your noble mind."

"Let me at least hear them," said the frog, somewhat flattered.

"You must know then, kind sir, that twenty years ago in Brahmapootra, I bit the son of Kaundinya," said the serpent. "Kaundinya was a holy Brahman, and his son died from my cruel bite. Seeing his boy dead, Kaundinya, in his sorrow and despair, cursed me with the curse that I should be a carrier of frogs. So here I am, waiting to do as the Brahman's curse compels me."

The frog, after hearing all of this, went and told it to Web-Foot, the Frog King, who quickly came to take a ride on the serpent. He was carried so carefully and was so delighted with his ride that he thereafter used the serpent all the time. But one day, seeing that the serpent was moving very slowly, he asked what was the matter.

"Please, your majesty," explained the serpent, "your slave has nothing to eat."

"Eat a few of my frogs," said the king. "I give you leave."

"I thank your majesty," said the serpent, and at once he began to eat the frogs. Before long he had eaten all of the king's frogs, and finished by eating the king himself.

May 30

The Young Sentinel

A STORY FOR MEMORIAL DAY

In the summer of 1862, a young man belonging to a Vermont regiment was found sleeping at his post. He was tried and sentenced to be shot. The day was fixed for the execution and the young soldier calmly prepared to meet his fate.

Friends who knew of the case brought the matter to President Lincoln's attention. "The boy was on duty one night," Lincoln's advisor explained. "The next night, he volunteered to take the place of a comrade who was too ill to stand guard. The third night he was called out again. Being utterly exhausted, he fell asleep at his post."

Lincoln nodded. "Let's prepare a pardon for the soldier immediately," he said. Lincoln signed the pardon and sent it to the camp. The morning before the execution was scheduled, the president had not heard whether the pardon had reached the officers in charge of the matter. He began to feel uneasy. He ordered that a telegram be sent to the camp, but received no answer. He sat at his desk, staring at a pile of state papers, but he could not banish the condemned soldier from his thoughts.

At last, feeling that he must know that the young man was alive, he ordered a carriage and rode rapidly over ten miles on a dusty road beneath a scorching sun. When he reached the camp, he found that the pardon had been received and that the execution had been stayed.

The sentinel was released and his heart was grateful. When the campaign opened in the spring, the young man was with his regiment near Yorktown, Virginia. They were ordered to attack a fort and he fell at the first shots fired.

His comrades caught up with him and carried him bleeding from the field. "Bear witness," he said, "that I have proved myself no coward and that I am not afraid to die." He choked and, in his last breath, said a prayer for Abraham Lincoln.

—ADAPTED FROM Z. A. MUDGE

May 31

The Sun and the Moon

A MASAI MYTH

The sun and the moon did not always live apart. No, dear, they did not. Once the two great powers were man and wife, and they ruled as one. Now this was a long time ago and no one quite remembers how or why, but one day the sun and the moon had a terrible fight. Words were spoken. Fists flew. The sky was filled with rage. The harm that they did to each other was so unspeakable that no one has spoken of it since.

After this happened, the sun was ashamed. The sun was so ashamed that he created a blaze so bright that from that point forward, no one could really look at him.

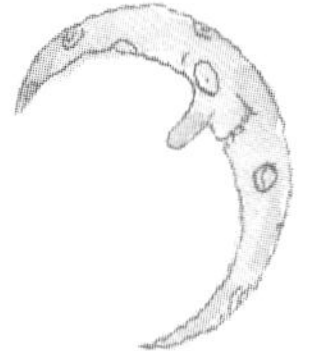

The moon was not so troubled by it all. She was able to forget. Each night, she just glides across the sky. Some nights, you can still see her bruises. She does not care who sees her or what they think.

JUNE

June 1

The Boy Who Told Fairy Tales

Once there was a fourteen-year-old boy named Ron. Ron was of ordinary height and ordinary weight. He had an ordinary mother and father and an ordinary ten-year-old sister. He wore ordinary clothes, watched ordinary television programs, listened to ordinary music, played ordinary games, and went to an ordinary school where he got ordinary grades. Almost everything about Ron's life was ordinary. *Almost* everything.

Ron loved to tell fairy tales. He had been telling them since he was six years old. The tales he told were all about his life and they were not ordinary. "My parents are giants," he told his teachers, "and they tear down houses, they stomp on trees and plants, and they live in a 100,000-foot castle in the sky."

He told his friends, "My brothers, Scott, Frank, and Steve, are warlocks and they are the most powerful men on earth. My sisters, Olivia, Jessica, Melanie, and Claudia, are witches and they are the most powerful women on earth. On Thanksgiving when we all get together they make the most special dinner appear. We eat as much turkey as we want, with all the ice cream it's possible to have, and we never get full."

He told so many fairy tales that sometimes even he forgot what was true and what he had made up. Each day his stories got grander and grander, and he became more and more popular. "Oh, Ron," his best friend Katie said one day, "you make up the best stories in the whole world. I love the story about how your dog and cat used to be king and queen until the mean witch put an evil spell on them."

"These aren't fairy tales," he yelled at Katie. "These are real stories about my life. You only think they're fairy tales because my life is so much more exciting than your life. You're just jealous that I have an exciting life, that's all."

Katie looked at Ron straight in the eye and told him, "Ron, no matter how much you want to believe your stories are true, they're just fairy tales that you made up. They are not your life, but it's plain to see you want them to be."

Ron was so mad at Katie that when he got home that night his mother, who had been turned into a giant turtle because she wouldn't reveal the secret for turning string into gold, his father, who was nineteen feet tall with a tiny head, and his sister, who had wings instead of hands because the stork who'd brought her got confused, were all eating diner and he walked

right past them and went into his room. He changed into his pajamas, which had been made for him by the six-headed visitor from the moon who came to his house every night when he was asleep. He closed his eyes and started dreaming.

The next morning when Ron woke up he stretched his rubber arms right up to the ceiling. As he walked past the mirror that only reflected the truth instead of seeing himself as a fourteen-year-old boy, he saw himself as a ninety-seven-year-old man. "No," he cried, "that can't be me. I'm only fourteen years old. I have to go to school."

But it was him. Ron had made up so many stories about his life that his real life had gone by so swiftly that he didn't even notice. Because he didn't cherish each moment, eighty-three years had gone by. It was only then that Ron realized he had been living in his dream world so long, he had forgotten to live a real life.

—JORDAN BURNETT AND DAVID FISHER

June 2

The Black Bull of Norroway, Part 1

AN OLD ENGLISH FOLKTALE

Once there lived a king who had three daughters. The eldest two were proud and ugly but the youngest was the gentlest and most beautiful creature ever seen. She was the pride not only of her mother and father, but of all the land.

One night the three princesses were talking about who they would marry. "As for me," said the eldest, "I will accept no less than a king." The second daughter agreed that royalty was a must, but she said she would stoop as low as a prince or even a duke. At that the third daughter giggled. "You are both so proud," she said. "Why, I'd be content with the Black Bull of Norroway."

No one thought more of the matter until the next morning at breakfast. At the castle door was the most dreadful bellowing, and who should it be but the Black Bull of Norroway! This was an awful development for he was the most horrible creature in the world. Everyone at the castle went into a complete panic. The king and queen did not know how to protect their beloved daughter. The king came up with the idea of putting a servant on the bull's back and saying it was his daughter. The bull stomped off with the servant on his back but when he realized he'd been tricked he threw the servant down and came back in a rage. The king and queen tried offering other servants and even the eldest two sisters, but each time the bull realized he'd been tricked, he'd throw off the rider and return in a rage. Finally the king and queen realized their youngest daughter had to go. With sorrow beyond words, they said good-bye, and she was gone.

The Black Bull took the princess through spindly forests and lonely wastelands until at last they came to a nobleman's castle. The nobleman wondered what such a lovely princess was doing with such a hideous bull, but he had seen stranger things, so he asked them to be his guests and spend the night. As the princess and the bull entered the main hall, the princess noticed a sharp pin in the side of the bull. She was kind and she thought it must hurt his flesh, so she pulled it out and when she did he was transformed into one of the handsomest princes ever beheld.

At once, the prince fell at the princess's feet to thank her. In removing the pin, the princess had broken a cruel enchantment. The prince and the princess told the nobleman and his court the extraordinary news and there was great rejoicing and feasting. But in the midst of the festivities, the prince disappeared.

The lovely princess could not believe that her fortunes had gone up and down with such speed and so little mercy. But she was a strong person and she knew what she wanted. She decided to find her prince no matter what.

For the next months and then years, she trod the lowlands and highlands. Her heart was determined but her body became weak and gray from hunger. One night, she wandered into a dark wood and lost her way. As night was coming on, she thought she would die of cold and hunger, but seeing a light coming through the trees, she went on until she came to a cottage. As she came to the door of the cottage, she collapsed.

June 3

The Black Bull of Norroway, Part 2

When the princess awoke, she could barely remember who she was or how she had happened upon the cottage. A kindly old woman was standing over her, patting her forehead and making her comfortable. The old woman gave the princess warm food to eat and fresh clothes. She asked how the princess had come to the dark wood and the princess told her sad tale. "You must continue your journey," the old woman told her. "But when your heart feels as though it will break and never be whole again, open one of these little nuts."

The old woman handed the princess three nuts and said good-bye. "Remember," the old woman said, "when your heart feels as though it will break, break one of these little nuts instead."

The princess felt better and continued her quest. She had not gone far when she chanced upon a company of lords and ladies on horseback. They were all talking merrily about the duke of Norroway's upcoming wedding. Then another procession of royalty passed, all bearing gifts and wearing finery for the duke's grand wedding. At last she came to the castle where cooks and bakers were busy in preparation. She was determined to find her prince, so she slipped into the kitchen and sidled down a long hall to get into the castle's center. Then she heard someone cry, "Make way for the duke of Norroway."

Who should ride past her but *her prince* and a beautiful lady!

You may be sure that her heart felt as though it would "break and never be whole again," so she broke one of the little nuts, and out jumped a wee woman carding wool. The princess then slipped up into the bedroom of the beautiful lady, carrying the wee woman in the nutshell. When the beautiful lady saw the wee woman, she was enchanted. The princess said, "I will give it to you only on the condition that you put off for one day your wedding to the duke of Norroway and that I might go into his room tonight."

So anxious was the beautiful lady for the wee one in the nutshell that she agreed, and so the princess went to the duke's room that night. The prince was asleep, and so the princess sat down by his bedside and began singing: *"Far I have sought you, near I have brought you, / Dear duke of Norroway, will you not speak to me?"*

The princess sang to the duke over and over again, but he never woke up. In the morning she had to leave without him even knowing she'd been there. She then broke the second nut, for her heart felt as though it would break, and a wee woman spinning popped out. Again the princess made arrangements with the beautiful lady: the lady could have the wee one in the nutshell if she would put off for another day her wedding to the duke.

That night the princess returned to the duke's bedside and sang to him. She sang and she sang and she sang, but the duke never woke up. In the morning when the duke was dressing, his servant asked him what all the strange singing had been about. The duke had no idea what his servant was talking about. The servant suggested that the duke try to stay awake that night to determine what was happening. The duke agreed that it was strange stuff and that he would unravel the mystery.

Meanwhile, the poor princess had nearly given up hope. She had but one little nut left and her heart felt as though it would break and never be whole again, so she broke it. Out popped a wee woman reeling, and on the same conditions as before, the beautiful lady got possession of it.

But the princess, who for so many years had pursued her great love, was losing her spirit. When she entered the duke's room on this final night, she sang in barely a whisper. The duke was pretending to sleep, but immediately he recognized even the faint sounds of his beloved's voice, and with surprise and joy he turned to her and held her close. He explained that he had long been in the power of a witch wife, whose spells over him had now happily ended since she had preserved and found him again.

The princess, happy to be the means of breaking this second evil spell, consented to marry him, and the wicked witch wife, who fled the country, has never been heard of since. As the castle had already prepared for a great wedding, the princess stepped in and boldly and beautifully took the place of the wicked witch wife, so ending the adventures of the Black Bull of Norroway and the wandering of the king's daughter.

June 4

The Black Bull of Norroway, Variation

The black bull story is told another way by Joseph Jacobs, a distinguished collector and editor of folktales. In his book *More English Fairy Tales,* the story begins with three sisters, each of whom has declared to her mother that it is time to seek her fortune. ("Mother, bake me a bannock, and roast me a collop, for I'm going away to seek my fortune.") All three go separately to the old wise woman in the woods. The first two are awarded a coach and horses. The youngest receives a great black bull.

The black bull takes her to three castles. The first two are those of the bull's eldest brothers and the third is his own. At the castle, the bull's maiden is awarded three pieces of fruit: a magic apple, pear, and then plum to use in dire straits. Then the bull deposits her in the woods, and tells her to sit at a simple throne and not to move hand or foot or he will never find her again. The bull must go to slay Old Un. If the bull is victorious, he tells her, everything will turn blue; if defeated, everything will turn red. Everything turns blue and the maiden is filled with joy, but she jumps up and in doing so leaves the throne, and that's when trouble begins. The bull returns and cannot find her. She weeps for a long time and then starts to wander. She ends up at a glass hill, which she cannot get over. At the bottom of the hill is a smith's house. He makes a deal with her: work for seven years as his helper, and he will get her over the glass hill. She is not in a position to negotiate, and so she agrees.

Seven years pass and she gets over the hill. She encounters the house of an old washerwoman. A gallant young knight has given the old woman some bloody clothes. Whoever gets them clean gets to be his wife. The old woman and her daughter can't get the laundry clean but the maiden, with little effort, gets the laundry pure and white. The knight appears, and the old woman lies and says it was her daughter who did the deed; the maiden, meanwhile, is seriously captivated by this knight and wants him for herself. She remembers the apple she was to use in dire straits. She breaks it, and gold and jewels come pouring out. She offers the loot to the old woman's daughter if she will put off the wedding for one day. The old woman gives the knight a sleeping potion, so when the maiden tries to wake him up and introduce herself, she cannot, though she cries, "Seven long years I served for thee, the glassy hill I clomb for thee, the bloody clothes I wrang for thee; wilt though not waken and turn to me?"

The next day, the maiden breaks open the pear, which was filled with even more gold and jewels. She makes the same arrangement with the daughter, but again the old woman has given a sleeping drink to the knight, so the girl's efforts are futile. The third day the knight's companion mentions that he heard a lot of noise and commotion coming from the knight's room. The knight decides to refuse the sleeping drink that night to find out what is happening. The maiden uses her plum to strike the same bargain with the old woman's daughter, and this time when she visits the knight, he is awake to receive her and fall in love with her. He causes the old woman and her daughter to be burned at the stake, and marries the maiden. They live happily ever after.

June 5

The Bride's Venture, Part 1

A GERMAN TALE

There once was a king's son who was secretly married to a princess he loved very much. One day, as he was visiting her, he received word that his father was dying and wished to see him one last time. "I must leave you," the prince said to his secret wife. "But I will give you this ring as a token of our love and when I am king I will come and fetch you."

Secrets can be a problem. After the prince made his long journey to the family castle, his father had a last wish for his son. He asked his son to promise to marry another princess from a distant land. "I will do anything you ask," the prince said, "but . . ." Before the prince could explain that he was already secretly married, the king died.

"My father died thinking I would marry the other princess," the prince thought out loud. "Now I must fulfill his last wish." The prince went to see his father's choice—a princess from a distant land—and purposely presented himself as a fool. He jumped on one foot and made silly noises. He was hoping she would refuse him, but instead she agreed to marry. The prince was devastated.

When the secret wife heard about all of this, she wept for seven days. Her father, who was also a king, was heartbroken to see his daughter in this state. "Isn't there something I can do for you?" he asked.

She thought for a moment and then said. "Yes, Father. I would like to have as companions eleven maidens who look exactly like myself."

The king did not question his daughter as to her intent, but sent messengers all over the country who finally found eleven maidens who looked just like the princess. When they arrived, she ordered twelve identical hunting costumes to be made. She gathered her maidens, dressed them in the hunting clothes, and bid her father farewell, as they all rode away to the castle of her great love. Once she was there, she sent a message to the prince, who was now a king, saying that she was the chief huntsman and that she and all her companions wished to be taken into his service. When he came to meet them all, he did not recognize his secret wife in the hunting costume. He was pleased and asked them to stay.

It happened that the king had an unusual lion who was able to tell truth from lies and also uncover secrets. One night the lion said to the king, "You are mistaken if you think you have engaged twelve huntsmen. They are maidens."

"That is ridiculous," said the king. "Can you prove it?" The lion said he could prove it easily. What would the king think if he found out that his chief huntsman was really his secret wife?

June 6

The Bride's Venture, Part 2

The king loved his friend the lion, but he could not believe his silly accusation that the huntsmen were really maidens in disguise. "If you are so sure about this, you must prove it," the king told the lion.

The lion had a plan. "We will strew peas in the antechamber and you will see. A man has a firm step and is unlikely to be aware of something so small and delicate as a pea. If they are men, they will crush the peas without so much as a thought. If they are women, however, they will walk around the peas carefully," he said.

To humor the lion, the king had peas spread about, but a kindly servant who had overheard the king and the lion speaking warned the twelve huntsmen. When the huntsmen passed, they walked through the peas with a firm, heavy stride.

"They walk like men," said the king to the lion.

"Yes," said the lion. "But they knew about the test. Give them another trial. Place twelve spinning wheels in the antechamber. A man would be thinking about what's ahead and will not notice them, but your huntsmen will be fascinated and will stop to look."

Again the young huntsmen were warned and they passed by the spinning wheels without so much as a glance. The king patted his lion friend on the head. "I think you need some rest. Your mind is playing tricks on you," the king said.

Not long after, the king was on a hunting trip with the twelve huntsmen when word came that the king's bride was approaching. By this they meant the king's second wife. The king's secret wife, in her disguise, could not bear to see her beloved with another woman. The very thought made her swoon and fall. The king ran to her, thinking it was his chief huntsman, and when he raised her up, her glove fell off.

There, on her finger, was the ring the king had given her so long ago. When the king saw the ring, he looked up and stared earnestly at her face. It was his true love. His secret wife.

"Now that you are here, truly here, we must never be separated again," he said to her.

The king had a long talk with his second wife, who was greatly disappointed but glad the secret was told and that she could live in truth. She returned home with a gift of gold from the king, enough for her to live in splendor for a long time. The king and his true wife celebrated their marriage with the entire kingdom, which was overjoyed to see their king look so happy and content.

The lion was returned to favor for, of course, he had spoken the truth.

—BROTHERS GRIMM

June 7

The Bird and the Clam

A CHINESE FABLE

A clam decided to take a nap on the banks of the River Yi. When the clouds passed, he felt cool in their shadow. When the sun returned, he felt warm. It was a good time to daydream, and so he did.

From above, a bird spotted the clam and swooped down and gave it a good peck. The clam, startled, clamped his shell down tight, catching the bird's beak.

"Remove your beak at once," ordered the clam, his shell lips pursed. But the bird was stubborn. Though she was able to pull out her beak, she refused.

"I will not remove my beak until you open your shell," the bird mumbled. Like the clam, she found it was difficult to speak plainly under the circumstances. Of course, the clam was not about to open his shell and place himself at the bird's mercy. But the bird pressed on.

"Open your shell or you'll be a dead clam," she said.

"Remove your beak at once," returned the clam.

"Open it!"

"Remove it!"

"Open it!"

Locked in this conflict, the two went back and forth for several hours. But as neither would comply with the other's orders, they stayed in such a state until a young man who happened to come their way grabbed the two of them and carried them off for dinner!

June 8

Why the Tides Ebb and Flow

A MALAYSIAN MYTH

If you go to the ocean and sit, the rhythms of the water will lull you, as your mind with the waves goes back and forth, back and forth. The tides inch in and, then, reaching their mark, go back out. Staring ahead, you see nothing but water and sky. But beyond where even your eyes will take you, and deeper than your mind can imagine, there is a great hole in the ocean. In the hole lives a giant crab.

Twice a day the crab comes to look for food. To feed himself, this monster must scour the ocean floor and the sandy beaches of the world to see what he can find. And when he leaves his great hole the waters of the ocean pour into the canyon, and the seas pour into the ocean, and the rivers pour into the seas. All the waters are called to the hole and it is low tide.

Then, satisfied, the crab goes back to his hole. Slowly he lowers his huge body down, and when he does so, he fills the space, causing the waters of the seas to sputter and clash and pour out of the hole around him. As he nests himself in, the waters rise and the waves roll toward the shore, returning the waters of the rivers and of the seas and of the ocean to their native shores. It is high tide. And that is why the tides ebb and flow.

June 9

How the Maverick Changed His Ways

A TALE OF THE AMERICAN WEST

Three old cows were lying on the sunny side of a little knoll up near the North Platte one day, telling stories of roundups they had been in. One of them made a remark about a maverick, and a little calf who was playing nearby picked up his ears and said, "Please, tell me what a maverick is."

Roan, the oldest cow of the bunch, laughed at the calf's ignorance with the others, but decided she had better enlighten him. "A maverick is what you'll be if you don't mend your ways."

"But I'm a good calf," insisted the little fellow. "I go where I please and do no harm."

"That's just why you are drifting into maverickdom," continued Roan. "You go from one place to another across the prairie, and one of these fine days a cowboy will come along and rope you, or catch you napping, and put his branding iron on you."

"Suppose I don't belong to him? I belong to the Bar-L ranch, you know, and all the cowboys there like me and wouldn't hurt me."

"You belong to the Bar-L ranch now," explained Roan, "but if one of the X-Y-Z cowboys gets hold of you, he'll change your mark of ownership real quick."

"Why would he do that?" asked the calf.

"Because you are a maverick. You go romping around the country, disobeying all orders about not going off the Bar-L range, and one of these fine days you'll see where you wind up."

"Were you ever a maverick?" the calf asked.

"No, not myself, but I have seen several. Aunt Bess here was one when she was young."

"Tell me about it," said the little calf, coming closer. "Does it hurt to be a maverick? Is the branding iron very hot?"

"Hot? I should say so!" exclaimed Aunt Bess, as she shifted her cud and cleared her throat. "It is hotter than anything I could tell you about. If you don't want to feel its sting, stay close to home."

"But how did you come to be a maverick?" inquired the calf.

"I was young and foolish, just as you are," replied Aunt Bess. "And one day, I ran away from home. I had been raised on the J-U-J ranch, and wanted to see more of the world than I was able to see there. I slipped out of the herd one morning and started north. After I had gone perhaps thirty miles, I got lost in the sand hills. I was awfully thirsty and my feet were sore by nightfall, but I didn't know how to get back. So I lay down to sleep and I was mighty happy to see a bunch of cattle grazing down in the valley the next morning. I went to where they were and asked for water, and an old bull showed me where to go. I told the cattle I wanted to join them, and the bull said all right, as long as I didn't lead any of the other calves astray. For ten days, I was as happy as a young calf could be, and then one evening several cowboys rode up and made camp. 'What are those men doing here?' I asked a young steer. 'Just you wait and see,' he said, and that was all the explanation I got.

"Early next morning, the cowboys began to ride around and separate the cows and calves from the steers. And do you know what happened to me?"

"I can't imagine," answered the little calf, whose eyes were fairly popping out of his head.

"They caught me, and before I knew it I had a red-hot branding iron slapped on my side and it wasn't the J-U-J brand either. As one of the cowboys took his knee off my neck to let me get up, I heard him say, 'This sure is a fine maverick.' "

As the old cow finished her story, the little calf said, "Aunt Bess, I want to thank you for telling me what a maverick really is. I'll never leave the Bar-L ranch again." And he never did!—EUGENE O. MAYFIELD

June 10

Through the Mouse Hole, Part 1

A CZECH TALE

In times long past, there reigned a king with three sons who were approaching manhood. They came to him one day and said, "Kingly father, it would be well for us to know more of the world. Do we have your leave to travel to other lands?"

Now the king did not think this a bad idea, but he made one condition: "You are all of an age when young men seek a wife. I will not tell you what princess to choose, but I command you to return in a year and a day with a gift from your intended, that I may know what sort of maiden has pleased you." The princes agreed at once, and decided that each would shoot an arrow into the air and begin their adventures in whatever direction the arrow fell.

They took their crossbows to an open field. The eldest son's arrow flew to the east, and the second son's to the west. But the arrow of the youngest son, whose name was Yarmil, flew after a mouse that had just run past. "O ho!" cried the brothers. "See where you must go, Yarmil! Into a mouse hole!" They thought it a great joke, but Yarmil was undaunted.

"I may find my fortune through a mouse hole as well as any other way," said he, approaching the mouse hole on his horse. Suddenly the small opening grew large, and he rode in quite easily. He found himself in open country, with nothing but a white marble castle standing before him. He did not see a living soul until he entered the castle gates, when a lady, dressed all in white and leading a snow-white steed, came forward and beckoned to Yarmil to mount this other horse. As he did so, they rose through the air and came to another splendid castle.

When Yarmil dismounted, his white horse disappeared. No one answered his knock at the castle, but the door swung open by itself. The first room was a great hall ablaze with gold and jewels. Beyond, Yarmil passed through a succession of chambers, each one more splendid than the last. In the eleventh room there was a crystal tub with gold pipes, but the twelfth chamber had little in it but a diamond pan in the middle of the floor. On top were inscribed words that Yarmil found strange: "Carry me near your heart and bathe me each day, so you will set free one who is bound."

Yarmil lifted the diamond cover from the pan, and inside what did he see but an ugly toad! His first thought was to run away, but instead he lifted the toad out and clasped it to his bosom. For a few moments, the toad's touch chilled him, but then he felt strangely happy.

Straightaway he went to the eleventh chamber and washed the toad carefully in the crystal tub. Many, many days passed like this: Yarmil ate fine meals served by unseen hands, and greatly enjoyed a splendid music room and library. Never once did a human being appear, and at first Yarmil was lonely but grew accustomed to his solitary splendor. And each day, he carried the toad near his heart and bathed it gently. Still, it remained a toad and, in fact, seemed to grow even uglier.

It was nearing the end of the year when he had to return to his father with a gift, and Yarmil was growing anxious. On the very last day, he saw a sheet of paper on his writing table that read: "Dear Yarmil—Be patient as I am patient. A gift for your father you will find in the pan. Give it to him, but do not stay too long at home. Put me back in the pan."

Yarmil found a lovely casket in the twelfth chamber, and when he went outside the castle, the white-robed lady appeared to him and escorted him back through the mouse hole. The brothers had brought impressive gifts, and Yarmil was rather nervous for he knew not what he was offering his father. The king opened the casket and was amazed to find a mirror no bigger than one's thumbnail, in which the king could see not only himself, but the whole great hall in which he sat. "Here is a princess who knows what is what!" cried the king. And Yarmil could not regret the year he had spent caring for the toad. After the feasting was done, the king commanded his sons to return to their princesses and bring back a portrait of them in another year and a day. Now what was Yarmil to do?

June 11

Through the Mouse Hole, Part 2

Back through the mouse hole Yarmil went, to the castle, where nothing had changed. He hurried to the twelfth chamber and took the toad out of the diamond pan. Now he bathed it twice each day, but to his grief it grew uglier. How could he take home the portrait of such a princess?

At last the day was near on which he must return. He looked continually on his writing table and finally found a sheet of paper whose silver letters read: "Dear Yarmil—Be patient as I am patient. You have my portrait in the pan. Give it to your father, but do not stay long. Put me back in the pan."

Yarmil took a jeweled casket from the pan without looking at it and returned to his father's palace. His father examined the portraits his brothers had brought back. Of each princess he said, "This is a beautiful lady. She pleases me. Still, there are fairer than she in the world." Yarmil handed over his casket with trembling hands. The king opened it and looked fixedly at what lay within, unable to utter a word. Was it a portrait of a toad that lay there? "Ah," cried the king at last, "I had not believed in all the world such a lady was to be found!" Everyone crowded around, including Yarmil, to look on the face of the princess. Such loveliness was unbelievable! There was nothing to regret about the two lonely years Yarmil had spent caring for a toad.

The king sent his sons off the next day on a final trip. "In a year and a day," he commanded, "bring back your princesses for the celebration of your weddings."

Yarmil hurried through the mouse hole to the castle and the twelfth chamber, hoping to find there his wondrous fair princess, but in the pan was the same ugly toad as before. He put the little creature near his heart, and for a year washed it three times a day. The toad, however, grew uglier and even seemed to shrivel. And now it was time to bring this creature to his father as his chosen bride.

Still, he would not give up hope and he stuck to his task till the very last day. On that day, to his surprise, he found the toad missing, and he began frantically searching the castle, for after all, he loved the creature. His astonishment when he reached the twelfth chamber was great. There stood a lady even more beautiful than the portrait. She turned to him and said sweetly, "My dearest, know that I am the daughter of a mighty king. My people and I were turned into toads by a wicked wizard because I would not marry him. You have endured much, but now at last your faithful devotion has set me free from the spell. Come, let us be off to your father's house."

She took him by the hand and led him out of the castle to where a splendid carriage with four white horses was waiting. Through the mouse hole they went and arrived at Yarmil's home with great pomp. No one even looked at the princesses that his brothers had brought with them, for Yarmil's bride was the fairest maiden anyone had ever seen.

The king rejoiced at his youngest son's good fortune, and the weddings were celebrated the next day. When the feasting was over, Yarmil set out with his wife to their kingdom. They found the mouse hole had become a magnificent gate leading to a great city, in the middle of which stood a golden castle. Now there were throngs of courtiers and servants who greeted their mistress and new master with mighty applause, thanking Yarmil at the same time for their liberation. The royal pair were goodness itself, and henceforth they all lived happily beyond measure.

June 12

Little Chicken Kluck

There once was a little chicken called Kluck. A nut fell on his back and gave him such a blow that he rolled on the ground. So he ran to the hen and said, "Henny Penny, flee! I think the sky is falling!"

"Who told you that, Little Chicken Kluck?"

"Oh, I know because part of it fell on my back."

"Then let us run," said the hen.

They hurried to the cock and said, "Cocky Locky, run! The sky is falling."

"Who told you that, Henny Penny?"

"Little Chicken Kluck, for part of it fell on his back."

"Then let us run," said Cocky Locky.

They ran to the duck and told him, "Ducky Lucky, run! The sky is falling."

"Who told you that, Cocky Locky?"

"Henny Penny. And Henny Penny heard it from Little Chicken Kluck."

They spread the word to Goosy Poosy and Foxy Coxy, then ran into the woods as fast as they could. Then the fox said, "I must now count and see if we are all here. I, Foxy Coxy, one; Goosy Poosy, two; Ducky Lucky, three; Cocky Locky, four; Henny Penny, five; and Little Chicken Kluck, six. Hey! That one I'll snap up." And then he said, "Let us run. . . ."

So they ran farther and farther into the woods. Then he stopped them once more and said, "Now I must count again and see that we're all together. I, Foxy Coxy, one; Goosy Poosy, two; Ducky Lucky, three; Cocky Locky, four; Henny Penny, five. Hey! That one I'll snap up."

And so he went on until he had eaten them all up.

June 13

Rapunzel

Once upon a time, a man and his wife lived all alone in a little house. They had long wished for a child, but in vain. Now at the back of their little house was a little window, which overlooked a garden full of lovely flowers and fine vegetables. But no one ever ventured into the garden, for there was a high wall around it and it belonged to a witch of great might.

One day the wife noticed that one of the garden beds was filled with fresh lettuce and she began to wish for some. Knowing she could not have it, she wanted it even more. This went on for days, and she grew pale and miserable.

Her husband asked, "What is the matter, dear wife?"

"Oh," answered she, "I shall die unless I can have some of that lettuce from the garden."

The man, who loved her very much, resolved to try. At twilight he climbed over the wall and plucked a handful of lettuce. As he headed back home, he suddenly saw the witch and he was terribly frightened. "How dare you come into my garden and steal my lettuce," the angry witch cried.

"Oh," begged the man, "be merciful! I only did it for my wife. She would have died without some of your lettuce."

The witch replied, "If that is so, you may have as much as you like—on one condition. The child who will come into your lives must be given to me."

The man made this promise, and sometime later a baby was born to his wife. Then the witch appeared, and giving the child the name Rapunzel, she took it away with her.

Rapunzel was the most beautiful girl in the world. When she was twelve years old, the witch shut her up in a tower in the middle of the woods. The tower had neither steps nor door, only a small window above. When the witch wished to be let in, she would stand below and cry, "Rapunzel, Rapunzel! Let down your hair!"

Rapunzel had long, lovely hair that shone like gold. When she heard the witch's voice, she would undo her braids and let her hair hang out the window, and the witch would climb up.

It happened that one day the king's son was riding through the woods. As he drew near the tower, he heard a voice singing so sweetly that he stopped to listen. It was Rapunzel, passing her lonely hours in song. The king's son wished to go to her, but he could see no way into the tower. So he rode home, but the song had entered his heart.

He went back to the woods each day, and soon enough he saw how the witch got into the tower. So the next night he rode there and cried, "Rapunzel, Rapunzel! Let down your hair."

Rapunzel was very frightened when the king's son climbed into her room, but he was so young and beautiful and he spoke so sweetly to her that she forgot her terror.

The king's son came back each evening, and soon he asked Rapunzel to marry him. She gladly agreed and, had it not been for a slip of the tongue, the witch might never have known a thing. When the witch was visiting one day, Rapunzel asked, "How is it that you climb up here so slowly and the king's son is with me in a moment?"

"O wicked child," cried the witch. "What is this I hear? I thought I had hidden you from the world, but you have betrayed me!"

The witch seized Rapunzel by her beautiful hair and cut it all off. Then she took Rapunzel away to a desert, where she lived in great woe and misery.

When the king's son came to the tower the next evening, the witch was waiting for him. She let down Rapunzel's shorn hair when he called up. As he climbed through the window, he saw not Rapunzel, but the wicked, glittering eyes of the witch. "Aha!" she cried. "You came for your darling, but the sweet bird sings no more. Rapunzel is lost to you forever."

In his grief, the king's son jumped from the tower and the thorns he landed on put out his eyes. He wandered blind through many forests for several years, weeping for Rapunzel. At last he neared the desert where she lived. Drawn by the sound of a voice he thought he knew, he came upon Rapunzel singing. She recognized him and embraced him tearfully. As her tears fell upon his eyes, they became clear again and he could see as well as ever.

Then he took her to his kingdom, where he was received with great joy, and there they lived long and happily.

—BROTHERS GRIMM

June 14

The Wedding of Widow Fox

A GERMAN TALE

Once upon a time there lived an old fox who, strange to say, had nine tails. He had a snug home in the woods and all else he needed, yet he was not happy. For the fox was eaten up by jealousy, and was convinced that his wife was not true to him. When he could stand it no longer, he devised a cunning scheme—and foxes, as we know, are very cunning—to test her faithfulness.

The old fox stretched himself out on a bench and lay motionless, holding his breath, so when Mrs. Fox came into the room, she believed him to be dead. Overcome with grief, she locked herself in her room. Only hunger drove her to call for the young cat who was her maid and ask for dinner.

The news of the old fox's death had spread quickly in the nieghborhood, and several suitors for Mrs. Fox's hand were gathered at the door already.

The young cat was busy frying sausages when she heard a knock. Answering it, she found a young fox at the door who said, "Oh, it is you, Miss Kitty. What are you doing?"

"Well, I'm getting supper ready for my mistress. Will you come in, sir?"

"Thank you, my dear, but what is Mrs. Fox doing?"

"Oh," replied the cat, "she does nothing but sit in her room and cry her eyes out."

"Then go and tell her that a young fox is here who wishes to court her."

The cat scampered upstairs and gave this news to Mrs. Fox, who was disbelieving at first, but then asked, "What is he like?"

"He is a handsome young fox," replied the cat. "With a bushy tail and such whiskers!"

"Ah!" sighed the widow. "But has he nine beautiful tails as my poor husband did?"

"No," answered the cat. "Only one."

"Then I won't have him!" cried the widow.

The cat gave the message to the suitor and sent him away. But soon after there was a knock at the door again. Another young fox wished to court the widow, and he had two tails, but no greater success than the first. And so they kept coming, one after the other, each with one tail more, but Mrs. Fox refused them all. Even a wolf, a stag, a bear, and a lion came calling, but she would have nothing to do with any of them.

By this time the old fox was beginning to think he had been mistaken about his wife. And besides, he was getting hungry and could not pretend to be dead much longer. He opened his eyes, and was just about to spring up and announce his resurrection, when the cat came into the room.

"Madame Fox," she exclaimed. "There's a young gentleman fox downstairs and he's so handsome. He has nine tails, a scarlet tongue, red stockings, and a pointed nose, and he wishes to become your suitor."

"That is just the husband for me," cried Mrs. Fox, much to everyone's surprise. "We'll have a splendid wedding. But first, let us throw the old fox out and bury him."

At this the old fox jumped up from his resting place and gave Mrs. Fox a terrible scolding. Then he turned the young cat and all the other servants and the suitors out of the house, and Widow Fox after them. So he had the place all to himself, and made a firm resolution never to die again, if he could help it.—BROTHERS GRIMM

June 15

Doctor Know-All

A GERMAN TALE

A poor peasant named Crabbs was once driving two oxen and a cart with a load of wood through town when he had the chance to sell it to a doctor for two dollars.

When he went in to receive his money, the doctor was at dinner, and the peasant looked at all the good things at the table and began to long for them, and wish he had been a doctor.

He remained standing for a while after he had been paid, and at last asked if he could not also become a doctor.

"Yes, that can be easily managed," replied the doctor. "You must first buy an ABC book. Then you must sell your wagon and oxen and buy a suit of clothes such as a doctor would wear. Lastly, have a sign painted and hung over your door that says, 'I am Doctor Know-All!' "

The peasant followed the doctor's advice, and soon had a few patients, but not that many.

About this time, a nobleman in town was robbed of a great deal of money. He announced he would give a handsome reward to anyone who could discover the thief or return the money.

The nobleman was told of the clever Doctor Know-All, and decided to invite him to dinner to see if he could be of assistance. "I am more than willing, my lord," said Doctor Know-All, "if my wife, Grethel, can accompany me."

The nobleman was agreeable and picked them both up for dinner in his carriage. As soon as they were seated at the dinner table, the servants began waiting upon them. When the first servant placed a dish on the table, the doctor quietly said to his wife, "Grethel, that is the first."

He only meant the first servant to bring the different courses, for he wished her to notice what a number of servants waited at table in a great lord's house. The servant, however, thought he was speaking to him as the first of the thieves, and as this was the truth, he was terribly frightened. When he got out into the hall, he said to his companions, "That doctor knows everything we have been doing! He has just said that I am the first."

On hearing this, the other servants were afraid to go into the dining room, but they were obligated to perform their duty. Another servant came with the second course.

As he placed the dish on the table, he heard the doctor say, "That is the second."

The servant got out of the room as quickly as he could, and it was the same for the third and the fourth servant. At this point, the nobleman, wishing to prove the cleverness of his visitor, asked him to say what was under the covered dish the fourth servant brought.

Now it happened to be a crab, which of course the doctor did not know, so he was in a great dilemma. To himself he said in a low voice, "Crabbs, Crabbs, what will you do?"

The nobleman heard only the word "Crabbs," and he cried eagerly, "Yes, it is a crab, and I see now that you know everything. You will be able to tell me where my money is."

The servants were very alarmed and signaled to the doctor to come out in the hall. There they offered him a reward to not betray them. To this he agreed, if they showed him where the stolen money was. They showed him, and a fifth servant hid in the dining hall to listen.

Back in the dining room, the doctor said, "My lord, I will now consult my book," and he opened his ABC book and pretended to consult various pages. As he browsed through the book, the doctor exclaimed, "You are there, but you will have to come out!"

The hidden man, supposing the doctor spoke to him, sprang out from his hiding place and cried, "This man knows everything!"

Doctor Know-All took the nobleman to the place where the money was concealed, but he did not tell who the thieves were. So in addition to the reward offered for the discovery of the money, he also received a sum from the servants for not betraying them, and became a man of great renown.—BROTHERS GRIMM

June 16

Doctor Know-All, Variation

The Doctor Know-All motif spans three continents—Africa, Asia, and Europe—and appears in some four hundred different stories. Running throughout all of these tales is the central character who saves or makes his reputation by a fortunate accident or coincidence.

The Italian version begins with a king who has lost a valuable ring and issues a proclamation that if any astrologer can find it he will reward him handsomely. A poor peasant named Crab, who aspires to be an astrologer, convinces the king to sponsor his search. The king gives him a room in which to "study." Of course, Crab cannot even read but he pretends to be the great scholar, scribbling phony notes and turning pages in books. Over time he impresses the servants who bring him food and provisions daily. The servants, who stole the ring, begin to worry that Crab is onto them.

Crab's wife comes to visit him in the room and he tells her to hide under the bed and to say "that is one" when the first servant enters; "that is two" when the second servant enters; "that is three," and so on. The servants are frightened at hearing the voice and figure that they are discovered. They confess to Crab.

Crab promises not to betray the servants and tells them to take the ring to the courtyard and to make the turkey there swallow it. They comply, and with great flourish Crab reports to the king that after much toil he has discovered the ring's whereabouts. When the turkey is cut open the ring is found and Crab is a hero.

A banquet is held to celebrate the recovery of the ring. At this grand meal crabs are served. Crabs are a very rare delicacy and few in the kingdom know them by name. The king challenges the astrologer to identify the crustacean. The poor astrologer is very much puzzled and nervously starts to mutter, "Ah Crab, Crab, what a plight you are in now." The food is thus identified and all who did not know his name was Crab proclaim him the greatest astrologer in the world.

June 17

The Farmer and His Sons

A farmer, being on the point of death, called together his sons. Though he was not a wealthy man, he did want to show his sons the way to success in farming.

"My children," he said, "I am now departing from this life, but all that I have I leave you, and you will find it in the vineyard."

The sons, supposing that he referred to some hidden treasure, set to work with their spades and ploughs and every implement that was at hand, and turned up the soil over and over again. They found no treasure but the vines, strengthened and improved by this thorough digging, yielded a finer vintage than they had ever yielded before, and more than repaid the sons for all of their trouble.—AESOP

June 18

The Farmer and His Two Daughters

A TALE FOR FATHER'S DAY

A farmer had two daughters. As it happened, one married a gardener and one married a potter. Wanting to see how his daughters were faring, he went for a visit. First he went to the gardener's home.

"How goes it, my dear?" he asked his daughter.

The daughter replied that all went well except for the weather. "We have everything we want but we are praying for a heavy storm so that the rain might water our plants."

The farmer promised to pray for rain and went to visit the potter's home.

"How goes it, my dear?" he asked his other daughter.

The daughter replied that all went well except for the weather. "We have everything we want but we are praying for hot sun so that the heat will bake our tiles," she said.

The farmer became confused. He wanted what was best for each of his two daughters. "What am I to do?" he asked, looking to his Good Maker. "One daughter wishes for rain and the other for hot sun. What I am to pray for?"

But the farmer received no answer. Again, the farmer asked the Maker: "What am I to pray for? One daughter wishes for rain and the other for hot sun." Still, no answer.

Not long after, a storm blew in and it rained for several hours. Then the sun came out and dried up the land. You see, the Good Maker is a father, too. And a good father would never choose between two daughters.

June 19

The Man and His Two Wives

In the days when a man was allowed more wives than one, a middle-aged bachelor, who could be called neither young nor old and whose hair was just beginning to turn gray, fell in love with two women at once and married them both. The one was young and blooming, and wished her husband to appear as youthful as herself; the other was somewhat more advanced in age, and was as anxious that her husband appear a suitable match for her. So, while the young one seized every opportunity of pulling out the good man's gray hairs, the old one was just as industrious in plucking out every black hair she could find. For a while, the man was highly gratified by their attention and devotion, until he found one morning that between the one and the other, he had not a hair left!—AESOP

June 20

The Emperor's New Clothes

Vanity breeds fools, and a fool was precisely what the emperor had become. The emperor was so in love with his own image that he'd ordered the palace walls to be lined with mirrors, and now he spent his days admiring himself from every possible angle. If people laughed at him for his conceit, he was too proud to notice.

One day, two tricksters pretended to be cloth merchants and came to the emperor's palace asking to see the emperor. The so-called merchants told the servants that they had come from a distant land bringing finely woven material, grander than any the emperor had seen. When the emperor learned of their wares, he ushered the twosome into his private chambers at once. "Show me what you have," he demanded, his fingertips dancing. He was beside himself as the tricksters began to pull out from a long wooden trunk bolt upon bolt of what they described as the finest material in the world. "This fabric is so superb," began the first, "that it has the magical quality of being invisible to anyone who is a fool." The emperor blinked—he could see no cloth at all. While the merchants unrolled the fine material, the emperor pretended to be enthusiastic, but really he could see nothing.

The emperor called in his wife and courtiers to see the cloth, and though no one could actually see it, they all pretended it was lovely, for no one wanted to appear the fool.

The emperor and his court continued to ooh and ahh over the material that did not exist so the tricksters decided to take the prank a step further. "Would Your Majesty like us to take measurements for a suit so we can transform these fine materials into a royal garment?" asked the first trickster. "We will do it from start to finish, for we would trust no one else to cut it and stitch it."

The emperor agreed and the tricksters were given a special sewing room and very particular instructions for sewing the jacket and coat. They fussed about the emperor and promised to have the royal ensemble ready for the next day.

In the morning when the new clothes were ready the emperor went through the motions of being fitted by the duplicitous cloth merchants. He stood before a long mirror looking to this side, then that one, but he could see no clothes at all. He called for the opinion of his chief minister, who was speechless to see the emperor with no clothes on. Yet the minister knew that the fabric was invisible to fools, so he flattered the emperor: "Why, Your Majesty, how magnificent you look! Perhaps you should wear your new suit of clothes at your birthday procession next week."

In truth, the emperor was somewhat surprised because he always believed the chief minister was a fool, but he didn't say anything. And since he did like the idea of having the whole kingdom admire him at his birthday procession, he had his messengers spread the news that the procession would be the following week, and that he would be wearing the finest clothes in the land. Word also got around that to fools the clothes would be invisible, so everyone planned to pretend to see the clothes rather than be regarded as a fool.

On the day of the procession, the emperor took great care dressing, even though he still could not see the fine garments. He rode through the streets of his kingdom without a stitch of clothing on, while the crowds lining the streets pretended to admire his invisible frocks. The emperor was somewhat surprised to discover there were no fools in his empire, until a cry came from a young boy, who was sitting up in a tree so as to better view his emperor. "Oh, dear," the boy cried. "What happened to our emperor's clothes? He has on nothing at all."

At first, the crowd shushed the boy, then a few people started to laugh. Finally, a man shouted out: "The boy is right. The emperor has no clothes on." With that the crowd started to roar with laughter, and the emperor realized that only a fool would believe in magic clothes.

The tricksters, of course, were run out of town, and no one knows for sure how they were punished. As for the small boy, the emperor declared him the wisest person in the whole kingdom. "You alone were not afraid to speak the truth," said the emperor with a grateful heart. When the boy became a young man, the emperor promised he would be chief minister.

June 21

The Gnat and the Bull

Gnats are tiny bugs that make a humming sound when they fly. This gnat was flying over a valley one day when he became weary. He looked for a place to rest and spotted a bull grazing on some grass. He landed on the bull's nose and took an afternoon nap.

When the gnat woke up, he spoke to the bull. "Excuse me, dear sir. I just wanted to thank you for allowing me to rest on your nose. I had a good nap, I feel refreshed, and I'm ready for the rest of my journey."

The bull looked at the gnat and said, "I don't know what you are talking about. I didn't even know you were there."

The smaller the mind, the greater the conceit.—AESOP

June 22

Howleglass the Quack

A GERMAN FOLKTALE

Howleglass paid a visit to the city of Nuremberg. On this occasion he entered the city, put posters on church gates, and trumpeted the news that a great doctor, a mighty expert at his art, was coming to town. About this time there were lodged at the hospital a number of patients who were stubborn and constantly complaining.

The keeper of the hospital told Howleglass that he would be paid well for curing the patients. Howleglass said, "Sir, if you will give me a hundred crowns from the sick fund I will rid you of these patients and I will not take a shilling until I have cleansed the hospital of them all."

This was an excellent arrangement for the keeper and the hospital's governors. Everyone shook hands and went their own ways. Howleglass did not waste a moment and began to see the patients, one by one, taking notes of the full nature of each one's complaint.

Then, confiding secretly to each, he told the patient the nature of his cure. "I have come here to cure all of you, of course, but I cannot do that without killing one of you to make a remedy of him, which the rest of you will take. The more sick and diseased the fellow is, the better he will suit our purpose, and I will certainly choose one who cannot walk. Next Wednesday I will come with the keeper and the governors, and the patient who appears weakest will be made into a medicine for the rest. Ha!" Howleglass then burst into a gale of sick laughter and walked away.

As you can imagine, the patients were most distressed with the nature of the cure, and they took every measure to recover their health as quickly as possible. On the appointed day, the patients were on alert. They dressed as well as they could and most of them had packed a bag. Even those who had been bedridden—one for ten years—were up and about and ready to go. Rather than stand around waiting for the call to be made into a medicine, they all checked out of the hospital.

The keeper and the governors were delighted to pay Howleglass his excessive fee, and upon being paid, Howleglass fled. In the course of three days, however, all the patients returned complaining of their infirmities louder than ever. "What is the meaning of this?" asked the keeper. "I paid a huge sum to have you all cured."

"True," they replied with one voice. "But did you know that Howleglass threatened to have the last of us who should remain in bed killed to make a medicine for the rest?"

The keeper could see that he had been fooled. But there was little he could do but take the patients back in, to no small regret of the governors and their bankers.

—ADAPTED FROM THOMAS ROSCOE

June 23

How the Tortoise Got Its Shell

Centuries ago, people believed in many gods. One of the most powerful of those gods was Jupiter. It happened that Jupiter was to marry, and so he planned a great wedding banquet to which he invited all the animals of the world. On the appointed day, the lion, the elephant, the horse, and all of the others came to the feast, but not the tortoise.

Jupiter was quite put out by the tortoise's absence, for it was highly insulting for the tortoise to ignore Jupiter's invitation. When next he saw the tortoise, he asked the reason for this snub. "Oh, I don't care for going out very much," said the tortoise. "I would rather stay home, for there's no place like it."

Jupiter was so annoyed by this reply that he issued a decree to punish the tortoise's rudeness. From that time forth, the tortoise would carry its house upon its back. Never would the tortoise be able to leave home, even if it wanted to.

June 24

Urashima

A JAPANESE TALE

Many years ago a boy lived by the sea, where the great green waves came riding in to break on the shore in clouds of salty spray. The boy, named Urashima, loved the ocean, and was often out in his boat from purple dawn to russet evening. One day as he was fishing, something tugged at his line, yet when he pulled it in, it was not a fish but a wrinkled old turtle.

"Well," said Urashima, "if I cannot catch a dinner for myself, at least I will not keep this old fellow from his." And the kindhearted Urashima heaved the turtle back into the sea. This made a big splash, and the splash became a spray, and from the spray emerged a lovely girl who got into the boat.

"I am the daughter of the sea god," she said. "I was that turtle you just threw back. My father sent me to see if you were as kind as you seemed. Will you come live with us in the dragon palace far below the green waves?" Urashima was glad to go, and away they sped.

Long before the purple haze of evening had settled on the earth, Urashima and the Dragon Princess reached the twilight depths of the under sea. The fish scudded about them through branches of coral and trailing ropes of seaweed. The roar of the waves above was only a trembling murmur down here.

The dragon palace was made of seashell and pearl, coral and emerald. It gleamed with all the thousand lights and tints that lurk in the depths of the water. Fish with silver fins rushed to wait on them, and the daintiest foods the ocean holds for her children were served to them. Seven dragons with golden tails hovered at their sides, anticipating any wish they might have.

Urashima lived in great happiness with the Dragon Princess for four short years. Then he remembered his home and longed to see his family. The princess was sad, but she understood. "I will not keep you, but I fear letting you go. Take this box of mother-of-pearl and let nothing happen to it. I know you will wish to come back, but if you open the box, you will never be able to return."

She placed Urashima in his boat, and the waves quickly carried him to the sands where he used to play. But strangely, his father's cottage was no longer there. As he drew near his village, the houses there looked strange too, and he could not recognize a soul. Urashima stopped an old man. "Can

you tell me, sir, where Urashima's family has gone?"

"Urashima?" replied the old man. "Don't you know he drowned four hundred years ago while out fishing. His brothers, their children, and their children have all lived and died since then!"

Gone! Urashima could hardly believe it. But now he had to hurry back to the dragon palace, as it was the only home he had left. How to get back, he was not sure. He walked along the sand, thinking, but not remembering the princess's warning. Urashima opened the pearl box and a white cloud rose from it. As the cloud floated away, he thought he saw the face of the Dragon Princess. He reached out toward the cloud and saw that he was suddenly growing old. His hands were shaking and his hair had turned white. Urashima was melting away to join the past in which he had lived.

When the new moon hung her horn of light from the branches of the pine tree, there was only a small pearl box on the sand shore, and the great green waves were lifting white arms of foam as they had done four hundred years before.

June 25

The Lion, the Bear, and the Fox

A lion and a bear happened upon the carcass of a fawn. Unwilling to share even a bit of it, they had a long fight. It was an ugly contest. They fought until they were half-blind and too weary to eat, and so for the longest time they lay on their backs, panting. The two were so weak they could not even muster the strength to nibble at the prize between them.

About this time a fox chanced to pass. Seeing the helpless state of the bear and the lion, he stepped in between the combatants and carried off the tasty prize.

"What foolish creatures are we," said the bear, still breathing hard. "We spent all our strength injuring one another, merely to give the rogue fox a delicious dinner!"—AESOP

June 26

Silly Jura

A CZECH FOLKTALE

Jura was the youngest of three brothers and the dreamer of the family. His two older brothers, who were shiftless and dishonest, were full of schemes to better their station in life. They thought Jura was useless and silly and they constantly made fun of him.

One day the two older young men announced their plan to leave their village and find themselves wealthy wives. "You stay home, Silly Jura," they said. "You'd never find a good wife anyway."

But Jura followed them off into the forest, where he had heard there was an enchanted castle. As night fell he came across the ruins of a castle, where there seemed to be a light in the cellar. But there was no one in the cellar but a cat, who said, "Welcome, dear Jura!"

Now Jura was frightened to hear a cat speak and was about to run away. But the cat pleaded with him to stay. No harm would come to him and he could be her servant.

It was an easy job, for all Jura had to do was gather firewood. He never saw a cook, but there were meals set out in the storeroom each day. At the end of a year, the cat told him to make a great pile of logs. Then she said, "You must set the pile afire and throw me into it. And no matter how I beg, you must let me be consumed by the fire."

"I can't do that!" said Jura. "I've had a good time here and I'm fond of you. Why should I repay your kindness in such an evil way?"

"Believe me, we will find great happiness if you do as I say," replied the cat.

So Jura reluctantly followed her orders, and when the fire died down, he fell asleep. When he awoke, the castle was no longer in ruins. There were servants scurrying about, and from a distant room he could hear lovely music. As he was wondering how this transformation had come to pass, a beautiful woman came up to him and asked, "Don't you know me, Jura?"

"How would I know your ladyship?" Jura said, puzzled.

"I am your friend, the cat," the lady answered. "A witch had put a spell on me that turned me from a princess into a cat. You freed me from the enchantment by doing as I asked."

Jura was overjoyed at this news, and a few weeks later the two were married. Jura's wife learned of his many humiliations at the hands of his brothers and suggested paying them a visit.

Jura and the princess left the castle in a magnificent carriage and splendid clothing, but just before they got to Jura's village, the princess told him to put his old clothing on. Then she hailed a ragged beggarwoman and told Jura that the two of them should walk to his brothers' house.

When Jura and the beggarwoman got there, the brothers—who had also married, but not to the wealthy wives they hoped for—jeered at him. "Look at Silly Jura! He's still the same and is bringing home a ragged old bride." They refused to let Jura in the house.

Jura left the village and joined his real wife in the carriage where he changed to his fine clothes. When the carriage stopped before his brothers' cottage, they didn't even recognize him at first. But when they learned how well he had married, they fell all over themselves trying to make the couple welcome. "You have sneered at Jura all your lives," said the princess. "And see how things have turned out for him. If you two cared less about appearances and more about the person inside, your lives could have been as happy as his."

And with those words, Jura and the princess left the brothers' cottage forever.

June 27

The Squire's Bride

A FOLKTALE FROM NORWAY

Once in Norway there lived a squire who was very wealthy. But he was also lonely, for his wife had died many years before. During the day, he walked his land and at night he counted his money. That was his life.

Just down the road there lived a neighbor who had grown from an impish little girl into a beautiful woman. Her father owed the squire a lot of money, which got the squire to thinking: maybe he could marry the girl and cancel the debt, sort of a trade.

"Well, that's the dumbest idea I've ever heard," said the girl. "You're way too old for me, no matter how rich you are!"

The squire was hurt. Then he got angry. How dare she speak to him that way! So he went to the girl's father and told him to pay up or else.

The girl's father thought that trading the girl for the debt was a sensible idea. He'd owe no money and she could lead a life of luxury. "Don't worry," he told the squire. "I can reason with her. I promise you her hand."

The farmer went back and pleaded with his daughter. But nothing the girl's father could say would convince her she should marry the old squire.

For the squire, the whole affair had become a terrible insult.

"Have her ready to marry or I'll close down your farm, and everything you own," he told the farmer, his face twitching with anger.

The squire had all of his servants begin baking and preparing for the wedding. Invitations were sent to all of the most important people in the village. Flowers were cut and made into huge, colorful bouquets. When everything was ready, the squire sent one of his farmhands to go and fetch what he had been promised. "And make it quick," he called out as the boy went on his dubious mission.

The boy knocked on the farm girl's door. "Halloo! I come from the squire, who demands that you send him what you promised."

The father peeked out from behind a curtained window. "But of course," he said. "Go down to the meadow and take her with you."

In the meadow the boy found the girl. She was bundling hay. "I am here to take what your father promised the squire."

"Doubtless he wants our little mare. Go get the horse yourself. She's hitched to the fence post over there," the girl said.

The farm boy was a good rider. He jumped on the horse and rode her back to his master, and then went to report that his mission was accomplished.

"Did you bring her back?" the squire asked. The boy assured the squire that he had and indicated that he had left her in the front yard.

"Take her to the guest bedroom then," the squire ordered.

"What?" asked the boy. "Are you quite serious?"

The squire gave the boy such a look that the boy did not want to discuss the matter further. He rounded up some of the servants and hoisted the mare up to the guest bedroom, where there was a beautiful wedding gown and veil laid out on the bed.

The boy reported to the squire that he had brought "her" up and that she was in the guest room. The squire then ordered the lady servants to "go up and dress her."

"But, master," they all protested. "Do as I say!" the squire barked.

Meanwhile, all of the most distinguished villagers, from the town mayor on down, began to arrive in carriages to witness the squire's elaborate wedding.

As the guests strolled onto the property, the lady servants went up and dressed the mare in pure white finery, putting a wreath of beautiful flowers on as a finishing touch. "Are you ready to see her?" they called down to the squire, giggling like schoolgirls.

"Yes," said the squire, suddenly pleased. "Bring the lovely lady down and I will receive her properly."

All at once there was a huge commotion, and a terrible ruckus on the stairway as the mare took a tumble and fell down the stairs. Hearing the noise, the guests ran in from all over, only to see the horse in a wedding gown licking the very red face of the squire. The villagers roared . . . and the squire swore off women for the rest of his life.

June 28

The Three Wishes

A SPANISH FOLKTALE

One summer night many years ago, an old man named Pedro and his wife, Joanna, sat at the dinner table in their house in a little village. Now Pedro and his wife had all the necessities of life, but instead of being grateful for this, they spent all their time wishing for the good things their neighbors possessed.

"Bah!" cried Pedro. "This wretched little hut of ours is only fit to house a donkey! If only we owned a fine house and farm like our neighbor, Diego!"

"Aye! Diego's house is far better," answered Joanna. "Still I could wish to have such a mansion as the grandees possess—like that of Don Juan de Rosa!"

"That old donkey of ours is good for nothing," went on Pedro sullenly.

"O aye! Diego's mule is better than our donkey," said Joanna. "For me, though, I would like a fine white horse with trappings of scarlet and gold, like Donna Isabella's. It is strange how some people have only to wish for a thing in order to get it. We have never had such luck."

Scarcely were the words out of Joanna's mouth when before the old couple appeared a beautiful little woman. She was not more than eighteen inches high, and was dressed in filmy white garments, and carried a golden wand with a sparkling ruby at its end.

"I am the Fairy Fortunata," she said. "I have heard your complaints and am coming to give you what you desire. Three wishes you shall have—one for you, Joanna, and one for you, Pedro—and the third you shall agree upon between you. I will grant it in person when I return at this time tomorrow."

Then the fairy disappeared in a cloud of smoke. The old couple was delighted. Three wishes to come true! They began to think at once of what they most desired in all the world, and wishes were soon swarming to them as thick as bees to a hive. In fact, they had so many that they agreed to postpone their decision until the next day, and began idly talking about their wealthier neighbors again.

"I dropped in at Diego's house this morning," said Pedro, "and they were making black puddings. Um! but they smelled good! Diego can buy the best of raisins and everything else."

"True, true!" said Joanna. "I wish I had one of Diego's puddings here this minute!"

The words were not out of her mouth when on the hearth appeared the most delicious pudding that could possibly be imagined. As she stared back in amazement, Pedro jumped up in rage.

"You foolish creature!" he cried. "You have used up one of our precious wishes—and on a poor little pudding! It makes me wild! I wish the pudding were stuck fast to your nose!"

At that—whisk! There flew the pudding and hung from where Pedro pointed. And shake her head as she might, Joanna could not free the pudding from her nose. "See what you have done, petty creature!" she wailed. At that point the dog and cat, sniffing the savory pudding, came leaping up and began pawing at Joanna, hoping for a lick. "Down! Down!" shrieked Joanna, as she wildly defended her nose. "I will agree to nothing but that our third wish is to have this miserable pudding taken off me."

"Wife, for heaven's sake," cried Pedro. "What of the new farm I wanted?"

"I will never agree to wish for it!"

"But listen to reason! Think of the golden palace you desired! Or let us wish at least for a fortune, and then you shall have a golden case with jewels to cover the pudding on your nose!"

"I will not hear of it," answered Joanna.

"Then, alas, we shall be left just as we were before!"

"That is all I desire. I see now that we were well enough off as we were."

Nothing Pedro said could alter his wife's determination, so when the fairy appeared the following night and asked their third wish, they answered, "We wish only to be as we were before."

So that was the wish she granted.

June 29

The Three Wishes, Variations

"The Three Wishes" (also known as "The Ridiculous Wishes" and "The Poor Man and the Rich Man") is a classic rendering of the fate of ordinary individuals granted instant power and/or wealth. Generally, these characters make a mess of it. It is usually the husband who gives his wife first crack at a wish. Then the husband enters the wish-making process at this point and flubs the second wish. The third wish is usually designed to undo the first two.

This story can be amended by storytellers by changing the foolish choices made by the main characters, or by completely changing the outcome by having the characters make wise choices. In the case of the latter scenario, a Christ or Buddha figure might come to offer the ordinary individual three wishes—or chances to choose wisely—and the tale might be used to illustrate a tenet of faith or morality.

June 30

The Wolf and the Sheep

A wolf had been hurt badly in a fight and was unable to move. A sheep passed by and the wolf appealed to him.

"Kind sheep, I have had nothing to eat or drink for days. Won't you please fetch me some water so I may get up my strength to eat solid food?"

The sheep was moved for a moment by the wolf's plight, but came to his senses quickly.

"Solid food?" he said. "And who might that be? If I brought you a drink it would only be to wash down the likes of me!"

Mercy can be misappropriated.—AESOP

JULY

July 1

The Cat and the Parrot

AN INDIAN FOLKTALE

Two friends, a cat and a parrot, decided to spend more time together.

"Let's have dinner at each other's houses, turn and turn about," suggested the parrot.

"That's a wonderful idea," said the cat. "We can dine first at my house."

The cat was very stingy. When the parrot went to have dinner there, he was served a bit of milk, a thin slice of fish, and dry biscuit. The parrot thanked the cat politely but he did not have a very good time.

When the cat came to dine at the parrot's house, it was another story. He had a roast of meat, a pot of tea, a basket of fruit, and five hundred little cakes. The parrot gave 498 cakes to the cat and saved just two for himself.

To the amazement of the parrot, the cat swallowed the food in a single gulp. Then he looked around and said, "I'm starved. Do you have anything to eat around here?"

The parrot offered the cat the two remaining cakes, which the cat put down in an instant. "Gee, I'm really working up an appetite here. What else do you have?"

The parrot was starting to get annoyed. "Well, I don't really have anything more unless you want to eat me!" he said, thinking his friend would be ashamed. The cat licked his chops and amazingly: slip! slop! gobble! Down his throat went the parrot. His *friend.*

An old woman saw the whole thing and chastised the cat for his behavior. "What's a parrot to me?" the cat. "I've got half a mind to eat you too." And with that: slip! slop! gobble! he ate the old woman.

The cat started down the road to the village. Along the way he saw a man driving a donkey. "Out of my way, cat," said the driver. "My donkey might step on you."

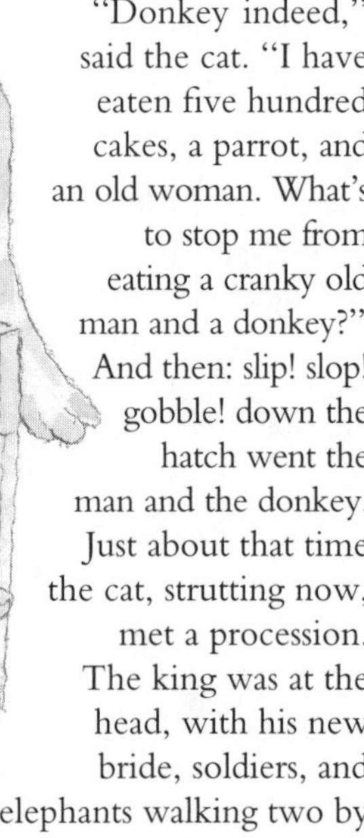

"Donkey indeed," said the cat. "I have eaten five hundred cakes, a parrot, and an old woman. What's to stop me from eating a cranky old man and a donkey?" And then: slip! slop! gobble! down the hatch went the man and the donkey. Just about that time the cat, strutting now, met a procession. The king was at the head, with his new bride, soldiers, and elephants walking two by

two. The king said, "Step aside, little cat. My elephants might hurt you."

"Hah!" said the cat. "I've eaten five hundred cakes, a parrot, an old woman, and an old man and a donkey. I doubt any of you could hurt me."

And with that he downed the king, his bride, the soldiers, and the elephants: slip! slop! gobble!

Two land crabs crossed the cat's path. "Move, old cat!" they squeaked.

The cat doubled over with laughter: "I've eaten five hundred cakes, a parrot, an old woman, an old man, a donkey, and a king and his whole entourage. Now I'll eat you too!" Slip! slop! gobble! Down went the two crabs.

In the cat's stomach, the land crabs were surprised at what they saw: the king in a corner, trying to console his bride; the soldiers pacing; the elephants trying to form into pairs; the old woman and old man having a conversation; and a great pile of cakes upon which a parrot was perched.

"Let's get to work!" said the crabs. Everyone in the cat's stomach began snipping away at the cat's side, and when the hole was big enough, out went the king and his bride, the soldiers in step, the elephants two-by-two, the old man beating his donkey, the old woman, and last of all the parrot, holding a cake in each claw. (Remember? Two cakes was all he wanted.)

The cat spent the whole day sewing up the hole in his side.

July 2

The Cat and the Parrot, Variations

Swallowing is a big theme in folktales. In the previous tale, the cat swallows five hundred cakes, a parrot, an old woman, an old man and his donkey, a king and his entourage, and two crabs. Other animals have swallowed enough men to have an entire card game going on inside their stomachs; monsters have had entire buildings and towns within; a louse in one Indian tale swallows a crow, a loaf of bread, a goat, a cow buffalo, a wedding procession, an elephant, and a tank of water among other things.

The swallowing motif is great fun for the improvised story told at home. Here again, a central character of your own making can encounter anyone along the way. The "way" can be the past or the future, a city or a country road. Your swallower can devour anything from a bus filled with lawyers to a nasty old aunt.

July 3

DOG DAYS BEGIN

The Bad Dog

Once there was a bad dog. He was so out of control that his master put a muzzle around him to prevent him from biting the neighbors. The dog, who was as stupid as he was bad, thought the muzzle spoke well of him, and paraded around the neighborhood, shaking his nose this way and that to gain attention. He looked like a fool!

A cat called out to him from a distant hedge, "I know you did not ask for my advice, but I feel it my duty to tell you: the less parading you do, the better. You are not in your right mind if you think a muzzle is a badge of honor."

The clueless canine thought over the cat's comments. As he was not in his right mind, he continued his parade and became the laughingstock of the neighborhood.

People often mistake notoriety for fame and would rather be noticed for their sins than not noticed at all.—AESOP

July 4

INDEPENDENCE DAY

Fourth of July Pies

Billy Ambrose was five, and very curious for his age. Today he was wondering about the Fourth of July. "Why do you always fry chicken for the Fourth of July picnic?" he asked his mother, who was standing over a huge cast-iron skillet filled with chicken legs gurgling in hot oil. "I mean, why not pork chops?"

"It's a tradition, honey," his mother said, "an Ambrose family tradition. When I married your father, we made an agreement. He promised he would love me for the rest of his life if I would love him *and* fry chicken for the Fourth of July picnic. That's just the way it is."

A few hours later, Billy and his sister, Jesse, and Mr. and Mrs. Ambrose took a big basket filled with fried chicken to the town square, where just about all of Canton was gathered for the annual Fourth of July parade. The parade was a democratic affair; half of the town marched, while the other half watched. After the parade, everybody gathered for the picnic. As long as anyone could remember, every Fourth of July the people of Canton ate fried chicken and ham and pickles and deviled eggs and biscuits, followed by Mrs. Janson's pies. Mrs. Janson had scary eyebrows and Billy wasn't crazy about her or her pies.

Billy and Jesse carefully laid out the blue-and-white-checked blanket on the grass and went to the buffet to fill their plates with food. Billy's mom was handing out chicken and Mrs. Janson was slicing pie. Everything was exactly the way it had been last year.

This made Billy curious.

"Jesse, why do we always have the same things at the picnic every year?

We always use this blue-and-white blanket and have a parade and eat Mrs. Janson's pies. Why is it always just the same?" he asked.

"Well," said Jesse, who was eleven and enjoyed explaining life to Billy, "I guess we do it because it's a tradition. On Thanksgiving, we always have turkey. I guess it would be a nuisance to have to come up with a different meal every year. So we do the same thing every Fourth of July. That's just the way it is."

Just about that time Billy's dad sat down. His plate was piled high. "Great Fourth, huh, Billy? Boy, your mom sure knows how to fry chicken."

"Sure," Billy said. "But next year can we have spaghetti on the Fourth of July?"

Mr. Ambrose looked hard at Billy. "I thought you liked mom's chicken, Billy. We've been having the same picnic for three generations in Canton. That's just the way it is."

Billy was starting to get the message. No one knew why they did all of this on July Fourth. They'd done it for so long they didn't know what they were doing.

Finally, Billy's mother came over and sat down beside him. "Mom, next year can we celebrate July Fourth on July third. I mean, just for a change?" he asked.

"Why, Billy. July Fourth is our country's birthday," Mrs. Ambrose said. "A birthday is a birthday—we can't change the date!"

It was a birthday party? Billy was curious. No one had ever mentioned a birthday before. He thought the United States had been around—well, as long as the sky. "How old is our country?" he asked.

"The United States is just a little more than two hundred years old. We are a young country and we are made up of people from all over the world. And even though Americans are all different—we go to different churches and we believe in different ways of life and we live in different neighborhoods—we all have one thing in common: we love and cherish our freedom. Freedom is what brought us together and what keeps us together.

"I guess we've gotten so caught up in the chicken and the pies and the parade, we forgot what the holiday is all about," his mother said, somewhat wistfully.

Mr. Ambrose turned to Billy. "You ask a lot of questions, son. And I'm glad."

Billy decided to push his luck. "So . . . next year . . . since this is a birthday party . . . can we have a cake instead of pies?" All of the Ambrose family looked hard at Billy and he blushed.

"I know, I know," he said. "That's just the way it is."

—CHRISTINE ALLISON

July 5

The Clever Elfe

A GERMAN TALE

Once upon a time a man and a woman had a daughter who was so canny that they gave her the name of the Clever Elfe. One day the father said, "You know, our daughter is grown up now, and we must get her married soon."

"Yes," agreed the mother, "if we can find anyone who will have her."

Soon after this a young man named Hans came to ask for their daughter's hand in marriage, on one condition. If he did not find her as clever as they said, he would not marry her.

"Oh, you'll not be disappointed," said the mother. "She can see the wind running through the streets and hear the footsteps of flies on the ceiling."

What they did not tell Hans was how much their daughter disliked work or any bother, and that she spent most of her time just sitting around.

They arranged a dinner for the couple, and everyone seemed very happy. Presently the mother said, "Elfe, go into the cellar and draw some beer." Clever Elfe took the jug and went downstairs. Then she fetched a chair and placed it in front of the cask of beer so that she would not have to stoop and tire her back. As she waited impatiently for the jug to fill, she happened to notice a crossbar in the ceiling that must have left there by accident.

Clever Elfe began to weep, having suddenly developed a superstitious fear that the crossbar would fall and kill someone. She stayed there so long weeping and wailing that her parents came down to investigate and joined in her lamentations. At last Hans went to the cellar to discover what was the matter. "Oh, dear Hans," said the Elfe, "I have a premonition that if we marry this crossbar may fall on your head and kill you."

However silly the fear, Hans was flattered by her concern. "I believe you are a clever Elfe to weep on my account, and I want nothing else to make my household complete but a clever wife."

He took her by the hand and led her back to the dinner table, and they were married soon after.

After several weeks of idleness, Hans was beginning to suspect that his bride did not like to work. As he set off for his job one morning he said, "Dear wife, do you think you could cut down the corn in our little cornfield today?"

"Yes, my dear Hans," she replied. "I will if you wish it."

After he left she went to the field, but decided to lay down and nap first before she began her work. Soon she was fast asleep, which is how she spent the whole day. Hans returned home, expecting his dinner, but no one was there, nor anything ready. "What a clever Elfe she is!" Hans thought. "So industrious that she cannot even come home for dinner."

But as evening neared he decided to go out and look for her and see how much corn she had cut. To his surprise, none had been touched and he finally found his wife fast asleep in the field.

Hans fetched a poultryman's net covered with little bells, which he spread over her, but she continued to sleep as soundly as before. So Hans returned home and locked the cottage door.

At last when Clever Elfe woke from her long sleep and rose to leave the field, the bells around her tinkled at every step she took. This puzzled her so much that she began to wonder whether she was really Clever Elfe or not.

"I know," she thought, "I will go

home and ask Hans whether I am really myself or someone else. He is sure to know." The bells tinkled in the dark as she ran to the cottage. Finding the door locked, she knocked at the window and cried, "Hans, is the Elfe at home?"

"Yes," he answered. "She is at home."

How frightened she felt when she heard this. "Oh, dear!" she exclaimed. "Then I am not the Clever Elfe after all."

Then she went from one neighbor's door to another, but when they heard the bells jingling no one would admit her. At last she ran away from the village and has not been heard of since. So, after all, it is better to be industrious than clever.—BROTHERS GRIMM

July 6

The Clever Elfe, Variation

One of the best-known twists on "The Clever Elfe" is called "Bastinelo," the Italian version of the tale. This tale begins like "The Clever Elfe," with the bride lamenting a calamity that has not occurred. The wife goes to the cellar to get some wine to serve to her future husband, mother-in-law, and father-in-law. When she gets there, she begins to cry, thinking that if she marries and has a son and names him Bastinelo, the child will die. Through her tears, she is unaware that she has tipped the wine over and that it is leaking all over the cellar.

The future mother-in-law comes down to see why the girl is so delayed, and hearing the girl's foundless concerns, begins to weep also. The future father-in-law follows suit. When the groom-to-be comes down and sees what is happening he storms out, saying that he will not marry the girl until he finds three fools greater than she.

The groom's journey to find fools is the core of the story. At first he is unlucky and can't seem to find anyone stupider than his wife. Then he stumbles upon a man who is covered with water and in a sweat from trying to fill a sieve with water. This fool obviously qualifies as the first one.

The groom continues his journey until he comes to a man and a woman. The man is jumping out of a tree, trying to aim for a pair of pants his wife holds outstretched for him. When the groom inquires about what they are doing, the man explains that he does not know how to put on his pants and that he thought by jumping from a tree he could get into them. The groom has now found a second fool.

The groom-to-be now approaches a city where there is much commotion. He discovers that it is the custom for brides to enter the city on horseback and there is a great discussion on this occasion between the groom and the owner of the horse because the bride is tall and the horse is high and they cannot get through the city gate. The horse's owner does not want the horse's legs cut off and the groom does not want his bride's head cut off, hence the commotion.

The groom-to-be approaches the bride and slaps her back, which makes her lower her head. Then he kicks the horse, and so they are able to pass through the city gate and enter the city.

The grateful couple asks the groom-to-be how they can repay him for settling the matter, and he will accept nothing. He has already been paid. He has just found the third fool.

The groom-to-be returns to his bride and marries her.

July 7

Momotaro, Part 1: The Gods Send Down the Peach Boy

A JAPANESE TALE

It was a spring afternoon like any other, pink with cherry blossoms but otherwise unremarkable, until a giant peach came tumbling down the river where the honorable old woman washed her clothes.

The old woman's eyes went wide.

The peach was luminous, unlike anything the honorable old woman had ever seen before, and she knew she must take it home. It had bobbled down the stream out of her reach so she called the peach to her side, almost like one might beckon a bird. When it rolled into her wrinkled hands, she placed it gently on top of her pile of washed clothes. Then she took the peach home to share with her husband, the honorable old man.

When the honorable old man came home, he could not believe what he saw. "This peach is a blessing," he said. The honorable old woman nodded and bowed, and then drew a sharp silver knife and sliced into the velvety peach. Suddenly a muffled voice could be heard.

"Honorable old woman, please be careful!"

It was not the peach that spoke, but a child, who with great effort pushed his way out of the center of the peach.

A child!

The honorable old man and woman had prayed for a child but long ago they had given up the prayer. Now the gods had answered it, and had sent them the peach boy, whom they named Momotaro.

Momotaro grew to be a fine young man. He honored his mother and father. He respected their land and their home. Sometimes the old man and the old woman wondered at their great fortune, but fortune is not constant.

Fortune changed one morning when Momotaro came to his parents and told them he must leave. The honorable old man and woman could not bear the thought of losing their son, but saw

that he was firm in his wishes. "On a small island in the north of Japan there lives a tribe of demons," Momotaro explained. "They wreak havoc and death on the innocent; they steal from rich and poor. The demons are the enemies of Japan and it is now my duty to stop them."

Momotaro was not only leaving, but he was off on a dangerous quest. His parents mourned his departure, praying that the gods who sent the peach boy would continue to protect him. Still, they worried. Through their tears, the old man and woman packed Momotaro some clothes to wear and dumplings to eat. Even Momotaro, who was wise and knew so much, could not have imagined the pain his parents felt as they said good-bye.

And so he left.

July 8

Momotaro, Part 2: The Peach Boy Fights the Godless Ones

Were it not for the terrible demons, Momotaro would never have left his devoted parents. But the gods had called him to make the lonely journey and to save Japan from these enemies of goodness.

The young man started his journey on a black, starry night, with just a few clothes and some dumplings. He saw no one, until a barking dog suddenly accosted him.

"This is my land," said the dog. "Be gone."

Momotaro replied, "I am off to fight the enemies of Japan. Get out of my way or I will fight you too."

The dog had never heard a voice so forceful. Now he felt so humble. He begged the mighty Momotaro to accept him as a comrade to rid Japan of its enemies.

Momotaro agreed, and the two shared a dumpling and then moved on, now climbing the mountains as the night turned to day. As they reached the summit, a monkey dropped from a tree onto Momotaro. "Forgive me," said the monkey, "but I hear you are off to slay the enemies of Japan. Might I join you?"

The dog was jealous, but Momotaro, who was a leader of animals as well as of men, assured the dog that the monkey would be an excellent vassal. The three shared a dumpling and went on.

A pheasant flew in front of the little

band of warriors, stopped at Momotaro's feet, and bowed.

"I have heard that you are the great Momotaro, off to kill the enemies of Japan," said the pheasant. "I would be so honored to join you." The dog was exasperated that a foolish bird might deign to join their war party, but when Momotaro accepted the bird, he kept quiet (though in truth, he was not happy).

Momotaro, who knew what the animals were thinking, warned them: "I cannot have jealousy and pettiness among my followers. We must stay united or we will surely fail," he said.

And so the four shared a dumpling and went on.

They came to the sea.

The animals, who had lived their lives on land, began to tremble. "I cannot travel the waters," said the dog. "I fear the sea," said the monkey. "I would die over such a pool," said the pheasant.

"You are fools and cowards," shouted Momotaro. "Go away, all of you."

But the animals, ashamed, did not want to leave Momotaro and begged him to let them stay. He secured a wooden boat and set sail, with the dog, the monkey, and the pheasant.

When they got to the island, the evil was palpable. The animals, more sensitive to good and evil, were frightened. They looked to Momotaro for their orders.

To the pheasant, Momotaro said, "Fly through the black iron gate and see what the demons are doing."

The pheasant did as told, and when he got to the demons, he called out, "Surrender now, you evil, godless ones. The great Momotaro is here to avenge the gods and slay all enemies of Japan."

The demons tossed back their heads with a laugh, showing their yellow teeth. The pheasant went and pecked at their heads, and then the dog and monkey stormed in, and in a terrible battle of fur and blood and nails and claws and flesh the animals took on the demons, one by one, laying them down for dead.

When the leader of the demons suddenly realized that all of his followers were dead, he froze.

"What is it you want?" he asked in a pleading, pathetic manner. "I will give you anything."

Momotaro stormed in and stood before the wretched man.

"You have killed and wounded hundreds of good men, stolen from the rich and the poor, trampled through villages of innocents. Now you will go back with me to the mainland, where I will see you die on a stake," Momotaro said.

Momotaro took the captive and gathered all of the riches the demons had amassed. To the delight of the honorable old man and the honorable old woman, he came back to live with them. The riches were theirs to keep, and their lives were prosperous for many years after.

Bright's Trip to Pike's Peak

A TALE FROM THE AMERICAN WEST

My father was a freighter and hauled things from the Missouri River up along the Platte to Pike's Peak. Back in those days, oxen were used to make the journey, and it generally took about four months for a round trip. Each huge wagon was pulled by a yoke of six to ten oxen, and often the wagon trains were nearly a mile long. The leaders for one of the outfits were Bright and Buck, two matched roan steers. Buck was as gentle and good as Bright, but unlike his mate, he would never talk, except to bellow for a drink of water or to tell the wagon boss that his shoes were loose. Bright talked whenever he got an opportunity, and that is how he came to tell me about his first trip across the western plains.

"I shall never forget my first wagon train to Pike's Peak," said Bright. "It was the late summer of '59. The weather was fine and the grass all that any ox could ask for. We made good time, and soon were pushing our way far into the unknown country, where Indians had roamed for ages and watering holes were a luxury.

"We passed along the trail unharmed, and I recall hearing one of the men say, 'Bill, if the Indians don't bother us, we'll soon be at Pike's Peak.' When I heard them say 'Indians,' I was mighty frightened, and I whispered to Buck that if they came we should slip our yoke and take the back track as fast as we could.

"Two or three days later, someone called out, 'There's Pike's Peak, away to the southwest.' I looked and, yes, I could see the mountains about 150 miles off, but I saw something else—what looked like a whole army of Indians on ponies, coming toward us on the dead run, yelling with all their might. 'Get ready to bolt,' I said to Buck. Closer and closer the Indians came, and I could stand it no longer, and said, 'Buck, now!' I backed up and gave the yoke a forward jerk, expecting to be free, and Buck did the same. Then we turned and looked at each other. Like a couple of simpletons, we had forgotten about our horns and the yoke would not come off. Worse, our driver saw us hanging back, and uncoiled his long bull whip and let it fly.

"As it turned out, the Indians weren't hostile. They were just having fun, and wanted to trade skins for flour and sugar. We got to Pike's Peak two weeks later, and after unloading and resting for a few days, started on the journey back.

"Around Julesburg, it began to get colder and snow a little. I guess your father knew what was coming, for that night I heard him say, 'Boys, it looks like a blizzard. Round up the wagons in a circle and put the cattle on the inside.' Soon after, the storm broke and the air was full of flying ice and snow.

"There was little feed and many an ox went to bed hungry that night. I remember that Buck cried until he fell asleep. The snow kept up for eleven days, and some of the best oxen froze or starved to death. The men would have died, too, if they hadn't chopped up the yokes and wagons to make fires.

"The morning of the twelfth day, it turned warmer and finally we were able to head home. But we had to leave our cargo where it lay and the whole outfit was in pretty bad shape."

Bright has been dead many years now, and the railroad makes the trip across the plains a lot easier. But I'll never forget his story, or the courage of the men and animals who struggled to settle the West.—EUGENE O. MAYFIELD

July 10

The Fox and the Cat

A GERMAN TALE

One day a cat met a fox in the woods. "Ah," thought the cat, "foxes are clever fellows. Perhaps I should chat with him and see what I can learn." So in a friendly manner she said, "Good morning, my dear Mr. Fox! How are things going with you?"

The fox, full of pride, looked the cat up and down, not knowing how to respond to this lowly creature. At last he said, "Oh, you poor little whisker-cleaner, you old, gray tabby, you hungry mouse-hunter, what possesses you to ask me how I'm getting on? Surely you haven't any knowledge you can share with me. Do you know any tricks at all?"

"I know only one trick," answered the cat meekly.

"And pray what is that?" the fox asked.

"Well," she said, "if the hounds are behind me I can spring up into a tree out of their way and save myself."

"Is that all?" cried the fox. "Why, I am the master of cunning and have a sackful of a hundred tricks. But I feel sorry for you, puss, so come with me and I'll show you how to baffle both hounds and men."

At that moment, a hunter with four hounds was drawing near them. The cat sprang nimbly up a tree and seated herself on the highest branch, where she was completely hidden by the foliage. To the fox still down on the ground she cried, "Take out your sack, Mr. Fox! Take out your sack!" But the hounds had already seized him and held him tight for their master.

"Ah, Mr. Fox," called the cat, "your hundred tricks were not of much use to you. Now if you had only known one like mine, you would be safe up here with me."

July 11

The Silver Penny

"Hurrah! I'm off into the world!" cried a bright new penny that had just left the mint. And so it was. A child held onto it tightly with warm hands, and a miser with cold and clammy hands. Old people turned it over and over many times, while children sent it rolling on at once.

The penny was a silver one, and it had been a whole year in the world when, one day, it went on a journey abroad. Its owner was traveling to foreign lands, and it was the last coin of his country that he had in his purse. Actually, he hadn't even known it was there. "Why, I've still got a penny from home!" he said, and the penny skipped and clinked for joy as he put it back into the purse. It lay there with foreign companions who came and went. One would make way for the next, but always the penny from home stayed behind.

Several weeks had gone by, and the penny didn't know exactly where it was. It heard from the other coins that they were French and Italian, and one would say that now they were in this town or that, but you don't see very much of the world when you're always in a bag. One day, noticing that the purse wasn't shut, it crept to the opening to peep out. Inquisitiveness is a good trait, but the penny was to pay for it. It fell out of the purse onto the floor and nobody noticed.

Eventually the penny was picked up, and it joined three other coins in someone's pocket. Well, it's nice to see the world! thought the penny. To know other people, other customs!

"What sort of penny is this?" somebody said. "This isn't our money! It's false! No good!"

Now let us hear how the penny felt about such an accusation. "False! No good! It wounded me," said the penny. "I knew I was of good silver and good mint. Surely they were mistaken and couldn't mean me! But, alas, they did. 'I'll have to pass this in the dark!' said the man who had me. And so I was passed in the dark and ignored in the daytime."

The penny would tremble each time someone tried to pass it off as lawful coin. "Miserable me!" said the penny. "Each time I was taken out I dreaded the eyes that would look at me, for I knew that I would be thrust back and flung on the counter, as if I were a cheat and a liar. Once I was given to a poor woman who got me in payment for her daily labor, and she was unable to get rid of me. I was a real trouble to her.

" 'I can't help it, I shall have to cheat somebody with it,' she said. 'I can't afford to hold onto a bad penny. The rich baker shall have it; he can best afford it. But I shall still be doing wrong.'

"So now I am going to trouble the woman's conscience!" I sighed. "Can I have changed so much?"

"And for many more years I was passed from hand to hand and from house to house, always being abused and always looked down on. Nobody believed in me, and I didn't even believe in myself anymore. It was a hard time.

"Then one day a traveler came and, of course, I was passed off on him, and he was innocent enough to take me for good money. He was about to spend me when I heard the cries of 'No good!'

"The man took a closer look at me. Then all at once his face lit up, as no other face ever had in the last few miserable years, and he said, 'Why, what's this? If it isn't a good honest penny from home! And they're calling you bad! I shall keep you and take you back home with me.'

"I cannot tell you how thrilled I was. The man wrapped me up in fine white paper so I shouldn't get mixed up with the other coins, and I was only taken out on special occasions when fellow countrymen got together, and then I was extremely well spoken of.

"And very soon after, I came home. My troubles were over and my joys were beginning. No longer was I a bad penny."—HANS CHRISTIAN ANDERSEN

July 12

The Three Spinning Fairies

There was once a young girl who was lazy and hated work, and no matter what her mother said, nothing would induce her to spin. At last the mother became so angry that she decided to give the girl a good beating.

But at the first blow, the girl began to scream so loudly that the queen, who was passing by in her carriage, stopped at the house to see what was the matter. "Why are you beating your daughter?" the queen asked.

The mother was so ashamed of her daughter's laziness that she told the queen a lie. "Oh, I cannot get her away from the spinning wheel even though we have no money to buy her flax."

"I love the sound of spinning," said the queen. "The humming of the wheel delights me. Let me take your daughter to the castle. I have plenty of flax and she shall spin as much as she likes."

The mother was delighted to send her with the queen. At the castle, the girl was taken to three rooms filled with flax. "Spin all this for me," said the queen. "If you finish I will give you my eldest son for your husband. I do not care that you are poor, for your hard work is dowry enough."

The girl was very distressed for she knew she could never spin all that flax if she worked day and night for a hundred years, and once she was alone she began to cry wretchedly. When the queen returned in three days, the girl had not even lifted a hand to begin. The queen was surprised, but the girl excused herself by pleading homesickness.

"Well, you had better begin tomorrow to work," the queen said sharply.

Alone again, the girl walked to the window, still without a clue as to how to begin this immense task. She noticed three strange-looking women coming towards her. One had a broad, flat foot, the second a large lower lip that hung over her chin, and the third an enormous thumb.

These women asked the maiden what was the matter, and when she told them, they offered to help on one condition. "You must promise," said one, "that we shall be invited to your wedding, and be allowed to sit at your table, and you must agree to call us your cousins without being ashamed of us." The girl readily agreed and brought them into the flax chamber.

The first woman turned the wheel with her foot and drew out the thread, the second moistened it, and the third twisted it with her finger, and as she twisted skein after skein of fine spun flax tumbled to the ground. In a very short time, all of the flax in the three chambers had been spun.

The three women made their farewells and said, "Don't forget what you have promised, for it will bring you good fortune."

The queen was delighted with all the beautiful thread and set the wedding day. The prince was quite pleased with the maiden. He admired her industry and cleverness and soon loved her dearly. Just before the wedding, he asked if he could grant her any favor. "Yes," she replied. "I have three cousins who have been very kind to me, and I should not like to forget them in the midst of my good fortune. May I invite them to the wedding?"

Of course the prince had no objection, and the three women came to the wedding beautifully dressed, but no clothing could hide their defects.

The bride greeted them kindly, but her new husband was most surprised at their appearance. Addressing the first woman, he asked, "How did it happen that you have such a broad foot?"

"From turning the spinning wheel," she replied.

He discovered the second woman's pendulous lip came from moistening the thread, and the third woman's enormous thumb was due to drawing and twisting the thread.

"If these are the consequences of spinning," exclaimed the prince, "then my beautiful bride shall never touch a spinning wheel again as long as she lives."

So the maiden was forever set free from the work she disliked, because she remembered her promise and was not ashamed to acknowledge the women to whom she owed so much.

July 13

The Donkey's Shadow

One hot summer's day a young boy hired a donkey and a driver to carry him from Athens to Megara. At midday the heat of the sun was so scorching that the boy dismounted to sit and rest under the donkey's shadow. But the driver disputed the place with him, declaring he had an equal right to it. "What!" said the young boy. "Did I not hire the donkey for the whole journey?" "Yes," said the other, "You hired the donkey, but not the donkey's shadow."

While they were thus wrangling and fighting for the place, the donkey took to his heels and ran away.

In quarreling over the shadow, we often lose the substance.—AESOP

July 14

The Wolf in Sheep's Clothing

Once there was a wolf who resolved to disguise himself, thinking that in doing so he could earn a greater livelihood. Believing he was clever, he clothed himself in sheep's skin and pretended to get among a flock of sheep. The disguise was quite convincing and, summoning all of his theatrical skills, the wolf fed along with the sheep so that even the shepherd was deceived.

When night came on and the fold was closed, the wolf was shut up with the sheep and the door was locked. The wolf could not believe his great fortune and was drooling just to think of what a fine supper the flock would make. But the shepherd was also hungry and, wanting something for *his* supper, went in to fetch a sheep. Mistaking the wolf for one of them, he killed the wolf on the spot.—AESOP

July 15

The Servant

Once there was a boy who lived alone except for his faithful servant. The boy and the servant were a comfortable twosome, not exactly friends, but more than simply a man in a child's employ. In the morning the elder would wake the boy with a proper "good day, master" and the child would bathe and dress and then have breakfast in a long dining hall. It was then time for lessons, out for some fresh air, lunch, more lessons, dinner, and bedtime. At night, in the child's room, they would sit together and stare at the fireplace, watching the flames dance in silence. Each day would end this very same way.

One morning the boy was in a curious mood. "Tell me, servant, what do you do after you leave me at night? Do you have friends? Do you have a family?"

The servant looked uneasy. He replied: "Good master, what I do when we are not together is unimportant. Come, it's time for breakfast."

"But I want to *know,*" insisted the boy. "I demand that you tell me."

The servant ignored the boy and took him to breakfast. The day passed without anything remarkable occurring. But in the middle of the afternoon lessons, the boy had an idea. "After my servant puts me to bed, I will follow him and see for myself what he does at night," he thought to himself.

After dinner, bath, and story, the boy and the elder stared blankly at the fire for nearly an hour. The servant, as always, seemed lost in his thoughts. Then, as was his custom, he bowed and left the room. When it was clear that the halls were empty, the boy crept out of bed and followed. The moon was so bright the boy could observe everything with perfect clarity. He watched as the servant passed through the garden and then stood at the roadside, as if waiting for someone. Minutes passed, then quite out of nowhere, a carriage approached. The carriage door opened, revealing a woman in a hooded cape. The servant embraced her lightly, gave her a parcel, and headed back for the garden. The little boy rushed back to his bedroom on tiptoe, his heart beating from the mystery of it all.

The next evening, the boy followed his servant once again. This time, the servant passed off a sheaf of papers to the strange woman and spent a few minutes speaking to her in low tones. At one point, the woman seemed to weep a little; the servant held her and then let go, and the carriage disappeared into the black night.

On the third night, the boy went directly to the garden and hid in some bushes near the roadside to gain a better view. The carriage pulled up and the door opened and suddenly the boy screamed. He saw one side of the woman's face and it was grotesque: where there had been an eye was only a blistered red lid, her nose was stretched wide and taut, and her skin was etched with gashes. But this is not what caused the boy to scream. It was when she turned the other side of her face to the moonlight that the young boy was overcome. Her face, you see, looked just like his.

The boy's screams panicked the woman and she slammed shut the door to the carriage. "Go quickly," the servant ordered, not knowing from where the scream came or from whom. When the elder turned and saw his young master crouched in the bushes, he gasped.

"Good master, you have made a terrible mistake," the servant said in alarm.

"But why," said the young boy shaking. "Who was that woman?"

The faithful servant was silent for several minutes. When finally he spoke, the words tumbled out weakly. "There was a fire . . . good master. . . ."

The servant sat down on a stone bench in the garden and pulled the boy to his side. "Several years ago, when you were just a few years old, a candle toppled in the night, while you and your mother and . . . I . . . slept. It produced a fire that ravaged the entire village. You and I escaped without injury, but your mother lost her arm and her face was disfigured so terribly that she felt like a monster. I told her it did not matter, but she did not ever want you . . . to see her like that.

"Every night, she comes from the convent, where she lives a life of isolation and prayer. I give her your schoolwork and your drawings, and a letter about your day," the servant continued. "She follows your progress with great joy."

"And my father? What became of him?" the boy asked.

"For years, you woke in the night screaming, living and reliving the blaze. Your mother wanted all signs and memories of your first life destroyed. So I took on the role of your faithful servant."

"But my father . . ." the boy insisted.

"I am your father," the servant said.

It was a strange reunion in that moonlit garden, but there the boy and the servant became again father and son. It took many months, but the boy soon persuaded his mother to come and live with them. In daylight, she would stay in her room. But when night fell, she would join her son and her husband and, having made a certain peace, the three would sit before the fireplace in the boy's room, watching the flames dance in silence.—CHRISTINE ALLISON

July 16

The Ant and the Dove

One day an ant went to the bank of a stream to have a little drink of water. Much to her surprise, she found herself slipping into a spring. "Someone, help!" she cried.

Fortunately, a dove was sitting on a branch over the stream and saw the ant fall in. Instantly the dove plucked a leaf off the branch near her and cast it into the stream. The leaf seemed like a life raft to the ant, who by now was struggling to stay afloat. The little ant clambered onto the raft gratefully and soon found her way to shore. The dove had saved her life!

Just as the little ant found harbor, she looked up and noticed a hunter laying a trap for the bird. She was afraid that her friend the dove would be his victim.

Without hesitation, the ant rushed to the hunter and gave him a good sting on the foot.

With a cry of pain, the hunter left his trap, giving fair warning to the dove of danger. She lost no time in flying off to safety.

One act of kindness deserves another.—AESOP

July 17

The Shepherd's Flower

A GERMAN TALE

Once upon a time there was a witch with two daughters. The witch loved the first daughter, who was wicked and ugly, but she hated the second one, who was her stepdaughter and a beautiful and good maiden.

It happened that the stepdaughter had a pretty apron, which made the first daughter jealous. "I must and will have that apron, Mother," she said.

"And so you shall," replied her mother. "Your stepsister should have been dead long ago. Tonight I will go into your room and cut off her head. Be careful when you go to bed to get in first."

Neither of them knew that the stepdaughter was hidden in a corner of the room and had heard this whole conversation. That night she stayed awake till her sister fell asleep, then she got behind her, near the wall, and lay still in fear and trembling until the darkest part of the night.

The witch entered their room with an ax in her hand and felt about the bed for the one who lay outside. Then she lifted the ax in both hands and cut off the head of her own child.

When she left, the terrified girl got up, dressed herself, and tiptoed out of the house. She fled to the home of her sweetheart, Roland, and told him her horrible tale. "Dearest Roland, we must take flight. When daylight comes and my stepmother sees what she has done, we will be done for it."

"But first," said Roland, "take away her witch's staff so she can't pursue us easily."

This she did, and they fled before dawn broke. In the morning, when the witch rose and called for her daughter, no one answered. When she went to the bedroom and saw she had chopped off the head of her own child, she was in a terrible fury. Now the witch was able to see a great distance, and when she looked out the window, she could see her stepdaughter and Roland fleeing, even though they were miles away. "It is useless for them to try to escape me," she cried.

The witch put on her one-mile shoes, which enabled her to travel an hour's walk in one step, and soon she caught up with the pair. But as the maiden saw her coming, she touched Roland with the magic staff and he was transformed into a lake. She turned herself into a duck and swam upon its surface. Try as she might, the witch could not lure her to shore. In her desperation, the witch leaned over too far, fell into the lake, and drowned.

Free from the power of the witch, the stepdaughter and Roland resumed their natural shapes, and Roland said, "Now I can go home and arrange our wedding with my father."

"I will turn myself into a flower and stay here and wait for you," said the maiden.

But on the way home, Roland met another maiden who so bewitched him that he quite forgot about the girl he had promised to marry. The poor forsaken girl waited a long time, until one day a shepherd saw her and decided to pick this lovely flower.

He took the flower home and laid it in his dresser drawer, and from that moment on, wonderful things occurred in the shepherd's house. When he rose each morning, his fire was lit and the room was swept, and at noon a nice dinner was always waiting for him. All of this pleased him, but also made him uneasy, so he went to a wise woman and asked her advice. "There is witchcraft behind this," said the wise woman, and she told him how to break the enchantment.

At dawn on the following day, the shepherd lay awake, ready to throw a white cloth over the first thing that moved, for this was the wise woman's advice. His drawer opened and the flower he had plucked came out. Quickly he sprang up and threw the cloth over the flower, which immediately was transformed into the beautiful maiden. She told him all that had happened to her, and he was so pleased with her goodness and beauty that he asked to marry her. But her heart still belonged to Roland, so she said no, but promised to continue to keep house for him.

The time came for Roland's marriage, and it was the custom for all maidens of the country to be present and sing in honor of the bridal couple. The true maiden was overcome with sadness, but knew she had to go. And on the wedding day, as soon as the song began, Roland recognized her voice. All the memories of their love came back to him. "That is my true bride," he cried. "I will have no other."

The marriage was indeed held, with the true maiden, and all of her sorrow turned into joy.—BROTHERS GRIMM

July 18

The Golden Blackbird

The great lord of a distant land fell gravely ill. His doctors were mystified by his illness and could not heal him. They finally summoned a physician from another country, who declared that only the Golden Blackbird could cure the dying man.

The lord called his son to his bedside and asked him to search for this marvelous bird, promising him great riches if he succeeded.

The son set out at once, but traveled for many days without finding a trace of the Golden Blackbird or even a clue as to its whereabouts. At last, he came to a spot where four roads intersected and there he met a little hare. "Where are you going, my friend?" asked the hare.

"I really don't know," said the son. "My father is very ill and only the Golden Blackbird can cure him. But no one can tell me where to find it."

"I can," replied the hare. "But you will have to journey at least seven hundred leagues."

"And how am I to travel such a distance?"

"Jump on my back," said the hare, "and I will take you."

The young man hopped on and the hare took off. At each bound it traveled seven leagues, and it wasn't long before they reached a grand and beautiful castle. "This is the home of the Golden Blackbird," said the hare. "It lives in a plain little cage right next to another cage made all of gold. Whatever you do, be sure not to put it in the golden cage."

Just as the hare said, the Golden Blackbird was standing on a wooden perch in a shabby cage, looking as stiff and rigid as if it were dead. "Perhaps it would revive if I were to put it in the beautiful gold cage," thought the young man. But the moment the Blackbird touched the bars of the golden cage, it awoke and began to screech. This alerted the castle guards, who quickly seized the thief and took him to the dungeon. When the young man explained that he needed the Golden Blackbird to cure his father, he was released on the condition that he find someone known as the Porcelain Maiden and bring her to the lord of the castle. The lord would then give him the blackbird in exchange.

Though the youth agreed, his heart was filled with despair, for here was yet another seemingly impossible mission. On the road outside the castle, he found the hare, and before he even spoke, the hare said, "You did not follow my advice, did you?"

"Alas, no!" the young man admitted.

"Well, do not despair. I know who the Porcelain Maiden is and where she lives. She is as beautiful as Venus and dwells not two hundred leagues from here. Jump on my back."

In no time at all, they were by the edge of a lake in another land. "The Porcelain Maiden will come here to bathe with her friends," said the hare. "While she is bathing, you must hide her clothes and do not give them back unless she consents to follow you."

The young man did just as the hare instructed this time, even though the maiden wept and begged most sweetly for the return of her clothes. And on the trip back to the castle of the Golden Blackbird, the couple fell in love. It was now out of the question for the young man to surrender the Porcelain Maiden to the other lord, so with the hare's help, he spirited the Golden Blackbird out of the castle and he and the Porcelain Maiden traveled like the wind back to his father's domain.

The Golden Blackbird did indeed cure his father, and one of the rewards bestowed on the son was the most splendid wedding the land had ever seen.

July 19

The Three Roses

A CZECH TALE

Once there was a mother and three daughters. On a crisp fall morning, the mother was feeling generous, and so she asked the three girls if she might fetch them anything from town. "Anything, anything at all!" she offered.

The first daughter prepared a long list. She wanted her mother to buy her a great many things.

The second daughter also had many wants and needs, and she did not hesitate to tell her mother about them.

The third daughter couldn't really think of anything she needed. She was quite content. "But, if you like," she said, "you can bring me three roses, please."

If she wanted no more than that, her mother was happy to bring them.

And so the mother went off to the market. She bought all she could, piled it on her back, and started for home. But night came earlier than she expected, as happens in the fall, and the poor old woman completely lost her way back home.

She wandered through forest and glen, hill and dale. Exhausted, the old woman stopped under an oak tree. She was so tired she wasn't paying much attention to anything, but when she looked up, she saw a magnificent palace. The palace was lit with candles all over the grounds and she could see a beautiful rose garden. Until that moment she had forgotten entirely her third daughter's request for three roses. "There are plenty of roses here," she thought to herself. "I'll pick just three and take them home."

She went to the garden and picked three roses. At once, an ogre came and demanded her daughter for the three roses. The mother was horrified "What have I done?" she cried out. She tried to throw the roses away, but the ogre would have none of it.

"Get me your daughter now or I will tear you to pieces," the ogre said.

Eventually, the beleaguered mother found her way home, and of course she had very bad news for the youngest daughter.

"Here are your roses, my love, but they came at a great cost," her mother began. "You must go to a palace on the other side of the woods to pay for them. Oh, my dearest one, I do not know if you will ever come back."

But the daughter was a cheerful character, so she said she would go without a lot of fuss.

The mother took her to the palace. The ogre greeted them at the door. He commanded the mother to go and the daughter to stay. The mother wailed and wailed to lose her daughter, but her daughter was not afraid.

The ogre then turned to the girl, and demanded she milk the royal cow for three days and bring him a cup of the finest cream to drink every day. This the girl did. On the fourth night, the ogre brought out a sword and told the girl to cut his head off.

"But I cannot do that," the girl protested.

"You must," snapped the ogre.

"I can't," said the girl.

But the ogre said that he would tear her to pieces if she did not cut his head off, so she did. To her horror, out of his neck came a long snake, hissing. The snake head told her to cut its head off, which she did not hesitate to do. At that, a beautiful youth emerged. The young man said, "This is my palace, and as you have delivered me from a curse, I will marry you."

The two fell in love and had a great wedding, and the bride carried roses.

July 20

The Lioness

There was a commotion among all of the beasts, as to which one could boast of the largest family. Finally, they came to the lioness.

"And how many, pray tell us, do you give at birth?" asked the animals gathered.

"One," responded the lioness, sweetly. "But that one is a lion."

Quality is a greater measure than quantity.—AESOP

July 21

The Boy Bathing

A boy was bathing in the river and ventured in too deep. He was on the point of sinking when he saw a stranger coming his way. The boy, knowing that this was his only chance, called out for help with all of his might. The man began to lecture the boy for his foolhardiness, but the boy cried out, "Oh, save me now, sir, please, and read me the lecture afterwards."—AESOP

The Hero Makoma

A TALE FROM AFRICA

When her young child began to speak with the voice of a man, Makoma's mother was not surprised. She knew her child was different. The only thing she did not know was in what *way* he would be different—would he be a great one or an evil one? But as the years went by, Makoma's mother knew her son was destined for greatness, and so she was prepared for the day when he came to her and said, "Dear mother, do not grieve, but I must say good-bye and make a home for myself, and become a hero." Before Makoma's mother could even bless her son, the boy flung a sack over his shoulder, picked up his iron hammer, and left to cross his country, Zambesi. It was the last time she would see him.

After wandering through some unusually hilly country, Makoma met a huge giant making mountains. Makoma greeted the giant and asked him his name.

"I am Chi-eswa, who makes mountains," the giant replied. "Who are you?"

"I am Makoma, which means 'greater,' as in greater than you!" said the young boy. Before the giant could respond, Makoma pounded him with his iron hammer and the giant shrank into quite a little man. "You are indeed greater than I," said the giant. "Please allow me to be your slave." Makoma, having absorbed all of the strength of the giant, agreed cheerfully to the proposition and dropped the little man into his sack.

It wasn't long before Makoma came upon another giant. This huge creature was digging up dirt clods and throwing them on either side of a long passageway. Makoma asked him his name.

"I am Chi-dubula-take, maker of riverbeds, and who are you?" the giant demanded.

"I am Makoma, which means 'greater,' as in greater than you," the boy replied. Chi-dubula-take hurled a huge dirt clod at Makoma, but the hero held his sack up like a shield and then rushed to hammer the giant to the ground. Chi-dubula-take groveled before the boy, becoming smaller and smaller as the boy took in all of the giant's strength and energy. The giant begged to be Makoma's slave and so the boy tossed him into the sack as if he were a piece of fruit.

Just about that time, Makoma found himself in a forest and he saw a giant who was much taller than the trees. The giant was painting the forest. Makoma called up to ask him his name.

"I am Chi-gwisa-miti, and I am planting these bao-bobs and thorns as food for my children the elephants."

"Leave off," said Makoma, "for I am greater than you and I would like to exchange a blow with you." With that Makoma struck the giant with a hammer and the contrite forest maker begged to be his slave. Makoma inhaled all of the forest maker's skills and wisdom, and popped what was left into his sack, and moved on.

Makoma continued his journey until he arrived at a rocky, barren plain, where he encountered a man eating fire. Makoma asked him his name.

"I am Chi-idea-moto," said the fire eater. "I can waste and destroy what I like."

"You are wrong," said the boy. "I am Makoma, which means 'greater,' as in greater than you!"

The fire eater laughed and blew a flame at the boy, but the hero sprang behind a rock, just in time because the ground upon which he had been standing had turned to molten glass. The fire eater dissolved into a tiny man, whom Makoma flung into his sack.

By now the hero had become a very great man indeed, for he had the power to make hills, the industry to make rivers, the foresight and wisdom to plant trees, and the power to produce fire whenever he wished. The four giants, who were now his slaves, loved and respected Makoma, giving him even greater powers.

After he conquered the fourth giant, Makoma knew his work was done, that he had become who he was meant to be. He was not surprised when Mulimo the Great Spirit approached him and said, "Makoma, you are now a hero so great that no man may come up against you. You must therefore leave the world and take up your home with me in the clouds." As he spoke, the hero Makoma became invisible to the Earth, and was no more seen among men.

July 23

Two Travelers and a Bear

Two men were traveling to a far-off village together when out of nowhere a huge bear appeared.

The first man, thinking only of himself, climbed a tree.

The second man was now face to face with this bear (and remember, it was *huge*). There was no escape, so the man collapsed. Actually, he pretended to collapse. He had heard somewhere that bears would not bother a dead body, so he figured he would play dead.

The bear sniffed around the man for a long time. He sniffed at his shoes, his legs, and his arms. Finally, he sniffed around the man's head. The man was steeped in fear; he knew that one movement would betray him—a cough, a breath, the flicker of an eyelash. The bear nuzzled at his hair and then, to the man's enormous relief, the bear loped off into the woods.

The first man, seeing that the coast was clear, came down from the tree. He was shaken, but not nearly so much as his friend, whom he had abandoned. He knelt down to speak to his friend.

"That was remarkable," the first man said, "It looked as if that bear was *talking* to you. What on earth did he say?"

The second man gave his friend a long, hard look.

"He said I was foolish to have a friend who would leave me in a moment of danger," said the second man. "Now, please, go on your way."

Crisis is the test of friendship.—AESOP

July 24

The Frog Prince

Long ago, when it was still of some use to wish for the thing one wanted, there lived a princess who amused herself by throwing her golden ball in the air as she sat by a cool well in her garden. One day the ball came down near the edge of the well and rolled in. She began to weep, and as she did so, she heard a voice say, "What is it, lovely princess? Why are you so sad?"

When she looked up, she could not believe what she saw. It was a frog, a fat, slimy frog who had stuck his head up out of the water. She explained that her beloved golden ball had rolled into the deep well.

The frog had a twinkle in his eye. "If I returned your ball to you, dear princess, would you give me anything I wanted?" he asked.

"Why, whatever you like, little frog," the princess answered.

He wasn't interested in her finery, her jewels, or even her golden crown. He wanted to be her friend and companion. The princess, thinking little of it, agreed.

In no time at all the frog swam to the bottom of the well and retrieved the princess's golden ball. The happy princess bounded away, forgetting completely about the frog.

The next evening, while the king and his family were having dinner, there was a knock at the door. A voice called, "Oh, Princess, it's me. The frog. Let me in!" The princess explained to her father that the frog had recovered her ball and that she had promised to be his friend. Her father had always taught her to keep her word, and so the princess invited the frog in and asked him to sit at the royal dinner table. After he feasted well, the frog announced he was weary, and the two went to play and rest in the princess's room.

When it was time to go to sleep, the frog jumped up on the princess's bed.

"Oh, no, little frog," said the princess. "You cannot put your slimy fat body on my silken bed."

She put him in the corner and the frog began to weep. "All I wanted was to be your friend, and now I see that in truth you think I am fat and slimy and unworthy of your company," lamented the frog.

The princess, who was kind at heart, felt pity. "Oh, what will I do with you, dear frog?" she said, shaking her head. She walked over and gave him a kiss.

With that, the frog was transformed. In his place was a handsome prince with clear, knowing eyes. The prince explained that a witch had put him under a spell from which only a beautiful girl could release him. By her kiss and her good heart, she had brought him back to life.

Eventually, the king gave permission for his daughter and the prince to be married. They were carried off in a splendid carriage to the prince's palace, where they lived in bliss.

—BROTHERS GRIMM

July 25

The Lion and the Mouse

It was a cloudy winter afternoon, and a lion lay asleep in the forest. His great maned head rested comfortably on his rounded paws and all was quite peaceful until a tiny mouse came upon him. The mouse, upon seeing the lion, panicked. And, instead of running away, the mouse jumped upon the lion's nose, which was located, as you might guess, just above his mouth. Suddenly, she realized she was in great danger.

Well, the mouse did what anyone in her predicament would do: she begged.

"Please, good king, have pity on a stupid mouse," she wailed. "If you let me go now, I will in turn do a favor for you someday."

The lion laughed. The idea that a mouse might be able to help him was one of the funniest notions he had ever entertained. It was so amusing, in fact, that he decided to let the mouse go.

"You might be stupid but you have nerve," said the lion. "Go on, but don't ever bother me again."

The mouse hadn't meant to be funny or nervy, but she was glad to be free. She thanked the Lion and went her way.

About a week later, the lion was hunting for his dinner when he suddenly became ensnared in a trapper's net. He was in a terrible tangle and it infuriated him. The whole jungle could hear him roaring in anger. The mouse, upon hearing the roar, raced to the Lion's side. With her tiny teeth she set about chewing the ropes, and finally set the lion free.

"When I promised to help you someday, you thought I was joking," said the mouse. "Now you can see that everyone has something to contribute, and even a mouse can help a lion."

The lion and the mouse parted as friends, the lion the wiser for it.

Do not underestimate others.—AESOP

July 26

Three Billy Goats Gruff

A NORWEGIAN TALE

There once was a family of three bearded goats, who were known by the villagers as the Three Billy Goats Gruff.

Since the village in which they lived was poor and even scraps of food were scarce, the Three Billy Goats Gruff often crossed a wooden bridge to the other side of the valley to chomp on the rich grass in the fields. But crossing the bridge was no easy matter, for beneath it lived a horrible-looking troll with a bulbous nose, warts all over his face, and oily matted hair that had never seen the likes of a comb. It would be one thing if the troll was just ugly, but this creature was also mad at the world, and it made him furious to hear the goats cross what he claimed was *his* bridge.

Therefore the goats knew that each time they crossed the bridge, they had to be very careful not to disturb the troll. One day while the troll was lying about he heard above him the sound of footsteps: trip trap, trip trap on the planks of the wooden bridge.

"WHO DARES TO CROSS MY BRIDGE?" bellowed the surly troll.

As it happened, it was the smallest

member of the Gruff family, who in a

meek voice replied, "Uh, it is me, the little Billy Goat Gruff."

"Then you shall be my dinner!" bellowed the troll, thinking how fine a morsel of goat would taste.

"Oh, please, oh, please, don't eat me," begged the little Billy Goat Gruff. "After all, I am just the smallest of my family. Allow me to go to the other side and I will eat lots of rich grass and grow fatter and even more delicious. In the meantime, you might wait for my brother, the middle Billy Goat Gruff. Surely a goat of his size would suit your appetite much better."

The troll thought the little Billy Goat Gruff had made an excellent point, and so he muttered, "All right then, you may pass. But I shall eat you next time, and that I can promise!"

Before the troll could even doze off again, he heard more footsteps: trip trap, trip trap on the planks of the wooden bridge above him.

"WHO DARES TO CROSS MY BRIDGE?" bellowed the troll once more.

This time it was the middle-sized Billy Goat Gruff, who answered, "It is me."

"Then you shall be my dinner," bellowed the troll.

"Why would you eat *me*?" answered the middle-sized Billy Goat Gruff. "After all, I am only the middle-sized goat in my family. Allow me to go to the other side and I will eat lots of rich grass and grow fatter and even more delicious. In the meantime, you might wait for my older brother, the big Billy Goat Gruff. Surely a goat of his size would suit your appetite much better."

The troll thought the middle-sized Billy Boat Gruff had made an excellent point, and so he said, "All right then, you may pass. But I shall eat you next time, and that I can promise."

About then the big Billy Goat Gruff came tromping across the bridge: trip trap, trip trap. This time, the troll knew exactly who it was. Nevertheless, he bellowed: "WHO DARES TO CROSS MY BRIDGE?"

"It is me, the big Billy Goat Gruff," answered the oldest brother.

"Then you shall be my dinner," bellowed the troll.

"I think not, ugly old troll. For I have horns and teeth and I will kill you first!" replied the big Billy Goat Gruff.

With that the troll ran out from under the bridge and attacked the goat with his gnarled fist, but the goat was ready with his sharp horns awaiting, and he lunged at the troll, who lost his balance and went somersaulting into the river below. The troll was never heard from again. And from that day forward, the Three Billy Goats Gruff came and went as they pleased, feasting on rich grass whenever they pleased, growing fatter and happier the rest of their days.

July 27

Three Billy Goats Gruff, Variation

In "Three Billy Goats Gruff" the intended victim convinces the would-be diner to put off eating him, at least for a time. This motif is used in a variety of stories. Generally, the main reason the character agrees is greed; he thinks he'll have tastier fare if he waits. The most commonly known version is Norwegian. In the Hungarian version, a wolf is pitted against the three goats. The only significant difference is in the ending. When the last Billy Goat Gruff appears, the wolf asks why he is not afraid. "Why should I be afraid? I carry a pair of pistols over my head and I've got a pouch between my legs. Gee willikers! That wolf got scared and took to his heels. And that's the end of it."

July 28

The Fisherman and the Genie

AN ARABIAN NIGHTS TALE

An old fisherman was so poor that he could barely make enough to feed his wife and three children. Despite his poverty, he had a rule that he would not cast his nets more than four times a day.

He went out to fish early one morning, before the moon had set, and cast his nets as usual. The first time, he seemed to have a heavy haul, but to his great disappointment his catch was nothing but a donkey. The second time he cast his nets, he pulled in a basket of stones. On this third try, he caught a mass of mud and shells.

As day began to break on the horizon, the old fisherman said a prayer and cast his nets for the fourth and final time. Instead of fish, he pulled in a large vessel made of yellow copper, with a seal on its lid. This actually pleased him, for he believed he could sell it to the smelter and thus buy some corn.

The fisherman examined the vessel and shook it, but heard nothing. The seal made him think it held something valuable, so he took his knife and pried open the lid. At once, a very thick smoke poured out and rose up to the clouds. It spread along the shore as a great mist, to the astonishment of the fisherman. Then the mist began to take a shape and became a genie, who was twice as tall as the greatest of giants.

The genie regarded the fisherman with a fierce look and exclaimed in a frightening voice, "Prepare to die, for I shall surely kill you!"

"But why?" asked the fisherman.

"Why would you kill me? Didn't I just now set you free? Have you already forgotten my kindness?"

"That won't save your life," said the genie. "I will grant you only one favor, and that is I will give you a choice in what manner you will die!"

"*This* is your reward for the service I have rendered you?"

"I cannot treat you otherwise," answered the genie. "But I shall tell you my story so that you will understand the reason. Solomon, the son of David, commanded me to acknowledge his power and obey his commands. When I refused, he had me shut up in this copper vessel and thrown into the sea. During the first hundred years of my imprisonment, I swore that if anyone should deliver me, I would make him rich. During the second hundred years, I made an oath that I would open all the treasures of the earth to anyone who set me free. In the third, I promised to make my deliverer a powerful monarch. At last, being angry to find myself a prisoner for so long, I swore that if anyone should free me, I would kill him without mercy and grant him no favor other than to choose the manner of his death. Timing is everything. What is your choice?"

The fisherman was very sad to hear this, but his pleas for mercy fell on deaf ears. "All right then, if I must die," he said to the genie, "I submit to the will of heaven. But before I choose my death, I ask you to swear upon the seal of Solomon that you will answer one question honestly."

The genie replied, "Ask what you will, but hurry up."

"I wish to know," asked the fisherman, "if you were actually in this vessel?"

"Yes," replied the genie. "I swear that I was."

"I cannot believe someone your size could possibly fit in this vessel. You must prove it to me."

The body of the genie dissolved and changed itself into smoke, and began to reenter the copper vessel. When all the smoke was inside, the fisherman grabbed the lid and hastily refastened it.

"Timing is everything, genie," he cried. "Now it is your turn to beg my favor. I will throw you back into the sea. And I will build a house upon the shore. Then I will tell all fishermen who come to cast their nets here to beware of such a bitter genie as you, who has sworn to kill the person who sets you free."

July 29

The Child Sold to the Devil

A FRENCH FOLKTALE

Long ago in France, there were a man and a woman who had many children, and who were graceless and perhaps a little stupid. The woman was a whiner and the man could not keep a job. When their tenth child came and the man still had no job, the woman said, "You're worthless! Why, the Devil would have been a better father!"

At that instant, to the woman's surprise, the Devil appeared. He looked rather like a person (and a handsome fellow at that) and since the woman was impressed with *anyone* who had a job, she treated the Devil hospitably. They chatted, and after the small talk was finished the Devil offered to help out with the family.

"Allow me the pleasure of giving you a small fortune—enough for a fine home, plenty of food and clothing, and anything your children might want. In return I would ask only for the soul of your new baby when he is seven years old," the Devil offered. For about two seconds the woman thought about it, then she listened to her children screaming in the background and shook hands with the Devil. "By the time the child is seven years old, I'll figure out something," she thought to herself.

The Devil kept his promise and the family lived like royalty. But when the child approached his seventh birthday, the woman began to panic and cried day and night. The thought of losing him grieved her terribly. One day the young child asked her why she was so sad.

"I'm afraid that seven years ago in a fit of desperation I sold your soul to the Devil," she answered. She explained the horrible bargain she had made and told the boy that their time together was almost at an end.

The boy dealt with the news quite well, which was a wonder in and of itself, but even more impressive, he came up with a plan.

"Give me a little bag and I will leave the country so the Devil cannot find me," he said. "I will live as a beggar and no one will be the wiser."

Certainly it was better than waiting around, so the woman fetched a little bag and kissed her beloved son goodbye.

For several months the boy lived as a beggar but he knew that he could not elude the Devil forever. After he had traveled nearly a thousand miles, he encountered the Devil in a mountainous village. After they chatted for a while, the Devil told the boy that it was time for him to take his soul.

"First, though, grant me a wish. I have heard that you make yourself as large or small as you like. Is it true?" the boy asked.

"Why, yes, of course," the Devil said, boastingly. "I could fill the sky or become as tiny as a flea," he continued.

"Do this last thing, then," asked the boy. "I could not see a flea, but if you became as small as a mouse I could see for myself your amazing powers."

The Devil chuckled. "Well, I suppose I could grant you this one small wish," he said. And without blinking, he turned himself into a mouse.

With that the young boy grabbed the mouse and stuffed it into his little bag. He then raced to the nearest village and found two blacksmiths, and asked them to place the bag on an anvil and strike it as hard as they could with two hammers. The blacksmiths were happy to help, but just as they were about to strike, the Devil called out, begging for mercy.

"I will give you your freedom, Mr. Devil, if you will release me from the foolish bargain my mother made seven years ago," the boy said.

"I agree, I agree, just let me out," called back the Devil.

At that point the boy opened the little bag and watched the wee mouse scurry off, giving the boy back his freedom. When the boy returned to his mother and recounted his adventure, she could hardly believe what had happened.

July 30

The Pied Piper

AN ENGLISH TALE

Newtown is a sleepy little village on the river Solent, but it wasn't always so quiet and peaceful. Once it was noisy enough, and what made the noise was rats. Newtown was so infested with rats that it wasn't fit to live in. There wasn't a barn or a cupboard that the rats hadn't gotten into. The number of rats was bad enough, but the squeaking and shrieking, the hurrying and scurrying, were so great that villagers couldn't hear themselves speak nor get a good night's sleep.

The cats of the town weren't up to such a monumental job and professional rat catchers had been unable to make a dent in the rodent population. The mayor and the council were at their wits' end. As they sat at a town meeting trying to figure out what to try next, a strange fellow came into the town hall. He was tall and thin, with piercing eyes, and his garb was in every color of the rainbow.

"I am called the Pied Piper," he began. "What might you pay me to rid Newtown of every rat?"

The council members haggled a bit, for they hated the rats but hated parting with money even more. They finally agreed to fifty pounds, which was a great deal of money back then.

The piper stepped out of the hall and raised his pipe to his lips. A shrill tune sounded through the streets. And at each note played, rats came tumbling out of holes. They crowded around the piper's heels and ran after him with eager feet. The townfolk came to their doorways and called out blessings on the piper as he strolled towards the river, accompanied by thousands upon thousands of rats.

When he got to the water's edge, he stepped into a boat, piping shrilly all the while, and the rats followed merrily, splashing and paddling out to deeper water. On and on he played until the tide went out, and each and every rat was sucked into the muddy ooze of the harbor.

The tide came back in and the piper stepped on shore, but not a single rat was alive to follow him. Now he asked for payment, but the townsfolk and the council members who had been cheering him earlier were strangely quiet. It seems the town money chest was almost empty, and surely fifty pounds was way too much money for such a simple job. After all, the man had done nothing but play a pipe and get into a boat. Perhaps he would take twenty pounds for his trouble.

"Fifty pounds was what I bargained for," said the piper. "And I'd pay up, if I were you, for I can pipe many kinds of tunes—as other folks have found out too late."

"Are you threatening us, you vagabond?" yelled the mayor. "The rats are all dead and drowned," he said to his neighbors. And turning back to the piper, the mayor said, "Do your worst!"

"Very well," answered the Piper, and he smiled a quiet smile. He put the pipe to his mouth and began to play a joyous tune, full of happy laughter and merry play. As he strode down the streets, the villagers snickered, but from every schoolroom and playroom came their children, following the piper's call with gleeful shouts.

The piper led them out of town toward the cool green forest of stately oaks. For a few moments, you could still catch a glimpse of the piper's many-colored coat, and you could hear the children's laughter. But soon sights and sounds faded away as the piper and the children went deeper into the forest. Watch and wait as they might, the townfolk never again laid eyes on the Pied Piper. Nor were they consoled by the occasional sounds of the children's song and dance that drifted from the forest.

July 31

The Travels of a Fox

A fox digging near a tree stump came across a sleeping bumblebee. The fox put the bumblebee in his bag and set off. At the first house he came to, he went in and asked the mistress, "Can I leave my bag here while I visit a friend?" When she said yes, the fox warned her not to open the bag at any time.

But as soon as the fox was out of sight, the woman took just a little peep into the bag and out flew the bumblebee. A rooster caught the bee and ate him up.

When the fox returned, he noticed his bag had been opened and asked the woman, "Where is my bumblebee?"

"The bee flew out," said the woman, "and the rooster ate him."

"Very well," replied the fox. "I must take your rooster then."

The fox put the rooster in his bag and continued his journey. At the next house he came to, he asked the farmer there if he could leave his bag in the house for a little while. When the farmer agreed, the fox warned, "Be careful not to open the bag!"

Once the fox had left, the farmer couldn't resist a peek and the rooster got free. He was chased by the farmer's pig and eaten up. The fox quickly saw that his rooster was gone and the farmer explained that his pig had gobbled up the bird. "Very well," said the fox. "I must have your pig then."

With the pig in his bag, the fox resumed his travels and soon came to a prosperous village where he stopped at the house of a farmer. The fox asked the farmer's wife if he could leave his bag in the stable while he visited a friend. She, too, failed to heed his warning about looking in the bag. The pig escaped and was gored to death by an ox. When the fox heard this tale, he demanded the ox in return.

The ox was stuffed in the bag and the fox journeyed on. The next house he stopped at was that of a poor woman and her son. This time the little boy peeked in the bag. The ox got free and the little boy broke off his horns. By the time the fox returned, the ox had died and so the fox told the woman, "I must have your little boy then!"

With the boy in his bag, he trudged on to the house of a merchant, where he asked the mistress, "Can I leave my bag here while I visit a friend?"

"I can't see why not," said the mistress of the house, who was in the middle of baking cakes.

"Be sure not to open the bag," said the fox.

The woman's children were crowding around her, begging for a piece of cake, and the little boy inside the bag could hear them and smell the delicious baking aromas. "Oh, give me a piece too," he cried. So the woman opened the bag and took the little boy out and put the family dog in the bag in the boy's place.

After a little while the fox returned and saw that his bag was still tied fast. He put it on his back and traveled off into the deep woods. Then he sat down and prepared to untie the bag, and you can be sure that if the little boy had been in there, he would have suffered an unhappy fate.

But the little boy was safe at the woman's house, and when the fox loosened the string of his bag, the dog jumped out, caught the fox, and killed him!

AUGUST

August 1

The Pelican and the Fish

For Mr. Fish, life was simple. A couple of times a day, he would go to the surface and gulp an occasional fly. The rest of the time he just stayed at the river's bottom, pretending to be a rock. It was a rather dull existence, but he never complained.

Mr. Pelican's life was more complex. He was a creature who liked to eat all manner of fish and he was willing to go to great lengths to acquire a satisfying supper. He also liked a joke at the expense of stupid creatures.

One day Mr. Pelican ventured over and saw Mr. Fish at the river's bottom, doing a poor job of imitating a rock. For Mr. Fish's benefit, Mr. Pelican said: "How will the poor creatures of this pool manage?" And in a louder voice: "This is a tragedy! A tragedy!"

Mr. Fish could not imagine what the pelican was talking about. His curiosity got the better of him, and he wriggled to the surface.

Breaking the water, he popped up and asked the huge bird, "What tragedy? What are you talking about?"

Mr. Pelican looked at the fish with great sympathy. "Dear fish, you did not know? A drought is coming. Within days the water of this river will be dried up and no life will survive. You don't have children, do you?"

"Why, yes," said Mr. Fish, worried now. "I have five sweet little baby fish."

"Five delicious, I mean, nutritious, I mean, uh, five babies?" said Mr. Pelican, who all but drooled out of his huge pocket mouth. "This is a tragedy indeed for I am afraid you all will perish. Unless . . ."

"Unless what?" demanded Mr. Fish.

"Unless I show you the pool two kilometers downstream," said Mr. Pelican.

Mr. Pelican then explained that he knew of a little pool that was surrounded by ferns and moss and shade trees. Of all the sites on the river, this deep shady pool would be the most likely to maintain water, even in a terrible drought. The fish family could live there until the river filled again.

"But the pool is too far away," lamented Mr. Fish. "There is no way the babies could swim that distance."

Mr. Pelican pretended to agree sadly. Then, as if he had just thought of it, he said, "What if I transported your family in my huge pocket mouth?"

Mr. Fish, who now was worried sick about his five babies, thought it was a brilliant idea. Mr. Pelican took Mr. Fish on a dry run and flew him to the pool downstream. Though Mr. Fish did not especially like riding in the dark, smelly interior of Mr. Pelican's mouth, he had to admit it was an adventure.

Mr. Pelican dropped the fish off at home, and Mr. Fish excitedly rounded up his wife and all the babies. "There's a drought coming, a drought coming. I've made arrangements to save our lives, but we must all be quick." As the fish family gathered their few, very few, things, Mr. Fish explained their escape plan. The children were excited to take a ride in the sky. Even Mrs. Fish, who was no more clever than Mr. Fish, enjoyed the prospects of an adventure.

As planned, Mr. Pelican dropped off Mr. Fish first. He then returned for his wife and children. It was an unlikely picture: five baby fish and their mother jumping up to the surface to be the first to enter the pelican's mouth.

Now, everyone knows that pelicans are the natural enemy of fish.

Mr. Crab knew. Mr. Crab could venture the water and walk on land; he knew the ways of the world and he knew Mr. Pelican had duped the stupid fish family into a ridiculous trap.

"Good day, Mr. Pelican," Mr. Crab said. "What's all of the fuss here?"

Mr. Pelican was about to digest the fish family but upon seeing Mr. Crab he thought he might complete his seafood dinner with some crab. "Why, there is a drought coming, good sir. I am transporting some of the locals here to a deep safe pool. May I offer you a ride?"

"Why, thank you, Mr. Pelican," said Mr. Crab, knowing it could not be true. "I'd appreciate that."

Mr. Pelican lowered his mouth to add a bit of Mr. Crab but when he did, Mr. Crab grabbed him with his claws around the neck and the bird's mouth opened and the mother fish and all her babies scrambled out and into the river again. Mr. Crab did not let go, and eventually, Mr. Pelican died.

And Mr. Fish is still waiting for his wife and little babies in the deep pool, doing his poor imitation of a rock.

August 2

Clever Manka

There was once a rich farmer who was always getting the better of his poor neighbors. One of these neighbors was a humble shepherd who was supposed to receive a prize cow from the farmer as payment for service. When the time came, the farmer refused to pay, and the shepherd took the matter to the burgomaster. The burgomaster was a young man, and not very experienced in his job as yet. He listened to both sides and then said, "Instead of rendering a decision in this case, I will give you both a riddle to solve. The man with the best answer shall get the cow. The riddle is this: What is the swiftest thing in the world? What is the sweetest thing? What is the richest? Bring me your answers tomorrow."

The farmer went home in a temper. "What kind of burgomaster is this?" he said to his wife. "If he had given me the cow, I'd have sent him a bushel of pears. How am I to answer his foolish riddle?"

His wife cheered him greatly by telling him she knew the answers. "Why, husband," said she, "our gray mare must be the swiftest thing in the world. No one ever passes us on the road. As for the sweetest, did you ever taste any honey sweeter than ours? And I'm sure there's nothing richer than our chest of golden ducats we've been saving these forty years!"

"You're right, wife," said the delighted farmer. "That cow will be ours!"

Meanwhile, the shepherd went home sad and downcast. His daughter, a clever girl named Manka, asked him what troubled him. He, too, told her of the riddle. She also had answers for him.

The next day the farmer proposed his wife's solution to the riddle. The burgomaster said, "Hmm," dryly. Then he asked, "What answers does the shepherd make?"

The shepherd bowed politely and answered, "The swiftest thing in the world is thought, for thought can run any distance in the twinkling of an eye. The sweetest thing of all is sleep, for when a man is tired what can be sweeter? And the richest thing is the earth, for out of the earth come all the riches of the world."

"Good!" cried the burgomaster. "The cow goes to the shepherd!" Later, he asked, "Who gave you those answers? I'm sure they didn't come out of your head."

The shepherd confessed they came from his daughter, Manka, and the burgomaster asked if he could try another test of Manka's cleverness. He gave the shepherd ten eggs, and told him to tell Manka to have them hatched and bring him the chicks by tomorrow.

When the shepherd gave Manka this task, she laughed and said, "Take a handful of millet and go right back to the burgomaster. Tell him that Manka says if you plant it, grow it, and have it harvested by tomorrow, she'll bring you the ten chicks and you can feed them the grain!"

The burgomaster was so pleased with her cleverness that he proposed at once. They were married shortly after. All the burgomaster asked was that Manka not use her quick wit to interfere with his job. In fact, he warned her that he would send her right back to her father if she did so. All went well for a time, but the day came when two farmers came to the burgomaster to settle a dispute. One of the farmers owned a mare that had foaled in the marketplace. The colt had run underneath the wagon of the other farmer. Now to whom did the colt belong? On that particular day, the burgomaster was thinking of something else as the case was presented, so carelessly he said, "Why, the man who found the colt under his wagon is the owner."

The owner of the mare told Manka of her husband's judgment as he was leaving, and Manka was ashamed of such a foolish decision. "Come back this afternoon," she told the man. "And bring a fishing net that you will stretch across the road." And she told him what to say when the burgomaster asked what he was doing.

The man did as she suggested, and when the burgomaster came out to inquire, he answered, "Why, I'm fishing!" Told that he was daft, he said, "Well, it's just as easy for me to catch fish in a dusty road as it is for a wagon to foal." This, of course, made the burgomaster realize the foolishness of his judgment, but he also realized that Manka had had a hand in this.

Quite angry, he told her she must go back to her father's house, but she could take the one thing she liked best back with her. Manka asked for the chance to make him one last dinner, and considering the circumstances, they had quite a pleasant meal together. The burgomaster grew drowsy after dinner, and when he was sound asleep, Manka carried him out to the wagon and took him to her father's house.

The next morning, when the burgomaster found himself at the shepherd's cottage, he roared out, "What does this mean?"

"Why, nothing, dear husband," said Manka. "But of all the things in the house, I liked you best."

The burgomaster laughed out loud and answered, "Manka, you are too clever for me. Come, my dear, let's go home." And after that he never scolded her again for interfering.

—PARKER FILLMORE

August 3

Raggedy Ann Rescues Fido

It was almost midnight and the dolls were asleep in their beds—all except Raggedy Ann. Raggedy lay staring straight up at the ceiling. Every once in a while she ran her hand through her yarn hair. She was thinking. Finally she announced aloud, "I've thought it all out."

At this the other dolls shook each other and sat up, saying, "Listen! Raggedy has thought it all out!"

"Tell us what you've been thinking, dear Raggedy," said the tin soldier.

Raggedy brushed a tear from her shoe-button eyes. "Have you seen Fido all day?"

"Not since early this morning," the French dolly said.

"I've been worried," said Raggedy. "When Mistress took me into the living room this afternoon, she was crying, and I heard her mother say, 'We will find him! He is sure to come home soon!' and I knew they were talking of Fido. He must be lost!"

"When I was sitting in the window about noontime," said the Indian doll, "I saw Fido and a yellow scraggly dog playing out on the lawn, and they ran out through a hole in the fence!"

"That was Priscilla's dog, Peterkins!" exclaimed the French doll.

"I know Mistress is very sad," said the Dutch doll, "because I was in the dining room at suppertime and I heard her daddy tell her to eat her supper and he would go out and find Fido."

"I think we should show our love for Mistress by trying to find Fido," declared Raggedy Ann. "Let's go see if we can track the dogs." She got out of bed and was followed by the rest. The nursery window was open, so the dolls helped each other up on the sill and then jumped to the grass below. At the hole in the fence, the Indian doll picked up the dogs' trail and the dolls followed him to Peterkins's house.

Peterkins was surprised to see the little figures in white nighties come up the path to his doghouse. But he said, "Come in," and all the dollies sat down while Raggedy told him why they had come.

"I was worried, too," said Peterkins. "But I had no way of telling your mistress where Fido was! He and I were having a romp in the park when a man with a funny thing on the end of a stick came toward us. Fido thought he was trying to play and went up too close. That wicked man caught Fido in the thing on his stick and carried him to a wagon with other dogs in it!"

"The dog catcher!" cried Raggedy Ann.

"Yes!" said Peterkins, as he wiped his eyes with his paws. "It *was* the dog catcher! For I followed the wagon and saw him put all the dogs into a big wire pen."

"Then show us how to get there, Peterkins!" exclaimed Raggedy Ann. "We must rescue Fido!"

Peterkins led the way up alleys and across streets, the dolls all pattering along behind him. A strange procession it was! At last they came to the dog catcher's place. Some of the dogs in the pen were barking at the moon and others were whining. Fido was all covered with mud. My, but he was glad to see the dolls and Peterkins! The dolls went to the gate, but the latch was too high for them to reach. Peterkins held Raggedy in his mouth and stood up on his hind legs so that she could raise the latch. The dogs, who were anxious to get out, pushed and shoved so hard at the gate that they knocked Raggedy Ann into the mud.

Fido helped Raggedy Ann to her feet, then they all ran after the pack of dogs, turning the corner just as the dog catcher came running out of his house. He stopped in astonishment when he saw the line of dolls in white nighties scampering down the alley, for he could not imagine what they were.

Fido and the dolls ran on home, and luckily found a chair in the yard and managed to drag it to the window and thus get into the nursery again. Before Fido went to his basket in the nursery he gave Raggedy Ann and the other dolls a big lick on their cheeks to show his gratitude.

The dolls lost no time in scrambling into bed and pulling up the covers, for they were very sleepy. But just as they were dozing off, Raggedy Ann sat up and said, "If it were not for the fact that my arms and legs are stuffed with nice cotton, I am sure they would ache. But I wouldn't mind for I know how happy Mistress will be in the morning when she discovers Fido safe at home."

And as the dollies, by this time, were all asleep, Raggedy Ann pulled the sheet up to her chin and smiled so hard she ripped two stitches out of the back of her rag head.

August 4

The Doctor and His Patient

A doctor had for some time been attending a young man. The young man was very sick, and over time his condition worsened until, at last, he died. At the funeral the doctor went about to the man's relations, saying, "Our poor friend. If only he had refrained from wine and attended to his body, he would not be lying there dead!" One of the mourners answered him, "Good sir, it is of no use saying all of this now—you ought to have prescribed these things when your patient was alive to hear them."

The best advice may come too late.—AESOP

August 5

A Golden Story

There was once a buttercup shining in the green grass. "You're a little golden sun that turns everything into gold," said a child who saw it. "Would you tell me a golden story?"

And would you believe it? The buttercup began without waiting a single moment. "A certain grandmother sits out of doors every afternoon in her chair. The hands resting in her lap are wrinkled and so is her face, and her hair is as white as the driven snow. All of a sudden two tiny smooth hands steal around from the back of her chair and cover her eyes. And the grandmother immediately says, 'It's my sweet grandchild; I'm sure of it because she never fails to visit me,' and she reaches up to touch a golden head."

"Why, the story is about me," cried the little girl. "Grandmother's guess is never wrong."

But the buttercup went on, pretending not to hear. "Then the child runs around in front of the chair and kisses her old grandmother. There is gold in that kiss, I am certain," said the buttercup, "because it leaves a mark of itself on the grandmother's face; it smooths out the wrinkles and it makes her eyes shine with joy.

"That's my golden story," said the buttercup, "and every child may go home and play it."

And the little girl was happy that what she did had been put into a golden story.—HANS CHRISTIAN ANDERSEN

August 6

Beth Gellert

A WELSH TALE

Prince Llewelyn of Wales had a favorite greyhound named Gellert that had been given to him by his father-in-law, King John of England. Gellert was as gentle as a lamb at home, but a lion in the chase. One day Llewelyn went off hunting and blew his horn in front of his castle. All his other dogs came to the call, but Gellert never answered it. So the prince blew a louder blast on his horn and called Gellert by name, but still the greyhound did not come. At last Prince Llewelyn could wait no longer and left without Gellert. He had little sport that day because Gellert, the swiftest and boldest of his hounds, was not there.

He turned back in a rage to his castle, and as he came to the gate, who should he see but Gellert come bounding out to meet him. But when the hound came near him, the prince was startled to see that his lips and fangs were dripping with blood. Llewelyn started back and the greyhound crouched down at his feet as if surprised or afraid at the way his master greeted him.

Now Prince Llewelyn had a little son a year old with whom Gellert used to play, and a terrible thought crossed the Prince's mind that made him rush toward the child's nursery. And the nearer he came, the more blood and disorder he found about the rooms. He rushed in and discovered the baby's cradle overturned, with blood all over it.

Prince Llewelyn grew more and more terrified, and sought his little son everywhere. But he could only find signs of some terrible conflict in which much blood had been shed. At last he felt sure the dog had destroyed his child, and shouting at Gellert, "Monster, you have devoured my son," he drew out his sword and plunged it in the greyhound, who fell with a deep yell, still gazing in his master's eyes.

As Gellert raised his dying yell, a baby's cry answered it from beneath the cradle, and there Llewelyn found his son unharmed and just awakened from sleep. But beside him lay the body of a great gaunt wolf, all torn to pieces and covered with blood. Too late, Llewelyn learned what had happened while he was away. Gellert had stayed behind to guard the child, and had fought and slain the wolf that had tried to kill Llewelyn's heir.

In vain was all Llewelyn's grief. He could not bring his faithful dog to life again. So he buried him outside the castle walls, within sight of the great mountain of Snowden, where every passerby might see his grave. Over it he raised a great cairn of stones, and to this day the place is called Beth Gellert, or the Grave of Gellert.

August 7

The Dog Who Fell in Love with a Fire Hydrant

One day a boy named David took his dog out for a long walk. His dog was named Kingfish, although he wasn't a king and he didn't look like a fish. He was a terrier, although David's parents like to tell people when they asked his breed that he was a "terror."

Kingfish would walk down the street as if he owned it. David knew that dogs marked their territory by leaving their scent on trees and plants and lamp posts and fire hydrants. But David did not know how much more information animals left as they passed. Because animals can't use the telephone, they leave long messages that only other animals, who have strong noses that work very well, can understand. As kingfish walked down the street he smelled all of the messages that had been left by other dogs. Sometimes he knew he had to leave his own answer. This was like e-mail for dogs.

But on this special day, as Kingfish learned all of the latest news and gossip from the other dogs in the neighborhood, he stopped at a fire hydrant. To David, it looked like an ordinary fire hydrant; it was red and had a silver top. It had nozzles on it for the firemen to screw in their hoses if they needed water. It even had a spray cap on the side so all the kids in the neighborhood could turn it on in summer and play in the spray. After letting his dog sniff at the fire hydrant for a few minutes, David started to pull him away. But Kingfish did not want to go. He dug his claws into the dirt. He tried to stand his ground. Finally, David was too strong for him and he was pulled away. But as he did he glanced over his shoulder at this beautiful fire hydrant.

The next day, Kingfish was waiting at the door when it was time to go for his walk. For the first time ever he held his own leash in his mouth. When David took him outside he didn't stop at his favorite tree to learn the gossip. He didn't pause at the usual plants to hear the news. Instead, with all his might he pulled David towards the fire hydrant. And when he got there he smelled and smelled. His tail stood up straight in the air. His ears were tall. And once again, when David wanted to leave, Kingfish fought him.

This happened every single day of the week. David told all of his friends that Kingfish had fallen in love with a fire hydrant and the story made everybody laugh. No one had ever heard of a dog falling in love with a fire hydrant. But Kingfish didn't care, he just wanted to go to the fire hydrant and stay there.

After two weeks of this David began to wonder if there was something wrong with Kingfish, so he took him to an animal doctor, a veterinarian. The veterinarian looked in Kingfish's mouth and ears and nose and said, "Nothing's wrong there." Then the doctor looked at his feet and his tail and listened to his heartbeat and said, "Nothing's wrong there."

"But what's wrong with him?" David asked. "I've never heard of a dog falling in love with a fire hydrant. It's embarrassing."

"I don't know," the doctor admitted. "This is very strange. It must be a strange disease going around. Until yesterday, I'd never heard of it. But a little girl came in with her little poodle dog. The poodle was very pretty and just like Kingfish, there seemed to be nothing wrong with her. But then the little girl told me that every time she took her dog for a walk she would stop at a fire hydrant and smell and smell and leave a message, and she never wanted to leave." The veterinarian paused. "David, where did you say this fire hydrant is?"

"On Maple Avenue," David said.

"Wow!" the veterinarian said. "That is truly amazing. The fire hydrant that the little poodle fell in love with is also on Maple Avenue. But it is in front of a brown house with white shutters."

David was very surprised. "It is?" he said.

The veterinarian then smiled knowingly. "That must be some very special fire hydrant," he said, "if two dogs have fallen in love with it."

The next day when David took Kingfish for his walk and they stopped at the fire hydrant David looked as carefully as he possibly could to see what was so special about this fire hydrant. It sure didn't look any different from any other fire hydrant in the whole neighborhood.

But for Kingfish it was the most special fire hydrant in the world. And that day, as he read the love letter the poodle had left for him, he knew for sure that David would never understand the true meaning of puppy love.

—JORDAN BURNETT AND DAVID FISHER

August 8

Old Sultan and His Friend

A countryman once had a faithful hound named Sultan, who had grown old in his service. Sultan had lost all his teeth and could no longer follow with the hunting pack.

One day the countryman said to his wife, "Old Sultan is no longer of any use. I shall shoot him tomorrow."

Sultan's mistress had great pity for the faithful animal and exclaimed, "How can you destroy him after he has served us for so many years? Surely we can keep him in his old age."

"No, he may as well go," replied her husband. "He's totally useless to us."

The poor dog, who was lying stretched out in the sun not far away, heard all that was said, and it made him very sad to know that tomorrow would be his last day on earth.

Now Sultan had a very good friend, the wolf, who lived in the forest nearby, and that evening he slipped out to visit him and tell the wolf of his fate.

"Listen, Grandfather," said the wolf, "take courage. I will help you out of your trouble. Tomorrow morning your master and his wife are going to the fields haymaking, and they will take their little child with them. While they are at work they will lay the child under the hedge in the shade. You lay yourself by him as if guarding him. Then I will run out of the woods, seize the child, and carry it away. You must spring after me with the greatest zeal, as you used to do in your hunting days. I will let the child fall and you will bring it back to its parents. They will believe that you have saved the child from me and will be so thankful that never again will they consider killing you."

The dog followed this advice and the plan worked perfectly. The father screamed as he saw the wolf run away with his child, and when poor old Sultan brought it back, his joy and gratitude knew no bounds. He stroked and patted the old dog, saying, "Nothing shall ever hurt you now, you dear old dog, and you shall never want for food and shelter as long as you live."

To his wife he said, "Go home and cook some bread and milk for old Sultan. It is soft and doesn't require strong teeth. And bring the pillow from my armchair. He shall have it for his bed."

And so from this time, old Sultan had every comfort and contentment that his heart could wish.

—BROTHERS GRIMM

August 9

The Dog and the Shadow

A dog had stolen a piece of meat out of a butcher's shop and was crossing a slow-moving river on his way home when he saw his own shadow reflected in the water. "This is my lucky day," the dog mused. "I'll just wrangle the meat from this stupid dog, and I'll be twice the winner."

Poising to attack, the dog snapped at the "other dog" to gain his piece of meat, but in snapping at the supposed treasure, he dropped the bit he was carrying. And so he lost it all.—AESOP

August 10

The House Dog and the Wolf

A lean hungry wolf chanced one moonshiny night to fall in with a plump, well-fed house dog. After the first compliments had passed between them the wolf asked, "How is it, my friend, that you look so sleek? How well your food agrees with you! And here I am striving for my living day and night, and can hardly save myself from starving."

"Well," said the dog, "if you would fare like me, you have only to do what I do."

"Indeed," said the wolf. "And what is that?"

"Why, just guard the master's house and keep off the thieves at night," answered the dog.

"I have nothing to lose," said the wolf. "I therefore will follow you."

Now as they were walking along together the wolf spied a mark on the dog's neck, and being a curious sort, could not resist asking what it meant.

"Oh, nothing at all," said the dog.

"But the mark is so deep and wide," pressed the wolf.

"Oh, a mere trifle," responded the dog. "Perhaps it is the spot where the collar is fastened to the chain. . . ."

"Chain!" exclaimed the wolf. "You mean to say that you can not roam as you please?"

"Why, not exactly," said the dog. "You see I am sometimes looked upon as fierce, so they occasionally tie me up at night. But it's nothing, really. My master feeds me off his own plate, and the servants give me their tidbits, and I am so adored . . . but wait! Where are you going?" asked the dog, seeing his companion leave their trail.

"Oh, good night to you," said the wolf. "You are welcome to your dainty treats but I prefer the hard life with freedom to the life of luxury with chains." And with that, the wolf slipped into the night and was not seen again.—PHAEDRUS

August 11

DOG DAYS END

The Dog and the Sparrow

There was once a sheepdog whose master treated him very badly. Rather than starve and endure the beatings any longer, the sheepdog ran away. As he trotted down the road, he met a sparrow, who stopped him and asked, "Brother, why do you look so sad?"

"I am sad because I have had nothing to eat for days," answered the dog.

"If that's all, friend, come to town with me and I'll soon get food for you," said the sparrow.

The sparrow led the dog to the butcher shop in a nearby village, and, while no one was watching, nudged some pieces of meat off the counter for the dog to eat. Once he was full, the dog suggested they take a stroll together.

They set off for the countryside but the sun was very hot, and the dog soon grew tired. "Take a nap," said the sparrow. "I'll look out for you while you rest."

The dog quickly fell fast asleep right on the road. In a little while, the sparrow noticed a wagon coming down the road, and she grew alarmed when it began to look as if the man driving the wagon didn't notice the sleeping dog.

"Take care, sir," the sparrow cried. "Watch out for my friend."

But the man simply laughed at her and drove his wagon straight over the sleeping dog, killing him instantly. "You have caused my brother's death," called out the sparrow. "And your cruelty will cost you your wagon and horse."

"Hah!" scoffed the man. "I'd like to see you try and take them from me!"

Now the man was carrying barrels of wine in his wagon, and the sparrow hid between them and began pecking away at the corks on the bottom of the barrels. Soon the wine was running all over the road, though it took the man a little while longer to notice that he wasn't pulling such a heavy load anymore. "Oh, how unlucky I am!" he exclaimed when he saw what had happened.

"Your bad luck has only just begun," said the sparrow, under her breath. "You shall pay even more for your cruelty." She perched on the horse's head and began pecking at his ears. When the man noticed her, he grabbed his axe and swung at the sparrow, but he hit his horse instead, and the horse ran away.

"What an unlucky fellow I am!" he cried. As he trudged home, the sparrow flew ahead of him, calling to her friends to join her. When the man reached his house and told his wife of his misfortune, she had more bad news for him.

"There are hundreds of birds in our barn!" she cried. "And they are eating all our grain!"

The man went to the barn and there, leading the birds in their feast, was his enemy, the little sparrow. "Surely I am the most unlucky fellow in the world!" he said in despair. He went back to his house and sat by the fire, brooding over the strange twists of fate which had cost him most of his worldly goods. But the sparrow was not done with him yet.

She perched at his window and when he spotted her there, he threw his axe at the little creature. But he only succeeded in breaking his window and letting the sparrow into his house. As she hopped about, he swung at her wildly, missing each time, but destroying his furniture in his rage. At last he grabbed the sparrow in his hands.

"Shall we wring her neck?" asked his wife.

"No, that is too kind for what she has done to me," said the man. "I shall eat her," and with these words he popped the sparrow in his mouth. But the sparrow fluttered and struggled and the man could not swallow her. "Wife," he cried, "take my axe and kill this bird."

The wife swung with all her might, but she missed the sparrow and hit her husband on his head, knocking him dead. The little sparrow escaped and flew away. As she had promised, the man's cruelty had cost him dearly.

—ADAPTED FROM ANDREW LANG

August 12

Dinner for Two

Two stray cats waited patiently at the back door of the village fish market. After the last customer had gone home and the money was counted for the day and the shade was pulled down for the night, the white-haired storekeeper would toss them scraps of fish. He knew the two cats would fight like dogs for the fish and it amused him.

One Friday evening, in the midst of the cats' usual scramble, an old hound wandered down to see what all of the commotion was about. He was hungry and when he saw the two cats were fighting over a pile of flounder, he asked if he could "help."

The two cats looked up from their future dinner. "You . . . help?" said the first one. "Are you quite serious?"

"Yes," said the dog. "If you like, I can end this argument once and for all."

The second cat, who invariably got shorted, thought the dog might be just the intermediary he needed. "Tell me, good friend, just what do you propose?"

The dog asked the cats if he might examine the flounder. "If you like, I will divide your fish into two completely equal portions," said the dog. "Each cat will have his own perfect piece, and then we all will have some peace!" said the hound, chuckling over his little joke.

The two cats were tired of fighting and thought the dog might have a good idea. So the dog took his paw and tore the piece of fish in two. Unfortunately, one side was decidedly bigger than the other. To remedy the situation, the dog simply nibbled the large piece down until it was the same size as the smaller piece. Only he nibbled a bit too much. And so to even the matter, he nibbled at the piece that now was larger.

"Just a bit here, just a bit there," mumbled the dog, his tail wagging in delight over the delicious flounder.

The cats were incensed. "What are you doing?" cried the first in indignation. "Give us back our fish," demanded the second.

The dog was simply making the two pieces equal, and he did so, until their was hardly anything left of either of them.

"Give us back our fish!" ordered the cats.

The dog looked at the two cats with mock seriousness. "I could not possibly do that. I realize now that if I returned the fish, you two would start fussing again. Actually, I should eat all of the flounder as a service to the neighborhood, which is tired of hearing you two fight every night!"

The old hound then polished off the last piece of flounder and headed home.

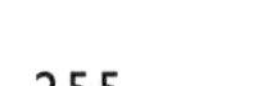

August 13

Rumpelstiltskin

A GERMAN TALE

There once was a poor miller who had a beautiful daughter. It happened one day that he came to speak with the king, and, to make himself seem more important, he boasted that he had a daughter who could spin gold out of straw. The king said, "That is an art that pleases me well. If your daughter is as clever as you say, bring her to my castle."

When the girl was brought to the king the next day, he led her into a room that was full of straw, gave her a wheel and spindle, and said, "Now set to work, and if by the morning you have not spun this straw to gold, you shall die."

And so the poor miller's daughter was left sitting there and could not think what to do. She had no notion how to spin gold from straw and she began to weep. Then the door opened and in came a little man who said, "Good evening, miller's daughter. Why are you crying?"

"Oh!" answered the girl. "I have got to spin gold out of straw and I don't know how."

Then the little man said, "What will you give me if I spin it for you?"

"My necklace," replied the girl.

The little man took the necklace, seated himself before the wheel, and—whirr, whirr, whirr!—three times round and the bobbin was full of spun gold. This went on till the morning.

When the king saw the gold, he was astonished and joyful, as he was very greedy. He had the miller's daughter taken to a much bigger room filled with straw, and as he left he told her that if she valued her life, she must spin it all in one night.

As the girl began to cry, the little man appeared again and said, "What will you give me to spin all this straw for you?"

"The ring from my finger," answered the girl.

So the little man took the ring and started the wheel spinning round, and by morning all the straw was spun into glistening gold. The king was ecstatic, but since he could never have enough gold, he had the miller's daughter taken into a still larger room full of straw and told her, "This, too, must be spun in one night, and if you accomplish it you shall be my wife."

As soon as the girl was left alone, the little man appeared. But the girl had nothing left to give him. So the man said, "Then you must promise me your first child when you are queen."

She made him this promise, upon which he began to spin. And in the morning when the king came and found all the gold, he held the wedding at once and the miller's daughter became queen.

In a year's time, she brought a fine child into the world and thought no more of the little man. But one day he appeared suddenly in her room and said, "Now give me what you promised."

The queen was terrified and began to weep, and the little man had pity on her. "I will give you three days," said he, "and if by then you can tell me my name, I will leave you your child."

The queen spent the whole night thinking over all the names she had ever heard, and sent a messenger through the land to ask far and wide for other names. When the little man came the next day, she tried all the names she knew, beginning with Casper, Melchior, and Balthazar, but after each the man said, "That is not my name."

The second day the queen had a list

of unusual servants' names. She asked the man, "Perhaps you are Roast-ribs, or Sheep-shanks, or Spindleshanks?" But he answered, "That is not my name."

The third day the queen's messenger reported, "I have not been able to find one single new name, but as I passed a small house I saw a bonfire burning in front of it, and around the fire danced a comical little man, who hopped on one leg and cried: 'Today I bake, tomorrow I brew my beer; the next day I will bring the queen's child here. Ah! luck 'tis that not a soul doth know that Rumpelstiltskin is my name, ho! ho!' "

You can imagine how pleased the queen was to hear that name. When the little man arrived, she said at first, "Are you called Jack?" "No," answered he. "Are you called Harry?" she asked again. "No," answered he. "Then perhaps," she said, "your name is Rumpelstiltskin!"

"The devil told you that!" cried the little man, and in his anger he stamped with his right foot so hard that it sank into the ground above his knee. Then he seized his left foot with both his hands in such a fury that he split in two, and that was the end of him.

—BROTHERS GRIMM

August 14

Rumpelstiltskin, Variation

In many tales, dwarfs, fairies, tiny old wizened men, and grotesque little devils appear as supernatural helpers. Often they come to the aid of a hero who has gotten himself in a jam on a dare or a boast. In "Rumpelstiltskin," the mission was to spin an impossible amount of gold in one night, but a wide range of other assignments can be used, from placing a spire on the top of a church to curing a dying animal.

The supernatural helper always demands payments, and these too can range widely. A common and to-the-point request: the first newborn child to take the "helper's" place in hell.

August 15

The Three Snake Leaves

There was once an old man who lived with his only son in great poverty. From one day to the next, they never knew if there would be enough food for the both of them. This troubled the young man, so one day he said, "Dear Father, I feel I am a burden to you. I believe I should go out in the world and see if I can earn my own living." Sorrowfully, the father gave him his blessing.

The youth took service in the king's army, and displayed remarkable courage and leadership in battle after battle. After a particularly important victory, the king promoted him to a high rank and made him his principal advisor at court. There the young man fell in love with the king's daughter, who was quite beautiful but as yet unmarried. This was because she had sworn to marry no man unless he promised that if she died first, he would take a vow to be buried alive with her. Understandably, this requirement had frightened a good many suitors.

The young man loved her too much to worry about the risk, and with the king's consent, he made her this promise and they were married in great splendor.

For a long time, they lived together in great contentment. But sadly, the princess was stricken with an illness her doctors could not cure. Her husband shuddered to think of the fate that awaited him, but knew he could not escape his vow. When the princess was laid to rest in the royal vault, he was sealed in there with her. Near the coffin stood a table on which were placed four candles, four loaves of bread, and four bottles of wine. But when these things were gone, he would have to die.

Each day the grief-stricken young man ate only a tiny mouthful of bread, and watched death creep nearer and nearer. As he sat there one day in his misery, he observed a snake slithering toward the coffin. He drew his sword and cried, "As long as I am alive, you will not harm her." Then he struck the snake and cut it into three pieces.

In a little while a second snake crept out, but when it saw the first one lying dead, it disappeared for a few moments and came back holding three green leaves in its mouth. These it laid on the three pieces of the dead snake and suddenly the pieces joined together. The snake was alive again!

The young man decided there must be a wonderful power to these leaves, so he laid them on the eyes and the mouth of his dead wife. And scarcely had he done this before life and color came back to her pale face. "Where am I?" she cried. He told her all that had happened and how he had brought her back to life. Together they pounded on the vault door till the guards heard them and opened it.

Wisely the young man entrusted the three snake leaves to his manservant, saying, "Keep them with you at all times, for they may help us in a time of need." For his wife seemed a changed person now that life had been restored to her. She forgot his faithfulness and her love seemed to have faded.

Some time later, on a sea journey to visit the young man's father, she fell in love with the captain of the ship and conspired with him to murder her husband. They threw him overboard while he slept and planned to tell the king some lie. Luckily, the manservant saw the conspirators at the ship's railing and let down a rowboat to rescue his master. By the time he reached him, the man was half-drowned, but fortunately the servant had the snake leaves. Once on land, these revived him.

They reached the king before his daughter did and told him of her wickedness. He found this hard to believe, but promised to put their story to the test when his daughter's ship returned.

At last she came back with a tale of how her husband had sickened and died on the voyage. The king cried, "I will bring the dead to life again," and called her husband out from a nearby chamber. The astonished lady fell to her knees and begged for mercy, but her father was deaf to her pleas. "He was ready to die with you and his reward was your attempt to murder him. You shall have no mercy."

She and the captain were put on a ship that was riddled with holes and set adrift on the sea to drown and never be heard from again.

August 16

Jack and the Beanstalk

AN ENGLISH TALE

There once was a widow who was very poor. All she had in the world was her son named Jack and an old cow named Milky Way. They depended on the cow to give milk for them to sell at the market. But one day Milky Way stopped giving milk completely. Jack and his mother decided that he would sell Milky Way for the best price he could get.

On his way to market Jack met a strange man who seemed very friendly. "Do you know how many beans make five?" he asked Jack. As quick as lightning, Jack replied to the riddle, "Two in each hand and one in my mouth."

Complimenting Jack on his quickness, the man pulled five beans out of his pocket and offered them to Jack, saying they were magic beans that would produce a stalk that would grow right up

to the sky. He said he would take Milky Way in exchange for the beans. It seemed like a good deal to Jack, but he had trouble explaining to his mother what he'd done when he got home. She scolded him for his foolishness, sent him to bed without any supper, and cast the beans out the window in disgust.

The next day, when Jack woke up, there was a huge beanstalk growing outside his window. It grew right up to the sky. Jack hopped onto it from his bedroom window and climbed and climbed until he reached the sky. At the top he found a long, winding road leading to a very big house. On the doorstep was an immensely large woman. Jack greeted her and asked politely if she could give him some breakfast. She replied that he'd better be careful that her husband the giant ogre didn't make a breakfast out of him, as he loved little boys broiled on toast. Just as the woman was sneaking some bread and cheese to Jack, there was a great thump-thump, indicating that the ogre was on his way. His wife scuttled Jack into the oven in the nick of time.

"What do I smell?" shouted the ogre.

"Fee-fi-fo-fum
I smell the blood of an Englishman!
Be he alive or be he dead,
I'll grind his bones to make my bread."

After breakfast the giant took out his bags of gold. He counted his gold coins until he began to yawn, then finally he nodded off to sleep. Slowly Jack crept out of the oven and past the ogre, grab-

bing a bag of gold as he went. He ran along quickly to the beanstalk, dropped the bag down into his mother's garden, then climbed down after it himself.

Jack and his mother supported themselves with the ogre's gold for some time, but finally it ran out. Jack climbed the beanstalk again, and this time, after a close brush with the ogre, he came back with a hen that laid golden eggs. By selling these, Jack and his mother were able to live comfortably, but Jack grew restless and mounted the beanstalk once more. This time he sneaked into the ogre's house and, after hiding in the copper pot, was just making off with the ogre's singing harp when the ogre saw him and followed him down the road. Jack swung himself onto the beanstalk with the harp, which cried out, "Master, Master!" to the ogre, who was not far behind him. Once on the ground, Jack asked his mother for an ax, which he used to give the beanstalk a good whack. One more whack brought the giant tumbling to his doom.

Jack and his mother grew rich by selling the golden eggs and displaying the singing harp. It is said that Jack eventually married a beautiful princess and lived happily ever after.

August 17

The Golden Lads

There was once a husband and wife who lived in a crude hut by the river, where the man made a meager living from the few fish he caught. But one day his fortunes changed, for in his net he found a remarkable fish. Not only was it completely gold but it spoke: "Fisherman, if you will just throw me back into the water, I'll turn your poor hut into a splendid castle. There is only one condition, and that is you must not tell a soul where your good fortune comes from. If you do, it will all vanish."

The man readily agreed and put the fish back in the water. Sure enough, on the spot where his hut used to be stood a magnificent castle. And his wife awaited him inside, nearly overcome with joy, "Isn't this wonderful! How can all this have happened?"

"Don't ask me that! I dare not tell you. It will all disappear if I reveal the secret. Put it out of your mind and go see if there's anything to eat in this castle," said her husband. As it turned out, there was a larder stocked with food, and when they had eaten their fill, the wife began badgering her husband for the secret to their good fortune. In exasperation, he blurted out the secret of the golden fish and their castle instantly vanished.

Back the man went to the fishing trade and, as luck would have it, he caught the golden fish a second time. "I can see that I am always going to fall into your hands," said the fish. "So take me home and cut me into six pieces. Give two to your wife to eat, two to your horse, and plant the last two pieces in your garden. They will bring you a blessing."

The man did exactly as the fish said, and from the two pieces planted in the garden grew two golden lilies. The horse had two golden foals and the wife gave birth to golden twin boys.

As the years went by, the boys grew tall and handsome, and one day they went to their father and said, "We want to mount our golden steeds and see the world." Their father protested, saying he couldn't bear not knowing how they fared. But the young men were persuasive, telling their father, "The lilies will tell you how things are going with us. If they prosper, we're well; if they droop, then we are sick; and if they fall, then we're dead." Reluctantly, the father gave his blessing.

Off they rode, and after several days' travel, they came to an inn. The people at the inn made fun of the golden lads and their horses, and one of the boys was disheartened by this, so he turned around and headed back for home. But his brother dressed himself in bear skins and rode on for many more days till he came to a village. There he met a maiden who struck him as being the loveliest creature in all the world. In a very short time, he asked her to marry him. And though her father was not terribly pleased that she wanted to marry a man who appeared to be a bear trapper, he gave his consent.

They lived together happily for several months until the night the golden young man dreamed of a hunt for a noble stag. That morning he told his wife he had to go to the great forest to search for this stag. She felt some premonition of evil and begged him to stay home, but he insisted.

He found his stag in the woods, but he also encountered a wicked witch, who turned him to stone. At that moment, back at his father's home, one of the golden lilies fell to the ground. His twin saw this and knew that his brother was in peril. Knowing not what kind of danger his brother was in, he called on a good witch and bought several potions that might heal his brother or reverse a spell.

From his brother's young wife, he learned that his twin had disappeared in the forest, and there, indeed, he found him turned to stone. Fortunately, the good witch's magic was enough to turn him back into human form and they were joyfully reunited.

And their father had the good news before anyone returned home, for just as the spell was reversed, the golden lily sprang to life and burst into bloom.

August 18

The Conceited Grasshopper

The other day, a very young grasshopper and an old rooster were out in a field together.

"I can jump higher than anyone in this field," bragged the grasshopper. The rooster said nothing, but opened his mouth, as if to yawn.

"Here I go," cried the grasshopper, and she jumped so high that she landed in the rooster's mouth. You know what the rooster did: he gobbled her up.

And that was the end of the grasshopper!—ANGELA M. KEYES

The Trial of Sunshine and Moonshine

A TIBETAN FOLKTALE

Long ago in a flourishing province a mighty Khan named Kun-snang lived. He had two sons, Prince Sunshine, who was born to him from his first wife, and Prince Moonshine, born to him by his second wife, the Khanin. The two brothers were close, but the Khanin knew that as long as Sunshine was alive, her own son would never inherit the Khan's throne. And so the ambitious woman plotted her stepson's death.

It began with a lie. The Khanin pretended she was ill and she took to her bed, demanding remedies of every variety. Nursemaids fluttered about, but no one could heal her mysterious illness. When the Khan, who could not bear to lose another wife, asked what he might do, the Khanin only shook her head, "The only cure that exists is a cure I would never allow."

The Khanin then told the Khan that the only thing that would save her was the heart of a prince, stewed in sesame oil. A human heart in sesame oil? It was horrible! "It matters not whether it be the heart of Sunshine or Moonshine, but Moonshine being my own son, his heart would not pass through my throat. But then how could I take the life of Sunshine? Therefore, O Khan, say no more, and let me die."

But the Khan fell for his wife's strange story. "If you need the heart of Sunshine to live, than I shall arrange for it," he said. Actually, he intended to have the heart of a goat used in place of his beloved son's heart, but he did not, of course, reveal this.

Now the story might have ended here, but unbeknownst to the Khan and Khanin, Moonshine was in the next room and overheard every bit of the plan to kill his brother. Within minutes, Moonshine was at his brother's side to tell him what he had heard.

Sunshine's heart was broken, as any son's might be. Fortunately, his will was strong. "I must leave tonight," he told Moonshine. Moonshine was disgusted with his parents' plot and decided to join his brother. The two brothers were filled with fear, and had no destination and only a few crumbs of food.

Uncertain of their path, elder brother Sunshine led the way. When they came to a muddy river, Moonshine was so overtaken by thirst that he drank of the clouded waters. The drink made him faint and then die. Sunshine could not believe his beloved brother was dead. "My dearest brother, how can I live without you?" He cried and prayed that in Moonshine's next rebirth they might live again together.

Journeying alone, Sunshine came to a cave. An ancient hermit lived in the cave, and when the hermit saw Sunshine's forlorn expression he was overwhelmed with compassion. "Why are you filled with such grief?" the hermit asked the prince in exile. Sunshine told him of all that had happened, and the hermit gave him a vial containing life-restoring waters. Sunshine took the waters, and then the two went to find Moonshine's body, and urged the waters down the dead prince's throat. Slowly and miraculously, Moonshine was restored to life. The two princes decided to stay with the hermit, who adopted them and treated them like true sons.

Now the story might have ended here, but in this land there lived some Serpent Gods who every year required certain sacrifices. The Khan of this particular province (who was not as mighty as the princes' father) was responsible for appeasing the gods, and this year the gods required the life of a young man born in the Year of the Tiger, the year of . . . Sunshine's birth. Another cruel twist of fate! The Khan dispatched envoys to scour the land for such a sacrifice, which led them to the hermit's cave and to Sunshine. How they knew Sunshine was born in the Tiger's year was a mystery, but the envoys were sure of it, and demanded the hermit turn over his adopted son. When they found Sunshine hiding behind some wine kegs, they treated him brutally. "Unhand my son," cried the hermit, but his outburst was in vain, and as he was vastly outnumbered, he could only watch while his son was hauled off to his death.

The envoys dragged Sunshine to the Khan's palace, but along the way the Khan's daughter was looking out the window, and when she heard the youth was destined for the Serpent-sacrifice she was filled with compassion. "See how handsome he is! He is worthy to be saved—do not throw him to the Serpent Gods. If you throw him in, you will also have to throw me in." The envoys reported her words to the Khan, who was furious. "Let her have her wish," he screamed. "Throw them both into the water of the Serpent Gods."

Sunshine was aghast. "That they should throw me to the Serpent Gods is not so bad, but that this beautiful maiden who has dared to love me should be sacrificed also, this is unbearable!" When the Serpent Gods heard these laments, and saw how the maiden and the prince viewed each other with such generosity, they did something they had never done before: they granted the two lovers their freedom. Sunshine and the maiden married. The maiden introduced Moonshine to her sister, and they too fell in love and married. When the two brothers returned to their homeland, triumphant with brides and wealth, their father, the mighty Khan, was filled with joy. The Khanin, however, was overcome by guilt and spoke to no one, and eventually died.

August 20

The Water Elf of the Millpond

There was once a miller who lived with his wife in great contentment. For a long time they were prosperous, until one year, as sometimes happens, their fortunes turned, and soon the man was barely holding onto his mill. He rose one morning before daybreak to walk around his pond, when suddenly he heard a rippling sound in the water. Turning, he saw a beautiful woman rising out of the water and he knew he was looking upon a water elf, which in olden days was called a nix.

The nix called to him in a sweet voice and asked why he was so sad. The miller told her of his troubles and she said to him, "Be easy. I will make thee richer and happier than ever before, only thou must promise to give me the young thing which has just been born in thy house." The miller quickly swore to do so, thinking perhaps a new kitten or puppy had been born at home.

To his great surprise and dismay, he found that his wife had just given birth to a baby boy. The cunning nix must have known this full well, and it was with great sadness that he told his wife of his promise. But as the nix foretold, prosperity returned in great measure to the miller's house. The miller could not rejoice over his wealth, however, for his bargain with the nix tormented his soul.

Whenever he passed the millpond, he expected her to rise from the waters and remind him of his debt, so he would never let the boy go near there. But the years passed and the nix did not show herself. The miller's heart grew a little easier. His son grew up to become an excellent huntsman, and the lord of the village took him into his service. In the village lived a beautiful and true-hearted maiden, whom the son married and loved dearly.

One day the young man was chasing a deer out of the forest and did not notice that he was now in the neighborhood of the dangerous millpond. After shooting the deer and skinning it, he went to the water to wash his hands. Scarecly had he put them in when the beautiful nix arose from the water, smilingly wound her dripping arms around him, and pulled him down under the surface. When evening came and the huntsman did not return home, his wife grew alarmed. Since he had told her of the danger to him from the nix, she suspected the worst. And when she found his hunting pouch by the edge of the millpond, she no longer had any doubt.

The wife spent many hours at the millpond, weeping and cursing the nix, till at last she fell into an exhausted sleep. As she dozed, she dreamt of a kind old woman who offered her help. The old woman gave her a golden flute and said, "Wait until the full moon comes, then take this flute and play a beautiful air, and when thou hast finished, lay it down and see what happens."

The wife awoke to find a golden flute beside her and did as the old woman instructed. A mighty wave rose up from the depths of the pond, and the body of her husband ascended in the air, caught in a water spout. He quickly sprang to shore, caught his wife by the hand, and fled. But they had gone only a small distance when the whole pond rose with a frightful roar and flooded the countryside. The husband and wife were torn apart by the flood and carried far away.

When the waters receded, neither knew where the other was, and they found themselves in strange and distant lands. The husband and wife were separated by hundreds of miles! Both took up sheepherding and many long, sorrowful years passed.

As chance would have it one spring, they both brought their herds to the same valley, and though they did not recognize each other, they were glad for the companionship. One evening, on the night of a full moon, the man pulled a flute out of his pocket and began to play a beautiful but sorrowful air. When he finished, he saw that the shepherdess was weeping. "Why art thou sad?" he asked.

"Alas," answered she, "it was a full moon when last I played the flute and saw my beloved." He looked at her and it seemed as if a veil fell from his eyes, and he recognized his dear wife. And when she looked at him and the moon shone in his face, she knew him also. They kissed and embraced, and the sorrow of their years apart soon faded to a dim memory.

—BROTHERS GRIMM

August 21

The Young Crab and His Mother

A crab and his mother were walking along a beach one summer morning. Suddenly the mother pulled back and studied her walking son. "Why on earth do you walk like that?" she asked him. "You seem to be going sideways, not straight forward with your toes turned out."

The young crab had never given much thought to how he walked. He just knew that he usually was able to get where he wanted to go.

"I'm sorry, Mother," said the young crab. "Show me how I am supposed to walk. I really want to know."

As it happened, the mother crab had never really thought about the proper way to walk. So when she tried to walk straight forward, she tripped and fell on her nose. She could only walk sideways, like her son!

Before you tell others they are wrong, make sure you are right.—AESOP

August 22

The Knight Bambus

A CZECH TALE

There once lived a gameskeeper who had little money. He was never happy because he always thought about what he didn't have, and what he mostly thought about was gold. "I'm getting older and poorer every day," he would say to his wife. "What's the point?"

One morning when the gameskeeper went to work, his chief said, "Do me a favor. Every day a fox crosses my path, and as many times as I have tried to shoot it, I've missed. I usually see it near those old ruins. Do you mind taking a look?"

The gameskeeper went to the ruins and spotted a huge fox. Quickly the gameskeeper loaded his gun with five charges. The fox disappeared for a moment, and then returned with a young fawn in his mouth. The gameskeeper shot at him—boom! The fox ran into the bushes. The gameskeeper figured he had injured the fox, enough to consider his mission accomplished. He decided to poke around the ruins when he came upon three lamps burning and three glittering bags of gold.

The gameskeeper couldn't believe his eyes. "Why, with that money I would live like a king!" he thought to himself. Suddenly, quite out of nowhere, an old knight appeared. "What are you looking for, gameskeeper?"

"Well, I shot a fox and I am wondering where he might have gone," the gameskeeper said, telling a white lie.

"I'm afraid you will never find that fox, for I am he," said the old man.

"But, but . . . why?" stammered the gameskeeper. Mystery made the gameskeeper very nervous.

"I am King Bambus, and these forests belong to my castle. I used to steal and as a punishment, I have to stand guard here, with this gold."

"But how long will you be tied to this spot?" asked the gameskeeper.

"I have to give three poor people two bags of gold each. You're the first and I have been here for three generations. I think it is going to take a while," the knight said. The knight went to fetch two leather sacks filled with gold. Then he explained to the gameskeeper that he must keep the gold all for himself and his family and that he must tell no one—not even his wife—where he got the money.

So the two men shook hands and the gameskeeper left the ruins. His wife was waiting for him in front of their cottage. "Where have you been, my dear? I have been looking for you for three days."

The gameskeeper was so excited he blurted out, "The Knight Bambus has given me two sacks of gold pieces. Have a look!"

But when they opened the sacks they found only dried leaves—no gold at all. The gameskeeper then remembered that he was not to say anything about it. He sulked and his wife wept day and night. They lived as poor people, always thinking about what they did not have, for the rest of their lives.

August 23

The Oak and the Reeds

A stately oak tree once grew on the banks of a river. A terrible storm blew up one day and the winds were ferocious. The oak tried to stand tall and straight in the face of the gale, but much ominous creaking was heard in its branches. The storm somehow found new fury, and the oak tree was uprooted and fell into the river. For a while it drifted downstream, and it happened that it passed some reeds growing on the riverbank. The oak asked, "How is it that you, who are so frail and slender, have managed to weather the storm, whereas I, with all my strength, have been torn up by the roots and hurled into the river?"

The reeds replied, "You were stubborn and fought against the storm, which proved to be stronger than you. We, on the other hand, bend and yield to every breeze, and when a mighty wind comes, we do not fight it. Thus we are still standing here, while you are done for."

—AESOP

August 24

The Donkey Carrying Salt

A certain peddler, hearing that salt was being sold cheaply at a seaside mill, drove his donkey there to buy some. He loaded the poor donkey with more than the beast could bear. As they passed a slippery ledge, the donkey stumbled and fell into a stream below, and the salt dissolved into the waters. The donkey, of course, felt much relieved and marched onward in far better spirits.

The next day, the peddler took the donkey back to the salt mill and loaded him up, this time with even more salt. Again, as the donkey passed the slippery rock, he slid into the stream below, and again the salt all dissolved in the water.

The peddler now saw that the donkey had learned a trick, and so on the third day when he returned to the salt mill, he loaded sponges onto the donkey's back, rather than salt. When the donkey stumbled and fell into the stream, the sponges became thoroughly wet, and instead of lightening his burden, it more than doubled its weight!—AESOP

August 25

The Stag and His Reflection

It was morning and the stag was drinking from a glorious clear spring. As he drank, he pondered his image in the clear water. "Truly, my antlers are a work of art," he said to himself. "Graceful, curving, balanced in every way. But my legs. They are pitiable! No better than sticks, they are! What a curse."

Just then, the scent of a panther crossed his nose. The stag did not hesitate but bounded quickly away from the treacherous predator. But as he raced through the woods his antlers caught in some trees and bramble, and soon the panther caught up with him and attacked.

As he lay dying, the stag realized that the legs he so cursed would have saved him but for the antlers he so admired.

We often overestimate the worth of mere ornament.—AESOP

August 26

Now I Should Laugh If I Were Not Dead

AN ICELANDIC TALE

Once two married women had a dispute about which of their husbands was the bigger fool.

One of the women, to make her point, played a trick on her husband. When he came home from his work, she took a spinning wheel and carders, and sitting down, began to card and spin, but neither the farmer nor anyone else saw the wool in her hands for there was none. Her husband, observing this, asked if she was crazy to be spinning without any wool.

"Have you gone mad?" he asked.

She said that she scarcely expected that he should see what she was doing, for the kind of linen she was spinning was too fine to be seen with the eye. Of this she was going to make him clothes.

The husband marveled at how clever his good wife was and was looking forward to wearing the marvelous new clothes. When his wife had spun enough to make a suit, she set up her loom to weave. Now remember, there was no wool and therefore nothing to weave, so the suit she was making actually did not exist. Yet when the woman announced she was "finished," her husband ran to her. She ceremoniously dressed him, putting on him nothing at all, and though he was standing stark naked, he thanked her for the fine clothes.

The first wife's husband was so stupid that the second wife wondered if she might have the lesser fool. When her husband came home from work, she asked him why in the world he was up and going about upon his feet. The man was confused by the question and said, "Why do you ask this, wife? I don't understand the question."

The woman replied that it didn't matter. "Forget it," she said.

The woman then persuaded her husband that he was very ill and told him he had better go to bed. After some time had passed, the wife said that they ought to find a priest and have last services for the man, for death would be coming soon. He agreed to last services but was feeling rather hungry and so he asked for a bowl of soup. "What are you talking about?" said his wife. "Don't you know that you died this morning?" The man, of course, was shocked. But before he could respond, the woman said she had better go buy his coffin and was out the door.

The poor man believed his death to be true, and when the woman returned he agreed to be put in the coffin. His wife then arranged the burial and hired six men to bear the casket. She had a window made on one side of the coffin, so her husband might see what was happening as the coffin was carried through the village. When the hour came for removing the coffin, the naked man came, thinking that everyone would admire his delicate linen clothes. But far from it. The coffin bearers were sad, yet nobody could stop themselves from laughing when they saw the naked fool. And when the man in the coffin saw him, he cried out as loud as he could, "I would laugh if I were not dead."

The burial was put off and the man was let out of the coffin.

Now it came out that these women had thus tricked their husbands and they got a public whipping at a parish court.

August 27

The Peddler's Dream

This is a story about a peddler and a dream.

We do not know the peddler's name, but we do know that he lived hundreds of years ago in a village called Swaffham in the county of Norfolk in England.

Almost every night, this man had a dream. The dream was always the same: a voice would come to him and tell him that if he went to London Bridge he would learn something that would change his life.

After a while, the dream started to bother him and the voice became more demanding. It got to the point where the peddler dreaded sunset because he knew that once the sun went down it would be dark, and that eventually he would have to go to sleep, and that once asleep, the voice would come in a dream and start nagging him: "Go to London Bridge, go to London Bridge."

"This is more than I can bear," he said one morning to his wife "I must go to London Bridge and be done with it."

It was no small decision. The City of London was very far away, and the peddler would have to walk for days and days to get there. But his dream was driving him crazy. He could not stand it one more night. And so he left for the big city.

Once he got to London, the bridge was not hard to find. But the peddler didn't know what to do. So he stood on London bridge and waited. He watched the boats and the carriages and the people, but nothing happened.

Now he felt like a fool.

He was just about to return to Swaffham when a shopkeeper spoke to him, "My shop is just across the way and I have noticed you standing here at the bridge. May I ask why you are here?"

The peddler was ashamed of his foolish enterprise, but he told the shopkeeper all the same.

The shopkeeper started to laugh. He laughed and laughed and laughed.

Finally, after he collected himself, he said: "You shouldn't pay any mind of dreams, good man. Dreams don't make sense. Why, I had a dream that instructed me to go to a worthless village in Norfolk—Swaffham, of all places! My dream told me to ask for the peddler's cottage, where I would find a grove of huge oak trees. Under the largest tree, I find an old box filled with gold. A box of gold! Can you imagine?" The shopkeeper doubled up with laughter again.

The peddler thanked the shopkeeper and left him laughing. He hurried home to Swaffham. Without even greeting his wife, he raced to the grove of oaks behind his little cottage and began to dig.

Within moments, he uncovered an old box filled with gold.

The peddler was a good man, and so he gave some of the gold to the poor people in his village. The rest he used for his wife and children, and bought each one a handsome bed on which to dream.

August 28

Little Annie

There once was a king who had such a large flock of geese that he had to hire a lass to tend them. Her name was Annie, and so they called her "Annie the goose girl."

At this time, the king's son was searching for a wife. He happened to pass by Annie as she sat in the meadow, sewing a quilt and watching her geese. "Sitting all alone there, are you, little Annie?" asked the prince.

"Yes," said little Annie. "Here I sit and put stitch to stitch. I'm waiting today for the king's son."

"Him you mustn't look to have," said the prince.

"No, but if I'm to have him, have him I will," answered little Annie.

The prince eventually sent portrait painters to other countries to bring him likenesses of the fairest princesses. One in particular caught his eye and she accepted his proposal of marriage.

When she arrived in his country, Annie the goose girl warned her of the stone the prince kept by his bedside. It could tell truth from lies and would reveal a person's true nature when it was stepped on. The princess grew alarmed at this warning and begged Annie to take her place in the prince's bed that night. After he was safely asleep, Annie could leave, so that the prince would find the right bride by his side in the morning.

When Annie stepped on the stone in the darkness of the prince's chamber, he asked, "Who is this that comes to my bed?" And the stone replied, "A maiden pure and fair." So they lay down to sleep and a little later, the princess crept in and took Annie's place.

But in the morning, the prince asked

the stone, "Who is this that steps out of my bed?" And the stone answered, "One who has had three children."

The prince immediately renounced his bride and began his search all over again. But the next woman he selected as his intended bride had, so said the stone, six children.

The last princess who came to the kingdom had the most children of all, but the prince didn't know that yet. He did know that something peculiar was going on in his chambers at night for the pure maiden that got into his bed did not seem to be the same person that got out. When this last princess heard little Annie's warning about the stone, she made much the same bargain with her. They would trade places in the prince's bed. But this time, the prince put a ring on his bride's—Annie's—finger while she slept. The ring fit so tightly she would never be able to get it off and the prince would have a way of identifying the woman later.

In the morning, when the stone revealed that the latest princess was the mother of nine, the prince threw her out of the palace in a rage. When he asked the stone what was going on, it revealed how he had been tricked and that the pure maiden he sought for a bride had been Annie the goose girl.

If Annie was the one wearing the ring, the prince thought he had best go ahead and marry her, so he went to the meadow where she tended her geese. She had tied a rag around her finger and said she had cut herself, but the prince insisted on seeing. There, of course, was his ring!

The prince took little Annie to the palace and had her attired in regal clothing, then whisked her off to their wedding. And so Annie the goose girl came to marry the king's son after all, just as she knew she would from the very start.

August 29

The Laborer and the Snake

A snake lived underneath the porch of a cottage. One day, no one knows why, he bit the cottager's infant son and the boy died. The parents were sadder than they ever thought possible.

The father resolved to kill the snake and the next day when the snake came out of his hole for food, the cottager took up his axe in a rage but missed the snake, cutting off a portion of his tail rather than his head.

Now the cottager was afraid, and with cause. He knew that the snake would be furious and would bite him also. In a pathetic attempt to make peace, he brought the snake some bread and salt.

The snake hissed, then said, "Your offering is ridiculous, dear man. Even a fool could see that there could never be any peace between us. Whenever you see me, you will be thinking about the death of your son; and whenever I see you, I will be thinking about the loss of my tail."

It is hard to forget injury in the presence of him who caused it.—AESOP

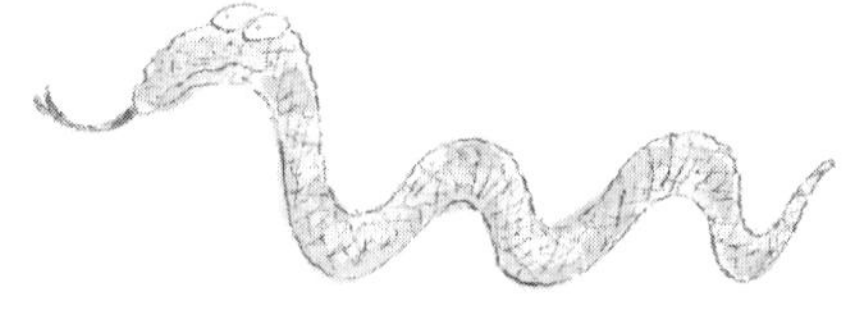

Dan and Billy's Bad Day

A TALE FROM THE AMERICAN WEST

"Move over, Dan, and don't take up all the room, or when Rattler comes back he won't be able to get into the hole."

"Move over yourself," replied Dan, giving his chum a pinch with his sharp teeth. Dan and Billy were chubby little prairie dogs who lived together in a big snake hole on the western plains. They had come over from another range the year before and had "squatted" in the home of Rattler, the largest snake on the North Fork of the Platte River. He was a monster with seventeen rattles, and it was sort of surprising that he'd adopted the two little prairie dogs as companions. But now everyone on the North Fork knew them as "Rattler's Kids."

Billy and Dan had left at sunrise that day to visit some friends up the valley. They had expected to find Rattler home from his hunt when they got back. "I can't see what on earth is keeping Rattler," said Billy, as he returned from his twentieth trip to the mouth of the hole.

The evening wore on and night gathered over the range, but Rattler did not return. At midnight the two prairie dogs cuddled down close together to go to sleep. Just as Billy began to snore a wee bit, Dan shook him and said, "Remember, Billy, if Rattler is dead then I'm the boss of this hole."

"Not if I can help it," muttered Billy, as he went back to sleep.

Both of the dogs woke early the next morning and went out to see the sun come up. Billy turned to his friend and said, "Dan, there is no use in worrying. Rattler will come back if he is alive, and if he is dead, why, then, I'll see you don't starve." They set out for the riverbank to dig some wild artichokes for breakfast, but they couldn't find any that day and returned to their hole in disgust.

Of course they checked the hole for Rattler right away but there was still no sign of him. Dan noticed that he didn't see any sign of other prairie dogs either. "Seems awful lonesome out here. I wonder where all the dogs can be."

"I was just thinking the same myself," replied Billy. They checked from hole to hole in the prairie dog colony, but there was no one around but themselves. "Something's happened!" cried Billy. "Only two things could have made everyone run away. Either a sandstorm is coming, or the water supply has given out."

Dan had lost all desire to be the leader with Rattler gone and he began to cry. "Don't worry, pal," said Billy. "We'll figure this out. Let's get some lunch first." After eating the buds and leaves of a friendly sage bush, they went down to the river for a drink. It was as dry as a bone and their little throats were mighty parched too.

"What does this mean?" cried Dan.

"It only means that the river has sunk out of sight on this side and has probably come up on the other side. It's happened before."

"And the colony and Rattler must have left for that reason," said Dan. The only thing left for the two little prairie dogs to do was to cross the dry sand dunes of the river themselves. As they popped their heads up over the rise on the opposite side, they saw hundreds of their old friends hurrying about digging new homes. And there was Rattler, lying in a great coil on a sunny mound.

"That was a good joke on you two, wasn't it?" Rattler said, as Dan and Billy came up to him.

"Why didn't you tell us?" asked Billy. "We wouldn't have treated you that way!"

"The river began to sink soon after you left the village. I knew you'd find us. I could have left some of the colony there to tell you, but we all thought it would be funny to make you hunt us."

Dan and Billy didn't see the humor in this at all, but there was no time to be cross, for like all creatures of the plains, they needed shelter before night fell. When their new hole was dug, they grudgingly let Rattler join them, but they didn't forget their bad day, and his bad joke, for a long while.

—EUGENE O. MAYFIELD

August 31

Tiki's Way Home

There once lived an elderly couple who were lonely because their only son married and moved away. They decided to buy a pet—a six-inch African brown-headed parrot—to keep them company. They called the parrot Tiki, and in no time they grew to love the little bird. They taught him how to say, "Hi, I'm Tiki," "I love you," and "What's for dinner?" Tiki wasn't friendly to strangers and even bit them from time to time. But he loved the old couple dearly and they in turn loved Tiki as if he was their own child. Soon the couple celebrated their eighty-fifth birthdays. They knew that they didn't have many years left to live. Tiki, however, might live for another fifty years. The couple decided to ask their only son to take care of the bird when they were gone and he agreed.

Two years later, the couple died. By this time, their son had a wife and a little ten-year-old girl. The family was so happy to have the little bird, but Tiki seemed sad. He never talked, never said, "Hi, I'm Tiki," "I love you," or "What's for dinner?" He just stayed on top of his cage until nightfall, when he would quietly slip into his cage until morning. The daughter knew how much Tiki had loved her grandparents and was determined to make the little bird happy again.

Little by little, Tiki started to warm up to the girl. He perched on her shoulder and soon he was talking again. The girl made up a bedtime song for Tiki, and when he heard it he would get all fluffy and cluck proudly like a chicken.

Years passed and soon the little girl

grew into a young woman, ready to go to college. She asked the people at the college if she could bring her bird along, but the answer was no. With tears in her eyes, she said good-bye to Tiki and headed off to school.

Once again, Tiki perched quietly on top of his cage, only to put himself in at night. He never said his name, never said, "I love you," and never asked, "What's for dinner?" One spring night the girl's parents accidentally left a window open and when they awoke, Tiki was gone. They put up posters in the neighborhood, even offered reward money, but he had just disappeared. The daughter, of course, was devastated by the news. She knew she would never forget her beloved bird.

Years passed and the girl grew into a young woman. She graduated from college, married, and had a daughter of her own. The woman would often tell her daughter bedtime stories about her little bird named Tiki. She would tell her how cute he was—just six inches tall, with a brown head and a green body. Then she would sing the bedtime song that used to make Tiki all fluffy and cluck proudly like a chicken. The little girl loved to hear about Tiki.

Like her mother, the little girl grew up into an adult with a life of her own. It was a sad day when she kissed her mother good-bye to become a teacher in a town a hundred miles from home.

One day, after teaching school, the young woman stopped at the village pet shop, where she found the most adorable kittens, puppies, turtles, and birds on display. As she strolled through the store she noticed a little parrot above a cage in the back corner of the shop. She noticed his brown head and little green body. She immediately asked the owner about the little bird.

"Oh, he's not for sale," said the owner. "He's a mean thing, he even bites people. A couple found him a while back. They tried to keep him but they couldn't tame him one bit. They brought him here. He's hopeless."

The young woman looked hard at the bird and although the owner said he was vicious she wasn't afraid. She walked up to the bird and stared straight at him. He stared back. Then in the softest voice, she started to sing the very song her mother used to sing to her little bird.

In less than a minute, the bird became fluffy and started to cluck proudly like a chicken. The woman uttered the word "Tiki," and just as she hoped, the bird said, "Hi, I'm Tiki," "I love you," and "What's for dinner?"

With tears in her eyes she told the owner that she had to buy the little bird, no matter what the cost. Reluctantly, the owner agreed, and the woman and Tiki went home. The days following were joyous, the best, perhaps, when the woman's mother would come to visit and together they would sing to Tiki as he proudly clucked away.—CAROL BOSWELL

SEPTEMBER

September 1

SCHOOL DAYS

The First Day of Fish School

Joe the Fish was a born worrier. When he was just a few days old and his big brother was showing him around the coral reef, he came up with his first real worry. "What happens if I nick myself on the coral?" he asked.

"Fish don't nick themselves on coral," his brother replied. "Just look where you're swimming."

"Yes, but what if another fish bumps into me and knocks me against the coral and I cut myself? What then?" he insisted.

"Let go of it, Joe," his brother said. "It isn't going to happen."

But still, Joe worried. He worried about sharks, jellyfish, shipwrecks, and of course humans. He worried about other fish. He worried that other fish didn't worry. Sometimes it seemed like his mind just spun around and around, faster and faster, whirring with worry.

Worrying is a hard life, and Joe was about to have his first day at fish school. He would be swimming with all of the big guys, patrolling, feeding, checking out the scene. Everybody told Joe not to worry. "You're a fish, Joe. You are programmed to do the right thing, There is no way you will mess up," his dad told him.

But Joe wondered what he would do if an octopus showed up, or a squid. "How do I know who eats whom around here? How do I know if I am at risk?" he asked his mother.

"Joe, listen to me. Everything is going to be fine. Tomorrow morning when the light begins to stream through the water, the fish school will pass by our place and you will join them. You will swim with them and patrol, feed, and check out the scene. This is the way it has been for millions of years, Joe. Try to relax," his mother said.

That night Joe tossed and turned. He couldn't sleep. "What if I don't wake

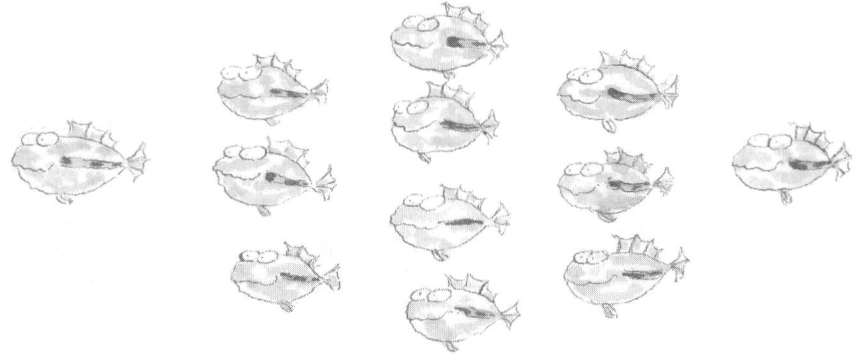

up on time? What if the school of fish passes by and I oversleep?" he thought to himself. He worried so much that he got very little sleep that night.

The next morning when the light began to stream through the water, about five hundred fish passed by Joe's place. Joe reluctantly joined them. There was not one familiar fish face, though all of them resembled Joe, with the same orange color and green stripe down the side. No one said anything, not even hello, but they swam in a magnificent formation, and though he didn't know how or why, Joe knew what to do. He knew where to swim and when to lean this way or that way, when to speed up or slow down. He stayed the perfect distance from the fish above him and below him and on each side. For an hour or so, he didn't even worry. When he came home from his first day at fish school, he actually had a smile on his face.

"So how was it, son?" his father asked. "Did you survive your first day?"

"Today was great," Joe said. But then he paused as a thought crossed his mind. "But what if tomorrow is different?" Joe looked at his dad, and then thought some more. He knew the answer. Tomorrow *would* be different, but there was no use worrying about it. And that was the best lesson of all from Joe's first day of fish school.—CHRISTINE ALLISON

September 2

SCHOOL DAYS

The Master and His Pupil

AN ENGLISH FOLKTALE

There was once a very learned man who knew all the languages under the sun and all the mysteries of creation. He had a large black leather book with an iron clasp, which he kept chained to a table. This book, which only he touched, contained all the secrets of the spiritual world. It told how many angels there were in heaven and what their jobs were. And it told of evil demons and how they might be summoned to serve men.

Now the master had a foolish servant, a young boy who aspired to be his pupil in the mysteries of the universe. But so far he had not even been allowed to enter the master's private study, and his curiosity was so great that he often couldn't sleep at night.

One day, when the master was out, the boy slipped into his study. There was the master's equipment for changing copper into gold, and there was the mirror in which the master could see all that was happening in the world, and there too was the seashell that the master could hold to his ear and hear all the words being spoken by anyone. But the boy saw only his own reflection in the mirror and when he held the shell close, he heard only indistinct murmurings, like the breaking of distant seas.

"I can do nothing," he said to himself in disgust. "I don't know the spells to utter and they are locked up in the book." But when he next turned around, he noticed that the master had forgotten to lock the black volume. He rushed over to the table and opened the book, but little on its pages made sense to him. Putting his finger on one particular line, the boy spelled out the letters there.

At once the room grew dark and the house trembled as a clap of thunder was heard. There before the boy stood a horrible form, breathing fire, with eyes like burning coals. It was the demon Beelzebub, whom the boy had inadvertently summoned.

"Give me a task," he said to the boy, with a voice like a blast furnace.

The boy shook in fright and his hair stood on end.

"Give me a task or I will strangle you," roared Beelzebub. But still the boy could not speak, for his terror was that great. Beelzebub stepped towards him and put his burning hot fingers around the boy's throat. "For the last time, give me a task!"

"Water that plant!" cried the boy in despair, pointing to a geranium on the windowsill.

Beelzebub vanished for an instant, but returned with a barrel of water on his back, which he poured over the plant. Again and again, he disappeared and came back till the water in the room was soon ankle deep.

"Enough, enough!" gasped the boy but the demon ignored him, for those were not the right words to stop Beelzebub's watering. Barrel after barrel filled the room, and the boy climbed on the table but the water had reached his shoulders now.

Just as it seemed likely the boy would drown, the master returned, for he had remembered that he had failed to lock his book. In the nick of time, the master spoke the incantation that returned Beelzebub to his fiery home. For some reason, the master never did take on the hapless boy as his pupil.

September 3

SCHOOL DAYS

The Master and His Pupil, Variation

One of the great modern storytellers is Tomie de Paola, and his "Strega Nona" is a story all children love. The story parallels "The Master and His Pupil." In Paola's retelling, the Italian Strega Nona (Grandma Witch) is the keeper of magic and various potions. She advertises for a helper to garden and keep house, and hires Big Anthony. All of his instructions are routine, except for one: do not touch the pasta pot.

The pasta pot, like the master's book and like the apple in the Garden of Eden, becomes altogether too tempting. Big Anthony overhears Strega Nona standing over the pasta pot, singing, "Bubble, bubble, pasta pot/Boil me some pasta, nice and hot/I'm hungry and it's time to sup/Boil enough to fill me up." After a nice meal of pasta, Strega Nona sings a good-bye verse to the pot and blows three kisses. But Anthony does not see or hear the three kisses.

Soon after, Strega Nona leaves to visit a friend. She warns Big Anthony not to touch the pasta pot, which of course he cannot wait to do. The moment she is gone he summons the pasta from the pot ("Bubble, bubble, pasta pot") and invites the whole village to come and enjoy it. Soon it is apparent that too much of a good thing can be a big problem. The pasta overflows from the cottage to the village and Big Anthony, unaware of the three kisses that need to be blown to stop the pot from producing pasta, has the entire village drowning in a mess of noodles. The priest and the sisters begin to pray. Fortunately, Strega Nona comes home just about that moment. She sings her magic song, blows three kisses, and the pot stops its boil. Big Anthony agrees to make reparations. He is given a fork and it is clear what he must do.

September 4

A Pot O' Brains, Part I

AN ENGLISH FOLKTALE

Once in these parts, and not so long gone either, there was a fool who wanted to buy a pot o' brains, for he was always getting into scrapes through his foolishness and being laughed at by everyone. People told him he could get all of the smarts he needed by going to the wise woman who lived on the top of the hill and dealt with herbs and potions and spells and things. So he told his mother and asked her if he could seek the wise woman and buy a pot o' brains.

"Well, you should," she said, "because you truly need some brains. If I died, who would take care of you? Go to the wise woman, but mind your manners and speak to her pretty, for those wise folks are sensitive and easily displeased."

So the fool went after he finished his tea, and there she was sitting by the fire, stirring a huge pot.

"Hello, missis," he said, removing his hat. "It's a fine night."

"Aye," the wise woman said and kept stirring.

"Maybe it'll rain," he said, fidgeting from one foot to the other.

"Maybe," she said.

"And maybe it won't," he said, looking out the window.

"Uh, huh," she said.

He scratched his head and squeezed his hat. "Okay, then. That's enough about the weather. Let me see. The crops are getting along fine," the boy said.

"Fine," says she.

"And the cows are fattening up," he continued weakly.

"They are," said she.

"And, uh. Well, I reckon we can talk some business now, having done the polite talk and the like," he said. "Have you any brains for sale?"

"That depends," said she. "If you want king's brains or soldier's brains or schoolmaster's brains, I don't keep them."

"Oh, no," the boy said quickly. "I just want ordinary brains. Something clean and common like."

"Aye so," said the wise woman. "I might manage that." She looked at her pot. "Bring me the heart of the thing you like best of all and I'll tell you where to get a pot o' brains."

"But," he said, scratching his head, "how can I do that?"

"That's not for me to say," she said. "Find out for yourself if you don't want to be a fool for your whole life. You're also to read me a riddle so I can see that you've brought me the right thing. Well, I've got something else to see to. Good-bye."

The fool went home to his mother and explained what he had to do. "I guess I'll have to kill my pig, because she is a favorite thing," he said sadly.

"Then do it," said his mother. "You've got to do whatever she says."

So the fool killed his pig and the next day went off to the wise woman's cottage. "Good evening, missis," he said. "I've brought you the heart of the thing I like best of all."

He put the pig's heart on the table.

"Is that so?" said the woman, peering down at the pig's heart with her spectacles. "Then tell me the answer to this riddle: 'What runs without feet?' "

He scratched his head and thought and thought but he couldn't tell.

"Go your way then, fool. You haven't fetched me the right thing yet. I've no brains for you today," the wise woman said.

The fool went home to his mother. She had a strange look on her face when he walked in the door. "I'm so glad you are finally getting some brains. It's important that you be able to take care of yourself when I am dead and gone," she said. And with that, she dropped dead on the floor. Dead and gone!

The fool sat down. The more he thought about it, the sadder he felt. He remembered how his mother had fed him and tried to help him with his schoolwork and mended his clothes and bore his foolishness, and the more he thought about it, the sadder he got. He began to sob.

"Oh, Mother, Mother, who will take care of me now?" he wailed. "You shouldn't have left me because I liked you better than anything." Then the fool had a thought. "Maybe I should take my mother's heart to the wise woman, since it is my mother, not my pig, whom I really like best of all," he said to himself.

The fool decided that more than ever he needed some brains, so he put his dear mother in a sack and took her to the wise woman at the top of the hill.

"Hello, missis. I think I've got the right thing this time," the fool said, setting his sack, kerplop! on the doorstep.

"Maybe," said the wise woman. "But tell me this now. What's yellow and shining and isn't gold?"

He scratched his head and he thought and thought but he couldn't tell.

"You're a bigger fool than I thought," said the wise woman. Then she slammed the door in his face.

September 5

A Pot O' Brains, Part 2

The fool sat down on the hillside and cried and cried. By and by, a young lady came walking along. "What's the matter?" she asked. "Why are you crying?"

"I've lost the only two things I ever cared for and I have nothing else to buy a pot o' brains with," he explained.

"I'm sure I don't understand you," the young lady said. "Quit talking like a fool."

"I am a fool, only a fool wouldn't see that," said the fool. "I've killed my pig and I've lost my mother, and now there's no one to take care of me." Then he told her all about the wise woman and the pig's heart, his dead mother and the riddles.

"Well, I wouldn't mind looking after you myself," the young lady said.

"Can you cook?" he asked, looking up.

"Yes, I can," she said.

"Can you clean?" he asked.

"Yes, I can," she said.

"And can you mend my clothes?" he asked.

"I suppose I could do that," she said.

"Well, you'll do as well as anybody," the fool said, "but what will I do about that wise woman?"

"Oh, just wait a bit. Something may turn up, and if not you have me to take care of you now anyway," the young lady said.

The young lady took very good care of the fool, and before long he realized that indeed he liked her best of all. But this presented a problem.

"I figure now that I like you best of all, I'm going to have to kill you and bring your heart to the wise woman," said the fool. The young lady couldn't believe it.

"There's something wrong with the way you think," she said. "Why don't you take me to the wise woman alive? You'll have my heart, just as she asked, and I'll be able to help you answer the riddles to boot."

The fool scratched his head. "The riddles might be too hard for women folk," he said.

"Oh, really," said the young lady. "Try me then."

"What runs without feet?"

"Why, water, of course."

"What's yellow and shining and isn't gold?"

"Why, the sun."

The fool scratched his head. "Faith be," he said. "Let's go to the wise woman at once."

The two went up the hill to the wise woman's cottage. "Hello, missis," said the fool. The wise woman looked at them both through her spectacles.

"Can you tell me first what has no legs and then two legs and then ends with four legs?" the woman asked.

The young lady whispered into the fool's ear, "A tadpole."

"Maybe a tadpole?" said the fool.

The wise woman nodded her head. "That's right," she said. "and you've got a pot o' brains already."

"Where are they?" the fool asked, digging through his pockets.

"In your wife's head," the wise woman answered. "The only cure for a fool is a good woman to look after him, and that you've got, so good riddance to you." And with that she nodded to them and went back into her cottage.

The fool and his wife went home together and the fool never wanted a pot o' brains again because he knew his wife had enough for both of them.

September 6

Down the Drain, Part 1

"Loddie, bath time," her mother called.

Loddie was stringing the last tiny plastic bead on her bracelet. She had created a pattern of green, red, blue, repeating it over and over. There! it was finished.

"Coming, Mom!" Loddie answered.

Loddie's pink bathroom was steamy and smelled of bubblegum bubbles, and the water was up high, the way she liked it.

"Do you think it's okay to wear my new bracelet in the tub?" she asked her mother.

"Sure, honey. But hurry because your father and I are going to the opera tonight and I have to get dressed," her mother answered.

Loddie was eight—old enough to draw her own bath—but she still liked it when her mother did it for her.

"I'm going to leave you on your own now," her mother said. "I've got to find something to wear," her mother said. "Your father and I are . . ."

"I know, I know: going to the opera. I'm fine, Mom, go ahead," Loddie answered.

Loddie made a ball gown out of bubbles, and pretended she was the star of an opera. She admired her arm with the bracelet on it. Then she laid back and relaxed in the water, and let her hair float like a mermaid's. By now most of the bubbles had gone flat, so she got out of the tub, dried off, put on her nightgown, and went to brush her teeth. Then she made a horrible discovery. Her bracelet was missing!

Loddie turned to the tub and swept a hand across the few remaining drifts of bubbles. It wasn't there. It must have gone down the drain, Loddie thought to herself. *My best bracelet!*

Loddie ran to her mother's room and told her what happened.

"Oh, honey, I have to go now, but I'll help you look for it tomorrow. You can make another bracelet, can't you?" her mother said, clipping on one sparkling earring, then another.

"Make another one?" Loddie cried out. *"It was my best bracelet!"*

Loddie ran into her room sobbing. She had worked for hours with those tiny Indian beads, and just like that—the whole thing was gone. She went to the bathroom one more time to see if the bracelet was under a sponge or a face cloth. But she found nothing. She laid her head down on the edge of the bathtub for the longest time, thinking she had never been so sad. Then she had an idea. Maybe she could reach down the drain and get her bracelet. So she lifted the lever up and stuck two

fingers down. Whoosh! Wait. Where was she going? What was happening? A force was pulling her . . . down the drain!

Suddenly Loddie was going down a dark pipe, slipping and sliding as if she was in a giant tube at a water park. "This is fun," she said out loud, though no one was there to hear her. She felt so light and happy she started laughing.

Before she knew it, the slide stopped and so did she. A sign was posted with an arrow and the arrow pointed to a path. "Why not?" she thought. She had not walked far when she came a white gate with a strange little man in a white suit and white gloves standing guard. He snapped to attention, as if he was greeting a queen.

"Yes, Miss. Yes, Miss. Good, good, good. May I help you?" the man asked.

"Excuse me, sir?" Loddie asked.

"I said, that is, welcome, Miss. Welcome to the Lost and Found." The man cleared his throat. "You obviously have lost something and we can help."

"Well, I did lose my bracelet, my best bracelet, the one I made today," Loddie said.

"Ah, a bracelet. That'd be Gems, Precious Stones, and Other. Just follow the gold path and you'll see the sign," the man said. "And please, please let me know if there is anything else I can do for you." Loddie wondered for a moment if this was a dream. But she *did* want her bracelet back in the worst way. She started down the gold path.

September 7

Down the Drain, Part 2

Loddie followed the gatekeeper's directions down the gold path until she saw a sign that said, "Gems, Precious Stones, and Other." There stood another little man in a white uniform in front of a huge building.

"Oh, boy, oh, boy, *this is it!*" the little man said excitedly, rubbing his palms together. He snapped to attention. "Yes, Miss. May I help you?" he said, bowing so deeply his nose grazed his shoes and he almost fell over.

"I'm here, I guess, to get my bracelet back. What is this anyway?" Loddie said.

The man regained his balance and answered in a deeper voice than before, "This, my dear, is the Lost and Found. It was established at the beginning of modern plumbing to help individuals just like you. Our inventory includes bobby pins, plastic toy pieces, sponges, barrettes, shampoo lids, gooey soap chips, and, of course, gems, precious stones, and others. Everything is dated and catalogued for your convenience. To be utterly forthright, you are our very first client, so it is a particular honor to serve you! Now may I have a description?"

"Description?" Loddie said. "Okay, it was my best bracelet, my most favorite all-time . . ."

"Oh, dear, a sentimentalist. Now, dear child, to find your bracelet, I need a description. In other words: what does the bracelet look like?" the man said.

Loddie collected herself. "It was in a pattern: green, red, blue. The beads were very tiny and I had to use a needle to string them."

"Say no more. I'll be right back," the little man said.

Loddie waited. She felt sorry for the little men because they had so little business. Anyway, who knew? It's not like they advertised. The man came back, interrupting her thoughts. In his hand was a bracelet with emeralds and rubies and sapphires, all in a pattern.

Loddie tried to whistle. "Anyway, that's very pretty, but it's not mine," Loddie said. "Why don't you just let me go in and have a look around? If I can't find it, no big deal."

The little man agreed to let her into his vault of found items. It was immense, a wall of tiny compartments for as far as the eye could see, all filled with missing jewelry. There were pearls and diamond rings and tacky brooches and puka shells and even a Mickey Mouse watch. Loddie had never seen anything like it. But all she wanted was her best bracelet back.

She must have looked for an hour, when the little man came up from behind her and startled her. "Gotcha!" he said, laughing again. "Any luck?"

"Not really," Loddie said.

"That's because I have it!" the man said with a twinkle. Sure enough, he pulled her little Indian bead bracelet out of his pocket. "I went to check 'New Arrivals' and it was there in a pile with some chewed-up foam alphabet pieces. I've got a C, F, and N—are those yours too?" he asked. Loddie was so overjoyed to get her bracelet back she didn't answer.

"Thank you so much, I really appreciate it," she said, hugging the little man so hard his eyes popped. "I don't want to seem rude, but I would love to show my mother before she leaves for the opera. How do I get home?"

"Home, right, home, hmm . . ." said the little man. "I really wouldn't know."

"What do you mean you wouldn't know? How can I get to my bathtub?" For a minute, Loddie was afraid. She ran down the gold path to get to the main entrance of the Lost and Found. The first little man was not at his post, so she passed through the gate. How would she get home? Losing the bracelet was one thing, but being lost herself was another. What if she had to live in the Lost and Found for the rest of her life? Loddie laid down her head on the side of the cool white gate and thought she had never been so sad. Then she heard her mother's voice, "Loddie, Loddie darling, wake up. Your father and I have to go to the opera."

"What? What, Mom? Is it you? How did I get home?" Loddie asked sleepily.

But her mother interrupted. "Oh, honey, you must be exhausted. You fell asleep right here on the edge of the bathtub. Surely your bed would be more comfortable," she said smiling.

Then Loddie saw it. Her bracelet was sitting on top of the drain. Next to it were three chewed-up foam alphabet pieces: C, F, and N. Her mother saw the little pile, too.

"My goodness, your bracelet. You didn't lose it after all! And where did you get those foam letters, Loddie? Aren't they for babies?"

"Well, you see there was this little man and a huge building filled with Gems, Precious Stones . . ." Loddie's mother gave her a funny look.

"Oh, never mind," Loddie said. "Have a good time at the opera!"

—CHRISTINE ALLISON

September 8

The Story of the Mouse Merchant

A HINDU FABLE FOR LABOR DAY

Many a man, starting with modest capital, has ended by acquiring great wealth. But I built up my great fortune by starting with nothing at all. Listen and you shall hear how I did it.

My father died before I was born and my mother's wicked relations robbed her of all she possessed. So in fear for her life she fled from them and took refuge at the home of one of my father's friends. There I was born, to become the protector of my excellent mother.

Meanwhile, she supported our lives by the pittance earned through the hardest work. As poor as we were, she found a teacher who consented to instruct me in the simple rudiments of reading, writing, and keeping accounts. Then one day my mother said to me, "My son, your father before you was a merchant and the time has come for you also to engage in trade. The richest merchant is now living in our city. His name is Visakhila, the money changer, and I hear that it is his habit to make loans to the poor sons of good families to start them in business. Go and ask him for such a loan."

Straightaway I went to Visakhila, the money changer, and found him angrily denouncing another merchant's son to whom he had loaned money. "See that dead mouse upon the ground," he said scornfully. "A clever man could start even with such poor capital as that and make a fortune. But however much money I loan you I barely get back the interest on it, and I greatly doubt whether you have not already lost the principal."

Hereupon I impetuously turned to Visakhila and said, "I will accept the dead mouse as capital to start me in business."

With these words, I picked up the mouse, wrote out a receipt, and went my way, leaving the money changer convulsed with laughter.

I sold the mouse to another merchant as cat's meat, for two handfuls of peas. I ground the peas, and taking with me a pitcher of water, I hastened from the city and seated myself under the shade of a spreading tree. Many weary woodcutters passed by, carrying their wood to market, and to each one I politely offered a drink of cool water and a portion of the peas. Every woodcutter gratefully gave me in payment a couple of sticks of wood, and at the end of the day I took these sticks and sold them at market. Then for a small part of the price I received for the wood, I purchased a new supply of peas, and so on the second day I obtained more sticks from the woodcutters. In the course of a few days I amassed quite a bit of capital and was able to buy from the woodcutters all the wood that they could cut in three days. It happened soon afterwards that because of the heavy rains there was a great scarcity of wood in the market and I was able to sell all that I had bought for several hundred *panas*. With this money I was able to set up a shop and—as I am a shrewd businessman—I soon became wealthy.

Then I went to a goldsmith and had him make me a mouse of solid gold. This mouse I presented to Visakhila as payment of the loan and soon after he gave me his daughter in marriage. Because of this story, I am known to the world as Mushika the Mouse. And so it was without any capital to build on that I amassed a fortune.

September 9

Idleness and Industry

A GERMAN TALE FOR LABOR DAY

There once lived a young maiden who was very beautiful, but very, very lazy. She hated to do work of any sort, preferring to idle away her days.

When the maiden was required to spin flax, she was too lazy to untie the little knots in it, but would break the thread and throw down whole handfuls of flax on the floor to be wasted. This young lady had a servant maid who was as industrious as her mistress was idle. She collected these little pieces of flax, disentangled them, spun them into fine thread, and had them made into a beautiful dress for herself.

Now it happened that a young gentleman in the village had asked the idle maiden to be his wife and the wedding day had been set. But a few evenings before it was to take place, the bride and bridegroom were walking together near the village green, where several young people were dancing. "Look," exclaimed the bride with a laugh. "That is my little maidservant. She thinks herself so fine in my leavings!"

"What do you mean?" asked the bridegroom.

Then she told him that her servant had made that dress out of the tangled pieces of flax that she had thrown away because it was too much trouble to unravel the knots. On hearing this, the bridegroom began to reflect that a hard-working young maiden, although she might be poor, would make a better wife than a careless idle young lady with all her beauty. So he broke off his engagement to the fair maiden and married her industrious servant instead.—BROTHERS GRIMM

September 10

The Case of the Contrary Woman

A NORWEGIAN FOLKTALE

There lived an old woman who was almost impossible to get along with. If someone would say up, she would say down. If you were cold, she was hot; wet, dry; long, short; and so on. Most of all, this woman would rather be dead than agree with her husband.

And so it happened. On a Sunday.

The old woman and her husband, the old man, went out on a mild Sunday afternoon to see how their crops were faring. From the village bridge they could see that their crops were growing very well—so well, in fact, that the old man, who after fifty years of unpleasant conversation should have known better, made an idle remark: "Well, the crops are ripe already. We'll have to start reaping in the morning."

"Not reaping, old man. Clipping. Tomorrow we will start clipping the crops," the old woman said.

"What are you talking about?" asked the man. "We clip wool, not crops. Wool you clip, crops you reap."

"Ah, yes, clipping time," said the old woman, ignoring her husband. "Clipping time is here again. Clip, clip, *clip*." She said the last "clip" with a sneer, which made her veins pop.

The old man observed that the old woman looked uglier than usual when her veins were popping. But ugly or not, he was not about to let her prevail.

"Tomorrow is reaping day," he sang, getting closer and closer to her ugly face. When he finally was standing toe to toe with her, he screamed, "REAPING DAY!"

The woman was not flummoxed, not one bit. "Clip, clip clip," she said snipping at the man's nose with her fingers. She "clipped" at his ears, his chin, his beard, and then broke into a wild laugh that threw her off balance. She so lost her balance that she tripped off the bridge and fell straight into the river.

The old man went to her rescue, albeit slowly. When finally he was at her side, he yanked at her topknot and lifted her up so just her nose was above water.

"Clip, clip, clip," the old woman said, the words bubbling in the water.

"This woman is insane," the old man thought, and decided to push her under. But hardly had he pushed her under that she thrust her hand up into the air, clipping with her fingers as though they were a pair of scissors.

"That's it!" the man bellowed. He pushed her down once and for all.

The man left the woman to drown, and eventually she did. He did not think too much about her until a few days later, when his guilt began to gnaw at him. "It was unkind to let her drown. The least I can do is give her a proper burial," he thought to himself.

So he began his journey to find the old woman, trekking for miles downstream, where surely the waters had carried her. For many days he searched, but she was nowhere to be seen.

It was not until months later, when visitors came upon the old man, that he learned of his wife's fate.

"Five miles upstream we found an old nag," the visitors told him.

"But that's impossible," said the man. "My wife died five miles downstream, and the current must have carried her three times farther than that."

Then it dawned: the old woman had not only been contrary in this life, but in the After, too. Even her dead body had floated up, against the stream. The old man did not bother to guess where she had gone now.

September 11

The Case of the Contrary Woman, Variation

This story has many variations, most of them under the title "The Shrew." Everyone has a bit of the shrew in him or her, but in earlier times the nagging wife was a common character. In "The Shrew and the Ghost," a Turkish tale, we meet the cantankerous wife of a woodcutter. The woodcutter is a mild man (mild men and shrews seem to have attracted each other in these stories) and one day he saddles his donkey and sets off for the mountains. He asks that his wife not follow him, which of course, she does. The woodcutter pretends not to see her but when he realizes she is close to falling into an abandoned well, he calls out to warn her. She pays no attention to what he says and falls in.

To rescue her, the woodcutter drops a length of rope into the well and when he feels her grip, he laboriously pulls it to the surface. But instead of his wife it is a hideous ghost on the other end. The ghost is grateful to the woodcutter. "For many years I have lived in peace in this well until a horrible old woman fell down here and grabbed me and would not let me go," the ghost explains. "I must reward you for saving me from this creature."

The ghost explains his plan. He pulls out three linen cloths. "Tomorrow I will inhabit the sultan's daughter," the ghost says. "She will fall deathly ill and doctors will be unable to cure her. You will travel to the sultan's palace and place these cloths on her face. She will be cured, you'll get a reward, and that will be that."

It sounds like an excellent idea to the woodcutter, who promptly forgets about his wife and goes home. As the ghost intended, the sultan's daughter becomes deathly ill and the sultan offers her hand in marriage to anyone who can cure her.

Off the woodcutter goes to the palace. Using the three linens, he cures the girl and subsequently marries her. As it happens, the sultan has another daughter, whom the ghost decides to inhabit. She is becoming sicker by the day and the sultan asks the woodcutter to help, promising the second daughter's hand in marriage also (no limit on the number of wives here). The woodcutter begs the ghost to move on but he has no intention of abandoning his new home. "If you don't leave me alone, I'll see that you lose both women," the ghost says.

The woodcutter sighs dramatically. "The last thing I need is another wife. Do you remember my first one?" he says slyly. "Wait," says the ghost. "Is she here?" The woodcutter says his first wife is right outside the door. The ghost needs to hear no more. Not only does he leave the sultan's daughter but flees the city and the kingdom, and no one ever hears of him again. And so it comes to pass that the humble woodcutter has two royal wives and eventually inherits magnificent riches.

September 12

The New Improved Family-Sized Butterfly

"The butterfly was a beautiful little insect. With carefully colored wings, it would glide on the wind, stopping only to rest momentarily on a leaf."

If only that description could have lasted a little longer. My name is Ayel Ruperton, and ten years ago, in 2056, I began working on "Project Butterfly." I regret working on it. I think the entire X-crew does. The goal of the project was simple: the ordinary butterfly hadn't changed at all in several centuries. It was exactly the same as it had been before we built cities on the moon. With so many wonderful computer games and movies and television programs, most people had taken the butterfly for granted. All it did was fly around. It didn't fly very fast. Its colors were pretty basic. It didn't sing a single note; it couldn't even hum like a bee. It wasn't very big. For many years, people had practically ignored the butterfly. It just didn't seem to fit in anywhere anymore.

That's when Project Butterfly began. Our plan was to create a giant butterfly. Not only were we going to make it huge, we were going to add incredible colors to the wings—and then we were going to sell advertising on those wings. No one would miss the simple old butterfly when the new, big butterflies with messages in their wings flew into their yards.

I worked on this project with my friends Andre and Macc. We were getting paid $250 an hour and working ten-hour days. We were so excited about how much money we were making that we really didn't pay too much attention to the job. "When this job is done," Andre would say, "I will buy a new car and a new television set with every video game."

"Yeah?" Macc said. "Well, I'm going to buy a new house with a new bed and a new couch and two VCRs!"

I didn't know what I was going to buy, but whatever it was, I was going to buy a lot of it. I was thinking about that when it came time to add the new colors to the butterfly wings. I accidentally dropped in too much color.

When the first butterflies were hatched they were four feet tall, and their wings were red and orange and green and blue and purple and black and white and brown. In the middle of the wings there was a little ad for washing machine soap, but no one could see it. The first butterfly flapped his wings and flapped and flapped and just barely managed to get off the ground. He flew about six feet and landed on a tree branch. But he was so big the branch broke off and he fell to the ground.

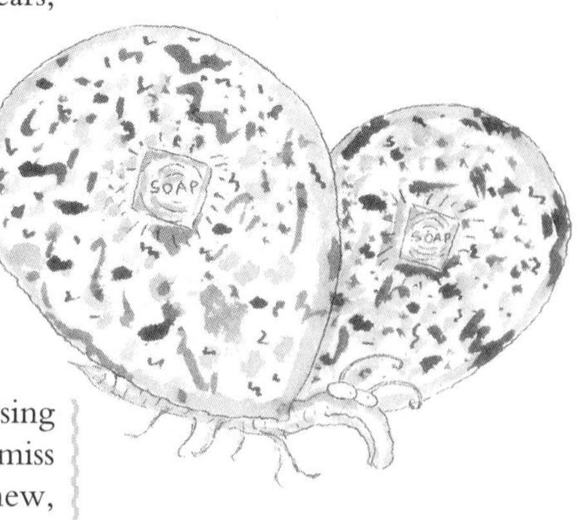

The butterflies were so big they needed to keep eating. They got too fat to fly. They couldn't even get into the air. And the colors on their wings were so bright that people couldn't even look at them without hurting their eyes. So as soon as anyone saw a butterfly come walking down the road they would turn their heads.

For the first time in years and years people finally noticed the butterflies. Whenever they saw them coming they would scream, "Help! Help! The giant butterflies are coming. Run for it!" So that didn't sell a lot of advertising. Our plan turned out to be a terrible thing.

So now, when I open a book and see how gentle and pretty the tiny butterfly used to be I feel very very sorry that I didn't realize some things are beautiful just as they are and there is no need to try to improve on nature.

—JORDAN BURNETT AND DAVID FISHER

How Brave Walter Hunted Wolves

Walter was six years old and about to begin school. He could not read yet, but he could do many other things. He could do cartwheels, stand on his head, throw snowballs, and he could hunt wolves.

One day in the spring Walter heard there were a great many wolves in the woods, and that pleased him. He was wonderfully brave when he was among friends or at home with his brothers and sister. He often told them, "One wolf is nothing, there ought to be at least four."

Indeed, some thought that the lad boasted a bit, but lacking proof to the contrary, what could they say. Instead they said, "Look, there goes brave Walter, who is brave enough to fight with four."

Walter was more convinced of this than anyone, and one day he set off for a real wolf hunt. He armed himself to the teeth with his popgun, his bow, and his air-pistol, and also took his drum and tin saber. He gave himself a menacing mustache with burnt cork, and stuck a red cock's feather in his cap so as to look fierce. His older friend Jonas was going to the mill with corn, so Walter hopped aboard the wagon, while Caro, the dog, ran barking beside them.

When they came to the mill, Walter asked if there had been any wolves in the neighborhood lately.

"Alas! Yes," said the miller. "Last night the wolves ate our best ram by the kiln not far from here."

"Ah!" said Walter. "Do you think

that there were many?" The miller didn't know and Walter replied, "Oh, it is all the same. I only asked so that I should know whether to take Jonas with me. I could manage very well alone with three, but if there were more, some might get away."

"In your place, I would go alone," remarked Jonas. "It is more manly."

"No, perhaps you had better come," said Walter. "There might be many."

"I haven't time," replied Jonas. "And besides, I doubt there's more than three. You can manage them very well alone."

"Certainly I could," said Walter. "But if one should bite me, I might have trouble killing the rest. If I knew for sure there were only two, then I should not mind, for I could grab one in each hand and give them a good shaking."

"I really don't think there will be more than two," answered Jonas. "There never are when they attack rams and children. And you can very well shake two without me."

"But, Jonas, I just remembered I am not quite as strong in the left hand as in the right. One of the two wolves might get away from me. But if you were there with a stout stick . . . Look, if there is only one, I shall take him with both my hands and throw him onto his back."

"Well, now that I think of it," said Jonas, "I am almost sure there will not be more than one."

"Come with me all the same, Jonas. These are new trousers and even one wolf could tear them."

"I am beginning to think you are not quite as brave as you say, Walter. First you would fight against four, then three, then two, and now you want help with one! I think you are frightened."

His pride wounded, Walter gathered his arsenal and marched off to the kiln alone. "It is best that I beat the drum," he thought, but it sounded dreadful, and an echo came out from the kiln that sounded like a wolf's howl. Sure enough, just then a shaggy reddish-brown wolf's head peered out at him from under the kiln. The brave Walter, who alone could manage four wolves, threw his drum away and took to his heels and ran as fast as he could back towards the mill.

Then, alas! The wolf ran after him, and Walter tripped, and the wolf jumped on him. But this was an extraordinarily friendly wolf who rubbed his nose against Walter's face.

Walter shrieked just the same, and luckily Jonas came running to his aid. "What has happened? Why did you scream so terribly?"

"A wolf! A wolf!" Walter cried, and that was all he could say.

"Where? I don't see any wolf." And then Jonas began to laugh till he thought his sides would split. "Down, Caro!" he called. "You ought to be ashamed to have put such a great hero to flight."

Walter got up feeling very foolish. "Well, it was only a dog. If it had been a wolf, I certainly would have killed him. . . ."

"Indeed!" laughed Jonas. "Are you at it again? Dear Walter, remember that it is only cowards who boast. A really brave man never talks of his bravery."

September 14

The Panther and the Shepherds

A panther, by some mischance, fell into a pit. Some shepherds discovered him and threw sticks at him and pelted him with stones. Others felt compassion for the poor beast and threw in some food to prolong his life, even though they knew he would soon die.

At night the shepherds returned home, not dreaming of any danger, but guessing that the next morning they would find the panther dead. The panther, however, had mustered all of his strength and freed himself with a sudden bound from the pit, racing home to his den.

After a few days the panther came forth in a rage and slaughtered the cattle, also killing the shepherds who had attacked him. Those shepherds who had spared his life, fearing for their safety, surrendered their flocks and begged only for their lives. The panther then replied, "I remember alike those who sought my life with stones and those who gave me food. Set aside, therefore, your fears. I return only as an enemy to those who injured me."—PHAEDRUS

September 15

Sandstorm on the Plains

A TALE FROM THE AMERICAN WEST

Poncho was a well-known cow pony whose master rode the range in Wyoming. I'd heard of him for quite a while before I finally met up with him near Casper. It took some persuading, but I got Poncho to tell me about the sandstorm that trapped him on the plains.

"It was late in September when Bill, my rider, and I left Jackson Hole country and started southeast. Bill is one the bravest and best cowboys ever to throw his leg over a bronco's back. There he is over there—tossing his sombrero up for the boys to shoot at," said Poncho, pointing with a foreleg.

"Anyway, Bill decided to take a shortcut home, even though the rancher we'd bunked with told us to stay a few more days. He was sure there was a sandstorm coming. 'I reckon I'll move on,' Bill said, and gave me a slap on the hip. Little did we know we'd just had our last food and drink for days.

"Late that afternoon I looked off to the east and saw a little black cloud coming up. At first it was no larger than your hat, but it grew to the size of a water tank mighty fast. Bill saw it too, but said nothing till I spoke: 'Bill, here comes that sandstorm.' 'Looks like it,' he replied, and a moment later the air was filled with shifting sand. The only thing to do was turn and try to find shelter.

"Harder and fiercer the storm raged till we couldn't see a yard in front of us. Mile after mile I galloped with the storm, sometimes half-lifted in the air, and other times half-buried in sand.

Occasionally Bill would reach over and pat my neck, saying, 'Good boy, old Poncho.' I made up my mind that if good horse sense and four strong legs could carry Bill to safety, we'd get there somehow.

"As night came on, the wind was worse than ever. Bill decided to stop and rest on the windward side of a sand dune. Both of us were hungry as a gray wolf, and would have given a great deal for a drink of water. Poor Bill—I felt sorrier for him than I did for myself, because I knew he had a sweetheart in Cheyenne, and if he never got back it would break her heart.

"Bill got off and loosened the girths of the saddle, then put one arm over my neck and turned his back to the storm. 'Poncho, we'll die game if we have to, won't we?' he said to me. All that night we stood there, digging the sand out of our eyes, waiting for morning to break. How long that night seemed! Near dawn, Bill must have dozed off, for I felt his arm slip from my neck. I knew if he lay down, he'd be buried in the sand pretty quick, so I nipped him good and hard on the shoulder, and he woke right away. 'Thanks, old fellow,' was all he said, but I knew he meant it.

"All the next day the wind swept across the desert, and the air was filled with sand, monstrous tumbleweeds, rushes from the Badlands. Darkness brought no relief, and Bill said, 'Poncho, I have to sleep,' and he crouched down on the sand. I wanted to do the same, but I knew that would mean neither Bill nor I would ever awaken again, so I stood on guard. I'd been so worried about the storm that I'd almost forgotten how hungry and thirsty I was, but now I felt like I would die at any moment. Life is sweet, however, even to a cow pony, and I fought off the stupor that kept coming over me. Every now and then, when the sand climbed up to Bill's face, I would paw it away. This kept my mind occupied.

"By morning the wind had died down some, and we left our sand dune. I would have been glad to carry Bill, but he knew I wasn't up to it. All day we traveled and as it began to get dark, Bill saw a light. It was a sheepherder's hut and we had shelter for the night.

"The next day the sun was shining and the fall birds were scooting through the air calling for their mates who had been blown away in the storm. All around the sheepherder's hut lay sheet after sheet of brown and white sand, but that was all—every sheep he owned had been buried, just as Bill would have been had I failed to do my duty."

As Poncho finished his story, a cowboy was walking toward us. "That's Bill now," said Poncho. I introduced myself and told him that I had asked to hear about the storm he and his horse had survived.

"Poncho's all right," was Bill's only reply. He swung up into the saddle and Poncho took off at an even gallop, headed for home, a hundred miles away.—EUGENE O. MAYFIELD

September 16

The Fairy and the Housewife

It is well known that the Fairy People cannot abide meanness. They like to be kindly dealt with when they beg or borrow from the human race and, by the same token, to those who come to them in need they are always generous.

Now there lived a certain housewife who had a sharp eye for her own interests and only gave away things she had no use for, hoping to get some reward in return. One day a fairy knocked at her door.

"Can you lend us a saucepan, good mother?" said he. "There's a wedding in the hill and all of the pans are in use."

"Should I give him one?" asked the servant who opened the door.

"Aye, to be sure," answered the housewife. "One must be neighborly."

But when the servant was taking a saucepan from the shelf the housewife pinched her arm and whispered sharply, "Not that one, you good for nothing! Get the old one out of the cupboard. It leaks and the fairies are so neat and such nimble workers that they are sure to mend it before they send it home. So I'll get on the good side of the Fairy People and save sixpence in repairs!"

As she was instructed, the servant fetched the leaky saucepan and give it to the fairy, who thanked her and went away.

When the pan was returned, just as the housewife had predicted, it was neatly mended and ready for use.

At supper time the servant filled the pan with milk and set it on the fire for the children's supper. But in a few minutes, the milk was so burnt and smoked that no one could touch it, and even the pigs refused to drink it.

"Ah, good-for-nothing servant!" cried the housewife as she refilled the pan herself. "There's a whole quart of milk wasted at once."

"*And that's two pence!*" cried a voice that seemed to come from the chimney in a whining tone.

The housewife had not left the saucepan for two minutes when again it boiled over, as burnt and smoked as before.

"*And that's fourpence!*" added the voice in the chimney.

After a thorough cleaning the saucepan was once more filled and set on the fire but with no better success. The milk boiled over again and was hopelessly spoiled. The housewife shed tears of anger at the waste and cried: "Never before did such a thing happen to me! Three quarts of new milk burnt for one meal."

"*And that's sixpence!*" cried the voice in the chimney. "*You didn't save on repairs after all, mother.*"

With that the fairy himself came tumbling down the chimney and went out laughing through the door.

But from then on the saucepan was as good as any other.

—ADAPTED FROM JULIANA HORATIA EWING

September 17

The Falconer and the Partridge

A falconer laid a net to trap a partridge. Having succeeded, the bird cried out sorrowfully, "Let me go, good Master Falconer, and I promise you I will decoy other partridges into your net." This meant that the bird would lure his own flock into the very trap that now ensnared him.

"No," said the man. "Whatever I have done, I am determined *now* not to spare you, for there is no death too awful for him who is ready to betray his friends."—AESOP

September 18

The Fox and the Horse

A GERMAN TALE

A farmer once had a faithful horse who had grown old and could not serve him well any longer. Since he had no wish to keep feeding the horse, he said to him, "I really do not want you anymore, for you are of no use to me. But if you can prove your strength by bringing me a lion, I will keep you as long as you live. For now, leave my stable and make your home in the fields."

The horse, feeling very sad, wandered till he came to a woods. A fox met him there and asked, "Friend, why do you hang your head and look so lonely?"

"Ah," replied the horse, "my master has forgotten for how many years I served him and carried him safely from place to place. Now that I am unable to plow any longer, he will not feed me and has sent me away."

"Without a second chance?" asked the fox.

"Oh, he gave me a second chance," said the horse. "He said if I was strong enough to bring him a lion, he would take me back, but he knows very well I couldn't possibly do that!"

Then the fox said, "Don't be downhearted. I can help you. Lie down here and pretend you're dead."

The horse did as he was asked and the fox left to find the lion whose den was not far off. The fox said to the lion, "Over yonder lies a dead horse. Come with me and you can have a good feast."

The lion went with him, but when they reached the spot the fox said, "This isn't a comfortable spot for a meal. I'll tell you what—I'll tie the horse to you by the tail. Then you can drag him to your den and dine at leisure."

The lion was pleased with this suggestion and he stood quite still as the fox began to tie the tail. He didn't know that the fox was twisting it around his legs so that he wouldn't be able to move them. When the fox had finished, he struck the horse on the shoulder and cried, "Gee up!"

The horse sprang up and galloped off with the lion dragging behind him. The lion roared in fury, but the horse ignored the racket and kept on through field and meadow to the door of his master's house. When the farmer saw his horse's accomplishment, he promised him, "Faithful horse, you shall have food and shelter with me as long as you live."—BROTHERS GRIMM

September 19

The Boy and the Broken Cart

There was a man who had many blessings: a good wife, lots of land, a sturdy house, and a fine son. Everyone in the village was envious of him. But the man was worried because he thought perhaps life for his family was *too* good and that his son in particular might get spoiled and soft.

And so the father was always on the lookout for some hardships.

One afternoon, the father noticed that the woodpile was dwindling down so he asked his son to go to the forest to fetch some more wood. The cart for hauling wood was old and falling apart, and the father thought it would be an excellent experience for the boy if the cart broke down in the forest.

The boy did not seem too concerned about the rickety vehicle. He inspected the cart, hooked up two oxen to pull it, and without saying much bid his father good-bye.

The father called to his son as he headed off: "Don't forget, if the cart happens to fall apart, Necessity will tell you what to do." The boy wondered who the person Necessity was; a friend of his father's, no doubt.

Sure enough, when the son reached the middle of the forest the cart fell completely apart.

"Hmm," mused the boy, scratching his head. "I guess I will have to call this fellow Necessity and get the cart fixed."

And so he called. "Necessity . . . say, Necessity! Can you hear me? Where are you? My father said you could tell me what to do if my cart broke down, and believe me, it's broken. . . ."

No one answered.

And so the boy called again: "NECESSITY!"

"Help me!"

"Necessity, tell me what to do!"

But, still, no one answered.

The boy was getting perturbed at his father's friend, who was no help whatsoever. "Forget this Necessity character," he thought to himself. "I'll just fix the cart on my own."

And so he did.

Using string and hammer and nails and spare wood, the boy rebuilt the cart, loaded it up with wood, and then hauled it all back home.

When he arrived home, his father was overjoyed to see the way the boy had handled the situation.

"I am glad to see what a capable young man you are," his father said, patting his shoulder.

"No thanks to your friend Necessity," the boy said. "I called for him over and over, but he didn't even respond. I had to fix the cart all by myself."

The father didn't understand, but figured the boy was tired and a bit confused. Before dinner, the twosome warmed their hands in front of a fire burning with logs won by "Necessity" and the boy's handy work in the forest.

The Donkey and His Master

A donkey and his master were ambling down a mountainous path when suddenly the donkey got it into his head that he wanted to go another direction. He pulled and tugged on the rope held by his master.

"What are you doing, little donkey?" cried the master. "If you take that path you will tumble over the edge and fall to your death."

Despite the kindly advice of his master, the donkey tugged in his own direction. He was so determined to have his own way that he would not listen to reason. As much as the master tried to keep the donkey on the path, he finally could not control him.

The donkey broke loose, tumbled down the mountain head over heels, and was never heard from again.

If you listen to reason, you will stay on the right path.—AESOP

Why the Earth Is Round

A mother is tucking her son into bed. "Will you tell me a story?" the boy asks, as he does each night. His mother, though weary from the day, turns to the window, and stares for a moment at the Adirondack Mountains in the distance and the stars twinkling in the night. "You know, of course, that the world was not always round. . . . Before the birth of our tribe, the world was long and flat, with edges, not curves. Listen, and I will tell you what happened."

It is summer festival night in the large village. The tribe is gathered around a crackling bonfire, and the heat of the day has not yet passed. Still, there is great rejoicing. The hunters and farmers celebrate their kill and their harvest: bear, moose, corn, beans, and squash. One man, Running Buffalo, stands alone before a crowd. Chief Sitting Sun points to Running Buffalo and says, "Here stands a true man. Someday, if you are worthy, you may stand in his place."

The young boys watch in awe. Running Buffalo has just returned from a great test of his manhood and strength. He had to swim the rivers and walk the plains to the edge of the earth. As he stands before the crowd, filthy and exhausted, he is held up by his pride alone.

"He looks as if he might faint," one boy whispers. "Perhaps he is no man at all," another says. "Someday, that will be me," says a third.

Like thousands of young men who proved themselves before, Running

Buffalo went to the end of the earth. For forty days and nights, he had to dig and haul a mound of earth a mile long and a mile wide. "Anyone can journey to the end of the earth," the tribe believed, "but only a true man can bring it back."

The males of the tribe—from the elderly to the toddling child—slowly form a line to see Running Buffalo's achievement. Carrying torches, they parade past the long houses and leave the festival and go to the see the great and noble mound of earth Running Buffalo had hauled from the Great Edge. It is a mile long and a mile wide. Like the true men before him, he has dragged his mound to a sacred place where it will stay besides thousands of others. In doing so, he has helped the world become the sphere it was meant to be.

"Mother, will I have to do that to become a man?" the young boy asked. Hauling that much earth sounded nearly impossible to him. "No, my dear. We believe it was the will of the Creator Spirit that the earth would be round, and that once our people fulfilled their mission, the tribe itself had passed a great test." The boy thought for a moment. "But what happened to the sacred mounds? Where is all of the earth our people brought from the Great Edge?" The boy's mother smiled. "Look out your window. These mountains are the work of your people."

A falling star crossed the sky over the Adirondack Mountains. The young boy, filled with thought, stared at the mountains for the longest time, and then closed his eyes and went to sleep.—GILLEA ALLISON

September 22

The Frog Maiden

A BURMESE FAIRY TALE

A childless couple, who had long hoped for a son or daughter, were delighted to discover that the wife was going to have a baby. But their delight turned to disappointment when the wife gave birth not to a human child, but to a little frog. It turned out, however, that the little frog spoke and behaved like a human, and so the parents and their neighbors came to love her and called her "Little Miss Frog."

Some years later the mother died, and the father took a new wife, a widow with two ugly daughters who were very jealous of Little Miss Frog's popularity.

One day the youngest of the king's four sons announced that he would perform the hair-washing ceremony, at which he would choose a wife. All young ladies were invited to the palace. On the morning of the appointed day, the two ugly sisters put on their best clothes and left for the ceremony. Little Miss Frog ran after them, pleading, "Sisters, please let me come with you."

The sisters laughed and said mockingly, "What, the little frog wants to come? The invitation was for young ladies, not young frogs!" Little Miss Frog walked with them, but they left her at the palace gates. She spoke so sweetly to the guards, however, that they let her sneak in.

The prince washed his hair in the pool and hundreds of young women did the same. But at the end of the ceremony, the prince still did not know whom to choose and so he decided to throw a bouquet of jasmine in the air. He would marry the lady on whom the bouquet fell. Everyone was most annoyed when it landed on Little Miss Frog, and the prince, to be truthful, was also disappointed, but he felt he should keep his word. So Little Miss Frog became Little Princess Frog.

Some time later the king called his four sons to him and said, "I am too old now to rule, so I must appoint a successor. As I love you all alike, I will give you a task to perform and he who is successful will be king in my place. The task is to bring me a golden deer at sunrise on the seventh day from now."

The youngest prince went home and told Little Princess Frog. "What, only a golden deer!" she exclaimed. "Rest easy, my prince, I will get it for you." And on the seventh day, she woke the prince, who rubbed his eyes to be sure of what he was seeing. On a leash, the princess led a pure gold deer.

Of course, this annoyed the older princes, who begged for another chance. The second task the king devised was for them to bring him rice that never grows stale and meat that is always fresh.

Once again, Little Princess Frog had no problem providing her husband with such amazing fare. The king was reluctant to give the elder princes yet another chance, but finally he agreed, saying, "This is positively the last task. On the seventh day from now, bring me the most beautiful woman on earth."

"Ho, ho!" said the three older sons. "Our wives are very beautiful, so one of us is sure to be declared heir. Our brother will be out of luck this time."

The youngest prince overheard them and was sad, for his wife was a frog and was ugly. But she told him, "Don't fret, my sweet prince. On the appointed day, you can take me to the palace and I will surely be declared the most beautiful." The prince looked at her in surprise, but he did not want to hurt her feelings, so he agreed to take her with him.

On the morning of the seventh day, Princess Frog took a great deal of time with her preparations, and the prince hoped against hope that she would somehow emerge from her chambers beautiful. After all, she had obtained the golden deer and the rice and meat. When she came out, however, she was still a frog, but the prince said nothing and they went to the palace. The other sons were there with their wives, and the king looked at the youngest prince with surprise, asking, "Where is your beautiful maiden?"

"I will answer for the prince, my king," said the Frog Princess. "I am his beautiful maiden." She then took off her frog skin and was transformed into a lovely young lady dressed in silk. The king declared her the most beautiful maiden in the world, the youngest prince became his heir, and the Frog Princess, at her husband's request, threw the frog skin in the fire.

September 23

Mr. Miacca

AN ENGLISH TALE

Tommy Grimes was sometimes a good boy and sometimes bad. And when he was bad, he was very bad. His mother would say to him, "Tommy, Tommy, please be good today. Don't leave our street when you go out to play, or Mr. Miacca will get you."

Now when Tommy was a bad boy, he would leave the street, and one day, sure enough, he was barely around the corner when Mr. Miacca caught him. He popped Tommy into a bag and carried him upside down to his house.

When Mr. Miacca got him inside, he pulled him out of the bag and felt his arms and legs. "You're rather tough," said Mr. Miacca. "But you're all I've got for supper, so you'll have to do. I suppose you won't taste bad boiled—especially if I add some herbs to the pot. Now did I forget my herbs? Sally! Come in here!" Mr. Miacca called to his wife.

Mrs. Miacca asked, "What do you want, my dear?"

"Here's a little boy for supper, but I've no herbs. Mind him, will you, while I go for them."

"All right, my love," said Mrs. Miacca.

Then Tommy Grimes asked, "Does your husband always have little boys for supper?"

"Mostly, dear," said Mrs. Miacca. "Especially when they're bad enough and get in his way."

"And you don't have anything else but boy meat? No pudding?" asked Tommy.

"Ah, I love pudding. But I don't get it often," replied Mrs. Miacca.

"Why, my mother is making a pudding this very day," exclaimed Tommy. "And I'm sure she'd give you some if I asked her. Shall I run home and see?"

"Now that's a thoughtful boy," said Mrs. Miacca. "Only don't take long and be back before supper!"

At those words Tommy tore out of the house, and for many days after, he was as good as good can be and never once did he leave his street. But Tommy could be good for only so long, and the day that he decided to go around the corner again, it was his bad luck to run smack into Mr. Miacca.

Mr. Miacca grabbed him and took him in his bag to his house. When he saw who he'd nabbed, he exclaimed, "Why, you're the youngster who tricked my missus and left us with no supper. Well, you won't do it again. I'll watch over you myself. Here—get under the sofa till the pot boils."

So poor Tommy Grimes huddled under the sofa, which Mr. Miacca sat upon. They waited what seemed like hours for the water to be ready. Mr. Miacca grew impatient and said to Tommy, "Here, you under there. I'm not waiting any longer, but I don't want you giving me the slip. Put out your leg."

Tommy put out a leg and Mr. Miacca chopped it off and popped it in the pot. Then he called for his wife.

When she didn't answer, he went into the next room to look for her. And while he was there, Tommy ran out the front door. For it was a leg of the sofa he had given Mr. Miacca.

Tommy Grimes sped home, and he never went around the corner again until he was old enough to be out and about all by himself.

September 24

The Fox Without a Tail

A fox was caught in a trap. Unfortunately, the only way he could get out was to sacrifice his tail for his neck, and so the creature escaped but did leave behind his major ornament, namely his red bushy tail. The fox looked strange without his tail and began to feel so disgraced by his appearance that he nearly wished he had died rather than come away without it.

He thought and thought about what to do.

An idea occurred to him, and so he called a meeting of all the other foxes. "I have a proposition to make," he said to the gathered clan. "You have no idea of the ease and comfort with which I now move about, having rid myself of that cumbersome tail. I would never have really believed it had I not tried it myself, but really, when you think of it, a tail is such an ugly, inconvenient, and unnecessary appendage that the only wonder is that, as foxes, we have put up with it for so long.

"I propose, therefore, my worthy brethren, that you all profit from the experience that I am most willing to offer you, and that all foxes from this day forward cut off their tails."

Upon this, one of the oldest stepped forward and said, "I do not find your conclusions to be honest,'" the gray fox said. "I think rather that you would not have advised us to part with our tails if there were any chance of recovering your own. Stop looking back and get on with your life."—AESOP

September 25

The Farmer's Daughter

One sunny morning a farmer's daughter was carrying her pail back to the barn when she began daydreaming.

"Let me see, let me see. . . ." she began to calculate. "The money we get from this milk should buy twenty-five dozen eggs, and the eggs should produce about two hundred and fifty chickens. If all goes well, the chickens will fetch a good price at market a few months hence."

She grew so excited she could hardly think straight. "Perhaps by the end of the year," she thought, "I shall have enough money to buy a beautiful new dress. Then I shall go to a dance and many handsome young men will want to marry me."

The farmer's daughter was just imagining how she would turn on her heel and walk away from the suitors who did not interest her when she lost her footing and let her milk pail fly down the path. She watched her dreams vanish as the milk flowed down the hillside.

Don't count your chickens before they hatch (or your milk before it's sold).—AESOP

September 26

The Twelve Lazy Servants

A GERMAN TALE

Twelve farm servants, who had been dawdling since dawn, were still at it when evening came. They lay sprawled in the grass, passing more time in idleness and boasting of their skill.

Presently the first spoke and said, "What is the use to me of leisure time? In fact, why get up at all? I don't like early rising. Noon would suit me best. And when I'm up, I find a resting place and lie down, and when the master calls me I pretend not to hear. If at last I am obliged to rouse myself, I go as slowly as I can. And so I pass my life away."

"I manage quite as well as you do," said the second. "I have a horse to take care of, but I can leave him with food in the manger and go sleep in the hayloft for hours. Sometimes I forget to give him his corn, but I always say he has had it. Why should I trouble myself?"

"Why must we bother ourselves with work?" asked the third. "No good comes from it. I know I take mine easy enough. I often lie in the sun and sleep. If it rains, don't think that I get up. I let the drops fall on me, for sooner or later they will dry."

"I think my plan is best," said the fourth. "Before I begin my work, I always lie in bed for an hour to spare my strength. Even after this, I move very slowly and ask everyone who comes near me to help me. In this way, I get through most of my work, which isn't very much after all."

"Oh, that is nothing compared to my laziness," cried the fifth. "My job is to remove the manure from the stables and load it in a wagon. I take it very easy, I assure you, for when I toss the manure on a pitchfork, I raise it only halfway in the air, and then rest for a quarter of an hour before pitching it in. It takes me a day at least to load the wagon, for I don't wish to kill myself with work."

"You ought to be ashamed of yourself," said the sixth. "I am not afraid of work, but I am quite expert at idling away the rest of my time. I sometimes do not take my clothes off for weeks. And suppose I have no laces to my shoes, what does it matter? I can drag one foot after the other slowly."

"Well, I have a different situation," said the seventh. "I have a master who examines my work, but luckily he is away from home all day. I can neglect nothing, but I finish my task quickly and sloppily so that I am free to sleep the rest of the day."

"Ah," exclaimed the eighth. "I can see that I am the only lively chap amongst you. If a stone lies in my path, I never bother to lift my leg and step over it. Why should I? It is easier to simply lie down. And if that gets me wet or muddy, the sun will dry me off soon enough."

"I can beat you all," said the ninth. "This very day my bread and cheese lay before me, and although I was starving, I was too lazy to reach out my hand and take them. A jug of water was nearby, but it was too heavy to bother to lift even though I was desperately thirsty."

"Well," said the tenth, "my laziness has gotten me a broken leg. Three of us were lying on the roadway with our legs stretched out. I heard a wagon coming along the road and I could easily have pulled my legs back but I was too lazy. So the wagon ran over me."

The eleventh idler now spoke. "Yesterday I gave my master my notice. I am tired of waiting upon him, brushing his clothes, and carrying his heavy books back and forth. Though in truth I'm surprised he didn't fire me first, for I let all his clothes become moth-eaten from neglect."

"I should not be here at all," said the twelfth. "Today I was sent with a wagon to the fields. I made a bed of the straw in the back and slept soundly. But when I awoke, I found that someone had taken the horse and harness, and the wagon had slipped into a ditch and gotten stuck. What was I to do but go back to sleep? When my master came along, he dragged the wagon from the ditch, tossed me out of the straw, and sent me on my business. Were it not for him, I would be sleeping still, not tiring myself out talking to you fellows."

As you can see, these twelve farmhands were no idle boasters.

—BROTHERS GRIMM

September 27

The Three Languages

AN ITALIAN TALE

A father had sent his son away to school for ten years. At the end of that time, the son came home for there was nothing more the school could teach him. The father decided to give a grand banquet in honor of his son's return. He invited all the noble gentlemen of the country, who made flattering speeches about the boy and toasted him.

Then one of the guests said, "Tell us some of the things you have learned abroad."

"I have learned the language of dogs, frogs, and birds," replied the young man.

At first the guests were silent, then they burst out laughing. They all left the banquet ridiculing the boy's foolishness and the father's misplaced pride. The father was so angry at this humiliation that he ordered his servants to take his son into the woods and kill him. The servants loved the boy and could not obey, so they only pretended to carry out his wishes.

The young man fled the country and one day stopped at the castle of a king's treasurer. Shortly after his arrival, a great pack of dogs gathered outside the castle gates. The treasurer asked the young man if he could explain their presence, and since the young man knew the language of dogs, he was able to tell the treasurer that the dogs knew that a troop of bandits was on the way. The treasurer posted soldiers in the woods around the castle to ambush the bandits, and was so grateful to the young man that he offered him his daughter in marriage. The young man thanked him, but said he had a journey to complete and could not stay.

After he left the castle, he traveled to the city where the king lived. The king's daughter was very ill because the croaking of frogs at the palace never allowed her to sleep. The young man, of course, could understand what the frogs meant with their incessant croaking. The princess had apparently thrown a cross in their pond, and as soon as it was removed, the croaking stopped. When the princess recovered, the king urged the young man to take her as his bride. Again, the youth said he must press on.

After leaving the king, he set out for Rome and on the way met three other young men who became his traveling companions. One hot day, as the travelers rested in the shade of a great oak, a large flock of birds flew over them, singing excitedly. "Why are these birds so joyful?" asked one of the traveling companions.

"They are rejoicing with the new pope, who is to be one of us," said the young man.

Suddenly a dove came to rest on his head, and though no one knew what to make of this at the time, it came to pass that the young man was elected pope.

The new pope sent for his father, and for the treasurer and king who had befriended him in his exile. He had them tell his father how grateful they had been for his knowledge of the language of birds and animals. The father began trembling in fear as he remembered how cruelly he had treated his son. But the son was quick to forgive his remorseful father. He lived with his son for the rest of his days and learned that not all wisdom can be taught in school.

September 28

The Street Musicians

A man once owned a donkey who had served him faithfully for many years. But at last the poor beast grew old and feeble, and could no longer do the jobs his master needed. With great alarm, the donkey learned that the man planned to shoot him, and so the donkey decided to run away to the nearest big town and become a musician.

He traveled for some distance before he came across a greyhound lying by the side of the road and panting heavily. "What is the matter with you, brother?" asked the donkey.

"I am old," said the greyhound, "and getting weaker every day. And because I cannot go hunting any longer, my master wanted to poison me. So I have left him, but how I'll survive, I don't know!"

"Well," replied the donkey, "I am going to become a street musician. The flute is my instrument. Why don't you come along with me? You could play the kettle drum perhaps."

The greyhound was pleased at this idea and the two set off for town together. Quite soon they met a cat with a face as long as three rainy days. "What has happened to you, friend?" asked the donkey.

"I am so depressed," answered the cat. "Because I am getting on in years and cannot catch mice anymore, my mistress was going to drown me. I ran away, but now what am I to do?"

"Come to town with us!" cried the donkey. "And try your fortune as a street musician!"

The cat was delighted to join them and the three friends journeyed down the road until they came to an inn. There they found a rooster crowing with all its might in the courtyard. "Why are you making such a racket?" asked the donkey. "It is not morning."

The rooster paused for a moment. "Tomorrow is a holiday and the inn is expecting many visitors. So the landlady has ordered that my neck be wrung tonight to make soup for tomorrow's dinner!"

"You'd better come with us," said the donkey. "You have a fine voice and can join our band."

They traveled all the next day, but still had not reached town by nightfall. The four were tired and hungry and had little hope of shelter for the night, till the rooster spotted the lights of a house in the distance. When they got there, the donkey, as the biggest of the friends, went to the window to check things out. "Well, greyhead, what do you see?" asked the rooster.

"I see a table with much food and drink," said the donkey. "But the men sitting there enjoying their meal look like a band of robbers to me."

"I wish we had food and drink," said the rooster. At that the four friends began discussing schemes to get the robbers to leave the house. They decided that the donkey should stand at the window, with his front feet on the sill, so that the greyhound should get on his back, with the cat on the greyhound's shoulders, and the rooster on the cat's head. Once there, they began to sing. The donkey brayed, the greyhound barked, the cat screeched, and the rooster crowed.

The robbers were quite startled by this horrible racket and as the glass of the windows began to break, they grew terrified. Thinking that evil spirits were invading the house, the robbers rushed out the door, never to return.

The four street musicians were very pleased with their new lodgings and with the success of their band. And as the house had everything they needed, they never did have to go out in the streets and earn their living making music.

September 29

Toads and Diamonds

Once upon a time a woodcutter found a baby girl in the forest, and so he took her home to live with his wife and his own daughter, who was just a little older. The young girl grew to be good and sweet of temper, and one of the most beautiful creatures ever seen. The mother and older girl, on the other hand, were selfish and lazy, and expected to be waited upon all the time.

Among her other duties, the young girl had to walk a mile and a half twice a day to draw water. One morning as she stood by the fountain, a poor woman came to her and begged for a drink.

"Gladly," said the pretty child, who held the pitcher for the poor woman and then got her more.

"You are so good and kind," said the woman, "that I am giving you a gift." For this was a fairy who had taken the form of a poor countrywoman in order to learn just how kind the young girl really was. "At every word you speak," continued the fairy, "there shall come out of your mouth either a flower or a jewel."

When the girl returned home, the mother began to scold her for staying so long at the fountain. "I beg your pardon, Mama," she answered. "But I could not make more haste." As she spoke these words, two roses, two pearls, and two large diamonds fell from her mouth.

"What is this I see!" cried the woman in great astonishment. "How did this happen?"

The girl told her the whole story frankly, not without dropping great numbers of diamonds.

"Truly, I must send my own dear child there. Daughter, look at what comes out of your sister's mouth when she speaks. Would you not be glad to have the same gift? Go at once to the fountain, and if a poor old woman asks for a drink, give it to her politely!"

"I would like to see myself going to draw water," said this proud, ill-natured creature, for she thought herself too fine to do work of that sort.

"I insist," said the mother, and sent the grumbling girl off.

No sooner had she reached the fountain than a magnificently dressed lady came out of the woods and asked for a drink. This was the same fairy who had appeared to her sister, but she had purposely taken another form so the older girl would not know her.

The girl never dreamed it was the same poor woman and answered her rudely. "Oho! I suppose you think I came here just to serve you with water! I suppose I carried this tankard all through the forest purely to please your ladyship! If you want a drink, get it yourself!"

"You are scarcely polite," answered the fairy calmly. "Well, then, since you answer me in such a way, I will give you an appropriate gift. At every word you speak, a toad or a snake shall come out of your mouth." And with that she disappeared.

When the girl returned home, the mother was horrified when, at the first word she spoke, a toad fell out of her mouth. The mother never thought of questioning the girl to see if she was at fault for what had happened to her, but immediately blamed the foster daughter. "You will pay for this!" the mother screamed. "Out of this house you go. At once and forever."

Then she drove the young girl out of the house and into the forest. The girl was sitting and weeping to herself when a king's son passed by. Seeing her so sad and beautiful, he asked her trouble.

"Alas, sir, my mother has turned me out."

The king's son, who saw five or six pearls and as many diamonds drop from her mouth as she spoke, was astounded and asked her to tell her whole story. As she did, he realized she was as beautiful in heart as in face and fell in love on the spot. He took her to the palace and married her.

As for the sister, snakes and toads kept falling from her mouth till she became so hateful to all that her own mother turned her out of doors. She wandered off into the forest and was never heard of again.

—ADAPTED FROM PERRAULT

September 30

The Great Turnip

Turnips are roots that grow in the ground, a vegetable favored by peasants and great chefs, but not beloved by children. Indeed, it is safe to say most children hate turnips. This is a shame because turnips actually are very tasty, but this is not a story about the virtues of turnips, but the harvesting of turnips—actually, the harvesting of just one of them.

Like all turnips, this particular turnip grew under the ground and somehow, even without peeking, the old Russian farmer who grew it knew it was special. He just knew! He harvested most of his turnip crop at the usual time but left this turnip in the ground much longer so it would grow bigger. Usually turnips are about as big as a fist, but this one grew to be big as a giant's fist, and (as you know) giants have really huge fists. When the old man decided the time had come to bring his great turnip to the surface, he took hold of the leaves and pulled. He pulled and he pulled and he pulled, but the turnip would not budge. And so he called his wife.

"Come, wife," said the old man, "come help me free this turnip from the earth." The old woman had arms like sausages. She helped the old man and together they pulled and pulled and pulled. But the turnip would not budge.

So the old woman called her granddaughter to come and help. Her granddaughter was very strong and had very thick ankles. This time the granddaughter pulled the old woman, and the woman pulled the old man, and the man pulled the turnip. But the turnip would not budge.

So the granddaughter called her dog. The dog was built like a barrel. Surely they could free the turnip from the earth! The dog pulled the granddaughter, and the granddaughter pulled the old woman, and the old woman pulled the old man, and the old man pulled the turnip. *But the turnip would not budge.*

So the dog called the cat. The cat was skinny but mean. The cat pulled the dog, and the dog pulled the granddaughter, and the granddaughter pulled the old woman, and the old woman pulled the old man, and the old man pulled the turnip. But the turnip stayed put; why, it didn't move an inch!

So the cat called the mouse. Calling the mouse was a pretty dumb idea, but no one else was around. The mouse pulled the cat, and the cat pulled the dog, and the dog pulled the granddaughter, and the granddaughter pulled the old woman, and the old woman pulled the old man, and the old man pulled the turnip and together they pulled, and pulled, and pulled as hard as they possibly could.

Just when they thought it would never come out, the turnip popped up and out of the ground, and everybody tumbled right down.

And then they ate it.

Well, all except the granddaughter. She didn't like turnips.

OCTOBER

October 1

The Story of Persephone

AN ANCIENT GREEK MYTH

Demeter, Goddess of the Harvest, loved all that she reaped, but her true love was reserved for her daughter Persephone. The mother and daughter were always together. Persephone would watch in awe as her mother Demeter would talk to the trees and the flowers and the fruits, marveling that with just a word or a touch, each plant would flourish. On hot days they would walk through fields of corn, and the husks would swell and the corn would ripen; when Demeter visited orchards the apples and pears would turn vivid crimson and gold and sweet. Her very gaze would paint the land with blooms and colors so fantastic that to this day the colors have yet to be named.

One morning Persephone asked if she could play with her friends while her mother went to tend some fields where the harvest was late. Thinking it perhaps was time her daughter gained some independence, Demeter agreed, warning Persephone not to stray too far. Persephone and her friends began to gather flowers to make garlands, and Persephone became so engrossed in her work that she lingered in the valley while her friends went on to gather more blossoms. She was happily working when suddenly the side of the mountain split and six ferocious black horses drawing a black chariot drove out the great divide. As she screamed for mother, the driver seized the girl and drove back into the mountain, leaving no trace.

Persephone's friends soon realized she was missing and when they could not find her, they called for Demeter. Persephone's voice had been carried by the wind, so the goddess had already heard her daughter's cries faintly and had began her search. For hours and then days and then weeks and then months, Demeter searched. While she searched she did not work, and crops failed, there were no blossoms or fruits, and farmers wrung their hands at the mystery.

As all were soon to learn, Persephone had been kidnapped. The god of the underworld, Hades, had plucked her from the earth, harvesting the earth's lovely goddess for himself. The underworld was a place of utter darkness, and though it was filled with beautiful distractions, Persephone was lost and discouraged. She would cry for her mother. She would not accept Hades' gifts and she would not eat. Hades wanted to marry Persephone and tried to please her, but she refused his affections, saying she only wanted her life in the light, with her mother.

When Demeter's search for Persephone failed she appealed to Zeus, the king of all the gods. Zeus was concerned for Persephone and he also saw that the people of earth were suffering, for Demeter had not touched so much as a crocus since her daughter had been stolen. Nothing was growing! Zeus, who was all-knowing, knew that Persephone was in the underworld, and he sent messengers there demanding her return. The messengers of Zeus appealed, but got no response.

Hades—who wanted nothing other than Persephone as his wife—was devastated, for the girl was weak and ill with hunger, and he knew that if she did not eat she would die. At last he found her favorite fruit, a pomegranate, and begged her to eat. Though Persephone did not love Hades, she was moved by his desire to please her. In a moment of weakness, she agreed to eat just six seeds of the pomegranate. Yet she did so at great expense, because once she accepted a gift from Hades, she belonged forever to the underworld.

When Demeter learned that her daughter had accepted the six pomegranate seeds, she was so despairing she had no heart to travel the earth as goddess of the harvest. Without Demeter, the crops failed utterly and people were beginning to die. The whole world was falling apart! Zeus sent his messengers to appeal to Hades once more. And Hades, who knew Persephone was bereft, decided that since the girl had eaten six seeds of the pomegranate, she should spend six months of the year with him in the underworld, but she could return for the other six months to the light, to be with her mother, Demeter.

Ever since, it has been so. When the leaves fall and the blooms wither in fall and winter, you know that Persephone has gone to the Underworld, and that her mother, Demeter, is grieving. And in spring and summer, when the earth is ripe with flower and fruit, it is Demeter in her happiness, reunited with her beloved daughter. This is why we have the different seasons and how powerful love can be between a mother and her daughter.

October 2

Pedigree

A KOREAN TALE

Under a large canopy of leaves, a fox, a hare, and a toad began to argue among themselves about who had the most respectable lineage. The fox lifted his pointy nose in the air. "What I have to say will humble you, dear friends. As it happens, my ancestors lived during the time of the Ha Dynasty—two thousand years before Christ! Refer to the classics! The fox is king! Which of you can boast of such a distinguished past?"

The hare, who had been resting on his haunches, shook his head patiently. "You are deluded, good friend. You dream of a distinguished past but it is just that—a dream! Long before the Ha Dynasty even existed, there was a moon. One looking at the moon on any clear night could see a cinnamon tree, beneath which was always a hare pounding medicines in a mortar. Please then acknowledge that my family, who has existed since the moon itself, has a pedigree far more distinguished than yours."

The toad could not contain himself. He was laughing so hard, he was snorting, and he was having a difficult time sobering up sufficiently to tell his story. "Okay, okay, I'm fine, really," the toad said, trying to be fine. "Ahem, dear friends," the toad said. "Long before the moon existed and of course *well* before the Ha Dynasty, the heavens and the earth were being created out of chaos. Miraculously, there lived three toads at this time and they were brothers. The first toad was crushed beneath the pillars of Heaven. The second one died when Pandora melted the five stones. The third one was killed when the first emperor of Chiu built his great palace. When I hear you making your ridiculous claims to respectability, I can only laugh."

While the toad was telling his friends of his noble ancestors, a tiger quietly joined the party. After the toad finished, the tiger stretched out his paw and brushed the toad to one side with a sniff of contempt. "We are not discussing feats of strength, noble sir," said the toad, "but respectability."

"Since you have no respect for strength," said the tiger, "maybe you can tell me what would happen to you if I placed a single one of my paws on you and kept it there for a few months." The tiger arched one of his eyebrows.

The toad answered without hesitation. "I could easily live by swallowing my own saliva, for toads rarely eat anything else. But may I ask, strong sir, what would happen to you while you were holding me under your paw for those few months? Isn't it true that, unlike toads, tigers require a bit more nourishment than saliva? Would you not starve to death?"

The tiger did not know what to say and so he walked away.

—ADAPTED FROM E. B. LANDIS

October 3

The Boy and the Filberts

The boy loved filberts, so when his mother told him to "help himself" his eyes got wide.

"Filberts, filberts, filberts," he hummed to himself, sticking his hand in the jar of nuts.

He grabbed a giant fistful, and . . . he couldn't get his hand out of the jar.

He pulled. He yanked. He tugged. but he just could not get his hand out of the filberts jar.

Unwilling to loosen his fist and give up a single filbert, the boy's hand was stuck. And all he could think about was how much he wanted a filbert.

He began to cry.

"My son," said his mother, advising him of the obvious, "if you would accept just half the nuts you could easily get your hand out of the jar." Half the amount was not what he wanted so he stood for a long time, his fist filled with filberts, without so much as a bite.

The greedy gesture sometimes yields nothing at all.—AESOP

October 4

The Hare and the Elephant

A HINDU TALE

Deep in the jungle there lived a rabbit. She was a shy little thing and she always feared that something terrible was going to happen. One morning she heard a great noise that made her jump sky high. She thought the world was coming to an end. Panic! She started to run to get out of the way.

Soon she passed a deer who was also a fearful sort. He ran to catch up with her.

"Where are you going in such a hurry?" the deer asked, running apace with her.

"The world is coming to an end and I'm running to get out of the way," answered the rabbit.

"Then I will run with you," said the deer. And away they went over hill and dale.

Soon the twosome passed a fox, who was sniffing about for something to eat.

"Where on earth are you two going? You act as though the world is coming to an end!" said the fox.

"Well, indeed it is," replied the rabbit, not breaking her stride. "If you want to save yourself, you'd better get out of the way."

The fox joined the rabbit and the deer, and soon they passed a jackal.

"For goodness sake, what's the rush?" the jackal asked.

"The world is coming to an end," the three replied in unison. "Come join us if you want to be saved."

The jackal did not hesitate, but joined the rabbit, the deer, and the fox straightaway, and together the four raced through the jungle at breakneck speed.

On the way they passed a tiger.

"Where are you going?" he asked, running alongside the four.

"The world is coming to an end, and if you want to save yourself, you'd better join us," the four replied.

Before long, the five came upon an elephant.

"Where are you going?" asked the elephant.

"The world is coming to an end, and if you want to save yourself, you'd better join us," replied the five.

Now elephants are slow but wise, and before this elephant was going to break into a sweat, he wanted to make sure it was well worth the effort.

"How do you know the world is coming to an end?" he asked the five.

"The jackal told me," said the tiger.

"The fox told me," said the jackal.

"The deer told me," said the fox.

"The rabbit told me," said the deer.

With that, everyone turned to the hare.

"How did you make this discovery?" the elephant asked the rabbit.

"Well, I heard a terrible noise," answered the hare rather shyly, for she was now unsure about the whole thing and wondering what she had started. "When I heard the noise, I thought it was a sign that the world was coming to an end."

"Was this the noise you heard?" asked the elephant, who then lifted his great trunk and made a huge sound that filled the entire jungle.

"Why, yes, that is the noise," answered the rabbit, now confused.

"What foolishness!" said the elephant. "I was just saying 'good morning' to the jungle."

The tiger turned to the jackal and the jackal turned to the fox and the fox turned to the deer and the deer turned to the rabbit, and the rabbit covered her face with her paws in shame. All five hung their heads and slipped away, while the elephant laughed and laughed.

October 5

The Sad Tale of Caribou and Moose

A NATIVE AMERICAN TALE

Caribou and Moose had been friends for so long that people mistook them for brothers. When it was time for the two boys to leave home and see the big woods and the mountains far away, they pledged to be steadfast and loyal.

After traveling just a day or two, the boys walked into a clearing where stood a girl so lovely and delicate that they were struck dumb. Never had they seen a creature so beautiful, nor had they ever seen a creature so ugly, for standing next to the girl was her mother. Jealousy and pettiness had turned the girl's mother into an awful old nag, and she was as grotesque as her daughter was enchanting. Caribou knew trouble was at hand, but Moose knew only that he was in love. In fact, Moose was so awestruck that even before saying hello, he asked the old woman for her daughter's hand in marriage. "Of course, my dear," the nag said, with a laugh. Caribou wondered why she was laughing, but said nothing.

That night, just before he went to bed, the girl gave Moose a warning. "Be careful," she said. "My mother may try to kill you tonight." Moose was so much in love that he did not find this odd. As the moon rose in the sky, the nag wandered into Moose's tent. "Here are some skins to keep you warm," she said. What appeared to be hospitality was quite the opposite. The old woman piled skin upon skin on Moose to suffocate him! Moose cut a hole in the skins for his nose so he could breathe and thought little of it.

The next morning, Moose was cheerful and rested, and the nag was not pleased. "I see you slept well," she said. "Now I would like you to saw off the great hanging branch from the hemlock tree." The nag was certain the gigantic branch would crush him, but Moose took a long pole, loosed the branch, and then jumped away quickly as it came down with a thunderous crash.

Caribou could not believe what was happening. "Can't you see this nag is trying to kill you?" he asked Moose. "If the woman is this devious, her daughter may be, too," he said. Moose was enraged. "A true friend would not say such things," he said. "Go your way and do not speak to me ever again." In this unfortunate manner, the two friends who were like brothers became strangers.

But before Moose could mull over the loss of Caribou, the old nag appeared. She had yet another plan to kill the foolish suitor. "Moose," she said, "please come with me to the enchanted island. I think it would be an ideal place for your wedding." Moose loved the idea and followed the old nag to her canoe. They paddled for hours in the blazing sun. Suddenly there appeared a treeless, rocky island. "Enchanted?" Moose thought to himself. It was not what he expected. The nag encouraged Moose to get out and to look around. While he was exploring, she paddled away, leaving him on the island to die. Slowly, Moose realized what had happened. The nag had tricked him and now he was doomed. He wailed at his foolishness, and his wailing was so pitiful that it attracted the attention of two sea gulls who happened to be passing by. The sea gulls asked the boy how they might help.

Moose told them the whole story, and they swooped down and carried him the great distance to the beautiful girl he loved. When Moose told the girl what had happened, her eyes got a strange look, and she started laughing and could not stop. "That settles it," she said, once she collected herself. "You must kill my mother so we can marry and our troubles will be over." Moose wondered at her laughing, but he was eager to get the nag out of his life, too, and so he searched until he found the old woman, who was docking the canoe. He picked the nag up and threw her down so hard that she broke into hundreds of pieces.

At last Moose and the girl were free to marry and they did so in great haste. But from one full moon to the next, the girl seemed to change into another person. Before long, she was cursing Moose and trying to trick him with devious schemes. The boy's heart was now weary and hard. The world was not as he thought it would be, and one day he just walked away and never returned.

Today, if you see Moose, he is usually alone in the forest. Caribou, on the hand, seldom travels alone. He is usually seen with five or six others, passing by Moose without saying a word.

October 6

The Thoughtless Abbot

AN ITALIAN TALE

In a city once there was a priest who became an abbot, which made him wealthy, and he soon had carriages, horses, and many servants. This abbot thought only of eating, drinking, and sleeping. All of his priests and his congregation frowned on him and called him "the thoughtless abbot."

One day the king happened to pass through the city and the abbot's enemies went to him to complain. "Your majesty, there is someone in this town wealthier and happier than you, and he is known as 'the thoughtless abbot.' "

The king mulled this over and replied, "I shall soon make this abbot think!" He sent for the abbot, and when he arrived, he was asked why all knew him as "the thoughtless abbot." The abbot replied it was because he was free from care, as his servants attended to everything.

The king said, "Well, then, Sir Abbot, since you have no cares in the world, you may do me the favor of counting all the stars in the sky—in the next three nights. If you cannot do this task, I shall behead you."

The abbot began to tremble like a leaf and went home fearing for his neck. At dinnertime he could not eat on account of his worry, but went outside instead, and began to count and write down the number of stars he saw. But by daybreak he had not finished, and, in fact, was not even close. His servants, seeing that the abbot did not eat or drink, believed he had gone crazy.

The three days passed without the abbot getting any closer to his goal, and he grew increasingly distraught. An old and trusted servant asked him his trouble, and when the abbot told him and said, "The king will surely cut off my head this morning," the servant tried to calm his fears.

"Leave it to me," said the servant, who went and got an ox hide, and told the abbot, "When the king asks Your Excellency how many stars there are in heaven, you will call me and I will stretch out the hide on the ground, and you will say, 'The stars in heaven are as many as the hairs on this hide."

The abbot ordered his carriage, and he and his servant went to the palace. All went as planned. The abbot pointed to the hide and exclaimed, "Your Majesty, the stars are as many as the hairs on this hide—which are in the hundreds of millions—and if you don't believe me, have them counted for I have brought proof!"

The king's mouth dropped open, and for a moment he had nothing to say in reply. Finally, he announced, "Go, and live as long as Noah, without thoughts, for your brains are enough for any man to live with."

The king dismissed the abbot and his servant, who was shortly made the abbot's steward—and great friend—and was rewarded with an ounce of gold for all the days of his life.

October 7

Androcles and the Lion

A slave named Androcles was so tormented by his master that he escaped from him and hid in the forest. He had not been there long when he came upon a lion who was moaning loudly. He was about to run away when he saw that the lion was groaning because he was in terrible pain. There was a thorn stuck in his paw, which was bleeding and swollen.

Androcles could see from the expression in the lion's eyes that the poor creature desperately wanted some help. He took the lion's paw in his own hands and very gently drew out the thorn. The lion licked Androcles' hand gratefully and hobbled off into the woods.

A few days later, both Androcles and the lion were captured by Roman soldiers. As punishment for running away, Androcles was sentenced to be thrown to the lion, who was kept without food for three days.

The emperor, the court, and all of Rome were invited to see the hungry lion tear apart the runaway slave limb by limb. Released from the cage where he'd been held captive, the lion bounded into the ring, wild with anger and hunger. But when he saw Androcles, he trotted over to him and licked his hands and face like a puppy dog. The emperor summoned Androcles to him, who told him the story of the lion and the sore paw. The emperor was so impressed that Androcles was freed and the lion was taken back to live in peace in the forest.—AESOP

October 8

The Troublesome Visitors

A GERMAN TALE

One day a cock and a hen decided to go for a little trip in the country to visit their old master, Dr. Korbes. They built a pretty carriage and harnessed to it four mice, then drove away.

They had not traveled far when they met a cat who asked, "Where are you going?"

The hen replied, "We are going to see Dr. Korbes, our old master."

"Take me with you," said the cat.

"Gladly," answered the hen. "But you must get up behind, so you don't fall." As they continued on their journey, they met a millstone, an egg, a duck, then a darning needle, and at last a pin, all of whom were given seats in the carriage.

When they arrived at Dr. Korbes's house, he was not at home, but they made themselves quite comfortable. The mice drew the little carriage into the barn, the cock and hen flew to a perch, the cat seated herself in the fireplace, the duck waddled to the spring, while the egg rolled itself up in a towel. The darning needle rested itself point upwards in a seat cushion, and the pin, jumping on a bed, fixed itself in the pillow, and lastly the millstone placed itself over the entrance door.

Dr. Korbes came home shortly after this, and as his servant was out, he went to the kitchen to light the fire. While he was doing this, the cat threw a great deal of ashes in his face. Dr. Korbes ran to the spring to wash them off, but the duck, who was swimming about, splashed so much water on him that he needed his towel from the house. As he picked up the towel, the egg rolled out and broke on his face, filling his eyes and making them stick together like glue.

After all this, Dr. Korbes wished to rest, but as he seated himself in his armchair the darning needle stuck him. Up he jumped in a rage and threw himself on his bed, but this was just as bad. No sooner did he lay his head on the pillow than the pin scratched his face.

At this last attack, the doctor cried out that the house must be bewitched and he ran for the front door. When he opened it, the millstone fell down on his head and killed him.

Dr. Korbes must have been either very wicked or very, very unlucky.

—BROTHERS GRIMM

October 9

Teeny-Tiny

Once upon a time there was a teeny-tiny woman who lived in a teeny-tiny house in a teeny-tiny village. Now one day this teeny-tiny woman put on her teeny-tiny bonnet to take a teeny-tiny walk. When she had gone a teeny-tiny way, she came to a teeny-tiny churchyard, and she saw a teeny-tiny bone on a teeny-tiny grave and thought, "This teeny-tiny bone will make me some teeny-tiny soup for my teeny-tiny supper." So she put it in her teeny-tiny pocket and went home.

Now when the teeny-tiny woman got to her teeny-tiny house, she was a teeny-tiny bit tired, so she went up to her teeny-tiny bed and put the bone into a teeny-tiny cupboard. And when she had been asleep for a teeny-tiny while, she was awakened by a teeny-tiny voice from the teeny-tiny cupboard that said, "Give me my bone!"

The teeny-tiny woman was a teeny-tiny bit frightened, but she hid her teeny-tiny head under her covers and fell back asleep. Soon she again heard, a teeny-tiny louder, "GIVE ME MY BONE!" This time the teeny-tiny woman was a teeny-tiny bit more frightened, so she hid her teeny-tiny head a teeny-tiny bit more under the covers and slept once more.

She had only been asleep a teeny-tiny time when the teeny-tiny voice said a teeny-tiny louder, "GIVE ME MY BONE!"

And this teeny-tiny woman was a teeny-tiny bit more frightened, but she put her teeny-tiny head out from her covers and said in her loudest teeny-tiny voice, "TAKE IT!"

October 10

Mother Holle

A GERMAN TALE

A widow had two daughters: one was pretty and industrious, the other was plain and lazy. The pretty one was a stepdaughter and she was made to be the drudge of the house. Every day the poor girl had to sit by the well and spin tell her fingers bled. One day she dropped the spindle in the well as she was trying to clean it off. Knowing that her stepmother would beat her for the missing spindle, she had no choice but to jump into the well after it.

For a little while, she knew nothing, but when she awoke she found herself in a beautiful meadow. The sun was shining on the flowers that grew around her. In time she came to a little house, where an old woman was peeping out the window. The old woman had such great teeth that the girl was terrified and about to run away when the woman called her back. "Don't be afraid, dear child. Come and live with me, and if you do the housework properly, all shall go well with you. You must take great care to make my bed properly and shake it up thoroughly so that the feathers fly about. When you do that, it will snow in the world, for I am Mother Holle."

The old woman sounded so kind that the girl took courage and went into the house. She did all the work to the woman's satisfaction for quite some time and had a very pleasant life. But after a while she began to feel sad and thought she must be homesick, even though she was better off with Mother Holle than back at home. At last she said, "I cannot stay any longer. I must go home."

Mother Holle answered, "It pleases

me that you wish to return home, and as you have served me faithfully, I shall help you." Mother Holle told the girl to stick her head out the door, and when she did a shower of gold fell on the girl so that she was totally covered. "All this is yours," said Mother Holle.

The door shut on the girl and she found herself back in the world not far from her stepmother's house. She was warmly welcomed there on account of the gold she brought, and the stepmother began to think it might not be a bad idea if her other daughter tried for the same good fortune. So she sat her by the well to spin and made her spindle bloody by putting her hand in the thorn hedge. Then the mother threw the spindle in the well and made her daughter jump in after it.

The idle daughter also found herself in the beautiful meadow and eventually made her way to Mother Holle's house. She knew beforehand of the old woman's teeth, so she had no fear and agreed to serve Mother Holle at once. The first day she was quite industrious and did everything Mother Holle asked. The second day she began to show her true self and grew increasingly lazy. The third day she was even lazier and would not even get up in the morning. Nor did she shake Mother Holle's bed so the feathers flew about.

Mother Holle was soon tired of the girl and told her she would have to let her go, which pleased the girl greatly as she expected the shower of gold. But when Mother Holle led her to the doorway, a great kettle of tar was emptied over her instead of gold.

"That is the reward for your service," said Mother Holle and she shut the door. So the lazy girl went home all covered with tar, which stuck to her for as long as she lived.

—BROTHERS GRIMM

October 11

The Flea and the Ox

A flea once questioned an ox: "What is your problem, being so huge and strong, that you sumbit to the wrongs you receive from men and slave for them day by day; while, I, being so small a creature, mercilessly feed on their flesh and drink their blood with little or no interference?"

The ox replied, "I do not wish to be ungrateful, for I am loved and cared for by men and they often pat my head and shoulders."

"Woe is me," said the flea. "This very patting you like, whenever it happens to me, brings with it my inevitable destruction!"—AESOP

October 12

COLUMBUS DAY

Columbus and the Egg

One day Christopher Columbus was at a dinner that had been given in his honor by a Spanish gentleman. Several of the guests were frankly jealous of the great admiral's success. They were proud, even conceited, and they soon began to try to make Columbus uncomfortable.

"You have discovered strange lands beyond the seas," they said, "but what of that? Anybody can sail across an ocean and anybody can coast along islands on the other side, just as you have done. It is the simplest thing in the world."

Columbus made no answer, but after a while he took an egg from a dish and said to the dinner guests: "Who among you can make this egg stand on end?"

One by one, those at the table tried the experiment. When the egg had gone entirely around the table and none had succeeded, everyone agreed it could not be done.

Then Columbus took the egg and struck its small end gently upon the table so as to break the shell a little. After that there was no problem in making it stand upright.

"Gentlemen," Columbus said, "what could be easier than to do this, which you said was impossible? It is the simplest thing in the world. Anybody can do it—after he has been shown how!"

—ADAPTED FROM JAMES BALDWIN

October 13

The City Mouse and the Country Mouse

One day the city mouse decided to visit her cousin, who lived in the country. Her country cousin was pleased to see her and welcomed her warmly. She considered the visit such a special occasion that she put together a meal of the best of everything she had in the house. It was only a few bits of cheese and bacon but the country mouse presented these with pride to her guest.

The country mouse enjoyed the treats she had set out, but the city mouse scarcely touched her meal. She was used to fancier things. Finally, the city mouse said, "Cousin, how can you bear to live like this? Your life is so dull and boring. Come with me and I will show you what you have been missing."

The country mouse was quite content with her life, but she agreed to go with her cousin to see what she had been missing.

Late that same night, the two mice arrived at the townhouse where the city mouse lived. "Follow me," she said and she led her cousin into the dining room where the remains of a fine feast were scattered about the table. The country mouse scampered behind her city cousin, sampling a bit of everything. She could hardly believe the wonders that lay before her—cranberry sauce, chocolate-covered mints, and all manner of cheeses and fruits.

"How could I have wasted my time in the country," she thought, "when I could live like this? This is heaven."

Just then the doors of the dining room were flung open and in came the servants and their friends to enjoy the leftovers of the feast too. Afraid for their lives, the mice flew from the table to the nearest hiding place and waited until the people went away. Just as they were about to venture out again, a large dog burst into the room, pulling at the tablecloth to get his share of the goodies.

When the dog went away and things seemed to have quieted down, the country mouse left her hiding place, eager to say good-bye to her cousin and return to the country. "You're welcome to city life, dear cousin, but it's not for me. I would far rather eat simply in the country than feast like this, not knowing what will happen next."—AESOP

The Tiger, the Brahman, and the Jackal

AN INDIAN TALE

To catch a tiger, one must be crafty. So a hunter in India dug a deep pit in the jungle and covered it with vines. At the bottom lay a cage that would snap shut when a large beast fell in. within a day, a tiger had been captured. Try as he might, the tiger could not bite through the bars of the cage.

By chance, a poor Brahman passed by the spot. "Free me, oh pious one!" cried the tiger.

"Nay, my friend," replied the Brahman. "You would probably eat me if I did!"

"I swear I will not! I will be forever grateful and serve you faithfully!" And the tiger sobbed and made so many promises that the pious Brahman took pity on him and opened the door of the cage. Out jumped the tiger, who seized the poor man and cried, "What a fool you are! I have been trapped a long time and I'm very hungry. Why shouldn't I make a meal of you?"

The Brahman begged for his life, pointing out how unfair the tiger was being. But his pleas won him only a postponement: the Brahman was to ask three others what they thought of the tiger's injustice and the tiger agreed to abide by their decision.

The Brahman first went to a pipal tree for its opinion. "What have you to complain about?" replied the tree indifferently. "Don't I give shade and shelter to everyone who passes by? And what is my reward? They tear down my branches to feed their cattle. Don't whimper—be a man!"

Next the Brahman described the situation to a water buffalo, who was at work turning the wheel of a water well. The buffalo was also unsympathetic. "You are a fool to expect gratitude! Look at me! While I gave milk, I was fed the choicest grains, but now that I am dry they yoke me here and give me scraps as fodder!" Sadly the Brahman walked away.

As he traveled down the road, he asked the road what it thought of the tiger's ingratitude. "My dear sir, you are foolish to expect anything else," replied the road. "I help everyone get where they need to go, and in return they trample me and kick me into dust!"

The Brahman sorrowfully turned back to where the tiger waited for him and met a jackal on the way. "What's the matter, Mr. Brahman?" asked the jackal. "You look miserable!" As the Brahman finished describing his problem, the jackal said, "How very confusing! Would you tell me again?"

So the Brahman repeated his story, but the jackal was still perplexed. "Perhaps," said the jackal, "if we went to the place where it all happened, I might understand it better."

When they arrived at the cage, the tiger, who had spent the time sharpening his claws, was waiting impatiently. "You've been away a long time," he growled. "Now let us begin our dinner!"

"*Our* dinner!" thought the wretched Brahman. "What a delicate way of putting it! Give me five minutes more, Mr. Tiger, so that I may explain matters to the jackal." When the tiger agreed, the Brahman told the story all over again, spinning it out as long as he possibly could.

"Oh, my poor brain!" cried the jackal, wringing his paws. "Now how did it all begin? You were in the cage and the tiger walked by—"

"No, you fool!" interrupted the tiger. "*I* was in the cage."

"Of course!" cried the jackal, pretending to tremble with fright. "I was in the cage. No, I wasn't—oh, dear! Where are my wits? Let me see—the tiger was in the Brahman, and the cage came walking by—no, that's not it either! Well, begin your dinner, for I shall never understand."

"Yes, you shall!" roared the tiger, in a rage at the jackal's stupidity. "I'll *make* you understand! Look here, I am the tiger and I was in the cage. Do you understand that much?"

"Yes—no—How did you get in the cage, Sir Tiger?"

"Why, the usual way, of course!"

"Oh, dear, don't be angry, but what is the usual way?"

At this the tiger lost patience, and jumping into the cage, cried, "This way! Now do you understand how it was?"

"Perfectly!" grinned the jackal, as he slammed shut the door to the cage.

October 15

The Bald Knight

A certain knight was growing very old and, as often happens with old age, his hair fell out, and he became bald. To cover this imperfection, the knight wore a wig. But one day as he was hunting with some friends, a sudden gust of wind blew off his wig and exposed his shiny bald head.

His friends could not help but laugh at the accident and the knight himself laughed as loud as anybody, saying, "How was it to be expected that I should keep strange hair upon my head when my *own* would not stay there?"

From then on, the knight contented himself that though his hair was lost he still had his humor.—AESOP

October 16

Wiley and the Hairy Man, Part 1

A TALE FROM THE AMERICAN SOUTH

Wiley's pappy was lazy. He would sleep while the weeds grew higher than the cotton. One day he fell off the ferry boat without a trace. The only clue was the sound of a big man laughing across the river. Everybody said, "That's the Hairy Man," and at those words everyone stopped looking for Wiley's pappy.

"Wiley," his mammy said, "the Hairy Man's got your pappy and he'll get you if you don't be careful."

"Yes, ma'am," he answered. "I'll look out. I'll take my hound dogs everywhere I go."

One day Wiley took his ax to the swamp to cut poles for a hen roost. His hounds went with him, but they took out after a pig and ran it so far off Wiley couldn't even hear them. "Well," thought Wiley, "I hope the Hairy Man ain't nowhere 'round." Just then the Hairy Man came through the trees, with a big grin on his face. He was sure ugly and hairy all over. His eyes burned like fire and spit drooled all over his big teeth.

Wiley quickly climbed up a bay tree. He had seen that the Hairy Man didn't have feet like a man, but like a cow, and he knew cows couldn't climb trees.

"Why you climbin' trees?" the Hairy Man called out.

"My mammy told me to stay away from you. What you got in that sack?"

"Nothin' yet." As he said this, the Hairy Man picked up Wiley's ax and began hacking at the tree.

But Wiley called out words he'd learned from his mammy, who knew conjure magic. "Fly, chips, fly, back in your same old place." The chips flew and the Hairy Man cussed and chopped some more till the sound of Wiley's hounds was heard nearby. The Hairy Man threw down the ax and took off.

When Wiley got home, he told his mammy that the Hairy Man had almost got him. She asked if he'd had his sack. "Don't climb a tree next time," she said. "Stay on the ground and say, 'Hello, Hairy Man.' Then say, 'I heard you're about the best conjureman 'round here.' He'll say, 'I reckon I am.' You say, 'I bet you cain't turn yourself into no giraffe.' You keep tellin' him he cain't and he will. Next you bet he cain't turn himself into no possum. Then he will, and you grab him and throw him in the sack."

"It don't sound right somehow, but I will," said Wiley. He tied up his hounds so they wouldn't scare away the

Hairy Man and went down to the swamp again. When the Hairy Man appeared, with his big teeth showing more than ever, Wiley did exactly as his mammy had told him. But after he'd nabbed the Hairy Man and thrown the sack in the river, he was mighty surprised, a little later, to see the Hairy Man in the swamp. Wiley had to scramble up the nearest tree.

The Hairy Man gloated. "I turned myself into the wind and blew out of the sack. Wiley, I'm going to sit right here till you get hungry and fall out of that tree. You want me to teach you more conjure?"

Wiley thought about his hound dogs tied up almost a mile away. "Well," he said. "You done some pretty smart tricks. But I bet you cain't make things disappear and go where nobody knows."

"Huh, that's what I'm good at."

"This rope I got tied around my breeches has been conjured. I bet you cain't make it disappear!"

"Huh, I can make all the rope in this county disappear." Wiley held onto his breeches as the Hairy Man hollered his spell.

"Here, dogs," yelled Wiley loud enough to be heard a mile off.

When Wiley and his dogs got back home and he told his mammy what had happened, she said, "He blew right out of the sack? That *is* bad. But you done fool him twice. If you fool him again, he'll leave you alone. I've got to study up a way to fool him a third time."

October 17

Wiley and the Hairy Man, Part 2

Late that evening, Wiley's mammy told him to go down to the pen and fetch the piglet away from her sow. When he did, she put it in his bed, then told him to go up in the loft and hide.

Wiley went up there and soon heard the wind howling. His dogs, who were tied up outside, were growling something fierce. He looked through a knothole and saw the dog at the front door looking down toward the swamp, with his hair standing up and his lips drawn back in a snarl. Then an animal as big as a mule with horns on its head ran out of the swamp past the house. One of the dogs jerked and jumped but he couldn't get loose. Then an animal bigger than a great big dog with a long nose and big teeth ran out of the swamp and growled at the cabin. This time the dog broke free and took after the big animal. "Lordy," said Wiley. "The Hairy Man is coming here, sure."

He didn't have to wait long, because soon enough he heard something with feet like a cow scrambling around on the roof. He knew it was the Hairy Man, because he heard him cuss when he touched the hot chimney. Seeing there was a fire in the fireplace, the Hairy Man came right to the front door. "Mammy," he hollered, "I've come after your baby."

"You ain't going to get him," Mammy hollered back.

"Give him here or I'll set your house on fire with lightning. I'll dry up your spring and send a million boll weevils out of the ground to eat your cotton."

"Hairy Man, you wouldn't do all that. That's mighty mean."

"I'm a mighty mean man. I ain't never seen a man as mean as me."

"If I give you my baby, will you go away from here and leave everything else alone?"

"I swear that's just what I'll do," said the Hairy Man, so Mammy let him in.

"He's over there in that bed," she said.

The Hairy Man grinned all the way over to the bed and snatched the covers back. "Hey," he hollered, "there ain't nothin' in this bed but an old suckin' pig."

"I ain't said what kind of baby I was givin' you! That pig sure belonged to me before I gave it to you."

The Hairy Man raged and stomped all over the house, gnashing his teeth. Then he grabbed up the pig and tore out through the swamp, knocking down trees right and left. It looked like a cyclone had hit it.

"Is the Hairy Man gone, Mammy?" yelled Wiley from the loft.

"Yes, child. That Hairy Man cain't ever hurt you now. We fooled him three times."

October 18

The Bat and the Weasel

A bat falling on the ground was caught by a weasel. When the bat pled for his life, the weasel merely laughed. "Birds are my natural enemy," the weasel explained. "You're doomed."

But the bat assured him that he was no bird, but a mouse, and the weasel, taking in the bat's strange appearance, decided to set the bat free.

Shortly afterwards the bat again fell on the ground and this time was caught by another weasel, whom he likewise begged for his life. "Good weasel, please spare me. For if you think I am your natural enemy you are mistaken. I am no bird but a mouse," the bat again made plain. The weasel, though, had a special hatred for mice, and thus explained, "Mice are my natural enemy. You're doomed." The bat then assured him that he was just kidding, that in actuality, he was a bird, and for a second time, he escaped.

When circumstances change, be ready to change your strategy.—AESOP

October 19

The Donkey Driver and the Thief

One day two thieves were walking down a country road and came upon a farmer leading his donkey by the harness. "I am going to trick that farmer and steal his donkey," said one thief.

"In broad daylight!" exclaimed the other. "How can you do that?"

"That farmer looks pretty stupid to me. Watch how easy this will be."

The farmer was plodding along, half-asleep, and the thief crept quietly up to the donkey, took off the harness, and put it on his own head. Then he beckoned his friend and motioned to him that he should hide the donkey in the woods. After the animal was safely away, the thief stopped dead in his tracks. The farmer did not look back, but merely yanked on the harness to get the beast going. When nothing happened, he yanked even harder. Still nothing. The angry farmer's eyes flew open and he turned to beat his stubborn donkey. To his astonishment, he found a man in the harness.

"Who . . . who . . . are you?" stammered the farmer.

"Why, I'm the donkey," replied the thief.

"But . . . but . . ."

"Let me explain," said the thief. He took the harness off and settled himself comfortably by the roadside. "Several years ago, I was human, just as you are. But I was very lazy and would not do my chores. My mother grew extremely angry with me, especially after she discovered I had begun thieving. She put a hex on me, transforming me into a donkey for seven years. But today was the last day of the enchantment and I am free to be human once again."

The astounded farmer immediately felt guilty for having worked the donkey so hard. "Let me apologize if I have treated you badly. If I had only known. . . . But congratulations on your freedom," the farmer said earnestly. "Here, let me give you some money for your new start in life."

The thief thanked the farmer and they said their good-byes. The thief joined his companion in the woods and they had a good laugh over the gullible farmer. Later, since they had no need of the donkey, they sold him in the nearest town.

A few days afterwards, the farmer came to that town to buy a new beast. While examining the animals for sale, he came across one that looked strangely familiar. "Is it . . . No! Can it be . . . ?" Suddenly he recognized his own brand on the back of the donkey he was looking at. "You scoundrel!" shouted the farmer. "Just a few days as a human being and you're at it again. No wonder your mother cursed you. When will you give up stealing?"

The donkey lifted its head and bared its teeth in a merry bray.

"That does it!" the farmer exclaimed. "You know perfectly well you understand every word I say. I'll show you! This time I won't buy you. I'll leave the likes of you to another master!"

And with that, the farmer, who was quite pleased with himself, walked away.

Baba Yaga

A RUSSIAN TALE

Once upon a time a girl lived by the edge of a great forest with her father and stepmother. When the father wasn't around the stepmother was very cruel to the girl, making her work like a servant and beating her often.

One day the stepmother told the girl, "Go to my sister, your aunt, and ask her for a needle and thread to make you a dress." Now the girl was no fool, and she knew that the stepmother was trying to get her killed, for the aunt was a Baba Yaga, a witch. So the girl went first to her real aunt for advice.

The real aunt gave her instructions: "There is a birch tree at the Baba Yaga's that would poke your eyes out. You must tie a ribbon round it. There are doors that would creak. You must pour oil on their hinges. There are dogs that will tear you to pieces, but you will throw them this bread. And finally there is a cat that would scratch you blind. Give it this piece of bacon."

The girl walked and walked into the woods until she came to where the Baba Yaga lived. It was a peculiar little hut that stood on chicken legs, and inside sat Baba Yaga Bony-Legs. Though she was quite afraid, the girl explained her errand to the witch.

"Very well, I shall look for a needle and thread. Meanwhile, sit and weave," said the Baba Yaga.

The girl sat down at the loom and the Baba Yaga went outside and told her maidservant to heat a bath. "Get my niece washed and do a good job. I mean to make her my breakfast."

The girl overheard this, and when the maidservant came in, she begged her to dawdle getting the bath ready, and gave her a handkerchief as a present.

The Baba Yaga's cat was in the hut, and the girl gave it the piece of bacon and asked, "Is there no way of escaping from here?"

"Here is a comb and a towel," said the cat. "Take them and be off. The Baba Yaga will pursue you, but lay your ear on the ground and you will hear her coming. When she is close by, throw down the towel. It will become a wide river. If the Baba Yaga should happen to get across the river, throw down the comb. It will become a dense forest that she will never get through."

As the girl fled the hut, the Baba Yaga's dogs would have attacked her, but she tossed the bread at them and they let her go. The squeaky doors might have given her away, but the girl had oiled their hinges. The dangerous birch tree let her pass when she tied a ribbon around it.

When the Baba Yaga returned to her house, she was outraged to find the girl gone and began beating the cat for not scratching out the girl's eyes. "As long as I've served you," said the cat, "you've never given me so much as a bone, but she gave me bacon." The dogs, the birch tree, the doors, the maidservant, all told the Baba Yaga the same thing.

Now the Baba Yaga traveled in a mortar, which she propelled with a pestle. She jumped in the mortar and set off in pursuit of the girl. The girl, however, heard her coming and flung down the towel, which became a very wide river. Foiled for the moment, the Baba Yaga returned to her hut and got her oxen. When she brought them to the river, they drank up every drop.

The Baba Yaga began the pursuit again and the girl threw down the comb. Instantly a very thick forest sprang up between her and the witch.

Then the girl ran like the wind, for she was almost home.

The girl's father had returned, and when she told him of the stepmother's plot, the father tossed his wife out of the house. And whether she reached her sister's hut, or whether the bears or wolves found her first, no one ever knew. But the girl and her father lived on happily in their house at the edge of the forest.

October 21

The Goblin Pony

A SPOOKY ENGLISH TALE

"Don't stir from the house tonight," Old Peggy said to the children. "For there is a terrible wind shaking the house and it is Halloween. The witches and goblins are out this evening. And they may be disguised as harmless creatures, but they mean to do evil."

But the children had plans to trap lobsters and crabs that night and were not interested in their grandmother's warning. Only the youngest child, Richard, hesitated a moment.

"Stay by my side, little Richard, and I will tell you beautiful stories," said Old Peggy.

But the others were leaving and Richard wanted to pick wild blackberries, so he ran out after them. Outside the children said, "What was the old woman talking about? There is no storm! Never has the night been finer or the moon brighter!"

Just then they noticed a little black pony trot up near them. "This is old Valentine's pony!" one of the boys said. "It must have escaped from the stable. Let's take it back." He jumped on the pony's back and his brothers joined him, including little Richard.

On their way they met some friends who also hopped on the pony. Strangely, the pony did not seem to mind the weight of all these children, but trotted merrily along.

The quicker the pony trotted, the more the boys enjoyed the fun. They urged him on, calling, "Gallop, little horse! Never have you had such brave riders before!"

Meanwhile, the wind had risen and the children could hear the howl of the waves from the beach. The pony did not seem to be headed back to his stable, but was galloping ever faster toward the ocean. The boys began to be a little bit concerned, and the eldest pulled at the pony's mane to get him to turn around. But all his tugging was in vain and the pony headed straight for the ocean.

As the pony felt the waves on its feet, it neighed with glee and moved even farther out into the billowing surf. By the time the waves came up to the children's knees, they were terribly frightened. "This cursed little black pony is bewitched! Why didn't we listen to Old Peggy?"

In just a few moments the pony was far out at sea. The waves covered the children's heads and they disappeared forever.

Old Peggy went out to search for her grandchildren at morning's light. She could not find anyone who had seen them, and they seemed to have vanished without a trace. Old Peggy stumbled home, her eyes so blinded by tears that she was not even sure, later, what she had seen. She thought a black pony galloped past her, neighing loudly and gleefully. But an instant later, it was gone.

—ADAPTED FROM ANDREW LANG

October 22

The Man on the Highway

A SPOOKY MODERN TALE

Fred and Jimmy had been driving for about three hours. "Let's stop for gas," Jimmy suggested for the fifth time. The needle on the dashboard had been hovering around the empty sign for about twenty minutes and Jimmy was getting very nervous.

"Oh, relax," said Fred. "We've got plenty of gas and I want to make good time."

They were winding their way through an empty valley in Wisconsin, when suddenly the car began to coast. That was it. No more gas.

"Hmm . . ." said Fred. "I really thought we had plenty. . . ."

"Don't talk," said Jimmy, who was furious.

As luck would have it, it began to rain, and as it was nearly midnight, the road was eerily quiet. The two roommates debated about whether to leave the car and walk to town for gas or wait for someone to come along and ask for help. Just about then some headlights appeared in the distance. A car was heading their way.

"I told you not to worry," Fred said to Jimmy. The two boys waved their arms wildly but the car didn't stop. "Right," said Jimmy. "Like I said: *don't talk.*"

Another pair of headlights emerged and whizzed right by them, despite their gestures for help. Then, some time later, a car appeared almost out of nowhere, approaching the two boys like it too was running out of gas, it was putt-putting along so slowly.

"Hi there," said the driver, a man in his sixties with silver hair and silver glasses. His car was about twenty years old, a real clunker. "You boys want a ride to town?"

The boys explained that they had run out of gas and the old man told them about a roadside inn about five miles down the road. "The gas stations are all closed now," the man said. "For a few bucks you can dry off, get a clean bed and a good breakfast, and start out tomorrow like new."

The boys agreed that they might as well stay over. They got their duffle bags out of the trunk and were loading them into the old man's car when a Mack truck, going well over the speed limit, skidded across the road and missed the old man and his car and the boys by only a fingernail. The two boys were trembling, but the old man acted like it hadn't even happened. The boys thought it was weird, but then again, it had been a weird night.

On the way to the roadside inn, the old man pointed out the little house where he lived and told the boys to come by if they had any more trouble. Then he dropped them off at the roadside inn, and they thanked him and said good night. When the boys went to check in, Fred reached for his wallet. "Oh, no," he said, turning to Jimmy. "I think I left my wallet in that old man's car."

"Don't talk," said Jimmy, who had had quite enough of Fred. Since the old man lived just a few doors down from the inn, the two boys decided to walk over straightaway and retrieve the wallet. When they got to the old man's house, they were greeted by an old woman. From the state of her robe and her weary eyes, it was clear she had been in a deep sleep.

"We're sorry to bother you, ma'am," said Jimmy, "but I left a wallet in your husband's car this evening."

The woman looked at the boys strangely and then narrowed her eyes.

"What do you boys want?" she said in barely a whisper.

"Just my wallet," Fred said sheepishly.

"What kind of cruel trick are you playing at one in the morning?" the old woman asked, looking at the two of them, one, then the other.

"Your husband picked us up tonight on the main road. It was raining. We were in trouble," Jimmy said. Then he noticed the back of the old man's car in the sideyard. The front of the car was crushed like a can.

"What happened?" Jimmy said in shock.

The woman looked at the boys hard.

"Twenty years ago tonight my husband was killed by a Mack truck that came barreling down the highway. He had stopped to help two boys who were in trouble. Everybody was killed."

Fred walked over to the car and peered into the backseat. His wallet was lying on the floor.

"Jimmy, come here," he said and showed his friend the wallet.

Fred didn't talk anymore that night. Neither did Jimmy.

October 23

The Golden Arm

A SPOOKY ENGLISH TALE

There once was a man in search of a wife. He searched high and low, courted young and old, rich and poor, pretty and plain. Yet he could not meet the woman of his dreams. As a matter of fact, he had given up his search when he chanced upon a woman who was fair and kind, and who also possessed a golden arm. He married her at once and thought that no man was so fortunate as he. They lived happily together and though he wished people to think otherwise, what he really loved about his wife was her arm of gold.

After years of marriage, she died. The husband put on his blackest black and wore a long sad face at the funeral but for all of that he got up in the night and dug up her body and cut off her golden arm. Horrors! He cut it off! He rushed home and hid his treasure, thinking no one in the world would know.

The following night he put the golden arm under his pillow and was just dozing off when the ghost of his dead wife glided into his room. Stalking up to the bedside, the ghost drew the curtain and looked at the husband accusingly.

He pretended not to be frightened.

"What happened to your rosy cheeks?" the husband asked.

"All withered and wasted away," replied the ghost.

"What happened to your rosy lips?" he inquired.

"All withered and wasted away," the ghost replied.

"What happened to your golden hair?" he asked.

"All withered and wasted away," said the ghost once more.

"What happened to your golden arm?" he finally asked.

"YOU'VE GOT IT!" screamed the ghost.

—ADAPTED FROM JOSEPH JACOBS

October 24

The Golden Arm, Variations

There are many ghost stories about the dead returning for missing parts. The key to telling "The Golden Arm" is to deliver the repetitive "All withered and wasted away" in a faint, sleepy tone so that the listener is lulled just prior to shouting out at the end.

Other chants that have been suggested (changing body parts as you like) are "Give me my silver toe," "Who took my ivory teeth," and "Who got my golden arm." The dead return in stories not only to retrieve missing body parts but pieces of clothing, which the teller can play with to great effect.

October 25

The Conjure Wives

A SPOOKY TALE FROM THE AMERICAN SOUTH

Once upon a time, when a Halloween night came on the dark o' the moon, a lot of old conjure wives was a-sittin' by the fire and a-cookin' a big supper for theirselves. The wind was a-howlin' 'round like it does on Halloween nights, and the old conjure wives was talkin' about the spells they was a-goin' to weave long come midnight.

By and by there come a knockin' at the door. "Who's there?" called a conjure wife. "Who-o?"

"One who is hungry and cold," said a voice.

Then the old conjure wives started laughin' and called out, "We's a-cookin' for ourselves. Who'll cook for you? Who? Who?"

The voice didn't say nothin', but the knockin' just kept on. "Who's that a-knockin'?" cried out another conjure wife. "Who? Who?"

Then came a whistlin', wailin' sound. "Let me in, do-o-o-o! I'se cold thro-o-o-o an' thro-o-o-o, an' I'se hungry too-o-o!"

The conjure wives laughed and sang out, "Git along, do! We's a-cookin' for ourselves. Who'll cook for you? Who? Who?"

Still the voice didn't say nothin', but the knockin' just kept on. Now the conjure wives began to get scared-like, so one of them says, "Let's give it somethin' and get it away before it spoils our spells."

And the voice didn't say nothin', but the knockin' just kept on. The wives, they took the littlest piece of dough, as big as a pea, and they put it in the fry pan. And when they put the dough in the fry pan, it began to swell and swell, and it swelled over the fry pan, and it swelled over the top of the stove, and it swelled out the door.

And the voice didn't say nothin', but the knockin' just kept on. Then the old conjure wives got scared and they ran for the door, and the *door was shut tight.*

And the voice didn't say nothin', but the knockin' just kept on. And the dough, it swelled and it swelled all over the floor and up into the chairs. The old conjure wives, they climbed up on the backs of the chairs and they were scareder and scareder. And they called out, "Who's that a-knockin' Who? Who?" Still the voice didn't say nothin', but the knockin' just kept on.

And as the dough kept a-swellin' and a-swellin', the old conjure wives began to scrooge up smaller and smaller, and their eyes got bigger and bigger with scaredness, and they kept crying out, "Who's that a-knockin'? Who? Who?"

And then the knockin' stopped and the voice said, "Fly out the window, do! There's no more house for you!"

The old conjure wives, they spread their wings and they flew out the windows and off into the woods, all a-callin', "Who'll cook for you? Who? Who?"

Now if you go into the woods in the dark o' the moon, you'll see the old conjure wives and hear them calling "Who? Who?" Only on a Halloween night you don't want to go 'round the old owls, because then they turn to old conjure wives a-weavin' their spells.

October 26

The Wolf and the Sheep

A wolf had been hurt badly in a fight and was unable to move. A sheep passed by and the wolf appealed to him.

"Kind sheep, I have had nothing to eat or drink for days. Won't you please fetch me some water so I may get up my strength to eat solid food?"

The sheep was moved for a moment by the wolf's plight, but came to his senses quickly.

"Solid food?" he said. "And who might that be? If I brought you a drink it would only be to wash down the likes of me!"

Mercy can be misappropriated.—AESOP

October 27

The Eagle and the Arrow

An archer took aim at an eagle and hit him in the heart. As the eagle turned his head in the agonies of death, he saw that the arrow was winged with his own feathers. His own feathers! He could not believe it.

"My death is much more painful," said the eagle in his dying words, "knowing that I have died from a weapon I myself supplied.—AESOP

October 28

The Changeling

A GERMAN TALE

A poor woman had a pretty child who was carried away by the fairies one day. In the child's place the fairies left a changeling, who had a large head and staring eyes, and ate and drank voraciously. The distraught mother went to a wise neighbor for advice.

"I will tell you what to do," said the neighbor. "Take the changeling into the kitchen, seat him on the hearth, make up a good fire, then fill two eggshells with water and place them on the fire to boil. That should make him laugh, and if he laughs you will get rid of him."

The mother was skeptical but she went home and did as her neighbor advised. When the changeling saw her fill the eggshells with water and set them on the fire he began to chant; "Now I am as old as a mine of gold; yet I never saw in my life before, water in eggshells boiled." And after this song he began to laugh.

The moment he laughed, a fairy appeared in the kitchen, holding the woman's own child. He seated him on the hearth and carried away the changeling.

—BROTHERS GRIMM

October 29

The Goose with the Golden Eggs

A farmer went to the barn one morning to check on his goose. There he found in the goose's nest an egg that glistened . . . like gold! When he lifted it, it felt more like a stone than an egg, and he was about to throw it away for he thought a trick had been played on him. But as a matter of curiosity he took it to show his wife.

His wife was overjoyed. "Throw it away!" she laughed. "You fool, this is gold. We are going to be rich!"

Every morning the farmer and his wife went out to the barn to fetch their golden egg, and soon they lived in great wealth and splendor.

The more the farmer had, the more the farmer wanted, and one morning he was greedy to get all the gold the goose could give so he killed the goose and opened it, only to find . . . nothing.

Greed can leave you with nothing.—AESOP

October 30

The Coffin Lid

A SPOOKY RUSSIAN TALE

For hours, the peasant and the old horse had been pulling the wagon filled with pots and pans. The animal was weary and thirsty and finally, at the graveyard, he just quit. The peasant could hardly blame the horse. It was past midnight and he was tired too. They had walked miles and had not sold a single pot that day. He let the horse graze a while, then he propped himself up against a tombstone and tried to rest.

The peasant couldn't sleep. He looked up at the broad, black sky and stared at the stars. He was lost in thought when a nearby grave began to open. The peasant froze. A dead man, wrapped in a white shroud and holding a coffin lid, jumped out, set down the coffin lid, and then ran off to the village. The peasant thought at first that his mind was playing tricks and vowed to get more rest. Yet there was the coffin lid, as real as it could be. He was examining it when suddenly the corpse ran back and began to holler.

"Give me back my coffin lid," he demanded, sounding rather like a spoiled child.

"I will not," replied the peasant. "I don't even know what—or who—you are. Tell me where you've been and what you have done."

The corpse explained that he had been to the village and had killed two ponies.

The peasant was horrified. "You what?" he said, standing tall. He couldn't imagine anything more senseless. "Unless you bring those horses back to life, you'll never see the roof of your casket again!"

It had been a while since the dead man had talked to anyone, but he knew one thing—he had to get that coffin lid back. So he directed the peasant to take a scrap of material from his shroud, go to the stable where the ponies were killed, pour live coals into a pot, and then burn the shroud. "There will be lots of smoke and incense and the ponies will be revived instantly," he assured the peasant.

The peasant was a man of his word, so he gave the dead man back his coffin lid and headed into town. He could hear the children crying for their dead ponies. When he finally found the stables, he did everything he was told to do and, sure enough, the ponies came back to life! The people of the village were ecstatic. But after they thought about the events of the evening, they became suspicious. "Just one minute," said one of the villagers. "If you knew how to bring our horses back to life, then you also must have killed them." The crowd turned to look at the peasant.

"You are wrong, dear people, though I can see why you might jump to that conclusion," he said. He told them everything about the corpse and the coffin lid. News of the strange encounter spread quickly and the whole village assembled and went to the graveyard to look at the grave from which the corpse had risen.

When they got to the gravesite, the village people tore open the casket and drove an aspen stake into the heart of the dead men. They also bought many pots and pans from the peasant, and sent him on his way with great honor.

—ADAPTED FROM WILLIAM RALSTON

October 31

HALLOWEEN

I'm Gonna Get You

A VERY SPOOKY STORY FOR OLDER CHILDREN

Once there was a little boy named Billy who wasn't afraid of anything. He wasn't afraid of snakes or spiders or scary movies or even the dark. On the playground, he would boast that he was "the bravest kid in the world," and though they got tired of hearing Billy say so, most of his friends would agree.

It was a winter night, and dark was coming earlier and earlier, and Billy had been lying in bed for just a few minutes when he thought he heard a noise. He was curled up under a pile of blankets and feeling pretty comfortable, so he didn't feel like getting up to inspect. But then he heard the noise again, so he threw off his covers, turned on the light, and looked around his room. Nothing! But Billy was the bravest kid in the world, so he didn't just leave it at that. He looked up and down the hallway, and even peered over the stairs. He didn't see anything, so he shrugged and went back to sleep.

The next morning at the sunny breakfast table, Billy's mom asked him if he had slept well.

"Not really," Billy said. "I thought I heard something in the night and I had to get up and investigate. It must have been the house creaking because I didn't see anything."

"That's strange," Billy's mother said. "I didn't hear anything, did you, dear?" she asked, turning to Billy's father. But Billy's father was deep into the newspaper, and so it was there that the conversation ended.

That night, after he had settled into

his cozy bed, Billy heard a noise again. This time it was a voice, and the voice said, "Billy, I'm on the first step."

Billy bolted out of his bed, raced to the door, and flicked the hall light on. But when he looked down the stairwell, he saw nothing.

The next night, Billy heard a noise, and then the voice, "Billy, I'm on the second step."

For the first time—maybe in his life—Billy felt just a wee bit afraid.

The next night, the voice said, "Billy, I'm on the third step." That morning, Billy went down to the sunny breakfast room, but as he did he counted the number of steps. There were eleven of them. That didn't give him much time to figure out where the voice came from—or what it wanted. But when he told his mother and father about it at breakfast, his mother just told him it was his imagination, patted his head, and told him not to worry. His father nodded and mumbled, "It's nothing, son," and put his face back into the newspaper.

But Billy was scared.

And that night, the voice said, "Billy, I'm on the fourth step." Like a bad dream, the voice came every night: "Billy, I'm on the fifth step, sixth step, seventh step," and so on. Billy was getting so scared he couldn't even eat breakfast in the morning and he couldn't eat dinner at night.

Then it was "Billy, I'm in the hallway." And then "Billy, I'm at your door." And then "Billy, I'm in your room."

Billy, the bravest kid in the world, was hiding under his blankets. It was pitch black when Billy heard his door open, and the sound of footsteps. And then "Billy, I'm standing by the bed and . . . I'M GONNA GET YOU!"

NOVEMBER

November 1

ALL SAINTS' DAY

Saint Cuthbert's Eagle

Once upon a time, there lived a saint named Cuthbert who went forth from his monastery to preach to the poor. He was a simple man, and wandered down dusty roads with only one young companion. On this day, the boy and Cuthbert had been walking for hours without food or water and were becoming weary.

"Young man," said the good saint, "do you know anyone on the road whom we may ask for food and a place to rest?"

"Hmm," mused the attendant. "I was just thinking the same thing. But I know no one on this road who might help us on our way. I was mistaken not to pack provisions for this journey."

"My son," said Saint Cuthbert, "learn to have trust in God. I know He will provide if we believe in Him."

Then, looking up, the saint saw an eagle in the sky. "Do you see the eagle?" the saint asked. "It is possible for God to feed us by means of this bird."

The bird soared above them, as they continued walking until they came to a river.

"Now then," said Saint Cuthbert, "run and see what God has provided."

The attendant ran and found a good-sized fish that the eagle had just caught. This he brought to the saint.

"Dear boy, did you forget about our friend the eagle?" asked the good man. "Cut the fish into two pieces and give the bird one, as her service well deserves."

The boy did as he was told and the eagle, taking half of the fish in her beak, flew away.

Then, entering a neighboring village, Saint Cuthbert gave the other half to a peasant to cook, and while the boy and the villagers feasted, the good saint told them about the love of God.

—ADAPTED FROM THE VENERABLE BEDE

November 2

The Famous Bubble Gum Boy

Beau Stevens loved bubble gum. Really, really, really loved bubble gum. When he woke up in the morning the first thing he would do was put bubble gum in his mouth and start chewing. And all day long he would add more and more pieces until his cheeks were as big as giant balloons. And each night, the last thing he did before going to sleep was to take out of his mouth the giant piece of gum and add it to the big ball of gum he was hiding under his bed.

Beau Stevens was the best bubble gum blower there ever, ever was in the whole history of the big city. He could make bubble gum bubbles in any shape he wanted. He could blow bubbles that looked like baseball players or cars or even the prettiest girl in town. One day, when the whole class was learning about France, he blew a bubble that looked exactly like the Eiffel Tower. Even his teacher, Mrs. Joyce, was impressed when he did that. He was as proud as it was possible to be.

But Beau Stevens's mom and dad did not like his bubble gum blowing. "Stop chewing bubble gum," they warned, "or all of your teeth will have cavities."

"Stop blowing bubbles," they warned, "or one day a big bubble will burst all over your face and smother you." "Stop chewing bubble gum," they warned, "or one day you'll have so much gum in your mouth that you'll never be able to open it again."

Beau nodded his head and pretended to listen to them, but when they weren't around he would start chewing all over again. And as soon as they came home he would take the gum out of his mouth and add it to the ball of gum under his bed.

The big ball of gum was getting so big that sometimes, when his mom and dad weren't home, Beau would take it out to play with it. Once he tried to bounce it. But because it was bubble gum it hit the floor and just stuck there. He tried to make it into really neat shapes, but it got all over his hands and he couldn't get it off. Beau began to worry about this ball. It was getting so big that soon he would have to find some other place to hide it.

Late one night, though, when he was fast asleep, he suddenly heard his mom shouting his name. "Beau," she yelled, "get up quick. The whole building is on fire." Sure enough, Beau could smell fire. And soon smoke began coming into his room. He could see that his mom and dad were really worried. Beau looked out his window and way down below, twenty floors down in the street, Beau could see the fire fighters trying to put out the fire.

But the fire climbed up the building. It was getting closer and closer. Beau's dad scratched his head. "I don't know what to do," he finally admitted. "We have to get out of this building."

Then Beau had an idea. "I know what to do," he said. He ran into his room and from beneath his bed he pulled out his ball of bubble gum. "Watch me." And very quickly he made a long, thick rope of bubble gum. When he was done, he tied one end around his bed post and dropped the other end out the window. "Mom, you go first," he said.

Beau's mother was afraid, so Beau went first. He tied the other end of the gum rope around his waist and jumped out the window. Slowly, slowly the gum stretched and stretched and stretched until Beau could feel his feet touching the ground. And then, when he untied his rope, the gum rope got smaller and smaller and sprang all the way back to his apartment. Soon his mom and then his dad came safely down the bubble gum ladder.

And that was how Beau Stevens became known as the Famous Bubble Gum Boy.

—JORDAN BURNETT AND DAVID FISHER

November 3

The Cunning Snake

AN AFRICAN AMERICAN FOLKTALE

One time a woman was walking through the woods when she found a snake's nest. In the nest was a great big egg. The woman really wanted the egg, but she was afraid to take it. That night she dreamt of the egg. When she woke up she said to herself, "I *have* to have that egg." She went back to the woods and found the egg and cooked it up for breakfast.

Soon the snake discovered that her egg was gone. She followed the thief's scent all the way to the woman's house. The snake looked this woman in the eye. "Where's my egg?" she demanded to know.

The woman said she hadn't seen any egg.

"Then what about that shell?" the snake said, nodding to a sad pile of crushed eggshells. The woman didn't say a word.

"Why did you tear up my nest and take my egg?" the snake pressed.

Still, the woman said nothing. She just shook her head and went back to work as if the snake wasn't even there.

"Woman, you stole my egg and killed my child. You'd better watch out for yours," the snake said and then slid away.

Over time, the woman had a baby, a little girl named Nancy. The woman loved her baby so, and remembering what the snake had said, she kept the child close on her back for safety's sake. Pretty soon, though, the child weighed as much as a big sack of rice and the woman got tired of hauling her around. She put the girl inside the house and showed her how to lock the door.

"Don't open the door," she said, "till you hear me sing my song." Then the woman sang, "Walla walla witto, me Noncy; Walla walla witto, me Noncy; Walla walla witto, me Noncy!" When the child heard her mother's song, she answered back "Andolee! Andoli! Andolo!"

The snake was coiled up in the grass, listening to every word.

For seven days, the mother left to do her work, and when she returned she would sing her song, and little Noncy would answer back "Andolee! Andoli! Andolo!"

But on the eighth night, just before the woman was due home, the snake went up to the door and tried to sing the woman's song "Wullo wullo widdo, me Noncy; Wullo wullo widdo, me Noncy; Wullo wullo widdo, me Noncy." The snake's voice was not sweet like the woman's but big and rough. The girl knew something was wrong and said, "No. Go away. My mother doesn't sing like that."

When the woman came back, the snake listened as hard as she could to hear how she sang to her daughter. The next day, the snake practiced the song backwards and forwards nearly four hundred times. When it was nearing sundown, she went to the house and sang the song. "Walla walla witto, me Noncy; Walla walla witto, me Noncy; Walla walla witto, me Noncy." The snake sounded just like the woman. The girl sang right back and opened the door!

She ran to hug her mother but the snake grabbed her and caught her in a coil. She squeezed her tight and then swallowed her whole without breaking a bone.

Soon enough, the woman came home and sang her song. No one answered. She sang again. Still no one answered. Then the woman saw the snake's trail on the road.

The woman quickly cut a cane from the swamp and started tracking down the snake. She was so mad she practically flew through the woods, and finally found the snake asleep in the grass. The snake was so full, she had gotten sleepy and just konked out.

The woman was furious. She saw the snake asleep on the ground and broke her head with the cane and mashed that snake flat. Then she cut that snake open and found her daughter, who looked like she'd simply been taking a nap. The woman took her home and washed her off, and as soon as the little girl opened her eyes, her mother sang her song, and Noncy sang back "Andolee! Andoli! Andolo!"

—ADAPTED FROM JOEL CHANDLER HARRIS

November 4

The Hare and His Ears

One day the lion king had goat for dinner. It was a delectable meal, but the lion had gobbled up the goat so greedily that the goat's horns scratched him and he had a few sore spots on his cheeks. The lion liked to blame others—even dead goats—and so he was very angry about the situation.

He decided that effective immediately, every animal with horns was to leave the kingdom.

The new rule spread quickly.

All of those who were so unlucky as to have horns began to pack up and leave. Even the hare who has no horns spent the night worrying. He got very little sleep thinking about his ears.

"But your ears pose no problem," a bird reassured him. "The new rule is about horns, not ears."

Hare was not so sure. He came out of his hole the next morning and the sun was shining bright. When he saw his shadow he jumped for a moment because it surely looked like he had horns.

"I'm off," hare said to the bird. "I'm not taking any chances. Who knows what the lion might do to me if he sees my shadow?"

After giving it a moment's thought the bird agreed that hare had a point. Knowing the lion as she did, she thought it was wiser to be on the safe side.

Your enemies will seize any excuse to attack you.—AESOP

November 5

The Brownie of Blednock

A SCOTTISH TALE

Did you ever hear how a Brownie came to the village of Blednock, but was frightened away by a silly young woman, who thought she was cleverer than anyone else?

Well, it was one November evening, just when the milking was done and before the children were put to bed. Everyone was standing on their doorsteps, talking of the bad harvest and other things, when the queerest humming noise started down by the river.

It came nearer and nearer, and everyone stopped their gossiping to look down towards the river. Up the road walked the strangest creature that human eyes had ever seen. He looked like a wee man, yet he looked like a beast too, for he was covered with hair from head to foot and wore no clothing except a little kilt made of green rushes. His hair was matted and he had a long blue beard, which almost touched the ground. His legs were twisted and knocked together as he walked, and his arms were so long that his hands trailed in the mud. He seemed to be humming something over and over, which sounded like "Hae ye wark for Aiken-Drum?"

The folks were scared. The children screamed and hid their faces in their mothers' skirts, and the dogs crept behind their masters. Only the grown men were bold enough to look upon the creature, and soon began making jokes about his appearance. Still, the poor little man went slowly up the street, crying wistfully, "Hae ye wark for Aiken-Drum? Any wark for Aiken-Drum?"

Old Grannie Duncan, the oldest and wisest woman in the village, was the first to say, "He may be a ghost or a bogle, but he may be only a harmless Brownie. I know that if he is an evil spirit, he will not dare to look on the Holy Book." So she ran into her cottage and brought out a Bible, which the odd creature took no more heed of than if it had been a song book. "He's just a Brownie," cried Grannie Duncan in triumph. "They're a kindly folk who will work hard for people who treat them well."

Looking closer, you could see that the wee man's hairy face was kindly and that his eyes had a merry twinkle. "Can you speak, creature?" asked an old man. "Where are ye from? What do ye want?"

"I cannot tell thee from whence I come," he said. "It is a nameless land, very different from this. There we all learn to serve, while everyone here wishes to be served. And when there is no work for us to do at home, we sometimes set out to visit thy land, to see if there is any work we may do here. I may stay in this place a while and help ye, but I seek neither wages, nor clothes, nor bedding. All I ask is for the corner of a barn to sleep in and a pot of oatmeal at bedtime."

No one knew quite what to say to this offer. But Grannie Duncan spoke up. " 'Tis but a harmless Brownie! Have we not been complaining about bad wages and bad times? And what about the corn that stands rotting in the fields and it's past Halloween already!"

That settled the matter, and the Brownie was given a corner of the miller's barn to sleep in. He turned out to be the most wonderful worker men had ever known. He got the corn safe in the stackyard within the week, and whenever there was a flock of sheep to be gathered together, or a sickly child to be sung to, or a batch of bread that would not rise, Aiken-Drum appeared in the nick of time. The odd thing was that almost no one ever saw him, and most of his work he did at night. Only the children saw him often, and to them he sang wondrous songs that they loved.

Soon it seemed as if Aiken-Drum had always lived in the village, and he would probably be there still were it not for one silly woman who thought she knew better than everyone else. She decided it was not right to have the little man work so hard for no wages, and could not believe that he worked for love. She took a pair of her husband's old breeches and laid them down one evening in Aiken-Drum's corner of the barn. The dear wee man's feelings were so hurt by being paid for his labor that he disappeared that very night and was never seen again. The children, though, say that they sometimes hear him singing, down by the mill, as they pass it in the gloaming, on their way home from school.

November 6

Snow White and Rose Red, Part 1

A widow lived in a modest cottage with her daughters Snow White and Rose Red. The girls were as beautiful as the flowers on the two rosebushes that grew by the cottage door. They were also blessed with virtue and good fortune, and wherever they went, no harm came to them.

One evening a large black bear knocked on their door. The young girls were frightened by the sight of him, but he said he was freezing to death and only wanted to warm himself by the fire. The widow felt sorry for him and invited him in. She and her daughters fussed over the bear, making him comfortable until even the lamb and the dove who lived with the family were not afraid.

The bear stayed the night with the family, then went on his way in the snow. He came back every evening to visit and let the children play with him. But when spring came, he announced that he would not be coming back for a while as he had to go deep into the forest to protect his treasures from the evil dwarfs. Snow White was so reluctant to let him go that the bear had to squeeze out of the door, leaving a piece of his hairy coat on the latch. Snow White thought she glimpsed gold glittering beneath the fur, but she wasn't sure. She knew this bear was going to be important in her life, and she did not want to see him go.

November 7

Snow White and Rose Red, Part 2

Snow White and Rose Red missed the bear terribly, but life went on as usual. Then one day, while gathering sticks in the woods, the widow's daughter encountered a crabby old dwarf with his beard caught in a half-split tree. The children tried to help, and after tugging away at the beard to no avail, Snow White whipped out her scissors and snipped off the end of the dwarf's beard. The ungrateful dwarf merely grumbled that she had cut off his beautiful beard and, cursing them roundly, marched off.

Not long afterwards, the maidens met the dwarf again, this time with his beard caught in his own fishing line. Once again the daughters tried to release him, and again they resorted to snipping off a bit of beard to do so. "You fool!" he raged at Snow White. "Do you want to totally disfigure me?" He muttered another curse upon them, then took a bag of pearls that appeared to belong to him and slipped behind a stone.

A few days later the girls were doing an errand for their mother when they saw an eagle swoop down out of the air, dip behind a rock, and reappear with the crabby old dwarf in his beak. The girls again came to his rescue, only to be criticized mercilessly for not being more gentle about it. With that, the dwarf went off to his cave with a bagful of precious stones.

On their way home, the maidens came upon the dwarf with his treasures spread out before him in the sun. Enraged to be caught with his stolen booty, the dwarf ranted and raved at the girls more loudly than ever before. In the middle of this, a large black bear emerged from the forest and came roaring towards the dwarf, who begged for his life and urged the bear to eat the two girls instead, as they would make a tastier meal.

The bear made short work of the dwarf with his enormous paw. As the girls ran off in fright, a voice called after them, "Snow White. Rose Red. Don't be afraid. Wait for me." They turned to see a handsome young man dressed in gold. He explained he was a prince who had been condemned by the wicked dwarf to live as a bear until the dwarf's death broke the spell.

In due course, Snow White married the prince and Rose Red married his equally handsome brother. The two couples shared the palace and all of the treasures the dwarf had collected. They invited their mother to live with them, and she brought the rosebushes that stood by the cottage door. And every year hundreds of beautiful red and white roses bloom outside the palace door.

November 8

The Boy Who Loved Bargains

Once there was a boy named Johnny who loved bargains. Johnny's favorite day of the week was Sunday, because the newspaper was filled with coupons—hundreds of dollars in savings! He loved to watch television, but when regular programming would come on he would change the channel because all he wanted to see were the commercials. Nothing thrilled Johnny more than getting a deal.

Sometimes Johnny's family worried about him. "Shouldn't he be playing baseball? Or chasing girls?" his parents wondered. His coupon collection spanned three giant file cabinets, arranged by subject, expiration date, and price. If someone was leaving for the store to buy something like shampoo or garbage bags, he would cry out "wait!" and check his data base for the very best coupon. Within seconds, he would know which store to go to and which brand to buy. When it came to saving money, Johnny was state of the art.

Johnny had an eye for bargains but sometimes he didn't think things through. Like the time his mother sent him to the store to buy some milk and bread. That day he had read in the newspaper that there was a sale on lima beans, six cans for one dollar, a very good deal! He went to the store and instead of getting milk and bread, he bought thirty cans of lima beans. But no one in his family liked lima beans. The family basement was filled with shelves and shelves of similar purchases.

One day, Johnny read that there was a big sale on televisions at Kendall's Appliances. He could get a nineteen-inch color television for sixty percent off! That sounded like a great savings. Johnny figured that if he bought three televisions he would save even more.

The store was very crowded. Everyone was standing in line to buy a television for sixty percent off. When it was Johnny's turn to make his purchase, he asked for three televisions. Instead of saving $100 on one, he would save $300 on all of them! He instructed the store to bill his parents. He was so pleased with his purchase he whistled all the way home.

But when Johnny told his parents, they were very unhappy with him. "What are we going to do with three extra televisions? We can't afford such things," they said. Johnny explained that if he had only purchased one television, he would have saved only $100. "This way, we save $300! A very good deal!" he said cheerfully. But his parents did not agree. They were afraid that Johnny's love of bargains would make them go broke.

Johnny tried to return the televisions, but since they were on sale the store would not accept them. "Oh, why did I have to buy three televisions?" he stewed. He went door to door trying to sell his televisions. He took the televisions to school and tried to sell them to his teachers. But he couldn't sell his televisions—even at sixty percent off. Then he had an idea. "I'll have a garage sale," he thought to himself. He hunted for a good price on poster board and made posters announcing the sale. He found a free classified ads circular to announce the sale. Things were looking better.

A few days before the sale, Johnny went to the storage area in his basement and began hauling items up to his driveway: thirty cans of lima beans, ten Pet Rocks, thirteen electric forks, two cases of rare tropical bird food, thirty-six rolls of glow-in-the-dark masking tape, five cassettes of Freddie and the Dreamers's Greatest Hits, seven pairs of left-handed wire clippers, and much much more. Over the years, he had purchased all of these items at very good prices but never had gotten around to using them.

The day of the garage sale arrived. People lined up to get a first look at all of Johnny's merchandise. He had arranged all of his bargains very neatly, presenting each item in a way that made it most attractive. He even wrote little descriptions of the merchandise, like "Lima beans: good in three-bean salad or warmed up with a little butter and parsley" or "Pet Rocks—for the child who has everything." People came from all over town. They enjoyed shopping at Johnny's garage sale. Even Johnny's parents seemed to enjoy themselves, especially when their friends complimented them on the variety of the merchandise and the very good prices.

In the crowd of shoppers was Mr. Kendall of Kendall's Appliance Store. He was most impressed with the way everything was priced, especially the televisions. Johnny was selling the televisions for $20 more than Kendall's Appliance Store! When Mr. Kendall went to pay for a Pet Rock and an electric fork, he asked Johnny if he would like to work at his store on weekends. "You seem to understand buying and selling in a way few grown-ups do," he said to the young boy.

Johnny felt very proud. It had been a wonderful garage sale, and so far he had sold all of the television sets and most of the merchandise from the basement. To have gotten a job offer on the same day was almost too good to be true. Johnny told Mr. Kendall he would love to work at his store. "Will I get an employee discount?" Johnny asked. Already he was thinking about making his very next deal.

—CHRISTINE ALLISON

November 9

Hansel and Gretel, Part 1

A GERMAN TALE

A woodcutter lived just outside a very large forest with his wife and two children from a previous marriage. The boy was called Hansel and the girl was called Gretel. Since there was no work and a famine besides, the family was struggling. Often at night they would go to bed hungry.

The woodcutter was overwhelmed. He didn't know how to provide for his family. His wife, the children's stepmother, said that the children must go. "I am tired of feeding those little wretches," she said. "Four mouths is two too many to feed." The woodcutter was so weary he did not argue with his wife.

The children, who were too hungry to sleep, overheard their parents talking. The heartless stepmother had devised a plan to take the children into the forest, light a fire, and give them each a piece of bread. "We'll leave the children there and they will be lost," the stepmother said with a cruel laugh. Hansel was angry and Gretel was heartbroken.

When Hansel calmed down, he reassured his sister. "Don't worry, Gretel. I have a plan as well." He crept out of the cottage and filled his pockets with white pebbles from around the house. The pebbles looked silvery in the moonlight. Hansel figured he could use the pebbles to mark a trail so the children would not be lost.

Before dawn, the stepmother woke the children and told them they were all going to the forest to collect wood. As they made their way to the very deepest part of the woods, Hansel dropped pebbles, marking the path. Once they were in the middle of the forest, their father made them a cozy fire and their stepmother gave them some bread. "Wait here, children," the stepmother said. "We are going to gather wood and we will be back in a few hours." Hansel looked at Gretel, knowing full well what was really happening. "Good-bye," they said quietly to their parents.

Hansel and Gretel ate their bread and soon became sleepy. When they woke up it was already evening, and the moonlight shone bright. With the help of the silvery pebbles, the two children made their way back to the cottage. When they arrived home safe, their father was relieved but their stepmother was furious. That night, the cruel woman made plans to abandon the children once again.

But because it was so late, Hansel did not have time to gather more of the pebbles that had served the children so well. The next morning, the father and stepmother led the children back out to the middle of the forest and, instead of pebbles, Hansel dropped breadcrumbs along the way. The parents left the children once again, but when Hansel and Gretel went to make their way back to the cottage, they were horrified. The breadcrumbs Hansel had dropped along the path had been eaten by birds. Now, truly, they were lost.

November 10

Hansel and Gretel, Part 2

Hansel and Gretel were lost. For the first time, Hansel showed some fear in his eyes. But he tried to be brave, and he took Gretel's hand and began to walk. "Surely we will be able to remember our way home," he said, not too sure about it at all. By and by the children caught sight of a beautiful golden bird, who seemed to want them to follow it. It led them to a cottage that appeared to be made of candy and cake. When they got close enough to look and taste, they took a nibble. The cottage was made of licorice, red hots, gum drops, candy canes, and gingerbread, with lots of frosting on the roof. Hansel and Gretel couldn't believe it!

They knocked on the door. Who lived in this magical cottage, anyway? The door opened and a frail old woman leaning on a cane came hobbling out. Hansel and Gretel hid the candy canes they had been eating behind their backs.

The old woman was very kind and invited the children in. She said they could eat all of the candy they wanted. She also prepared two little beds for them to sleep on. After they had had their fill of candy and cake, they snuggled into their little beds thinking all was well.

Unfortunately, the kind old lady was really a witch. And the house of sweet candies and cake was really a trap to capture the children. The witch wanted to fatten them up and cook them and eat them for dinner!

The next day, the witch told Hansel and Gretel how unlucky they were. "You foolish children thought you were saved, but instead you are doomed!" said the horrible old woman.

She locked Hansel up in her barn and forced Gretel to cook huge meals for him to plump him up. Each day the witch, who had very poor eyesight, would feel Hansel's finger to see if it was nice and fat, and each day Hansel would stick out a little bone for her to feel. Days passed and still he gained no weight. Finally, the witch was so frustrated she decided to eat him, fat or thin.

The next morning, as Gretel was making a fire in the oven, the witch announced her intention to cook Hansel that day. "Creep into the oven and see of the fire is hot enough, my dear," said the witch. Gretel did not think that was a good idea, so she asked the witch to show her what she meant. "Silly child, all I want you to do is stick your head in like this," the witch said, sticking her ugly wrinkled head into the burning furnace. Gretel gave the witch an enormous push, slammed the oven door, and then bolted it. Then she ran to the barn and released Hansel from captivity. "It's over," Gretel said to her brother. "Our nightmare is over. The witch is dead."

The two children hugged each other and then went into the cottage to get some provisions for their journey home. They discovered chests and chests of gold and jewels, and stuffed their pockets with the treasure. Loaded with riches, they were on their way.

Along the way, they came to a large body of water. Just as they were wondering how to cross it, Gretel spotted a duck. She asked the duck to help, and it obliged, carrying each child across the water, one at a time.

Once they were on shore again, the woods seemed familiar to them. Gradually, they found their father's cottage.

Their father cried and begged forgiveness for leaving the children alone in the woods. He told them that their stepmother had died several weeks before and that he had been searching for them every day. The children shared their treasure with their father, knowing that the three could now live together in peace and happiness. At last their troubles had ended.

—BROTHERS GRIMM

November 11

The Dancing Monkeys

A prince had some monkeys trained to dance. Being naturally great mimics of human beings, they showed themselves most apt pupils and when arrayed in rich clothes and masks, they danced as well as any of the courtiers. The spectacle was often repeated with great applause until on one occasion a jealous courtier, bent on mischief, took from his pocket a handful of nuts and threw them upon the stage.

At the sight of the nuts, the monkeys forgot their dancing and became (as they indeed were) monkeys instead of actors. Pulling off their masks and tearing their robes, they fought one another for the nuts.

The dancing spectacle came to an end amidst the laughter and ridicule of the audience.—AESOP

November 12

The Cat Who Married a Mouse

A GERMAN TALE

Once a clever little mouse met a cat, and the two were so pleased with each other that they decided to marry. Though the twosome were an unlikely couple, they spent a jolly spring and summer together. One day during summer, the cat said to his wife, "My dear, we must prepare for winter or we will die of hunger—and of course you, little Mousy, cannot venture anywhere for fear you will be caught in a trap." Mousy agreed, and so, the noble cat, whom Mousy called Tom, went out into the world to find their winter larder.

In a few days, Tom came back with an extraordinary treasure: a huge jar filled with meat. Mousy and Tom discussed where to hide it.

"I don't know a better place to hide it than the church," said Tom. "No one ever thinks of robbing a church."

And so the jar was carried to the church. But it did not stay there long.

Tom kept thinking about the jar and longing for a taste, so he invented an

excuse to get away from home. "Mousy," he said one day, "I've been invited by a cousin to the christening of her little son; he's a beautiful kitten, she tells me, and my cousin wishes me to be godfather."

"Oh, yes," replied Mousy. "Go by all means. But when you are enjoying yourself, think of me and bring me a drop of sweet red wine if you can."

Tom promised to do as she asked and went off as if he was going to see his cousin. But after all it was not true. Tom didn't even have a cousin.

Instead, Tom went straight to the church and located the jar of meat, and sat looking at it. He did not look long, for before he could stop himself he had licked the fatty surface of the meat and cleaned the top straight off! Then he took a lazy walk on the roofs of houses in the town and stretched out in the sun, stroked his whiskers, and thought of the delicious feast he had had.

"Oh, there you are again," said Mousy, who came upon Tom quite by accident. "Did you have a good day?"

"Yes, indeed," replied Tom. "Everything went off very well."

"Tell me, what did they name the young kitten?" inquired Mousy.

"Top-off," Tom said coolly.

"Top-off," said Mousy. "That is a curious and uncommon name."

"It is a very old name in our family," said Tom in a huff. Poor little Mousy made no reply, and for a while nothing more was said about Tom's cousins.

But Tom could not forget the jar of meat in the church, and before long he was obliged to invent another tale of a christening. So he told little Mousy that his aunt had invited him this time, and that the kitten to be christened was so beautiful that he could not refuse to be present.

"For one day, Mousy, will you do me this kindness and stay home?" Tom asked his little wife.

The good little mouse agreed and Tom ran off directly to the church. This time he feasted so greedily that when he finished the jar was more than half empty. When he returned home, Mousy asked what name had been given to the kitten this time.

Tom was puzzled to know what to say, but then at last he said, "Oh, yes, I remember. Its name was Half-gone."

"Half-gone," said Mousy. "What a strange name." But Tom ignored her remark, for now he could think of nothing but the remaining meat in the church.

But Mousy had not finished her thought. "Top-off and Half-gone are such curious names, Tom, that they ought to make one suspicious," she said.

"Oh, nonsense," Tom replied. "What can you know, staying at home all day? You know little of the world." Before long Tom had invented another christening, and when he returned from finishing the jar of meat and was questioned by poor Mousy, he snapped that the third kitten's name was "All-Gone."

Again Mousy thought it an odd name, but said nothing.

Then winter came, and it was a brutal one, and food was scarce. Mousy remembered the jar of meat Tom had hid in the church, and told him to go and fetch it.

The selfish cat told the mouse to go fetch it herself, and when she went to the church, she discovered nothing but an empty jar.

"Now I see why your little forays were named Top-Off, Half-Gone, and All-Gone," wailed the tiny mouse. "You stole all of our winter larder, and now because of your selfishness, we will both die from hunger."

"Not 'we,' " said Tom, in a rage. "For I am going to eat you." And before the unfortunate mouse could flee, the cat made a spring, seized the mouse, and gobbled it up.

Since then, it has been the world's way that cats and mice should never marry.—BROTHERS GRIMM

November 13

The Farmer and the Noses, Part 1

A BOHEMIAN FOLKTALE

There once was a very eccentric farmer who was also quite wealthy. He had a remarkably handsome daughter, named Teresa, who was admired by many of the students who attended a nearby university. So charming was Teresa and so rich was her father that many of her suitors pretended to be farmhands just to be close to the maiden and have a chance to win her heart.

The farmer, however, was shrewd and soon discovered their wily plot. For the future, he declared, he would only take servants who agreed to stay for at least a year—signified by the return of the cuckoo bird—and would permit him to cut off the tips of their noses if they became discontented. For his part, he would agree to cut off the tip of his own nose if he lost his temper with them. Amazingly, several of the university students agreed to his terms and entered his service.

Soon a student named Coranda arrived, determined to win the farmer's daughter's hand. At dinner the farmer began his usual tactics. He offered the young man nothing to eat yet smilingly inquired from time to time if he had had enough. Coranda always cheerfully replied that he was perfectly satisfied, but having no intention of starving, he reached across the table and helped himself to some bread and meat.

The farmer turned pale with anger. "Can it be that you have lost your temper, sir?" Coranda asked calmly. The farmer, realizing he had been caught, replied that no, he was perfectly satisfied.

The next day the farmer was preparing to go to church and instructed the servant to make a fine soup while he was gone. "And don't forget the parsley," the farmer said. "If the soup is not well seasoned, you'll regret it."

Coranda looked all over the garden but could not find any parsley. Then he remembered that the family dog was named Parsley, so he simply added the dog to the soup. When the farmer returned he was horrified at how fatty and foul the soup tasted. But he did not dare show his dissatisfaction.

"Where's the dog?" the farmer said. "This soup is perfect for . . . a dog." Coranda explained that since the farmer had insisted on parsley and since there was none in the garden, he was forced to use his beloved dog, Parsley, to season the soup. "If you are angry with me," said Coranda, "let me know so I may snip off the tip of your nose."

"Why, no, I am not angry. . . ." said the farmer, gritting his teeth, for he actually loved that little dog.

The next day the farmer had to go to the market. He instructed Coranda to do only what he saw others doing.

Coranda sauntered around the farm on the lookout for another chance to get even with his employer. He saw some roofers removing tiles from a building. Coranda lost no time in following their example. He got another ladder and began removing all of the shingles off the farmer's roof. When the farmer returned, he was furious, but he could not say a word. He stalked away in gloomy anger.

This sort of thing went on for some weeks. Try as he might, the farmer could not get the better of the quick-witted Coranda. Finally, the farmer consulted his daughter. What would she do if she were he?

November 14

The Farmer and the Noses, Part 2

The farmer consulted his daughter, Teresa, who thought for a moment about their predicament. Clearly, this Coranda was intent on having her for his bride. "I know," she said finally. "You told him he would have to stay until the cuckoo bird returned. Take him to the meadow behind the orchard. I will hide in the boughs and imitate the cuckoo's voice."

"You are as clever as you are handsome," her father cried with delight. Then he pretended to desire a conversation with the student and took him to the meadow. Teresa, of course, was hidden away behind some boughs.

"Cuckoo, cuckoo," she called out, so naturally that her father thought for a moment it was a real bird. As the sound reached their ears, the farmer promptly told Coranda it was time for him to leave.

"Very good, master," Coranda replied, "but this cuckoo is an early bird. I will have to have a look at her."

Before the farmer could stop him he ran to the orchard and caught sight of Teresa's dress hanging from the gnarled boughs of an apple tree, where she was hiding. He shook the tree and down she fell, into Coranda's arms.

"You dog," the farmer yelled at Coranda. "Be off at once or I will put an end to you."

"Why should I?" asked Coranda, trying to see Teresa's face, which was surely as red as an apple. "Are you angry, dear sir? It certainly was a lovely cuckoo."

"Begone," the farmer said.

"Then let me cut off the tip of your nose," replied Coranda.

"No, no, I cannot have that," said the farmer. "Take ten of my sheep and get out of our lives."

"That's not enough," said Coranda.

"Then ten cows," said the farmer.

"No, I would rather keep our agreement," Coranda said. He pulled out of his pocket a very large penknife and opened one blade. Teresa sprang forward in a cry of horror. Coranda turned to her. "Hush, dear lady," he said. "Your father may keep his nose but he must give you to me for my wife."

The farmer now forgot everything in his rage at the young man's boldness and in the midst of his storming, Teresa threw her arms around his neck and begged him not to sacrifice his nose; she was quite willing to marry this determined man.

The situation was not an easy one for the farmer but finally he admitted that his daughter had the best of the argument. And as the young man would not give up his advantage, the farmer finally gave the marriage his blessing.

The wedding was celebrated soon afterward and Coranda invited his fellow students, who came with a good grace. The farmer soon grew to like his new son-in-law and in due course was a great favorite of his grandchildren. If the grandchildren were naughty or appeared discontented, their father would threaten to cut off the tips of their noses, and then the old farmer might be seen to be tenderly rubbing his own.

November 15

The Great Turkey Roundup

If you'd lived in Millbank, you would have noticed Skip Schoonover. He thought he was a cowboy.

He walked like a cowboy, he talked like a cowboy, he dressed like a cowboy. He wore cowboy boots and a cowboy hat with a rawhide cord. His gloves were leather cowboy gloves and he had a buckskin jacket with fringe on it. Skip even had a pair of chaps, but he couldn't wear chaps to school.

There wasn't a cow within a hundred miles of Millbank.

Millbank, you see, is in New Jersey. It was just an ordinary town with a main street lined with shops and restaurants. There were two banks and four churches and a movie theater and a train station. The streets had sidewalks. The houses had big trees and big yards around them but they weren't ranches.

Except to Skip. When he was going home, he'd say, "Got to mosey back to the ranch." He called his house the Double Circle S, and he signed all his papers at school with his brand, like this: Ⓢ He called his bicycle his little cow pony, or his Appaloosa, and he had saddle bags draped over the back wheel. On his bike, Skip even had a sort of saddle that he made out of an old catcher's mitt. And he carried his lasso whenever he rode his bike on what he called a trail ride.

Skip was really proud of that lasso. He got it out in Wyoming, where he went to camp in the summer, and claimed it was a real cowboy lasso. He told us he practiced roping at home with his big white dog. "Yeah, right," we said. I guess we teased him more than we should have, but Skip was so different and he didn't seem to mind.

One Saturday morning in November we all rode our bikes to the deli on Main Street to get a doughnut. It was a cold morning, and Skip had on his cowboy gear—hat, jacket, gloves, chaps. When he walked into the deli, the guy behind the counter sang out, "Oh, give me a home where the buffalo roam. . . ."

Skip just laughed and ordered a cream-filled chocolate doughnut. We all took our doughnuts out to the side-walk and sat down on the benches. From there we could watch the traffic on Main Street, and we saw a big turkey truck come rolling along.

"He must be lost," somebody said. Nobody had ever seen anything like that in Millbank before—a great big truck loaded with cages of turkeys. They must have been on their way to the grocery store so that people could have their Thanksgiving dinners. Anyway, the turkeys were gobbling as the truck cruised down the street toward the railroad underpass.

We all realized at once that the truck wasn't going to fit.

Whoompf! The top cages hit the bottom of the underpass and there was a blizzard of feathers.

When the feathers floated down to the ground, turkeys were on the loose, flapping and fluttering all over Millbank.

"Yippee-ki-ay," said Skip, who hopped on his bike and took off after them, swinging his lasso.

He seemed to be the only one who knew what to do. The rest of us just stood there on the sidewalk, with all the people who came out of the deli and the other shops along Main Street. The turkeys went gobbling off in all directions. "Call the police!" somebody said. "Call the fire department."

But everybody just stood there and watched Skip.

He roped the first one in front of the drug store. He tied its legs together with a little piece of rope, just the way cowboys tie the steers in the rodeo, and then set off after a second one as it ran past the movie theater. Those turkeys could run fast but they weren't any match for Skip on his bicycle. He caught another one in the drive-thru

lane at the bank, and roped one under the awning of the fanciest restaurant in town. In front of the gas station Skip roped two gobblers and tied them to the gas pumps.

Most of the turkeys couldn't fly more than a few feet high, but one of them—it looked like the biggest turkey of all—had managed to flap up onto the railroad tracks. It got a running start and then it came flying down toward the deli, along Main Street. I know a turkey is just a bird, but it looked as big as a jumbo jet. We were all scrambling for cover when we heard Skip holler *"Yippee-ki-ay"* and saw his lasso flick through the air.

He roped that turkey in midair. The lasso pulled tight and thump! The big gobbler came down in a heap on the sidewalk at our feet.

Well, Skip was the town hero that day. Somebody had a video camera running the whole time, and that night they played the tape on TV stations all over the country. Maybe you watched as Skip roped those turkeys, riding his bike with no hands while he twirled his lasso.

After that, we didn't tease Skip the way we used to. As a matter of fact, a lot of the kids in Millbank started wearing cowboy boots, and some of us even got lassos of our own. On Saturdays, you can find us in front of the deli, just in case another load of turkeys comes to town.

—NICHOLAS GOODWIN AND STEPHEN GOODWIN

November 16

The Fighting Cocks and the Eagle

Two roosters lived in the same barnyard and this created a problem.

You see, roosters are not like hens. Hens like a lot of company and get along with just about any animal. Roosters want to be the only one of their kind; they want to be king of the barnyard, top dog, head honcho.

Two roosters cannot live in one barnyard happily, and so they fought.

They fought, and they fought, and they fought. Finally one day, after a knock-down, drag-out fight, one rooster triumphed.

He was so proud to be king of the barnyard that he got on the top of the barn roof and flapped his wings, crowing about his victory to all who would listen.

He crowed and he crowed and he crowed.

An eagle flying overhead heard the boasting rooster and swept down. In a single swoop, he picked the rooster up with his beak and carried him off to his nest—and then he ate him for dinner.

Now that his rival was carried off by the eagle, the remaining rooster came out of his corner. Without fanfare, he took his place as king of the barnyard. And that's how it all worked out.

Pride goes before the fall.—AESOP

November 17

Old Flea-Bag

A FRENCH TALE

Once upon a time there lived a king who had two daughters he loved greatly. But for some reason, he was unsure of them, and when they were grown he decided he would leave his kingdom to the one who loved him the most.

He called the elder princess to his chamber and asked, "How much do you love me?"

"As the apple of my eye," answered she.

"Ah, you are indeed a good daughter," exclaimed the king. Then he sent for the younger one and posed the same question.

"I look upon you, my father, as I love salt in my food," she replied.

But the king did not like her words and ordered her banished from court. She sadly packed her belongings and set off from the castle, having no idea what to do or where to go. Her pretty face, she knew, would be a hazard, so she covered herself with mud and made a tangle of her hair. Whenever she met someone on the road, she would scratch herself and wiggle about as if she were tormented by fleas.

At last she came upon a farm that sought a shepherdess. They badly needed help or they wouldn't have hired such a dirty creature, and they called her Old Flea-Bag.

One day when she was tending her flock in a lonely mountain valley, she had an urge to don her old clothing and, for just a few hours, be a princess again. She washed herself clean in a nearby stream and put on her royal robes. As luck would have it, a prince on a hunting trip passed through the valley and spotted her. She fled to the woods, and though he searched for hours, he could not find her.

The prince stopped at the farm for a drink and inquired about the beautiful maiden who was keeping their sheep for them. The farmer laughed uproariously at anyone describing Old Flea-Bag as beautiful. Thinking some sort of witchcraft was at work, the prince departed.

Still, in the months to come, he could not get the beautiful maiden out of his mind, and as he pined for her, he grew thinner and paler. His parents were greatly concerned, and as he could not tell them he had fallen in love with a woman known as Old Flea-Bag, he asked instead if they could get him some bread baked by the shepherdess on a distant farm.

This was a rather odd request, but they vowed to try. The farmer was told of the prince's desire, and Old Flea-Bag was summoned. For this task she washed herself and put on her rings, one of which fell in the dough during the kneading.

The prince found the ring as he ate the loaf of bread, and declared to his parents that he would marry the girl on whose finger the ring fit. The king issued a proclamation calling all unmarried women to the castle to try on the ring. After dozens of maidens had failed to get the ring on their hands, the prince remarked that the dirty shepherdess from the distant farm had yet to try.

Of course the ring fit perfectly, and the prince declared his intention to marry her. His parents were secretly appalled, but commented only that the girl was but a shepherdess, and a dirty and ugly one at that. At last Old Flea-Bag spoke up, announcing that she was as noble as anyone in the room, and if they gave her a few moments alone, she would prove it.

In a short time, she returned in a magnificent dress in all her beauty. She told the king and queen her sad story, and asked them to secure her father's consent for the marriage.

He, on his part, had long since repented of his harsh treatment of his daughter and was overjoyed to hear she was well. He not only agreed to the marriage but rushed to be there.

By order of the bride, her father's wedding breakfast was meat without any seasoning, and bread without salt. She asked if he was enjoying his meal. "No," he replied. "All the dishes are tasteless!"

"Did I not tell you, my father, that salt was the best thing in life? And yet, when I compared my love for you to salt, you drove me from your sight."

The king embraced his daughter, begging her forgiveness for his obstinate refusal to see how fundamental was her love for him.

November 18

The One-Eyed Man, Part 1

A NATIVE AMERICAN TALE

In times long ago, a chieftain lived with his beautiful daughter. Suitors came from near and far but the girl was never interested in marrying. The chieftain, who was getting old, was worried about how his daughter might live when he passed into the great unknown.

"Dear daughter," he said one day, "the most eligible men in the land have come and begged for your hand. Why do you refuse them?"

"Father, I am comfortable in my life as your daughter. I have everything I need, including my freedom. Why would I want to marry?"

"You are the chieftain's daughter. You *must* marry," her father said sternly.

"Father, it is time for you to hear these words: I am already pledged. When my mother died, the Sun Above claimed me and told me that though I would be courted by many eligible young men, I should never marry. If I remain true, Sun Above promised I would live to a great age."

This bargain saddened the chieftain, who had known the joys of human love. "So it must be," he sighed. And he promised to speak of it no more.

Life continued: spring to summer to fall to winter, and many seasons passed. One day, a poor young man entered the village. He was handsome and strong, but had only one eye. No one gave him room or food, and he lived alone, wandering and begging. One afternoon at a feast, the young nobles thought to play a joke. They told the One-Eyed Man about the chieftain's daughter.

"Go ask for her hand in marriage," the nobles encouraged. "She has refused all of us because we have two eyes. You must be the One-Eyed Man she's been waiting for!" Of course, this was not true, but the very thought that his deformity might have meaning filled the poor man with joy. Emboldened, the One-Eyed Man went to meet the girl. He did not know the whole village was laughing at him.

The One-Eyed Man stood patiently outside of the girl's lodge until she returned from the feast.

She arrived when Sun Above was just about to sink in the sky. She was surprised to see the One-Eyed Man there, and somewhat afraid of his appearance. Hastily, he sought to assure her.

"Do not be afraid, dear maiden. I mean no harm but have come to ask for your hand in marriage. I know how you have refused all who came before me. Unlike the others, I am a poor man and have nothing to offer but my heart and my one good eye," he said and stopped. "I am a fool. I should not be here."

The girl looked at him and her heart was moved. "My heart goes out to you, dear warrior. I have riches enough for both of us. If we marry, we will have everything," she said. She looked at him again and felt pity. "I will marry you."

Then she looked up at Sun Above. "Dear warrior," she said, "Sun Above has told me that I belong to him. You must go to his lodge and ask him for permission to marry. If he agrees, he will give you sight in your empty eye and that will be a sign. If he refuses, do not return to me."

The One-Eyed Man's face darkened. This task was beyond him. How would he find Sun Above's lodge? How does one meet with the Sun?

"Be Brave, One-Eyed Friend," the girl said gently, and turned and entered her lodge.

The One-Eyed Man looked as the great fiery ball in the sky dropped out of sight in the west. "Have mercy, Sun Above," he cried out, and began his journey to find him.

November 19

The One-Eyed Man, Part 2

The One-Eyed Man searched high and low for Sun Above's lodge, but no one knew where he lived. He asked people from other tribes, even the oldest and wisest. He asked the animals of the forest, and one night he even asked the trees. But no one knew where Sun Above lived.

The One-Eyed Man's moccasins were worn and his food was almost gone and his heart was weary. "Be brave," the girl had said. Yet he had walked for months, and still had no clue where Sun Above could be found.

That afternoon, he came upon a great mass of water. It was Forever Water, and no land appeared to be on the other side. "I have no hope or strength," the One-Eyed Man said in discouragement. "I will just lie down and die here."

But that night he had a dream, and in his dream the girl came to him on the backs of two swans and told him that Sun Above lived on the other side of the water. He woke with a start, for two swans were at his feet. When he asked if they could carry him to Sun Above, they nodded as if they had known for a long time that this day would come.

The swans took the One-Eyed Man across the water to a large island and showed him a path to Sun Above's lodge. Along the way he saw some fine bows and arrows and a shield, but he left them alone. Before long, a handsome young warrior bounded down the path and greeted the One-Eyed Man. "Who are you?" the warrior asked.

"I am the One-Eyed Man and I am looking for Sun Above."

"That's my father," the warrior said. "My name is North Star." Then a thought came into the warrior's mind. "Did you see some weapons on your way up?" he asked.

The One-Eyed Man told him he had, and the warrior was most impressed that the One-Eyed Man had not touched his property.

"I am glad that you have come," the warrior said.

The warrior introduced the One-Eyed Man to his father, who nodded approvingly when he learned that the young man had not touched his son's weapons. "My son needs a companion," Sun Above said. "Please stay with us."

Moon, who was North Star's mother, told the One-Eyed Man that he was free to roam wherever he liked except for the shore near Forever Water. "There are evil birds there, which swoop and kill. They have killed all of my sons except North Star. For the sake of Moon and Sun Above, stay away."

The young men went off and hunted every day and enjoyed each other's companionship. One day, despite the One-Eyed Man's protests, North Star wandered off to the shore near Forever Water. North Star was under attack when the One-Eyed Man caught up to him. The One-Eyed Man heard in his heart, "Be brave," and he took his bow and shot arrow after arrow until he had killed all of the birds. He supported North Star, whose leg was injured, and then took one of the dead birds to show Sun Above what he had done.

When the two boys arrived at the lodge, Moon and Sun Above were waiting for them. The One-Eyed Man handed over the dead bird and told them what had transpired.

"My son, you have done the work of a hundred warriors and I am in your debt. How can I repay you?" asked Sun Above.

The One-Eyed Man told Sun Above about the girl, and asked if Sun Above might release her to him to marry. With that, Sun Above slit open the bird and pulled out a human eye from its stomach. He blessed the One-Eyed Man and gave him his other eye.

"I have called you my son and now I know that truly you are he. Many years ago, you lost your eye to the birds at the shore, trying in vain to save the lives of your brothers. You left in bitterness to roam the world with a sleeping heart. When you met the maiden, your heart awoke, and as it was preordained that you should marry, you made your way home to complete your trial and become whole again," Sun Above explained. The One-Eyed Man was overcome to learn this truth, and fell in gratitude.

Without delay, the One-Eyed Man made his way back to the girl. There was great feasting in the village, and the two married and had many children and lived long and fruitful lives.

November 20

The Three Cranberries

A NATIVE AMERICAN FABLE

Three cranberries were living in a lodge together. They were sisters. One was green, one was white, and one was red. As it was the dead of winter, there was snow on the ground and it was getting dark. In the darkness the sisters worried, because all the grown-ups had gone on an outing and left them quite by themselves.

"What shall we do if a wolf comes?" they puzzled together.

The white one said, "If the wolf comes, I will hide myself in a kettle of boiled hominy."

The red one said, "If the wolf comes, I will hide myself under the snow."

But the green one said, "If the wolf comes I will climb the spruce tree."

Presently, some wolves did come and the three cranberries hid themselves as they had agreed. But as you can guess, only one of the three had judged wisely. The wolves immediately ran to the kettle and ate up the hominy, and with it the white cranberry. The red one was trampled to pieces by the wolves' feet in the snow. But the green one that had climbed the thick spruce tree escaped unnoticed and was saved.

November 21

The Frog King

Once upon a time, frogs lived as happily as could be in a marshy swamp, where they splashed and swam and were free of care. No other creatures bothered them, and they had to answer to no one. But some of the frogs felt this was not right. They needed a king. They needed a proper form of government.

So these frogs petitioned Jupiter, the king of the ancient gods, to send them a monarch to rule them and keep order. Jupiter laughed at their croaked request, and threw down into the swamp a great log. The frogs were terribly frightened by the huge splash the log made and all of them rushed to the bank to watch the log from a safe distance. After a time, seeing that the log did not move, a few of the bolder frogs swam out to the log and some even dared to touch it. Still, it did not move and nothing terrible happened. Then the bravest of the frogs hopped up on the log and began a merry dance. And still nothing happened. So other frogs swam out, and very soon they took to lying on the log and basking in the sun, and all went about their business as if King Log had never come amongst them.

This situation did not satisfy the frogs who had petitioned Jupiter for a king. "What kind of leader is this?" they asked. "We want a real king, one who will rule us."

Jupiter was annoyed by their complaints and decided to give these silly frogs someone they could really look up to. He sent a long-legged stork to the marsh, and for a few minutes, the frogs were thrilled. They crowded around the stork to pay their respects to their new king.

The stork looked around at the throng of frogs and began to gobble them up. Only a few escaped from his greedy beak.

"Well," said Jupiter, looking down at the scene, "they wanted a king. I just gave them what they asked for."

November 22

Why the Bear Is Stumpy-Tailed

A NORWEGIAN TALE

One day the Bear met the Fox, who was strolling along with a string of fish he had caught.

"And where did you get those?" asked the Bear.

"Oh, my lord Bruin, I've been out fishing and this is my catch," answered the Fox.

So the Bear had a mind to learn this skill of fishing and ordered the Fox to tell him how to go about it.

"Oh, it will be easy for you to learn," said the Fox. "You've only got to go out upon the ice and cut a hole. Stick your tail down into the hole and go on holding it there as long as you can. Don't mind if your tail smarts a little—that's when the fish bite. The longer you hold it there, the more fish you'll catch. Then all at once, when the fish are least suspecting it, give your tail a strong tug and pull it out."

The Bear did as the Fox instructed and held his tail a long, long time in the hole, so long that it froze fast in the ice. Then he gave it a strong pull and it snapped off short. That's why a bear goes about with a stumpy tail to this very day.

November 23

The Two Pots

Two pots, one of earthenware, the other of brass, were carried down the river in a flood. The brass pot begged his companion to keep by his side, promising to protect him.

"Thanks for your offer," said the earthenware pot, "but that is just what I'm afraid of. If you keep at a distance, I will float down safely. But if we come into contact, I will end up in a thousand pieces."

Avoid powerful neighbors. Should there be a collision, the weakest may be destroyed.

—AESOP

November 24

Thanksgiving Homework

A TALE FOR THANKSGIVING

"Why do they wear clothes like that? I would definitely die if I had to wear that kind of clothing," Brittany said to her friend Michelle, as a boy named Josh passed in front of the school. Josh's jacket was too small and was worn ragged. His jeans were a faded pink, probably a hand-me-down from his older sister. "Poor people disgust me," Michelle said. "They have no pride."

Brittany's chauffeur pulled up in front of the school, and the two girls climbed in. On the way home Brittany thought about Josh and how poor and unpopular he was. "Compared to him, I am the Queen of the Universe." Brittany's chauffeur dropped off Michelle and then drove to Brittany's house.

As she took the elevator up to her bedroom floor she reviewed her homework assignment. Her teacher, Mrs. Stevenson, had told the class to write a paper on "what you are thankful for." "Easy," thought Brittany, as the elevator bell rang and she stepped out into her huge pink bedroom. She placed her backpack on her pink-and-white king-sized bed and sat at her desk to ring for her butler, Charles. He came at once. "What may I get for you, miss?" he asked. Brittany thought for a moment and decided on a cherry soda. Then she decided to write her paper.

"I am thankful for my complete Beanie Baby collection and my 106 CDs," she wrote. "There, done," she said as Charles placed the cherry soda on her desk. Brittany didn't feel like writing about her horses or her private amusement park.

The next day, after all of the students turned in their papers, Mrs. Stevenson announced that the class would be having a Thanksgiving dinner. Each student would be assigned a Thanksgiving food to bring. Brittany was assigned cranberry sauce. "Oh, gee, I can't wait to stand in line at the grocery store," she said sarcastically. But buying cranberry sauce was the least of her troubles. That afternoon the students all got their papers back. Brittany got a 66. On her paper the teacher had written, "See me after school." "Yeah, right," thought Brittany. She was acting tough, but actually her failing grade bothered her. After school Brittany ran out the door so Mrs. Stevenson wouldn't see her and make her stay.

As she was looking for her chauffeur in the crowded parking lot, Brittany saw a piece of paper fluttering in the cool November air. It landed right in front of her limousine. She picked it up and told her chauffeur to take her to the grocery store so she could get some cranberry sauce. With nothing else to do, she began to read the paper she had found. It was Josh's Thanksgiving homework. *"I am thankful for my family and the love that we have for each other,"* the paper read. *"I am thankful that we have enough food to eat, and something to wear, and a place to live. Mostly, I am thankful that I am alive."* At the top of Josh's paper was a big 100.

The driver pulled into the grocery store. Brittany was in a thoughtful mood. When she went into the store, she saw Josh in line getting some cornbread for the Thanksgiving dinner. She started to go over and tell him she found his paper, but then she realized it wouldn't be a good time to interrupt him. He was counting out a lot of nickels and pennies, slowly and carefully, while the cashier waited impatiently. The people in line behind Josh were acting very annoyed, even though he was counting his pennies out as fast as he could. Brittany was filled with an indescribable feeling. She felt warm and a little sad, but it wasn't a bad feeling. She realized how lucky she was. For Josh, buying food for the school's Thanksgiving dinner was a hardship. He had to go through a lot to make it work. For her it was just a small bother, something to complain about. She had plenty of money and food; gosh, she even had a cook. She had beautiful clothes and she lived in a huge mansion. She had loving parents and a great friend, Michelle.

When she got home that afternoon, she decided to write a new paper: "What I Am Thankful For" by Brittany. *"I am thankful for my family and all of my friends. I am thankful for my teacher, Mrs. Stevenson, and all of my blessings: food, clothing, and my home."* When she turned in her paper, she wasn't concerned about what grade she would get. She knew she had learned something that would last her the rest of her life.

She was thinking about her Thanksgiving homework when she realized she had left off something very important. She ran back into her classroom. "Mrs. Stevenson, please may I add one more thing to my paper?" she begged. Mrs. Stevenson gave her a funny look, and then fished through the papers on her desk and handed Brittany's back to her.

Brittany had one more sentence to write. "What I am really thankful for," she put down in her best handwriting, "is to know someone as brave and special as Josh."—MAISIE ALLISON

November 25

How Indian Corn Came into the World, Part 1

A TALE FOR THANKSGIVING

Long, long ago in a beautiful part of this country, a Native American lived with his wife and children. He had very little, and he found it hard to provide enough food for his family. But though poor, he was kind and he always gave thanks to the Great Spirit for everything he received.

His eldest son, Wunzh, had a noble heart, too. He had just turned thirteen, the age when every boy in his tribe went on a special fast—eating nothing at all and drinking only water—so he could see in a vision the Spirit that would be his guide through life. Wunzh's father built him a little lodge apart, so the boy might rest there undisturbed during his days of fasting.

On the first day, Wunzh walked alone in the woods, filling his mind with the images of nature—flowers, rocks, and trees—that he might see in his night dreams. He saw how herbs and berries grew and knew that some were good for food, and others healed wounds and even cured sickness. This thought made him long to do something for his family and his tribe.

"Truly, the great Spirit made all things," he thought to himself. "We owe him our lives. But could He show us a way that we might gather our food without hunting and fishing? I must seek this knowledge from my vision."

Wunzh returned to his lodge and fasted and slept. On the third day, he became weak. He saw in his vision a young brave coming down from the sky. He was clad in yellow and green garments. On his head were pale green plumes and his motions were graceful, as if he were swaying in the wind.

"I am sent to you, Oh Wunzh," said the sky stranger, "by the Great Spirit who made all things. He knows you wish to do good for your people and that you do not seek strength in war, nor do you wish the praise of warriors. But only by overcoming me will you learn the secret."

Wunzh, though he was weak from fasting, arose and wrestled with the stranger. He fought as hard as he could, but he was weak, and the stranger kindly said, "That's all for now. I will come again tomorrow." And then he disappeared.

The next day the stranger came and Wunzh was weaker than before. But he wrestled bravely. "Have courage, my friend," said the sky stranger. "Tomorrow will be your last trial."

Wunzh was truly faint the next day, but he wrestled with the stranger and

though his body was weak, he grew strong in his mind and his will. He exerted all of his powers and finally overcame the stranger.

"Oh, Wunzh, my friend, you have wrestled nobly and met your trial well. Tomorrow I will come one last time, and you will wrestle me, and you will prevail. Then you must strip me of my garments, throw me down, clean the earth of roots and weeds, and bury me on that spot. When you have done so, leave my body on the ground. Come often to the place to see whether I have come to life, but do not let grass or weeds grow on my grave. If you do all of this, you will understand how to help your people."

Wunzh was mystified. He had come to admire and love his friend, and he did not want to see him die. But he knew he must do as the sky stranger directed, though he did not understand why.

November 26

How Indian Corn Came into the World, Part 2

Wunzh was thinking about the sky stranger's words when his father came to him and offered him some food. "Son, you have fasted long. It is seven days since you have tasted food and you must not sacrifice your life. The Master of Life does not require that."

"Father, wait until the sun goes down tomorrow. I wish to fast until that hour for a special reason," Wunzh replied.

Though Wunzh had fasted for seven days, he was beginning to feel a new power arise in him. When the stranger came, he grasped him with superhuman strength and threw him down. Finding him dead, he removed the garments and buried his friend as he had been told.

He then returned to his father's lodge and ate a meager meal. He stayed there for a long while, but he was faithful to his friend's grave, and visited it and cleared it of weeds and grass whenever it needed. Soon, to his great wonder, he saw plumes coming through the ground.

Weeks passed, and as summer drew to a close Wunzh took his father to the place. There, where the stranger had been buried, stood a tall and graceful plant with silken hair. Its stalk was covered with waving leaves and growing from its sides were milk-filled ears of corn, golden and sweet, each ear closely wrapped with green husks.

"It is my friend," cried Wunzh with joy. "It is Mondawmin, the Indian corn! No longer will we be forced to hunt so long as this gift is planted and cared for. The great Spirit has heard my voice and sent us food."

Then the whole family feasted on ears of corn and thanked the Great Spirit who gave it. It was in this way that corn came into the world.

—ADAPTED FROM HENRY R. SCHOOLCRAFT

November 27

The Rich Man's Grave

A GERMAN TALE

A rich farmer stood in his yard one day, looking with pride on his possessions. The fields were full of grain and the trees laden with fruit. With a sigh of contentment, he turned back to his house and went into the room where he kept his money chest. Suddenly he heard a voice: "Are you satisfied with all your gold and possessions, or do you still long for more? Have you taken care of the poor? Have you shared your bread with the hungry?"

The farmer's conscience answered: "I have been a hard and selfish man, never doing anything for my relatives or the poor. Were all the world in my possession, I should still have wanted more!"

As he thought this, the farmer's knees began to tremble and he had to sit down. At this moment, there was a knock on his door. "Come in," he cried, and as the door opened he saw one of his neighbors, a poor peasant who struggled to support his large family.

"I know," thought the poor man as he entered, "that my neighbor is as hard as he is rich. I do not suppose that he will help me, but my children are crying for food and I must try." So he said to the rich farmer, "My children are hungry. Will you lend me four bushels of wheat?"

The rich farmer looked at his neighbor, and for the first time a beam of pity melted his greedy heart. "I will not lend you four bushels," he said. "But I will give you eight, on one condition. You must promise to watch at my grave for three nights after my death!"

The peasant found this a troubling request, but as he was desperate, he gave his promise.

It was as if the rich farmer had foreseen what would happen, for a few days later he suddenly died and no one mourned for him. After he was buried, the peasant reluctantly remembered his promise, and at nightfall he went to the churchyard and sat himself near the grave. All was still, the moon threw her soft light over the tombstones, and only the hoot of an owl disturbed the peaceful silence. At sunrise, the peasant returned home unhurt, and the second night passed just as quietly.

When the third evening arrived, however, he felt an odd foreboding. In the churchyard he saw a stranger leaning against the wall. The man had a scarred face and sharp, piercing eyes.

"What do you want?" cried the peasant. "Are you not afraid here?"

"I want nothing," replied the man. "And I fear nothing. I am a discharged soldier, and I came to the churchyard to pass the night, for I have no other shelter."

"If you are not afraid," said the peasant, "then stay with me and watch this grave."

"Willingly," said the soldier. So they seated themselves by the grave and all was quiet till midnight. At that moment a shrill whistle pierced the stillness, and the Devil stood before them.

"Be off, you scoundrels!" he cried. "He who lies in this grave is mine and I am here to fetch him. If you do not go away at once, I will wring your necks."

"You are not my captain, Evil One," said the soldier. "So I cannot obey you. And I never learned fear. So take yourself off! We shall stay here as long as we please."

The Devil reconsidered and decided to try a bribe. He offered the men a purse of gold.

"Come now," said the soldier. "A purse is not enough. If, however, you can fill my boot with gold, we will leave the grave to you."

While the Devil went off to fetch gold, the soldier pulled off his left boot and cut off the sole, then hung it from a tombstone so that the foot was concealed in the long grass. Then he and the peasant seated themselves and waited, but not for long.

Back came the Devil with a small bag of gold. "Pour it in," said the soldier, pointing to the boot. "But I'm afraid there's not enough." And as the Devil emptied the bag, the money fell to the ground and the boot remained empty.

The Devil shook his head and left, returning in an hour with a large sack of gold. "That looks more like it," said the soldier, "but still I doubt it will fill my boot." The gold clinked as it fell, but the boot stayed empty.

"What abominably large calves you must have," cried the Devil.

"Now you insult me," replied the soldier. "Do you suppose I have cloven feet like yours? Go and fetch some more money."

The Devil left and came back with a sack so heavy that he was bent over under its weight. When the boot remained as empty as before, he became furious with rage. Just then the first beam of the rising sun appeared. With a loud yell of anger and frustration, the Devil had to flee.

And so the soul of the rich farmer was saved and the poor peasant's family hungered no more, for when he turned to the soldier to offer to divide the gold between them, the soldier had vanished.—BROTHERS GRIMM

November 28

The Frog and the Ox

An ox, grazing in a swampy meadow, set his foot among a collection of young frogs and crushed nearly the whole brood to death. One that escaped ran off to his pompous uncle with the dreadful news. "And, oh, Uncle, it was such a beast," he said, "a big four-footed beast."

"Big?" inquired his uncle. "How big? Was it as big as this?" he asked, puffing himself out to a great degree.

"Oh," said the younger, "a great deal bigger than that."

"Well, was it so big?" he asked again, puffing himself out even more.

"Indeed, Uncle, but it was," he replied. "And if you were to burst yourself, you would never reach half of its size."

Insulted, the uncle made one more attempt to puff himself out and burst himself indeed.

Do not attempt to greatness of which you have no claim.—BABRIUS

November 29

How the Parts of the Body Learned Their Place

A long time ago, the various parts of the body did not cooperate as well together as they do today. They resented the stomach. The teeth were most annoyed. All they did was chew, chew, chew away to feed the stomach. The heart was constantly pumping, and the lungs only got to slow down a little when the body was asleep. Every time the body wanted to go somewhere, the legs were forced to work. The eyes always had to be on the lookout, and only got to rest at night, and sometimes not even then. But the stomach! The stomach had a life of ease. "You live in luxury," said the other parts of the body to the stomach. "And you never do any of work. Not only do we have to do all the hard work, but we also have to minister to your needs. No longer! You can fend for yourself from now on."

They were as good as their word and left the stomach to starve. For a day or two, the other parts of the body took great delight in listening to the stomach's anxious grumbling. But after several days of no food, the other parts of the body began getting weak and soon they could barely do their jobs. They had to give in and feed the stomach, and all parts worked in harmony once more.

The other parts of the body learned their lesson and never revolted against the stomach again. But just so they never forget, the stomach occasionally growls and grumbles to keep them on their toes.

November 30

The Crow and the Pitcher

A crow was nearly dying of thirst when he came upon a tall pitcher, half full of cool, clear water. The crow leaned eagerly into the pitcher for a refreshing drink. But his beak was not long enough to reach the water. The crow was nearly wild with frustration until he thought what to do.

Beneath the windowsill where the pitcher stood were some pebbles lying on the ground. The crow flew down and picked up as many as he could carry. One by one he dropped the pebbles into the pitcher. Each time the level of the water rose a little bit higher. After many trips back and forth the crow had many pebbles. By the time he dropped them all into the pitcher, the water nearly reached the top. The triumphant crow was then able to drink his fill.

Where there's a will, there's a way.

—AESOP

DECEMBER

December 1

The Shower of Gold

A GERMAN TALE FOR ADVENT

Once upon a time there lived a poor little girl whose father and mother were both dead. The child was so poor that she had no home nor bed to lie on. The only clothes she had she wore on her back, and she had nothing left to eat but a loaf of bread given to her by a kind stranger.

Still, she was good and always believed that God would take care of her. On the day that the kindhearted person had given her the bread, she was walking along the road when she met a poor man who said to her, "Please, give me something to eat, for I am so hungry."

Immediately she offered him all of her bread, telling him, "Have this. Heaven has sent it to you."

Shortly after this she saw a little boy sitting by the roadside crying, and as she passed, the boy exclaimed, "Oh, my head is so cold! Do give me something to cover it."

Instantly the poor girl took off her own cap and gave it to the boy. A little farther on, she met another child, who said she was freezing for want of a jacket, so she gave up her own. As it grew dark, she entered the woods, intending to spend the night there. She had not gone very far before she encountered another small child, who appeared to be almost dying with cold. The good child thought to herself, "It is quite dark now. No one will see me."

So she took off all the clothes she had on, covered the poor shivering child with them, and went away. This little girl now had nothing left in the world at all. She began to cover herself with fallen leaves, when all of a sudden a golden shower fell around her from heaven. At first she thought that the stars were falling, but when the drops reached the ground, she saw they were pieces of gold. As she stood still under the golden shower, she found herself covered from head to toe with warm and beautifully fine clothes. She gathered up the gold pieces, carried them away, and shared her treasure with the poor all the rest of her life.

—BROTHERS GRIMM

December 2

The Magic Camera, Part 1

Once upon a time there was a girl named Iris. Iris was very unhappy. Her family had moved from California to New Jersey and none of the girls in Iris's new school were very friendly. But the most unfriendly person of all was a girl named Molly.

Molly was very rich and very snobby. The other girls liked her because on weekends she would take them horseback riding. Molly warned the other girls that if they were nice to Iris, she wouldn't take them horseback riding anymore. So Iris had to play all by herself. She was very lonely.

Two days before Christmas, Iris was searching all over the house for her presents. For the first time ever, she went up to the dusty, dim attic. When she looked behind an old cabinet she saw something she had never seen before. It looked like a camera, but it didn't look like her father's video camera or her mother's Polaroid camera, or even like her little brother's toy camera. It was covered with a thick layer of dust. As Iris blew the dust off this strange camera, she saw written on it, *"Be careful how you use this camera, because . . ."* The rest of the warning had been worn away.

She went to the window. The backyard was covered with snow. She pointed the camera at the snowman her father had built and snapped a picture. But when the photograph came out of the camera she was very surprised. It was a picture of the backyard on a beautiful day. Where there were icicles in the backyard, there were flowers in the photograph. She looked at the gloomy gray sky, but in the photograph the sun was shining brightly. Iris stared at the photograph. She thought it must be an old photograph that had been stuck in this strange camera.

On Christmas morning, Iris found a big box with her name on it under the tree. As she tore it open she heard a soft barking. Inside the box was the cutest puppy she had ever seen. Iris ran to get her camera. When she looked through the viewfinder she saw a little ball of yellow fur, happily wagging her tail. And that was the picture she took.

But the photograph she took showed a fully grown dog, sitting with five puppies surrounding her, happily wagging her tail. And Iris knew for certain that there was something very strange about this camera.

The next day she took a picture of her silly little brother. As she snapped the picture he stuck out his tongue and made a horrible face. But the photograph showed a handsome young man, surrounded by pretty girls, smiling sweetly. "That's my brother?" Iris thought, and fainted right onto her bed.

Could it be, she wondered, that this strange camera took photographs of the

3

future? She decided to experiment. The day Christmas vacation ended she was the first person in school. She went to the back of the room and took a picture of the fat green and yellow caterpillar. The photograph slowly came out of the camera. When Iris looked at it her eyes grew as wide as dinner plates. She was looking at a photograph of a beautiful black and purple butterfly.

In class that day Iris had a wonderful idea. Twice earlier that year someone had taken the teacher's glasses, broken them, and put them back on her desk. Iris wondered if she could use the camera to discover who had broken her teacher's glasses. When class was over that afternoon, she waited until everyone was out of the room, then took a picture of the teacher's desk. The photograph that came out showed Dan putting a pair of broken glasses on the desk. The mystery was solved. Iris left the telltale photo on her teacher's desk. But Iris didn't know that Molly had been watching her the whole time.

December 3

The Magic Camera, Part 2

Once Iris solved the broken glasses mystery, she should have been the class hero. But that is not what happened. The next day, the teacher found the telltale photograph on her desk. "Dan," she said, "please stay after class." Then she told the whole class what had happened and asked the person who took the picture to stand up. Iris didn't know what to do. And while she was deciding, Molly stood up. Iris couldn't believe it.

The whole class clapped for Molly. As Molly sat down, she looked at Iris and smiled.

Iris was very upset that Molly had taken credit for the picture, but she didn't tell anyone. Instead, she continued taking pictures with her magic camera. She took a picture of a chocolate cake her mother had just baked—and the photograph showed an empty platter with just a few crumbs. She took a picture of an empty lot down the street—and the photograph showed a new ice cream shop offering forty-five different flavors. One night as she struggled with her math homework she had a great idea. If she took a picture of the unsolved problems, maybe the answers would appear in the photograph.

But when she looked in her backpack the camera was gone! She searched everywhere, but she could not find the camera. It had disappeared. Iris started crying and couldn't stop.

In class the next day the teacher announced, "Only one person in the class got every math problem correct. And that person is . . . Molly." Iris couldn't believe it. Molly had never, ever gotten her math homework perfect before.

At recess, Iris got an even bigger surprise. As she walked towards the playground she heard Molly calling her name. She wondered what Molly wanted. Then she found out. "Look at my new camera," Molly bragged, "my father gave it to me last night."

It was the magic camera. Iris started to say something, but she knew no one would believe her. Molly tried to rub it in. "Please, Iris," she said, "I want you to take a picture of me and all my friends." The other girls all joined in.

Iris took the picture. She looked through the viewfinder. All the girls had their arms around Molly. When the picture came out, Molly grabbed it. "Hey," she screamed at Iris, "what did you do to my camera?"

Iris looked at the picture. In it, Molly was standing all by herself. Her friends had disappeared.

"I didn't do anything," Iris said. "I'll prove it. I'll take another picture." Again, all the girls gathered around Molly and Iris snapped their picture.

Molly was furious when she saw it. "What?" she screamed. Then she threw it on the ground and ran away crying.

The other girls picked it up. One of them, a girl named Lorraine, held it out to Iris. "Here," she said softly.

This was the most surprising picture of all. All of Molly's friends were at a birthday party. On a big cake was written "Happy Birthday, Iris." And in the middle of all of the girls where Molly had been standing when the picture had been taken stood Iris.

Molly didn't know what to do. That stupid camera, she thought, but she also wondered, "Am I really so . . . mean?" For the first time Molly realized how selfish she had been. Maybe, she thought, I shouldn't have been so mean to Iris. Maybe I should have let her go horseback riding with us. Maybe . . . maybe it wasn't too late to say she was sorry.

Iris was still standing with the girls when Molly returned. "Iris," she said loudly, "I'm sorry I was so mean to you. Can we be friends?"

Iris was so surprised she dropped the camera on the ground. "We can try," she said. With that Iris and Molly put their arms around each other and walked away, forgetting all about the final picture.

Lorraine picked it up and looked at it. It was the picture of the birthday party. But magically it had changed. In the picture, Molly was standing right next to Iris. And both of them were smiling happily.

—JORDAN BURNETT AND DAVID FISHER

December 4

The Bar of Gold

A WELSH TALE

Many years ago, there lived a poor working man who never knew what it was to sleep in peace. Whether the times were good or bad, he was haunted by fears of the future, and this constant worrying caused him to look so thin and worn that the neighboring farmers hesitated to give him work.

One day as he sat by the roadside with his head in his hands, a kindly doctor from the town close by stopped his carriage to ask him what was the matter.

"You seem in trouble, my good man," he said. "Tell me what I can do to help you."

Encouraged by the sympathy in his voice, Weeping John, as he was called, poured out his troubles. "If I should fall sick," the poor man finished by saying, "what would happen to my little children and my wife? Surely a more unfortunate family has never existed." Once more he buried his head in his hands while sobs shook his shoulders.

"Come, come," said the doctor briskly. "Get up at once, man, and I will do my best for you. I can see that if you do not kill worry, worry will kill you." The doctor helped the poor fellow into his carriage and told the coachman to drive straight to his mansion. When they arrived, the doctor took him to his library.

"See here," he said, pointing to a shining bar in a glass case. "That bar of gold was given to me by my father, who was once as poor as you are now. By saving and working as hard as he could, he was able to amass enough money to buy this bar of gold. By following his example and keeping a brave heart I now have a comfortable life. I no longer need this bar of gold so I am giving it to you. Now that you own it, you can be confident in the future. Do not break into it unless you truly need to, and remember, all of this whining and self-pity will get you nowhere." The worker thanked the doctor over and over, and sped joyfully home.

As he and his wife sat before the fire, John told her all the good doctor had said. "The knowledge that we have this gold, safely hidden in the cellar, will keep us from all anxiety," he explained to her.

From that day forward John was a changed man. He sang and whistled merrily as he went about his work. His cheeks filled out and his eyes grew bright. Instead of wasting time worrying, he dug and planted a little garden to feed his family and he even had enough left over to sell. The farmers who used to use him for part-time work vied to engage him permanently, and for the first time he was able to earn regular pay.

"The bar of gold has brought us luck," he would sometimes say to his wife, who held her tongue, although she was tempted to remind him that "luck" came after he stopped sitting around stewing about the future.

Long afterwards, on a summer night, as they sat on their wide front porch and watched their grandchildren play, a stranger came up the pathway and begged for coins. He was ragged and dirty, but he seemed gentle. The couple, full of compassion, invited him to rest. They gave him a good meal and some fresh clothes and when he tried to thank them, John put his hand on the stranger's shoulder.

"Friend," John said, "my family has been blessed. But once I was as poor as you seem to be and were it not for the kindness of a stranger, I would not be in this pleasant position." John went on to tell the stranger about the doctor and the bar of gold. After telling the stranger his story, he gave him the bar of gold, for it was time to pass it on.

The man, who understood the science of metals, was at first moved to tears by the kindness of the man and his wife. But upon feeling the weight of the object, he knew at once it was not real gold.

"I am astonished and grateful, but I must tell you that by its weight I can determine that this is not a bar of gold," he told the couple.

The wife took the gold bar and with the skirt of her apron began to polish it, as if to prove it was indeed gold. As she did so an inscription appeared that the couple had never before noticed. "It is less a matter of actual want," it said, "than the fear of the future that causes the unhappiness. Tread the path of life with courage and your journey will end well."

When the stranger paused there was dead silence for the old man and woman were thinking about many things. At last John offered the stranger an apology for the disappointment he must now be suffering through their innocent mistake.

"On the contrary," the stranger replied warmly. "The lesson that the bar of gold has taught me is worth more than any money you could give me. I will make a new start in life and remember that we fail through fear, and will now bear myself as a brave man should."

So saying, he said good night, and walked out into the fragrant twilight.

December 5

Fiddlers in Paradise

One day Saint Peter and Saint Paul had a quarrel at the gates of Paradise. Soon they came to blows and were fighting like ordinary apostles. In his anger, Saint Peter, the Prince of Apostles, hurled his heavy keys right at Saint Paul. He missed, and Saint Paul grabbed them and declared that from now on, he, and not Saint Peter, would be the guardian of the gates of Heaven.

As all of the fine points of the job of keeping the gates were not known by Saint Paul, he admitted many a soul who had no right to cross the sacred threshold. It was not long before the Devil himself came to the gates and yelled at him for letting in sinners. With a hurt expression on his grimy face, the Devil said he never thought he would see the day that a saint stooped to cheating a former archangel.

Among the persons that Saint Paul let slip into the dwelling place of the blessed were three fiddlers. Instead of behaving in a manner suitable to the place they had fraudulently entered, they began at once to play dance tunes lively enough to raise the dead, so to speak. Soon these musicians were surrounded by young male and female saints who quickly chose partners and began to dance, much to the indignation of the patriarchs and strict old saints. These elders went to the Lord and described the scandalous and unrestrained goings-on in Paradise.

Saint Paul, of course, was blamed for this sad state of affairs, and the Lord summoned him at once. "The keys must be given back to Saint Peter," commanded the Lord. And Saint Paul was further ordered to cast the three fiddlers out of Paradise.

Saint Paul now had a dilemma. He could not throw the fiddlers out by brute force since it was a rule that once inside the pearly gates, a soul, although it could leave of its own free will, could not be forced to depart.

The disorder in Heaven was continuing for the fiddlers had never left off fiddling. So long had they played that soon they would wear out their violin strings and bows. This presented Saint Paul with a solution. He summoned a herald, and placing him a little way outside the Heavenly gates, ordered him to beat on a drum and announce that he had for sale a good supply of strings, two dozen bows, and a large stock of rosin. He was also to declare that his prices were most reasonable and invite all to come outside the gates and inspect his merchandise.

When they heard this announcement, the fiddlers leaped with joy and rushed out the gates. They bought everything in sight, but when they tried to reenter Paradise, Saint Peter slammed the gates in their faces. And forevermore, he turned a deaf ear to both the fiddlers and the crowd of young saints who begged him to let the joyous musicians enter Heaven again.

December 6

THE FEAST DAY OF SAINT NICHOLAS

The Three Purses

Once there lived a nobleman and his three beautiful daughters. The nobleman had lost his fortune and as it was the custom for a bride to bring a dowry to her marriage, the father feared his daughters would never wed. By chance, the nobleman lived near the residence of Nicholas, the Bishop of Myra. Nicholas had an enormous heart. Each morning, before the city was awake he would go to his chapel to pray. He would pass the poor nobleman's home and see him, head in his hands, unable to sleep. The bishop felt the father's misery as if it were his own, and so one morning, when no one was looking, he crept to the open window and threw a silken purse into the bedroom. It fell gently on the bed of the eldest daughter.

When the daughter discovered the purse, she rejoiced, for it was filled with gold. She used the gold for her dowry and thus was able to marry the young man she loved.

A few nights later, when no one was looking, the bishop crept to the open window and this time threw a purse onto the bed of the second daughter. When she discovered the purse and its contents, she wept with joy and soon thereafter married the young man she loved.

The nobleman was overwhelmed with the mystery and joy of it all, and was so grateful that he decided to wait through the night to see if he could discover his benefactor and thank him.

When the Bishop of Myra came with a silken purse of gold for the third daughter, the nobleman ran to meet him. He nearly had to wrestle Nicholas to the ground, so intent was the bishop on remaining unseen. Catching him by his robe, the nobleman said, "Is it you Nicholas, Bishop of Myra? Why do you hide yourself thus?"

Nicholas was so confused and discomforted that his good deed had been discovered that he begged the nobleman to tell no one what had happened. But Nicholas's good deeds reached many people, and though he wished to remain unknown, his generosity became such a force in his time that people believed he was a saint. Good deeds last forever. Centuries later, Saint Nicholas continues to bring a mysterious joy to humankind.

—ADAPTED FROM WILLIAM S. WALSH

December 7

Belling the Cat

A family of mice and an old cat lived in a farmhouse quite peacefully. It was peaceful because the cat was too old to make much of a fuss over the mice, so the mice had the run of the place.

Then one day the cat died and the farmer brought in a new cat, who was young and fit and very mean. Things changed. The mice panicked. they called a meeting.

"What are we to do?" asked the oldest mouse, who considered himself far too old to handle this new development. "We can't live in constant fear of this monster's claws. Why, I used to take my constitutional whenever I darn well pleased, now I dare not stir!"

Many ideas were discussed but all of them fell flat.

Then the very youngest mouse rose to speak.

"I have an idea," she said. "It seems simple but I do believe it would work. All we have to do is hang a bell on the cat's collar. Then whenever we hear the tinkling of the bell, we would know at once that the cat is coming."

The mice, especially the older ones, were surprised they had not thought of that before. They started to rejoice at the excellent plan.

Then the old mouse made a comment. "The plan of the young mouse is excellent, but a question remains: who will bell the cat?"

An idea is not worth much if it can't be executed.—AESOP

December 8

The Fisherman and the Moor

The fisherman was not a poor man; indeed, he caught enough fish each day to make a good wage. He lived in a good house and had a comfortable life. But he knew that not everyone in Spain was so lucky, and so every feast day he would go into the poor parts of the city and find someone in need. He would take the poor man home, and give him clothing and good food and comfort.

One Christmas Eve, the fisherman was scouring the street for a poor wretch and he spied a thin, bedraggled Moorish slave. Though the Spaniards and the Moors were sworn enemies, the fisherman asked the slave's master if he could take him home for just one day. The master agreed and so the fisherman took the Moor home.

At his home, the fisherman gave the Moor clothes to wear and a meal fit for a king. The Moor could not believe his good fortune and could only babble his thanks. When the fisherman went to return the slave to his master, the Moor looked deeply into his eyes and then bowed.

Twelve months later, the fisherman was out at sea and captured by some Moorish pirates. At first the fisherman feared for his life, then he realized he was going to lose something just as precious: his freedom. As it happened, the pirates were slave traders, and the fisherman was one of dozens who were to be taken to the auction block and sold into slavery. One Moorish master after another came up and examined the fisherman, kicking him, pulling his chains, and viewing him with contempt. Before he knew it, he had been bought and loaded on a wagon with a host of other slaves.

When the slaves were checked into their quarters, their Moorish master came to greet them. The well-dressed Moor walked directly to the fisherman.

He stared into his eyes and bowed down.

"Did you take in a Moorish slave a year ago, and feed him and clothe him and give him comfort for a day?" the master asked the fisherman.

"I did," replied the fisherman, "but who are you?"

The Moor explained that he had been the slave and that he had been ransomed by his family. The Moor had returned home just a few months before and now was a wealthy master. "But one good turn deserves another," he said. "I will arrange to have you freed and shipped home. Just remember not to go to sea again. Our pirates will capture you and I will be unable to help."

The fisherman heeded his friend's advice and stayed at home for the rest of his days.

December 9

Hanukkah at Valley Forge, Part 1

A TALE FOR THE JEWISH FESTIVAL OF LIGHTS

Head down and deep in thought, Judah trudged the snowy path towards home. The icy wind tore at his scarf and tingled his face and fingers, but he was unconscious of the cold. For in two days the Hanukkah Festival would begin. And this was the third season without Father.

His mind flashed back to that morning in April when Father had burst in upon them in the kitchen. Word had just reached Philadelphia of the Battle of Lexington. Judah was only nine then. He wondered why his mother was crying. Father gathered his things hastily, held the family close to him for a long moment, snatched up his rifle, and was gone. Mother explained that all the patriots were joining the Continental Army to fight for liberty.

And now that same army, and Father with them, were at Valley Forge, such a short distance away. A furlough was out of the question because the Red Coats were all over Philadelphia.

What could he do? He kicked at the crusted snow. There would be some satisfaction in celebrating in the midst of the enemy. Almost like throwing defiance in their teeth—and King George's, too! Perhaps King George wasn't as wicked as Antiochus, the Syrian whose soldiers had captured the Temple and tried to force the Jewish people to worship heathen idols, but he was a tyrant just the same. As Patrick Henry had said, "He'd better profit by example."

Judah's chest swelled. If the war wasn't won soon, King George would have him to reckon with. His name wasn't Judah for nothing. He was indeed a Lion—and a Maccabee! If only he could be a drummer boy! But Mother wept when he mentioned it.

He was all she had—her twelve-year-old man of the house.

He was almost home when the idea came. He would take the lamp to Father—then all the Jewish soldiers could enjoy Hanukkah. It would be a long day's walk to Valley Forge, but he could do it. What about the sentries? If he carried the lamp boldly, right out in full sight, they might think he was visiting somewhere. But this year Hanukkah fell on the same day as Christmas. It would rouse suspicion to reach the camp then. He would wait until after the Sabbath and Sunday. If he left very early Monday morning he would get there at sundown, in time for the fifth light.

Here was his gate! He opened it and stamped off the snow as he walked up the steps. Lifting his chest, he opened the door.

December 10

Hanukkah at Valley Forge, Part 2

On Monday, December 26, 1777, at Valley Forge a ragged sentry paced his post. Stooping to adjust the rags that bound his one foot, he wondered what it would like to be warm, really warm, again. The last rays of the sun had disappeared, and the still cold bit through his very bones. The British soldiers were warm and snug in his town, only twenty miles away. He thought longingly of home. A single star came out. "Tonight they will be lighting the fifth candle, Esther and the boy," he said to himself. "These lights we light because of the miracles, mighty deeds . . ."

Miracles and mighty deeds! They had won that first great fight of the Jews for religious freedom almost two thousand years ago. How this struggling new nation needed them now. It was hard for men to feel heroic when their stomachs were empty and their bodies cold.

Suddenly, he was alert. Shadows were coming near and he could hear feet crunching through the snow.

"Halt! Who goes there?"

The spokesman was one of their own men. He carried a large bundle wrapped in his own torn coat.

"It's a boy, sentry. We found him in a snowdrift. We're taking him to the nearest cabin."

As they turned to go, the bundle stirred. "The lamp. Where is the lamp?" a weak voice said.

The sentry's heart skipped a beat. Judah's voice? His son? What had happened? He pulled back the ragged coat that covered the figure.

The boy's eyes opened. "Father? Oh, Father! The lamp—where is it?"

Strength came back to Judah and he struggled to his feet as his father clasped him roughly. "My son, oh, my son!"

In the excitement that folllowed the father explained to the soldiers that the boy had brought him the lamp for the special Hanukkah service.

One of the soldiers volunteered to see if the officer of the day would allow an exchange of sentries. At any rate, they would keep the boy safe until his father was free. The group moved on again with the boy.

Halt! Officers! General Washington himself was making the rounds.

The general listened quietly. "Let the boy come with me. I will order the exchange of sentries. The officer will understand. Tell the father to come to my quarters." He turned to Judah. "So it's come—the feast of the Maccabees?"

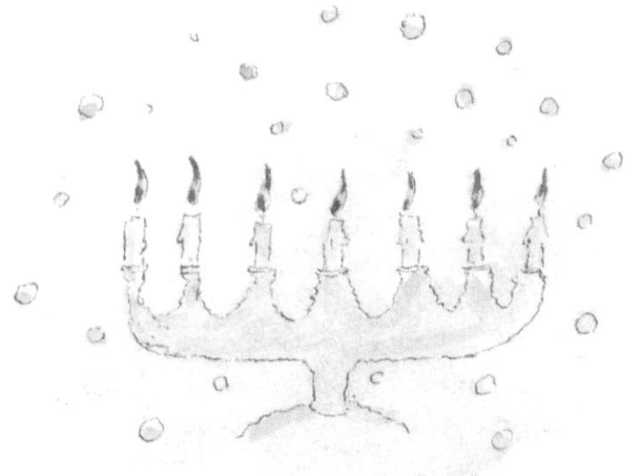

Judah nodded weakly as he followed the general inside.

Before long his father came in with the lamp, which had been found, one branch thrusting out of a snowdrift where Judah had fallen.

The boy forgot his twelve years and threw his arms around his father. The story poured out in a heap of words. "It had been so long, Father. And I thought all the Jews in camp could celebrate Hanukkah with you so I brought the lamp."

The father looked at General Washington. This was unheard-of behavior. But the general recognized the boy's spirit. "It's all right, man. He's a son to be proud of. We are all Maccabees here. This boy, too."

Judah looked at the general with wonder in his eyes. "Do you know about it sir? How Judah drove the tyrant from the land and cleansed the temple? And how the Maccabees threw down the idol?"

Washington nodded. "Yes, Judah. And we have a temple to cleanse today—the Temple of Liberty. It is that for which we are fighting. Please God we shall soon rekindle its lamp, the light of Freedom. Do go with your father. We must be about our duty."

The father saluted his chief, and the father and son went out together.

—EMILY SOLIS-COHEN

December 11

The Golden Bird, Part 1

In olden times there was a king who had a beautiful pleasure garden behind his palace. In that garden there was a tree that bore golden apples. The king was very proud of this tree, and when it was time for the apples to ripen, he posted guards at the tree each night to make sure none were stolen. But the sentries did not do a very good job, and one morning an apple was missing. So the king, who had three sons, sent his eldest to guard the tree.

But the prince fell asleep, and the next morning another apple was gone. The second son also dozed off and failed to catch the apple thief. The king had little hope his third son would fare any better, but here he was wrong. For the third son stayed awake and discovered that the apples were being plucked from the tree by a bird with golden feathers.

When he told his father, the king said, "That rascal is none other than the Golden Bird that was stolen long ago from my garden. He must be found!" The king summoned his eldest son and sent him out in search of the Golden Bird. The eldest son had great confidence in his own cleverness and thought this an easy task.

When he had gone some distance, he encountered a fox, whom he thought to shoot. "Do not kill me!" cried the fox. "If you spare me, I will give you some good counsel. This evening you will come to a village in which stand two inns. One is brightly lit and merry, but do not enter it. Spend the night in the other inn, even though it is very dingy and plain."

"Why should a wise fellow like me take advice from a silly beast?" thought the eldest son and shot at the fox anyway. But he missed, and the fox ran in the woods. Soon the son came to the village and decided he would be a fool to pass the night in the shabby inn. So he stayed at the lively one, and was so entertained by the revels there that he totally forgot about his father and the Golden Bird.

When some months had passed, and the eldest son had not returned, the king sent the second son out. Like the eldest, he encountered the fox and had soon joined his brother in idle amusements at the cheerful inn. The youngest of the king's sons, in contrast to his brothers, was modest and good-natured. When he took up the quest for the Golden Bird and met the fox, he said, "Be easy, little fox. I will do you no harm and will follow your advice."

The lad stayed the night at the shabby inn, and when he left the next morning, he again encountered the fox, who said to him: "I will tell you further what you have to do. Straight ahead lies the castle of a king who has your father's bird. In front of the castle, you will find a regiment of soldiers, but they will give you no trouble for they will all be asleep. Go straight through their midst into the castle and you will come to a chamber where the Golden Bird sits in a plain wooden cage. Close by, you'll see an empty gold cage that is very splendid. But that cage is all for show, and do not be tempted to put the Golden Bird in it."

When the son arrived at this castle, he found everything as the fox had described. But when he found the bird and saw the golden cage, he thought, "It would be absurd to leave this beautiful bird in this common and ugly cage." As he put his hands on the bird to move it, the bird gave a shrill cry, and the soldiers awoke and rushed in. The lad was dragged off to prison, and the next morning he was taken before a court of justice and sentenced to death.

The king of the country, however, decided to spare his life if he could bring him the Golden Horse that was known to run faster than the wind. In that case, he would also reward him with the Golden Bird. The son agreed to this bargain, but set off with a heavy heart, having no idea where the Golden Horse was to be found. In a short while, he met his old friend the fox, who scolded him. "This has happened because you did not heed my advice. But I will help you once more and tell you how to find the Golden Horse." At this, the son rejoiced and promised to obey the fox.

December 12

The Golden Bird, Part 2

The fox gave the youngest son directions to the kingdom where he would find the Golden Horse, but warned him not to use the lovely golden saddle that would be hanging in the stables. But, of course, the son could not resist the splendid saddle and was captured when the Golden Horse's neighing woke the guards. This time his life was spared on the condition that he travel to a distant country and rescue the Golden Princess. The king claimed she was his promised bride.

When the son departed, the fox was waiting for him in the middle of the road. "I ought to leave you to the consequences of your disobedience," said the fox. "But I pity you and will help you out of your trouble once more." He told the son that the princess walked from the castle to the bathing house each night. If the son could catch her then and kiss her, she would follow him anywhere. "But do not allow her to say good-bye to anyone in the castle," warned the fox.

Simple enough advice, but the son forgot it as soon as the princess tearfully begged to say farewell to the king there, her guardian. Once more, the youth found himself in prison, but the king was willing to let the Golden Princess leave with him if he could get rid of the hill that spoiled the view from the castle. "And you must finish your work in eight days," added the king.

The son began digging and shoveling at the hill at once, but after seven days, he could see that his task was hopeless. On the evening of that seventh day, the fox reappeared. "You probably don't deserve my help, but I have taken a liking to you. Lie down to sleep and I will finish the job."

The next morning the hill was gone, and the king had to turn over the Golden Princess to the son. They set forth at once and the fox joined them. When the princess heard she was to be the bride of the king with the Golden Horse, she began to weep. She was not promised to him, she said, and she wanted to go home with the king's son. And besides, the Golden Horse was hers, for that king had stolen it. The fox said, "If the princess chooses you, yours she must be. Let us go and recover the Golden Horse. You will have to trick the king. Thinking that he has the princess in his power, he will bring out the horse. Jump on it at once, grab the princess by the hand, swing her up on the horse, and gallop away. No one will be able to catch you."

All went as the fox had planned and now only the Golden Bird remained. The fox had a similar trick up his sleeve. "Ride into the castle yard with the horse and they will carry out the bird in his cage. Seize the cage and gallop away." This scheme, too, was a success, but as the son was about to leave for home with his treasures, the fox made his farewells. "I must part company with you now, but here is some final counsel. On your way home, do not sit at the edge of any well and do not help any thief or other criminal escape his punishment."

This was somewhat puzzling advice, but it wasn't very long before the prince came upon a hanging that was about to take place. The criminals were his two brothers, who were to be hung for their many thoughtless, evil deeds. The prince could not leave his brothers to die, so he paid their fines and they all rode off together. That afternoon, they came to a well in the woods and the older brothers suggested they rest there. No sooner had the youngest sat down—forgetting again the fox's warning—than his brothers pushed him into the well, and took off with his treasures and the princess.

Once they reached home, their father believed their many lies and the princess had been threatened with death if she told the truth. Fortunately for her, her prince had fallen into a well that was empty and filled with soft moss, and his friend the fox was nearby. The fox rescued the prince, but warned him that his brothers were on the watch for him just in case he escaped. He got the prince to switch clothes with a humble woodcutter and told him to stay in this disguise till he was safe in his father's presence.

It must be said that at the castle gates, the prince considered what a shame it was that he was arriving home in shabby clothing. But for once he heeded the fox's advice and no one recognized him as he made his way into the castle. Only the princess knew it was her beloved and the sight of him gave her the courage to tell the king of the elder brothers' foul deeds.

The king summoned the man in ragged clothes and, as the princess embraced him, rejoiced to find it was his youngest son. The wicked brothers were cast out of the kingdom, the prince married the princess, and the fox. . . . Well, every now and then he stopped in to see them, and, from time to time, even offered the prince his advice.

December 13

Prince Cherry, Part 1

A FRENCH TALE

Once upon a time there was a king who led so noble and praiseworthy a life that his subjects called him the Good King. One day, as he was hunting in the woods, a white rabbit being pursued by his hounds threw itself into his arms. The king was surprised, but told the little creature, "Since you have come to me for protection, I shall see that you are well cared for."

He took the rabbit home to his palace and ordered a hutch built for it, and that night, when he went to his chambers, a beautiful lady appeared to him. "I am the Fairy Candide," she said. She explained that she had heard of his reputation for goodness and had taken the form of a rabbit to see if he was as kind to dumb beasts as he was said to be to people. "You deserve to be called the Good King," the fairy said. "And I will always be your friend. You have only to ask what you most desire and, if it is in my power, I shall grant you that wish."

"Madame," said the Good King, "I have but one son, my beloved Prince Cherry. I wish for you to become his friend and protectress."

"Willingly," replied the fairy. "I can make him the handsomest, the richest, or the most powerful prince in the world. Which gift do you choose for him?"

"None of these, for I want you to make him the Best of All Princes. What use would riches or beauty be if he were wicked in heart? You know, Madame, that goodness alone can make him happy."

"You have chosen well," said the Fairy Candide. "But I cannot make Prince Cherry a good man. That is something each one must do for himself. All I can promise you is to give him good advice. I can point out his faults to him and punish him if he does not correct his wickedness."

The Good King was content with this promise, and shortly afterwards he died, leaving his throne to his beloved son. It was not long before the Fairy Candide appeared to Prince Cherry. "I promised your father I would be your friend, and so I have brought you a present." She put a gold ring on his hand and continued, "Take great care of this ring. Whenever you are about to do something wrong, it will prick your finger. Should you ignore the ring's warning, you will lose my friendship." And as suddenly as she had appeared, the fairy vanished. Prince Cherry would have thought her a dream, except the ring on his finger was very real.

For some time, he was so wise and good that the ring did not prick him at all. But one day he was in a bad humor, for his hunting trip had been a failure. When he returned to his chamber, his dog ran up to greet him, and began licking his hand and jumping on the prince. When the dog would not stop, Prince Cherry lost his temper and kicked him. Instantly, the ring pricked him, and he heard a voice that told him, "You have been guilty of three faults today: bad temper, anger, and cruelty. See that you do better tomorrow."

The prince, humbled and ashamed, promised to correct his faults, and for some time he kept his word. Still, he had always believed that a king could do anything he chose, and when he found that he, the king, had to learn to deny himself and govern his temper, it annoyed him. He began to do many a wayward, willful thing, and in this he was encouraged by some of his companions, especially a wicked foster brother. Only his former tutor, Old Suliman, dared still tell him of his faults.

Soon the ring was pricking him very often. Sometimes he stopped at its warning, but more often he did not. He insisted more and more on having his own way, and cared not how unjustly he treated those beneath him. He banished Old Suliman from court, and after that the ring annoyed him constantly. He lost all patience with its warnings, and wanting to be free to do as he chose, he flung it into the trash. Now he thought he would be the happiest of men, but oddly, the freedom to do whatever he wanted only seemed to make him more and more miserable.

December 14

Prince Cherry, Part 2

One day Prince Cherry encountered a young girl watching her sheep near his castle, and she was so beautiful that he fell in love at once and resolved to make her his wife. Being accustomed to getting everything he wanted, he was greatly astonished when he proposed to the maiden, whose name was Zelia, and she refused him. "Sire," she said, "you are most handsome, but I would be miserable with you. You make everyone obey your every will, and are most bad tempered."

At this Prince Cherry flew into a rage and had his guards carry Zelia off to his dungeon. It must be said that his conscience troubled him over this for a short while, but his foster brother convinced him that it was a disgrace for a humble shepherdess to defy him. That night the Fairy Candide appeared before him. "Prince, my counsel you have despised, my ring you have cast away. You have still the outward appearance of a man, but in your heart you are no better than a beast—a lion in fury, a serpent in vengefulness, a bull in stubborn willfulness, a wolf in ferocity. Bear henceforth in your outward form the likeness of all these animals."

To his horror, Prince Cherry found himself transformed into the monster the fairy had decreed. He had a lion's head, a bull's body and horns, a wolf's feet, and a serpent's tail. He was transported to the banks of a stream, where he could see the reflection of his ugly form, and heard a voice that said, "Look at thyself and know that the ugliness of thy body but expresses the ugliness of thy soul."

The prince dashed off into the forest, but almost at once fell into a pit dug by hunters. When they came by, they were delighted to have caught such a peculiar beast and dragged him off in chains to the capital of his own kingdom. There the prince could hear great rejoicing, for his subjects believed he had been stuck by a thunderbolt and they were free of his tyrannical rule. Suliman, his old tutor, had taken over his throne, but only as viceroy. The wise Suliman told the people that Prince Cherry would one day return to rule them when he was once again the good man of his youth.

Suliman's words touched the poor beast deeply and he quietly allowed the hunters to take him to the menagerie. The time had come when he was ready to admit that he deserved all that had happened to him, and he resolved to amend his ways, starting with being obedient to the keeper who cared for him. This was no easy task, for the man often treated the animals cruelly. One day, a tiger broke loose from his cage and sprang upon the keeper. For a moment, Prince Cherry was thrilled by the idea of revenge, but he quickly put that thought out of his head and wished he was free to help the keeper. With this good wish, his cage door swung open and Cherry saved the man from the tiger. As the man patted him in thanks, a voice was heard to say, "Good actions are always rewarded," and Cherry was transformed from a monster into a pretty little dog.

The zoo keeper eventually took him to the queen of a neighboring kingdom, who kept him as her favorite pet, and Cherry would have been well content were it not for thoughts of Zelia. It happened that a few days later, a young maiden was dragged from the palace gardens by a group of ruffians and Cherry saw it happen. Try as he might, there was not much a small dog could do to rescue her. "Ah, the wickedness of these men," he thought. "And yet did I not do the same thing to Zelia?" At that moment, he heard the voice in the air repeat, "Good actions are always rewarded," and suddenly Cherry took the form of a beautiful white pigeon.

The first use he made of his wings was to take flight in search of Zelia. Over many countries he flew until he came to a barren desert. There, in a cave, he found the lovely Zelia, who had taken refuge with a hermit. Cherry joyfully flew to her shoulder and perched there, using every means in his power to show her how happy he was to find her. Zelia was charmed by the gentleness of the little bird who seemed devoted to her. "Hast thou come to stay with me?" she asked. "Then I shall love thee always."

"What hast thou done, Zelia?" cried the hermit, for as she spoke the white pigeon vanished and in his place Prince Cherry appeared. And the hermit's white beard and ragged clothes also changed—into the lovely form of the Fairy Candide. "Prince," said she, "you regained your true form when you lost the last of the traits that made you beastlike and so won Zelia to pledge you her faith. She has always loved your true nature and now you shall live happily together for all time."

They were instantly transported back to Cherry's kingdom, where they reigned for many years, and the Fairy Candide restored to Cherry the valuable ring he had cast away. But it is said that he ruled so justly the ring never had to prick him again.

December 15

The Little Snow Maiden, Part 1

A RUSSIAN TALE

There was once a good man named Peter who lived with his wife, Anastasia, in a village at the edge of a forest in Russia. Though there was much happiness in their lives, they greatly regretted that there were no children in their home. The woman never had to run to her door and check to see that her little one did not wander away, because she had no little one. So Peter and Anastasia would stand at their window and watch the neighbors' children, and wish with all their hearts that one of these was their own.

One day they saw the little ones in their sheepskin coats playing in the snow. They made snow forts and threw snowballs, and rolled the larger snowballs into a snow woman, which they adorned with a kerchief and shawl. "Now there's an idea, wife," said Peter. "Let us go out and make a little snow girl. Who knows? Perhaps she will come alive and be a daughter to us."

"It's worth trying, at least," said Anastasia. And out went the two in their big coats and fur hats to their backyard, where no one could see them at work. They poured their hopes and dreams into building one of the loveliest little girls ever seen. Only towards evening, when the sky was opal and smoke colored, and the clouds lay purple on the edge of the earth, was she finished.

"Oh, speak to us, little white pigeon," cried Peter.

"Yes, speak, my darling," said Anastasia. "And run and laugh like the other children!"

Suddenly, in the twilight glow, the little maid's eyelids began to quiver, a faint blush bloomed on her cheeks, and her lips parted in a smile. All at once she skipped from her place and began dancing in the snow and laughing gaily.

"God be thanked!" said Peter. "Now we have a little girl to live with us! Run, wife, and fetch a blanket to keep her warm." She did as he said, and Peter wrapped her in it and carried the little maiden into the house.

"You must not keep me too warm," she warned. So Peter put her gently down on a bench farthest from the stove, and she smiled up at him and blew him a kiss. Anastasia got her a

little white fur coat, and Peter went to a neighbor's and bought her a white fur cap and a pair of little white boots with white fur around the tops. But when she was dressed, the snow maiden cried, "It is too hot here in the cottage. I must go out into the cold."

"Nay, little pigeon," said Anastasia. "It is time I tucked you up warm in bed."

"Oh, no!" cried the snow maiden. "I am a little daughter of the Snow. I cannot be tucked up under a blanket. I will play by myself in the yard all night." And out she danced into the cold.

Over the gleaming snow she tripped, down the silver path of the moonlight. Her garments glittered like diamonds and the frost shone about her head like a crown of stars. For a long time, the man and his wife watched her. "God be thanked for the little girl that has come to us," they said again and again.

In the morning she ran into the cottage with shining eyes. "This is porridge for me," she exclaimed, and showed the good woman how to crush up a little piece of ice in a bowl, for that was all she would eat. After breakfast, she ran outside and joined the other children at play. How the children loved her! And Peter and Anastasia were very proud.

Thus it went all through the winter. The little snow maiden was forever singing and laughing, and she was very good, too. She did everything Anastasia told her, only she would never sleep indoors. They were all very happy until signs of spring began to appear. The snow started to melt and tiny green shoots sprang up in the forest. The snow maiden seemed to be drooping and longing for something. What could be wrong with her?

December 16

The Little Snow Maiden, Part 2

Peter and Anastasia soon found out what troubled their little girl. She came to them one day and said, "Time has come when I must go, to my friends of Frost and Snow. Good-bye, dear ones here, good-bye. Back I go across the sky!"

At this, Peter and Anastasia began to weep loudly. "Ah, my darling, you must not go," cried Peter, and he ran and barred the door, while Anastasia put her arms about her darling and held her close near the stove. "You shall not leave us!" they said. But even as Anastasia held her tight, she seemed to melt slowly away. At least there was nothing left but a pool of water by the stove with a white fur coat, cap, and boots lying in the puddles.

Peter and Anastasia wept for hours, thinking they should never see her again. Anastasia carefully laid away the garments she had left behind, and often through the summer she took out the little fur cap and coat to kiss them and think of her darling.

But when winter had come agian, it happened one starlit night that the two heard a silvery peal of laughter just outside the window.

"That sounds like our little snow maid!" cried Peter, and off he hurried to open the door. And sure enough, into the room she danced, her eyes as shining as ever, and she sang, "By frosty night and frosty day, your love calls me here to stay. Here till spring I stay and then, back to frost and snow again!"

So Peter and Anastasia clasped the little snow maid in their arms. She put on her pretty white clothes again, and soon she was out playing in the gleaming snow, her garments glittering like diamonds.

Each springtime, off she went northward to play through the summer with her friends on the frozen seas, but every winter she stayed with Peter and Anastasia. In time, they came not to mind her going quite so much, for they knew she would come again.

December 17

The Rhinoceros and the Dromedary

A FRENCH FABLE

A strong young rhinoceros said one day to a camel, "Please explain, dear friend, why fate treats me so unfairly! You camels have a blessed life. That creature called Man, whose strength all lies in his cleverness, seeks your companionship, houses you, cares for you, shares his own bread with you, and thinks himself the richer as long as your number increases. Of course, I know that you lend your back to carry his burdens, his wife and children; and I admit willingly that you are swift-footed, gentle, steady, and indefatigable, but I am capable of the same virtues. I even think, if I may speak without offending you, that my brothers and I have much more to offer. Our horns and thick skin would be of good service in battle. Nevertheless, Man hunts us down, despises us and hates us, and forces us to flee from him."

"My friend," replied the camel, "do not be envious of our lot. It is easy enough to serve Man, but the hard task is to please you. You wonder why he prefers us to you, so here is the secret: we camels are humble. We have learned to bend the knee."

December 18

Snow White and the Seven Dwarfs, Part 1

A lovely queen pricked her finger with a needle while she was sewing by the window. Three drops of blood fell on the snowy white linen in her lap. The image caused her to dream. She thought to herself, "I wish I had a daughter with lips as red as blood, skin as white as linen, and hair as black as the ebony picture frame."

Before long, the queen's wish was granted and a beautiful baby girl was born to her. She named the child Snow White. Soon after the baby was born, the lovely queen died and the king married again. The new queen was beautiful but she was also vain and cruel. Each day she would look into the mirror and say, "Mirror, mirror, on the wall, who's the fairest of them all?" Usually the mirror replied, "You are the fairest one of all."

But one day the mirror answered that Snow White was the "fairest one." Furious, the queen instructed one of her hunters to take Snow White into the forest and kill her. She asked that Snow White's heart be brought back in a jeweled box to prove that she was dead.

The hunter could not bear to harm Snow White, so he told her to run off into the woods and to stay far away from the castle. On his way back to the castle, he killed a young boar and put its heart in a jeweled box. He gave this to the queen and she was delighted, thinking now that Snow White was dead.

Alone and afraid in the forest, Snow White searched for a safe place to sleep. She caught sight of a cottage that looked so inviting that she went up to it. She found the door unlocked. Inside, she saw that there was seven of almost everything: a little table set with seven knives and forks, seven bowls, seven mugs, and upstairs, seven little beds, side by side.

Snow White was exhausted and toppled onto one of the little beds, falling asleep at once.

While she slept, seven little men strutted through the woods on their way home. As they entered the cottage, they sensed that someone was there. When they looked upstairs, they found Snow White asleep. When she woke the next morning, she was amazed to see the seven little men and told them all about her wicked stepmother. She asked if she might stay and cook and keep house for them. The seven little men were delighted to say yes, but they warned her never to open the door to strangers and to stay very close to home, so the wicked stepmother would never discover her whereabouts.

Snow White agreed to be very cautious, and the seven little men and the beautiful young lady celebrated their new arrangement with a cup of tea.

December 19

Snow White and the Seven Dwarfs, Part 2

While Snow White and the seven dwarfs were making merriment, the wicked queen was making a terrible discovery. She had consulted her mirror, hoping to learn that once again she was the fairest of them all, but when she asked, the mirror responded, "In the woods where seven dwarfs dwell, Snow White lives both fair and well."

Realizing the hunter had tricked her, the queen decided to do away with Snow White herself. Dressed like a peddler, she set out into the woods with a bundle of combs and laces. One of the combs was poisoned and she intended to offer it to Snow White. As she drew near the cottage she began to yell, "Combs and laces for sale." Snow White remembered what the dwarfs had told her about opening the door but the queen persuaded her to crack it open just enough to pass a comb through. Snow White loved combs. She couldn't resist combing her hair with it. As soon as she did, the poison began to work and she fell to the floor.

Luckily, the seven dwarfs arrived home just in time to rescue Snow White from the effects of the terrible poison.

At the castle the queen consulted the mirror once again, only to hear that Snow White still lived. Livid, she disguised herself as an ugly old woman. She planned to put Snow White to sleep forever with an apple that was both yellow and red and soaked on the red side with poison. She hobbled off toward the cottage calling out, "Bright juicy apples for sale." Snow White loved apples. Once again, the evil queen tempted Snow White, this time with the apple through the open window. To show her it was perfectly good to eat, the queen bit into the yellow half herself and gave Snow White the red half, which was poisoned. Snow White bit into it and fell to the floor. The wicked queen hurried back to the castle, where her magic mirror assured her that she now was the "fairest of them all."

When the seven dwarfs found Snow White that evening, they could not revive her. They mourned her for seven days and nights, then placed her body in a glass coffin, with her name in gold on the outside. They put the coffin in a special clearing near the cottage.

One day a prince riding through the woods saw Snow White in her glass coffin. He thought she was so beautiful that he asked the dwarf's permission to take her coffin to his palace, where he could gaze at her forever. As the prince's men carried the coffin through the woods, one of them stumbled, dislodging the piece of poisoned apple that was in Snow White's mouth. She awoke from her deep sleep and was told by the prince that she was safe with him. "I want you to be my wife," he said. She accepted his proposal happily.

A magnificent wedding was held and everyone in the kingdom was invited. As the wicked queen was dressing for the festivities, she checked her magic mirror and was told that the mysterious bride was the fairest woman in the land. Incredulous, the queen rushed to see for herself. When she saw that the bride was Snow White, she collapsed and died. Snow White and the prince lived happily ever after for many years.

December 20

The Horse and the Stag

A horse had a whole meadow to himself until one morning when a stag came upon it. The stag romped and grazed and eventually made a terrible mess of the meadow. The horse was furious and pledged revenge.

With eyes of red the horse asked a man if he would help him to punish the stag. "Are you certain you want to do this?" the man asked more than one time.

The horse was so angry he said he would do anything to exact revenge on the stag.

"Anything?" the man asked, wanting to be sure.

"Anything," the horse replied.

The man shrugged. "I will help you find weapons if you will allow me to put a bit in your mouth and get up on your back," he said.

The horse, still in a rage, agreed even to that, and from that time forward has been the slave of man.

Revenge is too dearly purchased at the price of liberty.—AESOP

December 21

The Breakman

A TALE FOR CHRISTMAS

Once there lived way up in the sky, a little bit north of the clouds and just west of the sunrise, the man who ran the big machine that made things break on earth. It was his responsibility to make sure that cars overheated on the hottest day of the year, that television sets quit televising just before the detective told the audience who committed the crime, and that washing machines didn't wash. Every time a computer printed, *"The boy went to the myfetxgqw,"* he was very proud. When the lights went off during a storm, or the telephone sounded like it was underwater, or the hot water got very cold just when someone was taking a shower, he knew he was doing his job.

Because he was not a happy person, it made him feel good to make other people unhappy. Sometimes at work he would count the number of different languages in which people yelled at him for making things break. On the same day, he could start a big traffic jam in New York City and turn out all the lights in Beijing, China.

He wasn't the only breakman in the world—there were just too many things that had to be broken for one person to be able to break them all—but he was the best at what he did. He had learned that it didn't really make people angry when he broke things when they were home on Monday morning. They could just call the repairman and he would come and fix them. The best time to break things, he had learned, was on the night before a long holiday or on a Friday, when things just couldn't be fixed. His favorite thing of all was to break a car just before the family left for a long Christmas vacation.

Christmas came on Friday one year, which made him smile just thinking about it. That meant if he broke things on Wednesday night, it would be five whole days before people could get them fixed. He would ruin Christmas for many, many people, so he would have a very happy holiday. As the day came closer, he made long lists of the things he would break. He was going to break cars and trains and planes, he was going to break suitcases and cameras, he was going to break bicycles and talking dolls. Oh, it was going to be a wonderful holiday.

Finally, at 6 o'clock in Wednesday, he took a deep breath and turned on the big machine that broke things. The machine went "Rrrrr . . . ooooooo . . . bump." He pressed all the right buttons and pulled the lever again. And again the machine went "Rrrr . . . ooooooo . . . bump," and turned itself off. The breakman started sweating. He felt terrible—the machine that broke things was broken! He tried again and again but it wouldn't work. On earth, people started leaving on their vacations and there was nothing he could do about it. Their cars started, the television sets televised, and even the washing machines washed. He was very angry, and he tried to call the man who fixed the machine that broke things, but because it was Christmas the man wasn't working. "Call back Monday," the answering machine said.

There was nothing the breakman could do. He sat and sat and sat. He felt worse than he had ever felt in his life. He knew how much fun he was missing. And, for the first time, he understood how people on earth felt when he broke their things. There was a bad feeling in his heart and in his stomach and in his head, and he didn't like it at all.

On Monday, the man who repaired the machine that broke things arrived and took out his tools and tinkered and said "Hmmm" and "Hummm" and finally "Ahhh," and then said, "Okay, it's all fixed. You can break things now."

The breakman looked down and saw a woman carrying a big load of laundry and he decided to break her washing machine. But when he did and he saw her crying, he felt very bad. He knew, really knew how sad she was. So when no one was looking he fixed her washing machine. Breaking things was no longer any fun for him.

He had learned a very important lesson: Don't do things to other people that you don't want to happen to you. And he never ever broke anything again.

—JORDAN BURNETT AND DAVID FISHER

A Miserable Merry Christmas

A TALE FOR CHRISTMAS

Christmas was coming, but Christmas was always coming and grown-ups were always talking about it, asking you what you wanted and then giving you what they wanted you to have. Though everybody knew what I wanted, I told them all again. I wanted a pony, and to make sure that they understood, I declared that I wanted nothing else.

"Nothing but a pony?" my father asked.

"Nothing," I said.

"Not even a pair of high boots?"

That was hard. I did want boots, but I stuck to the pony. "No, not even boots. If I can't have a pony, give me nothing."

Now I had been looking myself for the pony I wanted, going to sales stables, inquiring of horsemen, and I had seen several that would do. But my father always found some fault with them. I was in despair. When Christmas was at hand, I had given up all hope of a pony, and on Christmas Eve I hung up my stocking along with my sisters'. I speculated on what I'd get; I hung up the biggest stocking I had, and we all went reluctantly to bed to wait till morning.

We did sleep that night, but we woke up at six A.M. I don't know who started it, but there was a rush. We raced to get first to the fireplace in the front room downstairs. And there they were, the gifts, all sorts of wonderful things, mixed-up piles of presents; only, as I disentangled the mess, I saw that my stocking was empty; it hung limp; not a thing in it; and under and around it—nothing. Each of my sisters knelt down by her own pile of gifts; they were squealing with delight, till they looked up and saw me standing there in my nightshirt with nothing. They came to look at my empty place. Nothing. They felt my stocking. Nothing.

I don't remember whether I cried at that moment, but my sisters did. They ran with me back to my bed, and there we all cried till I became indignant. That helped some. I got up, dressed, and went out to the stable and there, all by myself, I wept. My mother came out to me and tried to comfort me. But I heard my father outside; he had come part way with her, and she was having some kind of angry quarrel with him. She asked me to come to breakfast. I could not; I wanted no comfort and no breakfast.

I can feel now what I felt then, and I am sure that if one could see the wounds on our hearts, there would be found still upon mine a scar from that terrible Christmas morning.

After—I don't know how long, surely an hour or two—I was brought to the climax of my agony by the sight of a man riding a pony down the street, a pony and a brand-new saddle, the most beautiful saddle I ever saw. But the man came along, reading the numbers on the houses, and, as my hopes—my impossible hopes—rose, he looked at our door and passed by, he and the pony. Too much. I fell upon the steps, and having wept before, I broke now into such a flood of tears that I was a floating wreck when I heard a voice.

"Say, kid," it said, "do you know a boy named Lennie Steffens?"

I looked up. It was the man on the pony.

"Yes," I spluttered through my tears. "That's me."

"Well, then, this is your horse. I've been looking all over for you and your house. Why don't you put your house number where it can be seen?" he said.

"Get down," I commanded.

I could scarcely wait. The man adjusted the stirrups and then, finally, I rode, slowly, at a walk, so happy, so thrilled, that I did not know what I was doing. I was going to ride up, past Miss Kay's house. But I noticed on the horn of the saddle some stains like raindrops, so I turned and trotted home, not to the house but to the stable. There was the family, father, mother, sisters, all waiting for me, all happy.

"What did you come home so soon for?" somebody asked.

I pointed to the stains. "I wasn't going to get my new saddle rained on," I said. My father laughed. "It isn't raining," he said.

"Those are tears," my mother gasped, and she gave my father a look that sent him off to the house. Worse still, my mother offered to wipe away the tears still running out of my eyes. I gave her such a look as she had given him, and she went off after my father, drying her own tears.

But that Christmas, which my father had planned so carefully, was it the best or worst I ever knew? I think now that it was both. It covered the whole distance from broken-hearted misery to bursting happiness—too fast. A grown-up could hardly have stood it.

—LINCOLN STEFFENS

December 23

Solomon's Ghost

A respected old man, despite his years and the heat of the day, was ploughing his field by hand and sowing the grass into the willing earth in anticipation of the harvest it would produce.

Suddenly, beneath the deep shadow of a spreading oak, a ghost stood before him! The old man was paralyzed with fright.

"I am Solomon," said the phantom. "What are you doing here?"

"If you are Solomon, why do you ask?" replied the old man. "When I was young, I learned from the ant to be industrious and to accumulate wealth. That which I learned I still practice."

"You have learned but half of the lesson," said the ghost. "Go once more to the ant and she will teach you to rest in the winter of your existence, and enjoy what you have earned."

December 24

The Elves and the Shoemaker

A GERMAN TALE FOR CHRISTMAS

In a tiny village there lived a shoemaker, who made very fine shoes, but not nearly enough of them, and so he was very poor. He was so poor that he had but one scrap of leather left with which to sew some shoes. "This may be the last pair of shoes I make," said the shoemaker sadly. He looked around his shop in despair, wondering what to do.

The next morning when he went to his workbench, he was astonished to discover a pair of perfectly made shoes in place of the last scrap of leather. Each stitch was tidy and perfect! Knowing the shoes would draw a handsome price, the old man hung out his shop sign and put the shoes in the window for sale. Within minutes, a fine gentleman walked into the shop. The gentleman wanted to buy the shoes and offered the shoemaker an enormous sum for them.

The shoemaker now had enough money to buy food for his family and to buy more leather. Still pondering the mystery, the shoemaker cut out two pairs of shoes from his new scraps of leather. Neatly he arranged the pieces as he had the night before, all ready to be sewn up the next day.

In the morning, the shoemaker came to his workbench only to be astonished again. In place of the two scraps of leather were two pairs of perfectly sewn shoes. "Who on earth could have made such perfect shoes?" the shoemaker wondered.

Again, he placed the shoes in the shop window, and wealthy passersby stopped in at once to acquire the shoes, and always at handsome prices. The shoemaker would buy food for his family and then use the remaining sum to invest in leather. Each night he would cut out the pieces of leather and return to his workbench the next day, only to find pairs upon pairs of perfectly sewn shoes.

By now the shoemaker was earning superior wages, and for the first time the family not only had enough to eat but a little left over. The shoemaker and his wife were overjoyed, but they also were curious about the mysterious helpers who in the hardest times had come to help.

One night, the old man and woman decided to stay awake and spy. While the clock ticked, they crouched behind a curtain, waiting and waiting. Just as they were about to give up, dozens of little elves, no bigger than a finger, came pouring out of the walls and corners. Each of the little men picked up a needle and began to make perfect stitches on the scraps of leather that the shoemaker laid out for them. The old man and woman could not believe their eyes. The twosome stayed silent, while the elves transformed the scraps of leather into beautiful shoes.

To express their gratitude the old man and woman decided to make little outfits for the elves, and so they sewed them matching jackets and trousers, all in green. They made the elves little hats and boots, and as it was nearing Christmas, they put out the brand-new outfits with cookies and cakes, to thank the little men for their help.

The elves came again that night and they rejoiced to receive the gifts, feasting on the cookies and cakes and dancing about in their new clothes. In the morning, when the shoemaker and his wife came to investigate, they were thrilled to see that the clothes were gone and the cakes and cookies consumed.

That night, the shoemaker laid out the cut leathers again, but the elves never returned. The elves knew by the gifts of food and the clothes that fit perfectly that they had been seen, and since fairies do not like to be seen by humans, they never came again.

Though the shoemaker and his wife were saddened to have the elves disappear from their lives, they did not despair. The elves had helped them through their hardest times, and they were back on their feet again, with a reputation for fine shoes, enough leather with which to make them, food to eat, and a little left over.

—BROTHERS GRIMM

December 25

CHRISTMAS DAY

The Fir Tree

In a small cottage on the borders of a forest lived a poor worker who made a meager living as a woodcutter. He had a wife and two children, who helped him in his work. The boy's name was Valentine and the girl was called Mary. They were good children and their parents loved them very much. One winter night, this sweet family was sitting before the hearth eating their simple supper of dry bread and tea when a gentle tap was heard on the window. A child's voice cried, "Oh, please let me come in. I am hungry and have no home and I will die of cold if you do not let me in."

Valentine and Mary jumped up and ran to the door, and welcomed the little child in. Mary brushed the snow off the child and wrapped him in a blanket. "Sit down and have some tea," she urged him gently.

The stranger-child came in and warmed his hands.

"You must be tired," Valentine said. "You may sleep in our bed and we will sleep on the bench."

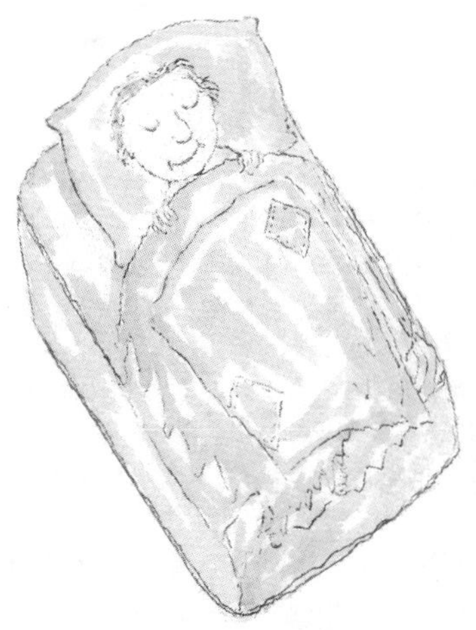

The stranger-child looked up in wonder. "You are so kind," he said and his eyes looked deeply into theirs.

Valentine and Mary took their guest to their bedroom, and laid him on the bed and covered him with worn blankets. "We should be so thankful," Mary whispered to Valentine, as she looked at the stranger-child, who already had fallen asleep. "We have a bed and a home and this child has only heaven for his roof and the cold earth for his bed."

The children fixed themselves a place to sleep on the bench near the hearth. They were filled with happiness. "The stranger-child will be so cozy tonight in our bed," said Valentine and drifted off to sleep.

A few hours later, Valentine and Mary heard voices just outside the window. They went to look and could not believe their eyes. In the east was a streak of rosy dawn, and in its light they saw a group of children standing before the house, clothed in silver garments, holding golden harps in their hands. They were singing: *"Oh, holy Child, we greet thee! Bringing sweet strains of harp to aid our singing. Thou, holy Child, in peace art sleeping, while we watch our house without keeping. Blest be the house wherein thou liest. Happiest on earth, to heaven nighest."*

Then, from their bedroom, emerged the stranger-child in a golden dress, with a gleaming radiance round his curling hair. "I am the Christ-child," he said, "who wanders through the world bringing peace and happiness to good children. You took me in and cared for me when you thought I was but a poor child, and now you will have my blessing for your kindness."

Near the house there grew a fir tree, and from this he broke a twig, which he planted in the ground. "This twig shall become a tree, and shall bring forth fruit year after year for you."

Just as the twig was planted, the Christ-child vanished.

But the fir branch grew and became a Christmas tree, and on its branches hung golden apples and silver nuts every Christmas.

This is the story told to German children every year. Though we know that the real Christ-child can never be wandering cold and homeless, still we may gather from this story the great truth—that anyone who helps a person in distress can be counted as if he had done so to Christ himself. "Inasmuch as you have done it to the least of these, my brethren, you have done it unto me."

Merry Christmas.

—HANS CHRISTIAN ANDERSEN

December 26

Elsa and the Ten Elves

A SWEDISH FOLKTALE FOR CHRISTMAS

Once upon a time there was a pretty, sweet-tempered little girl named Elsa, who lived on a prosperous farm. Elsa learned reading, writing, and singing, but she did not learn how to cook, sew, or care for a house. The truth was that Elsa was lazy and did not like anything that she called work.

When she grew older, many young men wished to wed her, but she chose her neighbor, Gunner, a handsome, industrious young farmer. So the two were married and went to live on Gunner's farm.

At first they were very happy, but as the days passed and Elsa did not direct the servants in their work or see that the house was kept in order, everything went wrong. The provisions in the storerooms were tumbled about, food was missing, and the house was dirty. Gunner was miserable, but he loved Elsa too much to say a word to her about it.

The day before Christmas came, and the sun had been up and people bustling about the house for hours. Still Elsa lay fast asleep in her bed. At last a servant came into her room. "Oh, mistress," she said, "the master and his men are ready to set off for the woods. What shall we pack in their lunch bags?"

"Don't talk to me," said Elsa sleepily. "Leave the room!"

Another servant came in to tell her the bread dough had risen and Elsa told her to go away too. A third servant tried to get Elsa's orders for Christmas dinner, with no better success.

At last Gunner could stand it no longer and went to her room. "Dear Elsa," he said gently, "my mother used to prepare things the night before so the servants could begin work early. She did not lie in bed when the sun was up. My men and I are off now with I know not what in our lunch bags. Surely you are ready by this time to rise. Remember that there is cloth on the loom waiting to be woven."

Elsa finally got up grumbling and yawning, loitered for a while in the kitchen, and then went off to the little house where the loom was kept. But when she got there, she slammed the door behind her and threw herself down on a couch. "No," she cried. "I won't do this weaving. I won't toil and drudge. Who would have thought Gunner would make me work so hard? Is there no one to help me?"

"I can help you," said a deep voice.

Elsa, raising her head in astonishment, saw an old man in a gray cloak and a broad-brimmed hat standing next to her. "I am Old Man Hoberg," he said. "And I have served your family for many years. You, my child, are unhappy because you are lazy. To be lazy makes any person miserable. I will give you ten obedient servants who shall do all your tasks for you."

At that he shook his long gray cloak and out tumbled ten strange little men. For a moment they danced about, then they swiftly put the room in order and finished weaving the cloth. When their work was done, they came running up and stood in a row before Elsa, as though awaiting her orders.

"Dear child, reach out your hands," said the old man.

Uncertainly, Elsa held out the tips of her fingers, and the old man cried, "Hop-o'-my-Thumb. Lick-the-Pot, Long-Pole, Heart-in-Hand, Little-Peter-Funny-Man, away all of you to your places!" In the twinkling of an eye, the little men popped into Elsa's fingers, and the old man vanished from sight.

For a moment Elsa sat staring at her hands. Then suddenly a great desire to work came over her, and up she jumped. "Why am I idling here?" she cried. Soon she was giving orders to the servants and setting things to rights everywhere.

When Gunner came home that night, all was clean and bright to welcome him. "Oh ho!" he cried heartily. "Some good fairy has been here!"

Elsa smiled and held up her fingers. "Ten good fairies," she said.

After that Elsa rose early each morning and went about her work sweet-tempered and happy. The farmhouse prospered under her hands, and health, wealth, and happiness came to stay when she learned how to manage those ten little elves.

December 27

The Olive Tree and the Fig Tree

The olive tree ridiculed the fig tree because while she was green all year round, the fig tree changed its leaves with the seasons. "How thin and wretched you look, Mr. Fig, while I am resplendent with silvery leaves all year long," mocked the olive tree. The fig tree was hurt by the olive tree's words but said little.

A few weeks later, a shower of snow fell upon them and, finding the olive tree full of foliage, the snow settled upon its branches. But the weight of the snow broke the branches down, and eventually spoiled the olive tree's beauty and killed it. The fig tree, void of leaves, stood unharmed, as the snow fell through its bare branches to the ground.—AESOP

December 28

The Fisherman and His Wife

A GERMAN TALE

A hardworking fisherman and his wife lived in a modest shack near the sea. Each day the fisherman fished from dawn until dusk. One day, after a long struggle, he landed the biggest flounder he had ever seen. To the fisherman's amazement, the flounder could speak, and he asked the fisherman to release him, explaining that he was no mere flounder but a prince in disguise.

The fisherman, who was a little taken aback, did agree to let the flounder go, for he had never seen a talking fish before, let alone one who claimed to be a prince. He threw back the flounder, went home, and told his wife what had happened. The wife, who was a bit of a shrew, berated the fisherman for not asking the flounder for some wishes, saying that whenever someone does a special favor for a creature with powers, they usually get something in return.

She instructed her husband to go back to the seashore, find the flounder, and ask for a cottage for the couple to live in.

"Prince, oh prince, if such you be
Flounder, flounder in the sea
My faithful wife, Dame Isabelle,
Has begged a wish against my will."

The flounder appeared when he was called and told the man that his wish was granted. When the fisherman arrived home, his wife greeted him from the gate of a pleasant little cottage.

The fisherman was very pleased, but his wife kept sending him back to the shore to ask more favors. She tired of the cottage and demanded a castle. Then she wanted to be queen of all the surrounding land. Next she had to be empress. Finally, she asked to be pope. When her husband thought there was not another thing in the world she could desire, she demanded to be lord of the sun and moon.

The fisherman returned to the shore once more and summoned the flounder. Reluctantly, he told the fish of his wife's latest demand.

This time the wife had gone too far. The flounder informed her husband that he would find her back in their modest shack, where first she lived. And there the couple remained for the rest of their days.—BROTHERS GRIMM

December 29

The Moon Maiden

A JAPANESE FOLKTALE

There dwelt once on the edge of the forest at the foot of Mount Fujiyama a bamboo cutter and his wife. They were honest, industrious people who loved each other dearly, but no children had come to bless them, and therefore they were not happy.

"Ah, husband," mourned the wife, "more welcome to me than cherry blossoms in springtime would be a little child of my own."

One night she stood on the porch of her bamboo cottage and lifted her eyes to the everlasting snows atop Fujiyama. Then she bowed to the ground and cried out to the Honorable Mountain, "Fuji no yama, I am sad because no small head lies on my breast. Send me, I pray, a little one to comfort me."

And as she spoke, from the top of the mountain there suddenly sparkled a gleam of light as when the face of a child is lit by a beaming smile. "Husband, come quickly!" cried the good woman. "See there on the heights of Fujiyama a child is smiling upon me."

The bamboo cutter thought it was probably just her fancy, but he loved her and said he would climb the mountain and see. He followed the trail of silvery light through the forest and up the steep slope, where Fujiyama towered white and still above him. At last he stopped by a tall bamboo where the glow seemed to come from. Cradled in the branches was a tiny moon-child, dainty, radiant, clad in filmy moonshine, more beautiful than anything he had ever seen before. "Ah, little shining creature, who are you?" he asked.

"I am the Princess Moonbeam," answered the child. "The Moon Lady is my mother, but she has sent me to earth to comfort the sad heart of your wife."

"Then, little Princess," said the man eagerly, "I will take you home to be our child."

The good woman was overjoyed, and took the little moon-child and held her close. As the little one's head nestled snug against her breast, the good wife's longing was satisfied at last.

As the years passed by, Princess Moonbeam brought nothing but joy to the couple. Lovelier and lovelier she grew. Her eyes were shining stars and her hair had the gleam of a misty silver halo. About her, too, there was a strange, unearthly charm that made all who saw her love her.

One day the Mikado himself came riding by in state. When he saw the Princess Moonbeam, he fell in love with her instantly. He would have taken her back with him to his court, but the Lady in the Moon had other plans for her daughter. Now that she was a maiden grown, and had fulfilled the longing of the earthly mother and father for a child, it was time for her to return to her sky mother.

"Stay! Stay with us on earth!" cried the bamboo cutter and his wife.

"Stay with me!" cried the Mikado, and he sent two thousand archers to guard her house so that none could take her. But when the moon rose white and full, a line of light like a silver bridge arched down from heaven to earth, and floating down that path came the Lady of the Moon. The Mikado's soldiers stood as if turned to stone. The Moon Lady wrapped her long-absent child close in a garment of silver mist and led her gently back to the sky. The Princess Moonbeam was glad to go home, yet as she went, she wept silvery tears for those she was leaving behind. And her bright, shining tears took wings and floated away to carry a message of love to comfort the Mikado and her earthly mother and father.

To this very day the tears of the Princess Moonbeam are seen to float hither and yon about the marshes and meadows of Japan. Children chase them with happy cries, saying, "See the fireflies! How beautiful they are!"

December 30

The Many-Furred Creature

There was once upon a time a king who had a beautiful wife with golden hair. Unfortunately, she fell very ill and when she knew that the end was near, she asked her husband, "If you must marry after my death, make no one queen unless she is as beautiful as I am, with golden hair like mine." After the king promised her this, she died.

For a long time, he was not to be comforted, but eventually his ministers told him he must marry again. So messengers were sent far and wide to seek a bride as lovely as his first wife. They spent years on this mission, which proved impossible. But meanwhile, the king's daughter grew to womanhood. The king noticed she was as beautiful as her mother, and announced he would take her as his bride.

His ministers were horrified at this idea, as was his daughter. She put him off by making what she hoped was an impossible request of him: "Before I do your bidding, I must have three dresses. One must be as golden as the sun, one as silver as the moon, and the last should shine like the stars. And I also want a cloak made of a thousand different furs." She underestimated his determination, however, and it wasn't long before he produced the cloak and dresses and announced their wedding.

The princess had no choice but to flee from her father's castle. She packed a few of her treasures: a golden ring and a tiny golden spinning wheel. She put the star, moon, and sun dresses into a nut shell, donned the many-furred cloak, and blackened her face and hands with soot. By the light of the stars, she traveled all night till she came to a great forest. Weary, she sat down inside a hollow tree and fell asleep.

It happened that the king who owned this forest was hunting the next morning, and when his hounds came to the hollow tree, they circled it in great excitement. The king told his huntsmen to see what kind of wild beast was inside. They reported that it looked like a strange animal whose coat was made of many different furs. The king ordered them to seize it, which was when they discovered that the beast was a maiden, who cried, 'I am a poor child, with no parents. Please, let me go with you."

The princess was taken back to the castle, where she was given a tiny room under the stairs and a job as the scullery maid in the kitchen. Because of her cloak, they called her the Many-Furred Creature.

One night a great feast was held at the castle and the princess asked the cook's permission to go watch the festivities for a while. "Be back in a half an hour to sweep up the ashes," said the cook. The princess hurried to her room, washed the soot from her face and hands, and put on her dress that was as golden as the sun. When she entered the feasting hall, no one would have know this beautiful maiden was the Many-Furred Creature. The king himself begged her for a dance, but when it was over she vanished. Quickly the princess changed and returned to her kitchen duties. The cook happened to ask her help in making the king's soup. And in the soup tureen, the princess dropped her gold ring.

When the king found the ring in his soup, he hoped it had some connection to the vanished maiden with whom he had fallen instantly in love. The cook confessed that it had been the Many-Furred Creature who had prepared the king's soup, but no one suspected that *she* was a beautiful princess.

Some months later, another feast was held and the Many-Furred Creature was again allowed to go upstairs and watch the dancing for a bit. She, of course, ran to her room, cleaned herself, and donned her silver dress. The delighted king took her out onto the dance floor, and while she was distracted, slipped the golden ring on her finger and found that it fit perfectly. But as the music ended, she again disappeared. On this occasion, she didn't have enough time to completely resume her disguise as the Many-Furred Creature, but simply threw the cloak over her silver dress before hurrying to the kitchen.

The princess dropped the tiny spinning wheel in the soup this time, and the king himself came to the kitchen to investigate. Though the princess had put ashes on her face, she had forgotten to dirty her hands in her rush to get back to her station, and the king noticed the glint of the golden ring on her finger. He grabbed her by the arms, and as she struggled to free herself, the fur cloak fell off, revealing her silver dress. The king ordered her face to be cleaned, and when she stood there in all her beauty, he cried, "You shall be my bride and we shall never be parted again!" And so they lived happily ever after.

December 31

Beauty and the Beast

A rich merchant had three daughters, one of whom was called Beauty. Though they all lived well for many years, one day things changed for the merchant and he lost everything he owned. All he had left was a small country cottage where he went to live with his daughters. The two older daughters were lazy and complained bitterly about their lost riches, while Beauty did most of the work and tried to make her father happy.

One morning the merchant received news that one of his ships, which he thought was lost, had arrived safely in port. He felt sure that if he went to the ship he could recover some of the fortune he'd lost. He asked his two daughters what gifts they wanted him to bring back. The two eldest asked for all kinds of finery; Beauty wanted only a rose.

When the merchant reached the port where the ship had docked, he found that his partners, believing him dead, had divided the ship's contents among themselves. The merchant was obliged to turn back home empty handed.

On his way home, the merchant passed through a dense forest where the snow was so deep his horse could barely move. Just when he was about to give up in despair, he saw a light shining through the trees. He discovered that it came from a great castle, which seemed to be empty, though a table was set in a small sitting room and a fire blazed cozily in the hearth. The merchant helped himself to the meal on the table as it seemed to have been prepared for him. He fell asleep by the fire and in the morning he awoke early, eager to find his host and thank him. In his search, he came to a garden with roses blooming. Remembering Beauty's request, he plucked one. At that moment, a hideous beast appeared, accusing the merchant of being a thief. "For this you must die," declared the beast.

The punishment seemed quite harsh. The poor merchant fell to his knees and tried to explain that he had promised his youngest daughter that he would bring her a rose. When the beast heard this, he said, "I will allow you to go if you will send one of your daughters to take your place. She must come willingly or you yourself will have to return in three months."

The merchant returned to his cottage and related to his daughters what had happened. The two older daughters blamed Beauty for causing all of the trouble. But without hesitation Beauty volunteered to take her father's place. Reluctantly, her father allowed her to go.

Three months later Beauty and her father traveled to the Beast's castle, where she explained to him that she had come willingly. The merchant left the next morning and Beauty found herself surrounded by luxury. Everything was arranged for her comfort and pleasure. During the day she was quite alone, but in the evening the Beast would come to talk to her. He was gentle and kind, but each time he came he would ask her to marry, and Beauty would always refuse.

Soon Beauty began to miss her father and to worry about him. She asked the Beast for permission to go home on the condition that she would return in eight days. He said if she did not return, he would die. He gave her a magic ring that would take her to her father, then return her to the Beast's castle.

Beauty's family was delighted to see her, though her sisters were jealous of her life in the castle. When the week with them was over they tried to trick Beauty into staying longer. Beauty lingered awhile but one night she had a dream that the Beast was dying. She quickly found her magic ring and rubbed it as the Beast had instructed. Almost instantly she was back at the castle, where she found the Beast lying in the garden. He appeared to be dead, and Beauty felt it was her fault for not having returned sooner. Then he opened his eyes, and she saw he was just barely alive.

"Dear Beast, you must not die," she cried. "You must live and be my beloved husband."

At that moment the castle began to glow with light and a handsome prince stood beside Beauty. He explained that her words had broken a magic spell that had forced him to take the form of a beast. The spell could be broken only when someone loved him in spite of his ugliness.

The prince and Beauty were married the next day, and her family joined in the celebration.

Credits and Sources

Appreciation is extended to the following for permission to reprint copyrighted material. Every reasonable effort has been made to trace ownership of all copyrighted stories in this volume. Any errors that may have occurred are inadvertent and will be corrected in subsequent editions, provided notification is sent to the publisher.

"A Miserable Merry Christmas," from *The Autobiography of Lincoln Steffens* by Lincoln Steffens; copyright © 1931 by Harcourt Brace & Company, renewed 1959 by Peter Steffens; adapted and reprinted by permission of the publisher. "Clever Manka: The Story of a Girl Who Knew What to Say," from *The Shoemaker's Apron: A Second Book of Czech Folktales* copyright 1920 by Parker Fillmore and renewed 1948 by Louise Fillmore, adapted and reprinted by permission of Harcourt Brace & Company. "Hanukkah at Valley Forge" by Emily Solis-Cohen, The Jewish Publication Society, Philadelphia. "Tiki's Way Home" by Carol Boswell; copyright © 1997 by Carol Boswell. "The Babysitter," "The Seed from Mars," "The Most Powerful Person in the Whole World," "The Boy Who Told Fairy Tales," "The Dog Who Fell in Love with a Fire Hydrant," "The New, Improved Family-Sized Butterfly," "The Famous Bubble Gum Boy," "The Breakman," "The Magic Camera," and "The Little Chicken," by David Fisher and Jordan Burnett; copyright © 1997 by the authors. "The Great Turkey Roundup," by Stephen Goodwin and Nicholas Goodwin; copyright © 1997 by the authors.

To put together a collection of this size the author pored through hundreds of books, journals, and research papers. The author would also like to gratefully acknowledge the following sources used in finding, rewriting, adapting, comparing, and compiling stories used in this volume:

Fairy Gold: A Book of English Fairy Tales, chosen by Ernest Rhys; J. M. Dent & Sons and E. P. Dutton, 1907. *A Book of Foxes Fairy Tales,* edited by Clifton Jones; Houghton Mifflin Company, 1914. *Near and Far Stories* by Lora B. Peck; Little, Brown and Company, 1920. *Italian Popular Tales* by T. F. Crane, 1885. *Czech Folk Tales* by Dr. Joseph Baudis; George Allen and Unwin, Ltd., 1917. *English Fairy Tales,* collected by Joseph Jacobs; David McNutt, 1898. *The Olive Fairy Book,* edited by Andrew Lang; Dover Publications, Inc., 1907. *The Big Book of Fairy Tales,* edited by Walter Jerrold; Blackie and Son, Ltd., 1911. *The Grey Fairy Book,* edited by Andrew Lang; 1900. *Children's Tales from Scottish Ballads* by Elizabeth Grierson; A. and C. Black, Ltd., 1906. *Russian Folk-tales* by W. R. Ralston; Smith, Elder and Company, 1873. *How to Tell Stories to Children* by Sara Cone Bryant; Houghton Mifflin, 1905. *More English Fairy Tales,* collected and edited by Joseph Jacobs; David McNutt, 1894. *Manx Fairy Tales,* collected by Sophia Morrison; David McNutt, 1911. *Outlook* 57, no. 11, collected by Clifton Johnson, 1897. *Raggedy Ann Stories* by Johnny Gruelle, 1918. *Popular Tales of the Norse,* collected by Peter C. Asbjornsen, translated by G. W. Dasent, 1859. *Tales from Turkey;* Simpkin, Marshall, Hamilton, Kent and Company, Ltd., 1914. *Celtic Fairy Tales,* collected and edited by Joseph Jacobs; David McNutt, 1892. *An Argosy of Fables,* selected and edited by Frederic Table Cooper; Frederick A. Stokes Co., 1921. *Cossack Fairy Tales and Folk-Tales,* edited by R. Nisbet Bain; A. L. Burt Company, 1894. *Up One Pair of Stairs of My Bookhouse;* The Bookhouse for Children, 1920. *Through the Fairy Halls of My Bookhouse;* The Bookhouse for Children, 1920. *The Diamond Story Book,* selected and edited by Penrhyn W. Coussens; Duffield and Company, 1914. *Holiday Stories;* Rand McNally, 1921. *Turkish Fairy Tales and Folk-Tales,* collected by Ignacz Kumos, translated by R. Nisbet Bain, 1896. *Jewish Fairy Tales and Legends* by Gertrude Landa; Bloch Publishing 1919. *Fairy Tales of the Western Range and Other Tales* by Eugene O. Mayfield, 1902. Donnell Van de Voort of the Federal Writers Project of the Works Project Administration, State of Alabama. *Fairy Tales from the Swedish* by Nils G. Djurklo, translated by H. L. Braekstad; Frederick Stokes Company, 1901. *Louisiana Folk-Tales,* collected and edited by Alcee Fortier; *Memoirs of the American Folk-Lore Society* 2, no. 6, 1895. *Mace's Fairy Book* by Jean Mace, translated by Mary L. Booth; Harper & Brothers, 1870. *Icelandic Legends,* collected by Jon Arnason, translated by George Powell and Eiriky Magnusson; Longmans, Green and Company, 1866. *Lousiana Folk-Tales in French Dialect and English;* Folklore Society by Houghton Mifflin, 1895. *Roman Legends* by Rachel Harriette Busk, 1877. *Popular Tales from the Norse* by G. W. Dasent, 1877. *Grimm's Household Tales,* translated by Margaret Hunt, 1884. *Le Folklore du Pays Basque* by Julien Vinson. *Contes Populaire de la Haute-Bretagne* by Paul Sebillot, 1880. *Spofford's Library of Wit and Humor* by Thomas Crofton Croker, 1892. *German Novelists* by Thomas Roscoe, 1826. Accounts of historians William of Newburgh and Ralph of Coggeshall. *Korean Folktales* by E. B. Landis; The China Review, 1896.

Subject Index

Authors & Titles Index